"You Are an Annoyingly Difficult Man to See."

Ah, so the woman had a tongue after all. Despite all her bravado, he could tell he scared her all the way down to her white kid slippers. Not particularly interested in giving up his advantage, lowered his lids to a predatory slant. "Possibly only difficult to people I do not want to see." He admired her more when she took another step forward, her cloak swinging around her as she placed the branch of candles on the table near him.

"I would not have sought you out in this manner if you had read my letters or permitted me an audience." Now that she was closer, he could see that her eyes were more blue than green, a subtle battle that changed with her surging emotions.

Rayne considered her for a moment. "Bedegrayne. Miss Devona Bedegrayne."

Her eyes lit up in delight, as if he were a pupil who had answered his governess's question correctly. "Yes. Yes, I am—that's me. I had feared your gargoyle—"

Amused, he interrupted. "Gargoyle?"

"Yes, that rude man who kept slamming the door on my footman."

"I fear it is not entirely Speck's fault. You see, I pay him to be rude and to slam the door." His statement hit its mark as he had intended, and to his delight her face suffused with color.

She glared at him, her gloved hands fisted at her sides. "See here, Lord Tipton. I am not normally so presumptuous. Do you think I do not know my reputation would be in shreds if word got out about this evening? However, you had refused all my appeals for your attention, and since there is so little time left . . ." Her voice faded, her eyes clouded with the consequences that only she understood. "A gentleman would not make me beg."

A LADY'S MISCHIEF

BARBARA PIERCE

ZEBRA BOOKS
KENSINGTON PUBLISHING CORP.
http://www.zebrabooks.com

For Mom

ZEBRA BOOKS are published by

Kensington Publishing Corp.
850 Third Avenue
New York, NY 10022

All Kensington titles, imprints and distributed lines are available at special quantity discounts for bulk purchases for sales promotion, premiums, fund-raising, educational or institutional use.

Special book excerpts or customized printings can also be created to fit specific needs. For details, write or phone the office of the Kensington Special Sales Manager: Kensington Publishing Corp., 850 Third Avenue, New York, NY 10022. Attn. Special Sales Department. Phone: 1-800-221-2647.

First Printing: August 2001
10 9 8 7 6 5 4 3 2 1

Printed in the United States of America

PROLOGUE

England, 1792

Rayne Tolland Wyman was certain of two things: today was his fifteenth birthday. The second, he was dying. He shifted in the darkness, only to discover he was being held in place.

His eyes rolled white then crossed as he focused on a circle of light that suddenly appeared. He did not know if it was real or just a fevered manifestation, nor did he care. It chased the shadows from his emaciated body, banishing them as it moved over his legs, traveling upward until it hovered over his bare chest. He choked back a sob, noticing for the first time the two fat leeches feeding on his chest, their slick, dark, flowing forms glistening in the faint light. Christ! If he listened carefully, he swore he could hear them sucking the life out of him.

"Mum," he croaked, his throat dry from screaming during the worst of the fever. His arm twitched, too weak to drop off the side of the bed and search for comfort. Gloved fingers reached out to him, clutching his limp hand. The coolness of the leather-clad fingers seemed impersonal, yet the fragile bones within were identifiable even in his befuddled state. He clung to that disembodied hand as if it was the only thing holding him to earth.

"Hush boy, I am here," she crooned.

His mum. The only grandmother he had living, and at times more of a mother to him than the one she had given birth to. She blended with the shadows, dressed in black as she was. A lace cap kept her gray hair tidy, and was bright enough to keep his dimming vision from sinking completely into the darkness. "I'm dying, Mum."

"Bother that," she snapped, her faded blue eyes filling with tears as she denied both their fears. "The fever has a strong hold on you, but you will fight it. Fight it for me."

The light faded, winking out of existence as if it had never been. He heard voices in the distance. His grandmother's? Maybe the surgeon called to attend him and his brother. Devlin. The eldest son. The most precious heir. He had fallen ill two days before the fever had taken Rayne's mind. Their mother had closed herself off from the household to pray at Devlin's bedside. To his knowledge, she had not visited her second son once.

Thunder rumbled in the distance. Rayne could almost taste the drizzle even though the air around him was stale. "Mum." She did not answer him this time. He turned his head, wondering why they had closed the bed curtains. Did they not understand he was smothering? Couldn't they hear him calling out? Fear had a taste, he decided. It was a combination of blood, the brine of sweat, and stale urine. Rayne swallowed, the blackness of the room pulsed with the contractions of the ravenous parasites that were slowly killing him.

"I want them off."

Lightning struck the house. The concussion vibrated his body. He gasped, sounding like a strangling man taking his last breath. The lightning struck again, then again, again. The storm outside seemed to mimic the seething torment he felt within.

If he had the strength, he would have ripped those feasting creatures off his chest and smeared their bloated guts across the oak floorboards. Such musings burned in his pained head, until the voices disturbed him again.

"Our man wants his meat fresh," the male voice warned.

"They don't come fresher than this. I heard tell the chap died two days past."

Died? Rayne's mind turned over the words, trying to make sense of them. Had Devlin died? Was that the reason for everyone's absence?

"Right shame, dying and not being able to tie it up proper, even at the end," the mysterious male continued.

"Naw, he come from gentry. Saw the old lady meself, all dressed up and blubbering with all the other black carrion. Heard he was diseased. They just lost the older one this morning. Business like this could make me a rich man."

"Diseased, eh?" The man paused, considering the ramifications. "I warrant our client knows our goods come damaged."

Another crack of lightning shook the house. Rayne flinched as nature's energy cracked open the roof. He could feel the rain beat down on his face, though he was too weak to do much more than lie there and allow it to wash away the sweat beading on his face.

"Move the glim closer, so we can have a look

at him." The man clucked his tongue. "Young. Fifteen if not a day. Our man said no smalls."

"We'll be getting two guineas for 'im. He's more man, than child."

Helpless, Rayne felt cold hands on the side of his head. Twisting and tugging they dragged him headfirst into the storm. Water clogged his mouth and nose when he tried to speak. His narrowed gaze caught a flash of light, and his mind dully registered that it was a knife. He felt his clothes being cut from his body.

"Aw, would you look at those wounds. Sucking leeches probably kilt him 'fore the fever done him in."

He was dead. Not exactly right, he amended. These men thought he was dead. They mentioned leeches, the fever. He was not in his bed. Devlin had not been the one to die. He had, or at least his family thought he had. Dear God, they had buried him alive!

"Give me a hand here. Bloody sack is soaked and I can't cram him in it. I'll hold him while you work it over his head."

Despite the cold rain, and his nudity, a warmth stole into his body. Pain seeped into his muscles as he willed his useless body to move, to show some sort of life. A heavy sack was being worked over his body, over his face. He could smell rain on the man's hands that hovered so close to his nose now. He could also smell earth, the earth that almost swallowed him whole, not caring that he was alive.

His hands shot up, manacling the wrists of his savior. The man easily broke the contact as he and his companion stumbled backward in surprise. Jackknifing into a sitting position, his blue-tinted lips sucked in the much-needed air his body craved, ignoring the babbling half-forgotten prayers his new companions evoked. He knew the sounds he made as his lungs ejected fluid and took in air made him seem more monster than human. He was too involved in bringing himself back to life to tell them he was harmless.

Later he would have time to be amused by the notion that two grave robbers, intent on stealing his corpse, had saved him from the hideous nightmare of being buried alive.

ONE

Fifteen years later . . .

"I warrant ye won't be getting yer way with this gent, missus."

Devona Bedegrayne did not seem upset by her footman's grim assessment of the situation. Being the fifth and youngest child of a baronet, she was not one to be put off by minor obstacles. Her older sister, Irene, described her nature as tenacious as a mouth full of nettles, something Devona had desperately wanted to put to the test every time her cheeky sister uttered her glib little phrase. Devona, realizing she was clenching her jaw, immediately relaxed.

So Rayne Wyman, Viscount Tipton, was proving to be a difficult man to visit. She had tried to be polite about gaining an introduction. Since Lord Tipton abhorred society functions, she had chosen to discreetly contact him by post. He had returned all her thoughtfully worded letters unopened.

Undaunted, she had tried to pay him a social call. She knew her family would disapprove even though she had called on the proper day, the proper time. Lord Tipton was not in, or so the rude little man had said before he slammed the door in her footman's face.

Devona was starting to think the man was purposely avoiding her, although she could not understand why. It was not that she had a fine opinion of herself, even if this very evening Lord Nevin had tried to flatter her by comparing her copper tresses to the constrained fire of Mount Etna. Personally, Devona just considered her unfashionably colored hair unruly and a source of distress when she was forced to look critically into a mirror. Still, what woman minded a little flattery? She frowned, staring at the imposing door that was keeping her from her goal. She doubted when she finally forced an audience with the elusive Lord Tipton that he would be comparing her hair to ancient volcanoes.

Barely disguising her sigh, she met the gaze of her loyal servant. "What did his man say this time, Gar?"

"He said"—Gar took a deep breath, trying to lessen the irritability in his tone at his lady's persistence—"that a *real* lady does not make social calls at midnight. His lord has no need to buy off the streets."

"Well, that certainly puts me in my place, does it not?" she said dryly, noticing even by the light of the carriage lanterns that Gar's ears had reddened. Her gaze strayed back to the secured door in the distance. "What we need is a better plan. Trying to pay a social call is not working. Lord Tipton is obviously beyond the notion."

"My lady, let's go onward home and try another day," Devona's maid, Pearl Brown, implored. "Even with us in attendance, this isn't respectable. Nor the night safe."

It took quite a bit of adventure to rattle Pearl,

and she looked like she had reached her limit. Of course, it did not help her staff that their stubborn mistress enjoyed testing the limits of everyone around her. "It was perfectly safe to travel to the ball this evening, and as you can see I have yet to step down from the carriage." Inspiration, sharp and bright as a lightning bolt, lit up her face. Of course, that was it! Devona clapped her hands together, dismissing the wary looks her servants gave her. She had a plan.

Minutes later, Gar was pounding his elbow against the door, while he grappled with the shifting weight of Devona and the yards of silk overflowing in his arms. " 'Tain't likely to work," he muttered.

"You underestimate my abilities. My future husband's gain is the stage's loss."

Pearl scowled. "The master is sure to tan all our hides when he hears of your latest mischief."

"Nonsense. Papa can be very indulgent," Devona reassured them, even if it was a tiny lie. It was up to her to keep her staff's spirits up.

"Only 'cause there's too many Bedegraynes to work up too much steam about," was Pearl's tart reply. "If your sweet mama was alive, she would have pruned the first bud off your hoydenish ways."

The comment aimed and delivered the guilt right where it was intended. It was a direct blow to her heart. Anna Bedegrayne had lost her life in a senseless accident. In the act of running after her mischievous three-year-old youngest daughter, she was struck in the temple by a heavy, wooden beam a workman had been maneuvering into position for some household renovations. The simple childhood game, and a generous gift from a loving husband, clashed, then went horribly wrong. Her brain hemorrhaged and she died. Devona accepted the blame for her mother's death. Being reminded of it by an impertinent servant was another matter.

"If I were you, I would tread carefully when speaking of my mother. You never know how a hoyden who is responsible for killing her mother might react."

Pearl, seeing her words had hurt her mistress, was instantly contrite. "Devona—"

The door swung open, ending their conversation. It was time for their performance.

"Make way, man!" Gar ordered, brushing past the stunned manservant before he could form a suitable dismissal. He carried Devona into the small hall and placed her on a plain walnut bench. "There, there, missus, all will be well."

On cue, Devona clasped her stomach and groaned. "The pain is worse, Gar. I—yes—I shall be sick!"

Lord Tipton's manservant stood firm. "She can't be doing that here. Off with you."

Stubborn man, she thought. Guards his master like an unyielding gargoyle. You'd think the man had countless women vying for his attention, though Devona knew better. Men considered demons were quite safe from the machinations of the *ton's* mamas. Crying out, she doubled over, her face lost in the folds of her skirts.

Gar drew himself up and used every inch he had on the man to tower threateningly over him. "See here. Our lady is ill. If you can't run for the doctor, then the least you can do is find a clean chamber pot before she disgraces herself on your floor."

Pearl put her arm around her, offering comfort. "And something to drink as well, if you can spare it." Concealing her nerves, she patted Devona's arm. "This crying will make you feel worse, my lady."

The manservant wavered as he glared at the trio. His duty warred with his instinct that these people were up to something. The suggestion that the sobbing woman might actually be a lady, had him grudgingly warning, "Don't move a hair. I'll see what I can do." He disappeared down one of the dark halls.

"Trusting soul," Gar murmured.

Devona lifted her head. Her face was clear of the agony and tears she had affected. "You owe me a shilling, Gar." She gave Pearl's hand a quick squeeze. "Since he went left, we shall search right." She was already heading in that direction.

"Miss Bedegrayne, how do you know his lordship will be this way?" Pearl whispered, close on her heels. She was determined not to be left behind.

"A simple deduction, really." She tried a door, and peered within. Empty. She moved on to the next door. "This side of the house is lit up. Besides, the gargoyle went the other way."

"Maybe the man went off to get his lord?" Pearl asked, growing more nervous with each step.

"Highly doubtful. He was about to throw a woman in pain out on the streets. We'll be lucky if he actually went off to get a chamber pot. Ahha!" Devona froze when she noticed the shadow and light under this next door flicker. Anticipation bubbled in her blood. After all, it was not every day a lady introduced herself to a supposed demon.

"Gar," she said, pitching her voice so the sound did not go beyond their small group, "you and Pearl return to the hall and await its guardian.

Distract him if you must, for I will need time to speak with his lordship."

Devona watched the dance of light and shadows as it escaped from underneath the door. She had not explained to Gar and Pearl her reasons for seeking an audience with Lord Tipton, nor the dire outcome if she failed to secure his help. He would help her, would he not? She had never thought until this moment that she would fail. Sensing their concern, she glanced at her motionless companions. "All will be well, once I speak to Lord Tipton. Go ahead, I shall be fine."

Without thought to the consequences, she quietly opened the door and blinked. What she saw within did not meet with her expectations. Why, the room was empty and . . . quite normal. It was not a large room, but it definitely was a male's domain. The walls were a plain pea green; the only adornments were several landscapes depicting the changing seasons of country landscapes and a huge ornate gold-foiled mirror that was suspended over a chimneypiece of cream-colored marble. A welcoming fire beckoned her to enjoy its warmth. No dainty, fashionable furniture was displayed to impress the visitor. Everything from the old French upholstered rococo armchair, the oversized Hepplewhite library cases spanning the length of two walls, and on to the geometrically precise library table serviced its owner with efficiency and comfort.

Who was this Lord Tipton? She had gleaned every bit of gossip bandied about the *ton,* and none of it added up if this elegant, private sanctuary reflected the man she had been desperately trying to meet. Her lower lip pouted a bit as she turned this latest intriguing tidbit in her mind.

So lost in thought was Devona that she failed to notice that she was being assessed as well.

A prickling awareness jarred her from her musings. Rubbing her arms to ward off an imaginary chill, she pivoted. Her gaze scanned the room again. There, in one of the shadowed corners, her gaze sought out, then faltered when she realized she was not alone. The mysterious Lord Tipton. This was the man the *ton* snidely called behind his back, Le Cadavre Raffiné. The Refined Corpse. She doubted any of the fashionable would have repeated such an insult to the man's face, if he had ever bothered to show himself.

She could tell even in the dim light that he was magnificent. Too fascinated to be wary, she took the branch of candles closest to her and brought the light to this man of shadows. He sat sprawled out in a corner chair, one leg propped up on a nearby chair while the other was bent close to his chest. His left arm rested casually across the surface of his knee. He held a smooth, flat stone between his fingers, which he slowly stroked with his thumb. Her attention caught the movement, and stared at his long, elegant fingers. He had large hands. A long scar ran from his wrist to his thumb. He possessed the hands of a warrior, a man who had battled for everything he claimed and won. The gentle stroking of the stone seemed contradictory and disturbed her on some level she could not define.

Lord Tipton cleared his throat. If it was her attention he wanted, he gained it. Her focus shifted to the thick column of his throat, then up to his face. What masculine beauty! It was a proud face, all chiseled angles that begged exploring. A day's growth of beard peppered his jaw, and drew attention to his full, sensual lips. His hair, a blend

of chestnut and honey, was unbound, and tangled
over his shoulders. There was a distinct streak of
blond or perhaps it was white that sprouted from
his right temple. Someone told her it was the
mark of *le compagnon du diable,* the devil's companion.

Wariness stiffened her stance as she realized the
man was half dressed. He wore a linen shirt, its
only adornment four linen buttons to connect the
front opening. His breeches were well made and
suede. His shoes were missing! She could feel the
heat in her face as she stared at his feet sheathed
in silk stockings. She had never seen her brothers
without shoes or coats.

Each studied the other; a unique male-to-female
alertness had electrified the space separating
them. Neither had said a word, and yet Devona felt
threatened. She gazed into eyes almost the color
of pewter, and she almost could believe the rumors about him.

"For a housebreaker, you aren't a very efficient
one," Rayne said, finally deciding it was time to
end the staring contest with his bold intruder.
"The last one who tried to make off with the bed
linen had cleaned out one of the bedrooms before Speck tackled him in the front hall."

She was not pouting anymore, a fact for which
he silently was grateful. His intruder had lips that
were made for kissing. He could almost imagine
how the soft resiliency of that bottom lip would
feel if he playfully bit it and sucked it into his
own mouth. He shifted slightly. Yes, better to have
her gape at him like he was addled than to have
her offer those sulky lips to him.

"Maybe it is disappointment that keeps you
mute. Considering my reputation, I suppose you

had expected to be greeted with disemboweling weapons and skeletons strewn about the room."

The woman blinked at the bitterness he could not keep out of his tone. Her hand came up to her face to brush an errant curl from her cheek. Teasing curls of fire framed her face, while the rest of her tresses, he had observed when she had first entered the room, had been plaited in a coil and secured in the back. A half handkerchief of lilac silk was pinned across the back of her head, with the embroidered ends hanging down past her shoulders. If he were to guess, he would say that his intruder had attended a ball before she had decided to rob him.

"You are an annoyingly difficult man to see."

Ah, so the woman had a tongue after all. Despite all her bravado, he could tell he scared her all the way down to her white kid slippers. Not particularly interested in giving up his advantage, he lowered his lids to a predatory slant. "Possibly only difficult to people I do not want to see." He admired her more when she took another step forward, her cloak swinging around her as she placed the branch of candles on the table near him.

"I would not have sought you out in this manner if you had read my letters or permitted me an audience." Now that she was closer, he could see that her eyes were more blue than green, a subtle battle that changed with her surging emotions.

Rayne considered her for a moment. "Bedegrayne. Miss Devona Bedegrayne."

Her eyes lit up in delight, as if he were a pupil who had answered his governess's question correctly. "Yes. Yes, I am—that's me. I had feared your gargoyle—"

Amused, he interrupted. "Gargoyle?"

"Yes, that rude man who kept slamming the door on my footman."

"I fear it is not entirely Speck's fault. You see, I pay him to be rude and to slam the door." His statement hit its mark as he had intended, and to his delight he watched her face suffused with color.

She glared at him, her gloved hands fisted at her sides. "See here, Lord Tipton. I am not normally so presumptuous. Do you think I do not know my reputation would be in shreds if word got out about this evening? However, you had refused all my appeals for your attention, and since there is so little time left . . ." Her voice faded off, her eyes clouded with the consequences that only she understood. "A gentleman would not make me beg."

There was that pout again! Rayne sucked in his breath at the impact of sexual desire. He felt helpless against it, and he had yet to get his hands on her, or press his face against her scented skin. She could bisect his emotions for all to see with just a glance. That vulnerability made him attack.

"There lies our problem, Miss Bedegrayne. I am no gentleman. If you know anything about me, you should know that I do not acknowledge the title or the civility."

He shot to his feet and took the remaining steps that brought her within arm's length. He reached out, tugging on the strings that held her Spanish cloak of white lace in place. It slipped from her shoulders and fell on the carpet. She was female perfection in his eyes. Her stature was small; the top of her head barely reached his shoulders. The gown she had kept hidden beneath her cloak was meant to heat a man's blood.

Her gown was lilac netting, with a white satin slip the only protection from his hungry gaze. The square neck was cut very low, as was the fashion, and framed a generous portion of her breasts, just begging a starving man to feast.

Rayne very much wanted to be that man.

She wore no jewelry except for the gold link bracelets attached to her upper arms, worn just below her short puckered sleeves. The need to touch her made him reach out for an area that would least likely get him slapped for it. His knuckle caressed one of the gold bracelets on her arm. Who did it hurt if he slipped lower and stroked the small area of skin just above her elbow? It was just as he imagined. Her skin was softer than silk. She shuddered, and the temptation to do more than touch made him pull back.

"I know I'm not a gentleman, but what about you, Miss Bedegrayne? Breaking into a man's town house doesn't quite make you a lady, does it? Shall we test this speculation?" Rayne leaned toward her lips. Perhaps the pleasure was worth a slap.

"I won't let you do it."

He was close enough to feel her breath on his lips. "Do what?" Knowing full well what she meant.

"I will not allow you to insult me."

She was not pouting anymore. In fact she looked mad enough to sink her teeth into his lower lip and draw blood. Self-preservation made him straighten to full indignant height. "Kissing me is an insult?"

She waved away the question, ignorant of how enraged he was. "You were not planning to kiss me."

"Wasn't I?" he asked, with enough menace to have her stepping back.

"I should have anticipated it sooner. You are a true strategist, my lord." Anger bringing her courage to the fore, she stepped up and poked him in the chest. "You block all my posts." Poke. "Ignore society so I cannot seek you out in a more acceptable manner." Poke. Poke. "You refuse all my calls, and when I finally confront you, you try to intimidate me by treating me like a courtesan!" She blew the errant curl out of her face. "By all rights, I should slap you so hard your teeth rattle and have both my brothers call you out. But you are Le Cadavre Raffiné, and no other man will do!"

"That little girl might be small, but that mouth of hers puts most hawkers to shame."

Rayne grunted in agreement to Speck's observation. Miss Bedegrayne and her harried servants had departed an hour ago, leaving the house disturbingly silent. He turned the tankard of ale in his hands, studying the dark brew as if it could divine answers to the more troubling questions of his life.

"An' what's this gargoyle nonsense she was muttering about? I never thought that man of hers was ever going to pry her fingers from the door frame."

"I think you were her gargoyle, Speck. You know . . . stocky, ugly, vicious guardian of the door. You struck terror into their hearts."

Speck smiled, showing his very pointed teeth. "You think? I kinda like that. Gargoyle, huh?"

Rayne swallowed his ale, trying to forget the look of despair he saw in Miss Bedegrayne's eyes when Speck rushed into the room with her two servants practically hanging on to his coat. The moment had erupted into complete chaos with everyone yelling at him at once. Deciding he had endured enough torment for one evening, he had ordered Speck to remove his uninvited guests from his home.

My lord, please allow me to tell you why I've come. Once you know my reasons, you will understand the urgency . . .

He never gave her a chance to explain. It appalled him all the more that he had felt the rising need to justify his reasons. She represented everything he had turned his back on fifteen years ago: the money, breeding, and the hypocrisy of the class.

He had thought he had cut that part of himself out like some malignant growth. Although, lately—he scowled. Just because you cannot see the seeds of disease did not mean the body was not fertile to grow them. It was as if all that absurd, feminine, outrageous poking had planted a restlessness deep within his chest.

It was strangling his resolve.

This would not do. He had been right to send the pretty Miss Bedegrayne on her way. He did not need to get involved in one of her absurd schemes. What did someone of her age and position know of hardship and dire consequences?

Nothing, he was certain of it.

He swallowed some more ale. Miss Bedegrayne would bother him no more, her parting glare said as much. Rayne reminded himself that he was glad he had seen the last of her. Partly, because the lust simmering in his gut would wane, but also he feared the next time they met, he might be tempted to help her.

TWO

Devona could not think of another moment in her life when she had felt more miserable. All her carefully laid plans to gain Lord Tipton's assistance faded into oblivion when he had ordered them out of his town house. She had tried to explain. Blast him, she had even begged, for all the good it had done. Sizing up the situation as a complete failure, Gar had hooked an arm around her waist and dragged her out of the house. Absolutely mortifying! She could trust Pearl and Gar to remain silent, and as for Lord Tipton . . . she doubted the odd man had any friends to tell about her humiliating debacle of an evening.

A clock somewhere in the house chimed the three o'clock hour. Devona snuggled deeper into the bedclothes, her back automatically seeking the warmth of her sister. Wynne, the eldest by two years, had been asleep when she and Pearl had slipped silently into the room to undress her. They had attended the same ball that evening. She was certain Wynne was curious as to why she had arrived home before Devona when she had been the one to leave early, pleading a headache.

Devona sighed. She should try to be more like her sister. Patient and practical, Wynne was too much of a lady to show up at a gentleman's residence, demanding to be seen. No one would ever scream at her that she was responsible for the death of a decent, young man.

"Your feet are cold," Wynne murmured, her voice thick from sleep.

"Sorry."

"And you are twitching. Stop it." She rolled over and placed her hand on Devona's shoulder. "Where did you go after you left the Fowlers'?"

"Who said I went anywhere?" She tried to sound innocent, and was grateful the room was dark.

"Because I left the ball shortly after you did and you were not here when I arrived."

Devona felt her sister move off the bed, she assumed to light a candle. "I guess you arrived when I was watching Gar and some of the other men play cards downstairs." The lie was a little weak. Maybe she could bribe Gar to back her up.

A small flame burst into life, filling the room with cavorting shadows. Wynne walked around the bed and placed the candle on a table close to Devona's face. "Papa might believe that tale, but I know you better." She picked up a discarded shawl and wrapped it around her shoulders. "Were you meeting a man?"

Devona mentally added *not an idiot* to her growing list of her sister's virtues. Giving up the pretense of sleep, she sat up in the bed. Wynne climbed back into bed and slipped her bare legs under the blankets.

"I vow it is still cold enough to freeze water. What is the time, do you think?"

"Three or after, I suppose. We should go to sleep." Was it too much to hope that her sister would take the hint? Obviously so, since her sister's next words confirmed her determination to continue their discussion.

"We would be, if you were not intent on tangling the bedding and I was not so worried about you." A small line appeared on her brow, as she critically studied her younger sister.

Devona supposed if she had to choose a favorite between her two sisters, she liked Wynne the best. They were the closest in age. Irene was eleven years older, married to a viscount, and the eldest of the Bedegrayne siblings. Brock, the heir, was next, then Nyle, Wynne, and finally herself. There had been another brother, Bran, but he had drowned two years before she had been born.

Wynne nibbled her lip and still managed to look lovely despite the late hour. They did not share the same temperament, or looks, for that matter. Although their height and build were closely matched, the similarities ended there. Wynne favored their mother. Her pale blond hair and cream and rose complexion gave her a fragile bearing. It was also misleading. One could see her strength by just looking into the cool, green pools of her eyes. With one glance she could make a man feel like he was king of her affections or slice off his head. Devona always admired that particular trait. A few years back, she had practiced those looks hundreds of times in front of the mirror without success. Whatever Wynne did, it was so much a part of her. She was now using those green eyes of hers to inspect and assess.

"This goes back to Mr. Claeg, does it not?"

Devona wrapped her arms around her waist, feeling the chill in the room. "A few years ago, he was simply Doran," she accused, lacking heat. "We all played together as children . . . fished and played near the same ponds."

"I know what he is, Devona. And what he is not."

"Wynne, he is going to die and it is all my fault!" Tears filled her eyes, as they always did when she thought about it.

"Who told you that?"

"Doran's mama and sister, two weeks ago. I came across them on Fleet Street while running errands." Wynne took her hand and squeezed it to offer comfort. "It was simply dreadful, the hateful things they said to me. The worst is that I agree with them."

"So what did they have to do with your absence this evening?"

Devona clutched her sister's hand to the point of pain. "First, swear. You mustn't tell a soul."

Wynne placed her cheek next to Devona's and sighed. "I swear."

Devona closed her eyes and began to recount her embarrassing encounter with Lord Tipton. Her sister quietly listened, rocking them gently, offering Devona comfort the only way she could. There was never any doubt that Wynne could be trusted with her secrets. After all, loyalty was at the top of that growing list of virtues.

Four days passed before Devona felt she could risk the blatant act of disobedience she was about to commit. Even understanding Wynne would have disapproved. With Pearl and Gar beside her, they traveled by hackney coach to their destination. Although reckless, Devona never considered herself a fool. She would pay dearly if her father's coach was recognized on Newgate Street.

Devona had visited Doran twice since his incarceration at Newgate. Horrified by his condition, she had told her family of the first visit at the urging of Pearl. Knowing they would never appreciate her true reasons for seeing him, she had argued instead that it was her Christian duty to offer him support.

Her ears were still ringing from her father's scathing lecture and threats. He thought he had her properly cowed, but her dear papa had underestimated her resolve and guilt. She used a little more cunning to arrange the next visit. She could not travel to the prison unescorted, so Pearl and Gar were enlightened and then sworn to secrecy. They had figured she was reckless enough to go without them, so they had agreed someone needed to protect her from her latest insane venture.

"So where does the family think you've wandered off to?" Pearl tartly inquired, now that she had had a few days to recover from what Devona privately dubbed the Tipton Tragedy.

"Cards at Mrs. Elizabeth Watts', I think."

" 'Tis a sad day for us all, when you can look me in the eye and have me believing it."

"Do not worry so, Pearl. It will be truth by the end of the day. I just fibbed a bit on our arrival time."

The coachman called out as the coach slowed to a halt. Gar opened the door and helped the ladies down. In an uncharacteristic nervous gesture, Devona smoothed the front of her simple brown-and-gold-striped carriage dress. A straw bonnet with matching ribbons and veil completed her attire. She wanted to look pleasing for Doran, but did not want to call too much attention to herself.

"Here, take this." Gar handed her a handkerchief soaked in vinegar. "Sir Thomas will have more than our positions if you are taken sick."

Doran was already waiting for them as they approached the gate. Heartsick, Devona feared he fought for a position near the gate daily, just so he would not miss her visit. Gar paid a greasy looking man two shillings so she could come within speaking distance.

"Miss Bedegrayne." He formally bowed, the simple courtesy reminding them both that he was bred for better surroundings.

"Mr. Claeg, I trust you are well."

His hazel eyes were eloquent, seemingly searching her face to commit it to memory. "No worse than most here."

"I—we—" She motioned to Pearl to step forward. "It is a basket of apples. I know it's not much. I was not even certain they would allow you to keep them." Before Doran could take the basket, the turnkey seized it. Satisfied after his quick search, he helped himself to an apple and took a huge bite.

Doran returned his wistful gaze back to Devona. "I have learned to treasure the simple gifts of humanity. Just seeing you, hearing your voice, makes the cold darkness I have to return to a little more bearable."

Her eyes were glassy with tears. "Oh, Doran." She closed her eyes; the tears left glistening channels on her cheeks. "Have you appealed to your father?"

"Appealed?" For the first time, anger cloaked the worshipful tone he always used when speaking to her. "Haven't you heard? My father has no second son. He disavowed my birthright the moment I was fettered by the magistrate." The bruises on his face gave him a sinister appearance. "He never bothered to ask if I was innocent."

Devona lowered the handkerchief from her face. "Is that what you are? Innocent."

He sagged against the metal gate and smoothed his knotted hair with a grimy hand. "Hell of a way to treat an innocent man, I say. Lock him up tight with a squirming mass of fetid squalor that even breathing air becomes a paying privilege." He gripped the grate separating them. "No air. No heat. No place to move. Only darkness, and the sounds of the dying as they lie in their own filth. All of us hoping there will be something left to identify us as human after the rats and roaches have had their feast."

"Enough!" Gar stepped in front of Devona to shield her from the ugliness lurking behind the stone walls of Newgate.

"I am so sorry, Doran. I do not know what I can do. I thought I might be able to—" She glanced away, feeling helpless. "I failed. You know my father has forbidden me to see you."

The harshness that had frozen Doran's features into a marble mask softened at her distress. "Poor pet. Always my fierce protector, eh? Had you been born male, you would have been invincible."

She choked on her laughter. "Had I been male, you would have looked awfully silly courting me with flowers." Devona held out her hand. "Here, take this." She pressed some coins into his hand when he did not take them. "Just enough to buy you some comfort, but not enough to get your throat slit." Gar pulled her back, and this time she did not resist.

Pearl shuddered as they moved through the crowd, away from the gate. "Lord, I feel like my skin is crawling with lice! If we had any sense, we would burn all our clothing and bathe in a barrel of vinegar."

"At least we can walk away from the despair. A good soaking, a freshly laundered gown, and we are the same." She glanced back. Doran was no longer visible. "I doubt Mr. Claeg will ever be the same man."

Gar made a sound of disgust. "Maybe you are just viewing the same man from a different viewpoint."

"What the devil does that mean?"

Gar never was given the chance to answer. Devona found herself facing Doran's formidable mother and his younger sister, Amara. The young woman had come out the same year as Devona. Despite the friendship between the two families, they had never been very close. She could tell by the expression on their faces that this accidental meeting would not be pleasant. Trying to appear pleased to see them, Devona said cheerfully, "Lady Claeg. Miss Claeg. I was just about—"

Lady Claeg cut her off with a look, then filled in the gap before she could take another breath. "I know what you are about, Miss Bedegrayne, and it will cease this moment. For the sake of my lord's long-standing friendship with your father, I have tried to hold my tongue."

"I meant—"

"To beguile my son, and then tell him he was not rich enough to keep you—"

Indignation dampened some of the guilt she was feeling. "I did no such thing, madam. If I had known what he was doing, for my sake or not, I would have dissuaded him from his plan. He is my friend."

"You heartless whore! He is going to die because of your greed." Lady Claeg sobbed, drawing the attention of those around them.

Devona shook off Gar's grip, stepping in front of Lady Claeg when she would have walked away. Triumphant in the public assassination of her adversary's character, the older woman was more than willing to dismiss her. It would have been better to let her walk away. She knew that and would have agreed with that direction later, after she had had a chance to settle her emotions. Unfortunately for the Claegs, Devona felt she had peeled off enough flesh on their behalf for one day.

"Madam, if you please," she said, with a clipped tone.

"Miss Bedegrayne," Pearl pleaded, recognizing the look in her lady's eyes.

"I have nothing to say, Miss Bedegrayne. Come, Amara."

Devona blocked their escape. "Good. I do. You are so willing to lay this tragedy at my feet, and I have taken it." Her voice hitched at the sudden lump in her throat. "Maybe I deserve every slur you have uttered. However, consider this. Perhaps if Doran had had the support of his family, he would have never have resolved his problems by falling in with a criminal element."

Lady Claeg's lips moved, her face becoming mottled with an unattractive shade of purple. "My son is innocent!"

"Possibly. More telling is Lord Claeg's disowning of his second son, do you not think?"

The slap Lady Claeg delivered snapped Devona's head to the left, knocking her bonnet askew. Dazed with pain and shock, she wondered if she would have ducked the attack if she had anticipated it. Her hands automatically were reaching to repair the damage.

"You will pay for your treachery. I will see to it!" The older woman whirled around, a hostile flurry of black bombazine. Amara, her eyes full of shock, met Devona's for a second, then turned away, hurrying after her mother.

Certain the encounter would soon reach the ears of the *ton* and more importantly, her father's, Devona chose the opposite direction to escape. Unshed tears of fury filled her eyes. How could she have been so foolish as to have allowed that selfish, cruel woman to goad her into fighting back? So blinded by her thoughts, she collided into someone.

"My apologies," she murmured, trying to disengage from the man's embrace. Firm hands held her by her upper arms, refusing to release her. She lifted her head, prepared to scream. Her eyes widened in recognition. "Lord Tipton."

"Mr. Tipton does me just fine, Miss Bedegrayne," he corrected. His gaze searched her face, finally settling on the red handprint on her face. A fine muscle in his jaw jumped, then tensed. "That woman hurt you. What is her name?"

He looked so fierce, yet his voice was gentle, coaxing. Seeing his face for the first time in daylight, she noted his eyes were not really pewter, but the lightest blue she had ever seen. She fought an irresistible urge to lay her hand against his cheek and soothe the anger her tart mouth had placed there.

"I deserved the slap and more, although I wish there was some manner of preventing my father from learning this."

"Why? Are you concerned about what your father will do to this woman?"

He truly was outraged on her behalf. His hands
on her arms vibrated with suppressed violence.
Devona had been defending her actions for so
long that his simple acceptance of her being in
the right without question left her breathless and
weak. She was halfway in love with him for his
faith alone. Giving in to the urge to smile, she
winced at the pain. "Lady Claeg is safe from my
father. I dread the matching handprint he'll place
on my backside for disobeying him."

Still not releasing her, he stared at her, his pale
blue eyes impaling the simple lighthearted defense she had erected to prevent herself from giving in to the urge to press her face against his
coat and cry. "If you were mine . . . uh . . . my
daughter—" the tension in his features increased,
as he fumbled his words—"I would punish the
person who dared to strike you."

"Mr. Tipton!" a man some distance away called
out and waved.

"Damn." He shook himself as if he just realized
where they were and how he was holding her.
Carefully, he loosened his grip and took a step
back. "I have a promise to keep. I must go." He
sent Gar a look, sizing the man up quickly. Apparently liking what he saw, he gave the footman
a nod. "See to it that your lady gets home without
further violence."

"Mr. Tipton, the time." His acquaintance was
almost upon them.

Lord Tipton touched her chin, forcing her to
meet his gaze. "I must go. Expect me to call on
you tomorrow."

"No!" The horror in her denial chilled the
warmth she had glimpsed in his eyes. It took her
a moment to understand her unintentional insult.
Instantly contrite, she dug her teeth into her

lower lip. "My lord, your card would be most welcome. It is just that no one in my family knows about my troubles, or that I sought out your assistance."

"And consorting with the likes of me could damage your reputation."

"You twist my words at my expense, sir. If I worry about anyone's reputation, I fear for yours." Nodding her head in his direction, she started for the hackney Gar had secured.

"Mine?" Stunned, he remained rooted to the ground. "Miss Bedegrayne, do you know what I am?" He ignored the persistent man at his side.

She turned back, her stance was challenging. "I know who you are, Lord Tipton," she said, so softly she was amazed he had heard her.

"There is no Lord Tipton, Miss Bedegrayne. He died fifteen years ago. If he is the man you seek, then your faith is misplaced." He might as well have kept silent. The woman who had haunted him since she had walked into his life was safely sheltered in the departing coach.

THREE

It never occurred to Rayne to simply ignore Miss Bedegrayne's imperial summons. Half expecting her to show up at his town house the night before, he had remained at home, magnanimously ordering Speck to allow her entry. To his disappointment, her reckless behavior had not placed her in his hands. His left hand fingered the note in his coat pocket.

Lord Tipton:
If it pleases you, will you attend us at Vauxhall Garden tomorrow. We will be watching Mr. Johnson's balloon ascension at three.
Yours,
Miss Devona Lyr Bedegrayne

Anticipation thrummed through his body as he threaded his way through the crowd, heading in the direction of the large red-and-white-striped balloon in the distance. Somewhere the beautiful Miss Bedegrayne awaited him, needed him. She did not look at him as a curiosity, a conquest, nor did she cross herself in horror when she saw him. He was just a man in her eyes. The novelty of the notion jumbled his insides. After seeing the little drama played out on Newgate Street the other day, he was inclined to agree that she might actually need his protection.

Instead of being mixed in the crowd, Miss Bedegrayne and a female companion sat apart from it on a blanket. An oversized wicker hamper kept them company. Increasing his stride, he looked forward to their meeting.

Her eyes and smile brightened when she saw him, causing his pulse to jump in his throat. She was so lovely, dressed in a celestial blue gown and a silk poke bonnet. Miss Bedegrayne said something to her companion and the other woman turned in his direction. If her expression was not as welcoming, perhaps even wary, Rayne did not care. All his attention was focused on the woman who said she needed him.

"Lord Tipton, please join us," she said, her voice breathless.

He sat as close as he dared without raising speculation. He had learned a long time ago that it took little to have people questioning his motives. "Miss Bedegrayne, how could I resist such a summons?"

Her hands fluttered up to her cheeks, as if to prevent him from seeing the pretty blush his words had stirred. "How arrogant you must think me! I suppose I should be grateful my note did not kindle your evening fire."

Giving in to the impulse to touch, he took her hand and kissed her fingers. "And miss the opportunity to see Mr. Johnson's balloon ascension? Perish the notion." He winked at her, and to his delight she giggled.

"You have firmly put me in my place, sir." Her gaze flickered to her companion, sobering a bit. "Lord Tipton, may I present my sister, Miss Wynne Bedegrayne. Wynne, this is Lord Tipton."

"Miss Bedegrayne." He bowed in her direction. At first glance the sisters looked nothing alike. Miss Wynne was a cool blonde, compared to her sister's cinnamon fire. Upon closer inspection, he concluded their eyes were similar in shape and there was a certain matching stubbornness in the way they lifted their chins.

"I have heard much about you, my lord."

It was an ambiguous statement that could be interpreted in several ways, none of them flattering.

"I told Wynne how I charged into your house uninvited," Devona volunteered, oblivious to the wariness of both her companions. "She was quite horrified, of course, and lectures me at every opportunity."

Miss Wynne glanced at her sister. "Little good it has done."

"I assume since you aren't locked in your room with only bread and watery soup to eat that yesterday's incident did not reach your father's ears?"

The sisters looked at each other, then laughed.

"No, truly, it isn't at all amusing." Devona attempted sobriety and failed. "Papa was furious. He was so busy yelling that we both missed our supper."

"I thought Papa was going to break his oath and take a leather strap to your backside."

Before Rayne could protest, Devona added, "Papa has a rule about using that form of punishment on girls above the age of thirteen."

"He was tempted to break that rule, Devona."

"I know."

"And would have, if he had heard the entire recitation of your misdeeds." Miss Wynne gave Rayne an icy glare.

"Fortunately for all, he settled on a different punishment."

"Which was?" Rayne prompted, when they did not elaborate.

"Brock," they said in unison.

Neither seemed upset with the punishment. Confused, Rayne asked, "Is it a person?"

Devona's eyes twinkled, begging him to share the great jest. "I have my doubts. He is, after all, our older brother. Papa figured I could not get in much trouble if Brock was on hand."

Miss Wynne wrinkled her nose. "Brock was entirely the wrong choice. At twenty-five, our brother has turned into quite a rake. Since our father intends to outlive us all, Brock has no need to take life seriously. It is all an adventure to him. He gambles, fights, whores—"

"Wynne!"

"It's all true, and we only hear the cleaned-up versions of his adventures. He was the wrong choice."

Rayne glanced around, searching for their guard dog. If there was to be a fight, he was one to hold his own. "Where is this adventurous brother of yours?"

Devona smiled again and Rayne felt his world tilt. "Why he's up in Mr. Johnson's balloon!"

Devona studied Rayne's profile while his attention was focused on the airborne balloon. Wynne had left them to speak with an acquaintance, giving her the chance to speak with him alone. What was he thinking, she mused. He kept shaking his head every few minutes and muttering under his breath.

"Did that brother of yours go willingly or did

your sister hold him down while you trussed him up?"

"Oh, that was the beauty of my plan. Brock was a victim of his need for adventure. A man like him could not easily dismiss an opportunity to float along with the clouds."

"Miss Bedegrayne, the balloon is tethered."

She dismissed the comment with a wave of her hand. "A minor detail. In the end, Brock and I both got what we wanted."

Rayne's fingers played with the rosettes decorating the hem of her gown, his eyes never leaving her face. "And what is it that you wanted?"

"W—why," she stuttered, finding it suddenly difficult to keep her voice steady. "To see you alone." Her reddish-brown lashes fanned across her cheeks as she stared at her lap. "That sounds indelicate."

He tapped her on the chin, luring her gaze back to his. "Perhaps. However, I happen to like where I am sitting."

Devona laughed, pleased to see humor lightening the seriousness in his eyes as well. "Well, thank you very much. A gentleman is supposed to deny a lady's faults."

The change from amused to cold struck faster than lightning in a spring storm. "I keep having to remind you that I am not a gentleman, Miss Bedegrayne. What will you do if I give in to the temptation and prove it to you?"

"Stop teasing me, sir! You would never do anything to hurt or embarrass me."

He hesitated, not sure how to accept her observation. "Since we just met, I am amazed by your conviction in my character. Placing people at such lofty assessments must lead you to be often disappointed."

"Rarely."

Rayne quietly watched Wynne hug a new arrival to the small group of women surrounding her. "Your sister would probably disagree."

"Wynne is merely protective. If you must know, she has no faith in my plan either."

"Ah, now we get to it. What kind of trouble are you in that forces you to lower yourself to dally with an outcast?"

Sensing trouble, Devona fidgeted with the strings of her reticule. "You are not the monster they say you are."

A cynical grin twisted his lips. "There is always a grain of truth to all rumors, Miss Bedegrayne."

"I have always admired you," she said softly, ignoring the quick sound of disbelief. "I was still in the nursery when I first heard the story. My brother told me it to frighten me. A young man mistakenly buried alive by his family only to be rescued by grave robbers. Quite harrowing. I am surprised no one published the account."

"You forgot the best part. When the young man arrived home, he learned that his brother had died from the same sickness, making him the heir to the title. Sadly, his family was not as overjoyed to see him. A superstitious group, they were convinced that the new heir was some sort of resurrected demon. Soon the entire parish was whispering about the differences that proved he was more than he seemed."

"Your family was grieving for the son they lost. They obviously did not understand how surviving had marked you."

Annoyance flared, then was snuffed. Devona had a feeling he was not used to people understanding, nor did he desire it.

"The tale is old, and bores me. I am satisfied

with my life." He became speculative. "So what does the story have to do with solving your troubles?"

Nerves sparked along her spine. She had to make him understand. If all efforts failed to release Doran from Newgate, his life depended on Lord Tipton's cooperation. She took a deep breath and jumped. "Are you acquainted with the Claeg family?"

"No."

"Oh, well, uh, my father thinks highly of Lord Claeg. Our country estates are rather close."

"Convenient."

Devona straightened her spine, and plowed ahead with a determination that most found admirable if not a little irritating when one was the focus. "I grew up playing with Lord Claeg's children. In particular, his second son, Doran." She did not like how Lord Tipton's gaze had narrowed to pewter-colored slits. "As we grew to adults, Doran started to view me not as a sister, but as a—ah, you know."

"Yes, I know," he grimly muttered. "Are you engaged, Miss Bedegrayne?"

"Yes. No." His glare was rather unnerving and her thoughts scattered for a moment like white petals on the grass. "He wanted to marry me, but Papa was against it. Doran is the second son of a baron. He was educated as due his position. He just lacks direction. Papa said that he was shorted the steel needed to hold someone like me. Whatever that means," she mumbled more to herself, and blinked in surprise when Lord Tipton replied.

"I think I do." He tapped his riding whip against his thigh. "So being the lovely, spirited, backward creature that you are, you decided to take on the opposition."

She frowned, thinking that his deductions made her seem a trifle nutty. "I am not backward."

He grinned, delighted by her reaction. "I also called you lovely."

"To soften the sting, I bet."

"Just remember you were the one who came calling. You must admire something about me?"

Devona glared at the mock sincerity on his handsome face and knew the truth would only get her in trouble. She scooted back when he reached for her hand. "What would you expect from an addled chit?"

He stared at her in awe. "Your eyes lose their blue when you have your back up."

"I do not—" She lowered her voice when she noticed her tone had caught the attention of a strolling couple. "This is getting us nowhere."

"Are you certain, Miss Bedegrayne? I am positively fascinated by the many facets of your character." He held up a hand, relenting when she started to search for something to hit him with. "Calm yourself, you maddening creature. You are too adorable when vexed. All right, so Papa has cast your beau onto the streets and you are feeling badly 'cause he's a dear friend. I doubt your father is going to accept my recommendation, even if I was inclined to give it. Which I'm not." He leaned forward, making certain she understood.

She did. "I do not need your word, sir. I need your skills as a surgeon."

He relaxed back into a slouch and gave her a roguish leer. "You look in splendid health to me. Trust me, I've examined you quite thoroughly."

Why, the man was actually flirting with her! She

gave him a playful shove. "Not me, you fool. Doran."

"I admire your loyalty, but if the man is ill, allow his family to see to him."

Always the hardest part to explain, she felt the sting of tears. "Not ill. He's going to die, and it is all my fault!"

"Why don't you tell me the rest of it?" he gently coaxed, sensing she was tightrope-walking across a thin wire of emotions.

Her hand shot out, a gesture of helplessness. "After Doran returned from a tour of Italy, he got it into his head that we should marry. Papa's refusal seemed to make him more determined."

"Do you love him?"

"How could I not? I have known him for most of my life."

His expression remained carefully blank as he mulled over her words. "Love has many degrees . . . the kind of love you have for one's brother is different from the love you have for a lover, a husband."

"Since I have never taken a lover nor a husband, I can not compare." She could not understand how the discussion had disintegrated into such an improper topic. Stranger still was the fact that she felt prompted to reply.

Satisfaction gleamed in his gaze. "Sometimes lover and husband are the same man."

If he had set out to distract her from crying, he had succeeded. Their conversation was definitely out of her element. Showing her displeasure, she squared her shoulders and made a production out of smoothing her skirt. "I appreciate hearing a surgeon's perspective on relations," she said with just enough tartness to have him grinning again, "However, the degree of my affection for Doran is not under consideration."

"My observations were merely that of a man. No more, no less, Devona Lyr Bedegrayne."

Her name was a purring caress from his lips. The sounds stroked her, making her feel hot and restless. He was dressed as fitting his station this afternoon, she noted, thinking back to all his claims that he was not a true gentleman. What was troubling to her was that she almost preferred him the way she had first met him, half dressed and barely civil. This teasing, playfully sensual side of him made her feel that each of her nineteen years had not prepared her for a man like him. Lord Tipton was indeed a wicked man.

He held up a hand, stalling her from retorting. "All right, enough. Let's continue. You were explaining how you are at fault."

Since the subject was a safer course for her, she gathered her thoughts. "He never gave up on the idea of having me. While trying to prove to my father his worthiness, he fell in with a criminal element. He was arrested three weeks ago for his participation in a coining ring."

"For most that is an automatic death sentence."

"It is for Doran. His father has disowned him. Who would vouch for him if he cannot call upon his own family? He has no money, no friends—he will hang."

"You feel responsible."

Tears streamed down her cheek. She was going to cry after all. "He did it for me. If he had not felt like he had to be more than he was, he would have never been driven to this crime." She listened for a second to the people, laughing and chatting around them. "I have to do something to save him."

"Where do I come into this scheme of yours? If you expect me to break him out, you are—"

Devona shook her head. "No. I would not ask this of you. I want you to resurrect him after they cut him down from the gallows."

Whatever Lord Tipton had expected, it was clearly not this. Rubbing his face, he looked away. "Do you know what you are asking?"

She grabbed his hands and squeezed. "You are Le Chirurgien de la Mort. They say you have made it your life's ambition to cheat death. You are a highly regarded surgeon, if anyone could resurrect Doran, you are the one."

"Christ, Devona!" Rayne jerked his hands from hers, tension knotting them into fists. "You have spent too much time listening to legends in the ballroom. I may not attend those affairs, but I know what I'm called. The Refined Corpse. Death's Surgeon, and a few other less savory sobriquets. Names. Just meaningless names made up by small-minded people for things they do not understand."

Was she so wrong? Despair intertwined with grief, choking her. "But your work . . . the people you have helped. I know."

He took her face in his hands, willing her to understand. "You are asking for a miracle. If this were fifty years ago before they started using the automatic drop, I would say his chances of surviving would have been about even. Think! His neck is going to have to support the weight of his body for fifteen minutes. I can't help you."

Her tears flowed over his fingers. "I will be responsible. I do not know if I can live with that."

A horn blew in the distance. Their gazes

locked, a silent battle of wills. They ignored the entertainment that was stirring up the crowd around them. He was not going to help her, she thought, her desperateness as wild as the rumble she heard in the distance, warning of the approaching storm.

Screams, surging over the landscape like a tidal wave, filled the air. Everything slowed at a time when Devona would have expected speed. Their heads turned in the direction of the commotion. The crowd cleaved for a runaway chaise driven in their direction by four thundering horses. Before the danger and the horror could fully register on her face, Rayne blocked her horrific view by tackling her. The ground spun as he rolled them out of the path of those killing hooves, wood, and metal.

Time returned to its normal tempo as the horses and chaise raced over the blanket, flattening the food hamper. Devona lay tangled in Rayne's arms, the warmth of his body barely keeping the chill she felt at bay. His hat was gone, the neat queue mussed so that one side was free, his long hair tickling her face. Both of them were breathing hard, and she could not decide if the pounding heartbeat she was feeling against her chest was his or her own.

"We could have died," she whispered, her voice raspy from dust and reaction. "You saved us."

Panting, he stared down at her, his eyes fierce and his body still battle-tense. He looked every bit the hardened warrior who had protected her body with his own. She wanted to comfort him, to tell him she was fine, but she could do nothing more than lay caged under him and tremble. Her lips parted to thank him and the warrior in him seized the invitation. Warm lips settled over her cool ones. Reverently, he used his mouth to reassure them both that they were alive. He stroked, he nibbled, and his tongue flicked her upper lip. Devona felt the ground whirl around her again.

"Release her, you bastard!"

Having nothing to do with pleasure, Devona closed her eyes and groaned into Rayne's mouth. Abruptly, he was yanked off her body. She watched him shrug off the two men who held him, his stance one of defiance and challenging confidence.

"I'm going to kill you for touching her!"

She knew that voice. Brock, finished exploring the heavens, had plummeted to earth like some arrogant golden god prepared to smite the mortal who dared to touch his baby sister.

Sitting up, she threaded her fingers through her hair and pulled out a small stick. The gravity of their situation was starting to hit her as she realized their near-death experience had drawn an audience. Wynne approached her, placing a shawl around her to conceal her torn sleeve. Why had she not noticed how terrible she looked? Her gown was torn, her bonnet gone, and her hair was unbound. Having been thoroughly kissed, she was certain she looked quite brazen. Wynne gave her a sympathetic hug.

Not liking the expression on her brother's face, Devona stood. "Brock, there is no need for this."

He did not acknowledge that he had heard her. His glare promised death and it was focused on Lord Tipton. "I demand justice for my sister."

"A duel for a kiss?" Rayne smirked. "Can I help it if your sister keeps throwing herself at me, Bedegrayne?"

Devona heard a collective gasp from several ladies. She closed her eyes and said a quick prayer.

Brock was not the only one feeling provoked and someone was going to pay. A scuffle broke out between the two men. Her brother swung and clipped Rayne in the chin. She winced as she heard his neck bones crack. Rayne repaid in kind by delivering a painful blow to Brock's kidneys. Men came forward and grabbed both budding pugilists before they could do any more damage.

Her brother struggled against the restraining embrace. "Name your choice of weapon and seconds, you devil's piss."

Devona jumped between them, silencing Rayne's taunting retort with a glare. "Stop it, both of you!" She grabbed her brother by the front of his ruined coat. "You will not challenge him. In fact, you will apologize—"

"Apologize!" he exploded.

"Yes! He was not attacking me, you simpleton. He saved my life. I would have been under the wheels of a runaway chaise if he had not rolled me away from their path. What was he supposed to do, ask your permission?"

Brock was still far from appeased. "And what was he doing with your mouth, Devona. Reminding you to breathe?" He renewed his struggle, pinning Rayne with a glare. "You are a dead man."

Rayne's face lost the answering fury, becoming carefully blank. "You tell me nothing new, Bedegrayne." Disgusted with all of them, he walked away.

FOUR

Rayne was surprised and disappointed that the bold Miss Bedegrayne had yet to figure out a way to contact him. If her father had any sense, he would have locked her in her room and set a guard at the door. Not that he thought such high-handed tactics would discourage the lady. Still, five days had passed. There had been no notes, no seconds pounding on his door, none of the usual chaos he had come to expect from a Bedegrayne. If he didn't know himself better, he would have had to acknowledge the edginess he was feeling as loss. Did he actually miss her? It was absurd.

It wasn't boredom, that was certain, he concluded while covertly watching the older woman across from him. His mother. At forty-seven, Lady Jocelyn was still magnificent. Excellent bones, he thought, one side of his mouth lifting as if he had made a joke. Her once-blond hair was streaked with white and darker undertones. She had a quiet dignity which demanded respect.

She also was petrified to sit in the same room with him.

Call it perverse, but Rayne saw no reason to alleviate her fears. Some might even say he went out of the way to provoke them. If she saw her only living son as some kind of monster that needed to be shunned or killed, then who was he to deny it? True enough, he had stopped being her son years ago.

"The reasons for this visit must be fairly life-threatening to abandon the safety of Foxenclover." He avoided the family's country estate, just as fervently as she avoided London. Unfortunately, there were times neither could avoid their duty.

She met his gaze, then faltered. "We must discuss your sister Madeleina."

"Madam, why would I wish to discuss your daughter?" He never thought about the younger sister his mother had conceived after his so-called rebirth. It galled him to know she existed because his parents had tried to create another heir to replace him, after it was clear they had not considered him worthy of his birthright.

"She is fourteen this summer. She has been allowed to roam wild and it has given her some rather eccentric notions. I have done my best on the limited funds you provide." Her tone sharpened despite her fear. "She needs proper guidance. A school for ladies, I think. Before long it will be time for us to think of presentation at Court."

He shrugged carelessly, sensing the action would infuriate Lady Jocelyn. "She could take up snuff and wearing breeches for all I care."

Her teacup clattered as she placed it on the table. "Care or not, the child is your sister. I will have you do right by her!"

"Polish or rough as gravel, I am certain I can find some farmer to remove her from our hands."

Her pale complexion became a blotchy pink. "What do you think your father would say if he was alive to witness such callousness? You have permitted the country house to fall to ruin, we have been reduced to letting go most of the staff. The small stipend you send for our care goes for our food, a few gowns, and precious else. Your grandmother would be horrified by your lack of honor, sir!"

It was a barb meant to sting, and it did. "Mum accepted who I was, more so than you and my sire." She had died four and half years after his illness, leaving a hole in him that never seemed to heal. Of them all, she had loved him best. Her death had severed his final emotional ties to the Wyman family.

"If it is your desire to punish me for all the sins of what I did and did not do, then that is your privilege. However, Madeleina is an innocent. She does not deserve this coldness."

To hear his mother defend her, when there was a time he had needed her support and had received silence, had made his sweet, eccentric sister his natural enemy. "How long will you be residing in the city?"

Dry-eyed, her hate plainly visible on her face, she stiffly stood. "I am returning to Foxenclover forthwith. I can see I made this visit in vain."

Rayne didn't bother to reply. She thought she was disappointed. Her presence reminded him of all the grief, anger, and hatred he had not put behind. It disturbed him to discover that he was still being haunted by a fifteen-year-old incident.

"You were not the one groomed to be Viscount Tipton. However, once we lost Devlin, and your father . . . I thought you would find purpose in the title, something you seemed to have lost." She started to walk toward the door, and then surprised him by stopping in front of him. "You are so removed from me, I cannot even fathom what you think of us. Are we a burden, or just an amusing instrument for revenge? Or maybe, just maybe we are a reminder that you once were human."

"Still telling the parish that I'm the devil's creature, Mother?" he taunted softly, the menace in his tone causing her to back up toward the door.

"Whatever you are, you are not my son. It would have been better if you had remained dead." She turned her back and walked out of the room.

Rayne reached into a pocket, removing the small, smooth stone he liked to rub while working out his problems. It would take more than guilt to get him to change his mind about how he dealt with the Wyman family. It was their poor luck that the man they hated also controlled the family's finances. It had to rankle his mother, and that amused him. Sadly, he had to take his joys where they landed. His thoughts drifted to Devona Bedegrayne, causing his smile to become genuine. She was the only one of late not wishing for his quick demise. He liked her spirit and her loyalty, something lacking in his own family. He ruefully shook his head, thinking what a handful she was. Rayne was also confident, if she were to be in any man's hands, it would be his.

Devona was enjoying herself this evening despite her unwanted chaperones. Brock had been dismissed as useless, much to his relief. He still wanted to put a ball into Lord Tipton for kissing her in such a carnal manner, but even Papa had to agree the man had rescued her, and in front of witnesses. Some allowances had to be made.

The duty of keeping control of the family's wild hair had fallen to Irene. Catching her older sister's eye from across the room, she made a face. Someone older might have been preferred, however Devona thought her sister was stuffy enough to fill the skin of three maiden aunts. According to their father, Irene was an excellent example of feminine grace in action. Married at seventeen to a viscount, she promptly gave him three sons in five years. Now thirty-one, she was expecting again, although she was not far enough along to show yet. Irene felt it was her duty to lend a hand since Devona lacked a mother's guidance. She was prepared to help their overwhelmed papa until it was time to leave for her confinement in the country. Her departure could not come soon enough for Devona. Still, she would have missed the Kissicks' ball if her sister had not been such a paragon.

"Miss Bedegrayne, we missed you the other evening at the Goodmans'."

Devona smiled at the man approaching her. "Mr. Lockwood, how are you this evening?" She glanced over at Irene and caught her approving nod. She tried not to groan. Obviously, her companion was on her sister's approved list.

"Fine and well. Just trying to avoid dancing this evening. I fear I twisted my leg dismounting from my favorite mount. Why are you doing your best to blend into the wallpaper? Not your usual behavior, I must say." The lines on his face deepened, his brown eyes teasing her into matching his grin.

He was a sweet man, she mused, close to forty if she were to guess. Someone once told her he had been engaged, but it had ended badly. She sensed he was attracted to her, and would pursue her if she had showed any interest. She hadn't. Whatever his feelings, he kept them in check, al-

ways prepared to be a cheerful supper companion
or partner in cards.

Still awaiting her reply, she opened her fan with
a Chinese motif. Lowering her voice, she spoke
behind her fan. "I suppose I have made the gossip rounds again?"

Oz raised his hand to a companion in the distance. "My dear, you have been very naughty if
my sources tell the truth."

"What have you heard?"

"Which drama shall I repeat?" he whispered
back in mock horror.

She closed her eyes. "Do your worst."

"I heard you were brawling with Lady Claeg,"
he said, his brows lifting, daring her to deny it.

"Old news, Oz. The woman hates me." Devona
held her chin up, but the tremor in her lower lip
ruined her haughty effect. She had never been
hated by anyone.

Seeing her distress, Oz gave her a sympathetic
pat on the hand. "Never mind Glenda Claeg. She
would despise anyone who could take her son
away from her. Speaking of Doran, how is he
holding up?"

"Weary. Desperate. Fearful. Like everyone else
behind that gate." Thinking of Doran made her
feel guilty for being there, enjoying the music and
the people around her.

"Have you had a chance to think on my suggestion? Any luck finding a surgeon?"

"I made some inquiries," she said carefully, noting her sister was moving in their direction. "I
approached Lord Tipton. Do you know him?"

"Only by reputation." His face took on a mien
of concern. "Tipton," he said, under his breath.
"Devona, when I suggested that you find a surgeon to help Doran, I meant someone not so no-

torious. Dangerous. Your name is already linked with him."

"Doran needed the best. Lord Tipton is that man. He saved my life, Oz. Everyone will forget that part, and turn his heroic gesture into something sordid."

"I hear your brother is prepared to call him out."

"Just wishful thinking on Brock's side. None of it matters anyway. Lord Tipton refused to help."

Oz's next words were interrupted by Irene's appearance at their side.

"Mr. Lockwood, you must cease from monopolizing my sister's attention, 'else there will be rumors that you are ready for the parson's mousetrap."

"Irene, please." It had been wishful thinking that she could endure an evening under her sister's direction without being mortified. "Mr. Lockwood has injured his leg and is content to remain at my side and listen to the music. There is no need to harass the poor man."

Oz, always prepared to charm a lady out of the sulks, gallantly kissed Irene's hand. "Viscountess, ignore this ungrateful child. How can a man be poor when surrounded by such beauty?"

Devona practically rolled her eyes at how easily her sister fell for the bait meant to distract her. "Did you have need of me, Irene?" she asked, thinking to spare Oz further torment.

Irene blinked, momentarily confused by the question. "Oh, Lord Nevin was searching for you. He thought he might escort you to supper."

"Hmm." She had neatly turned the conversation back to Irene's quest for finding her a proper husband.

"Why is it," she whispered to Oz, loud enough for her sister to hear, "that every married person is not content until the rest of us are as tightly leg-shackled as they are?"

Irene took her comment seriously. "Is this why you have been acting so recklessly? Do you use it as a means to escape marriage?"

Devona could not resist teasing her. "Marriage is like being trapped in prison."

"Where do you get these notions?"

"Well, it is a life sentence, is it not?" Her sister was staring at her as if she had just crossed her eyes at the king. Oz coughed, trying to conceal his merriment behind his hand.

Devona's eyes gave her away. Irene's narrowed, looking so much like their mother. "I do not understand how Wynne tolerates your jests." Prepared to make a dramatic exit, she spoiled it by touching her stomach. "Oh."

Instantly contrite, Devona put her arm around her. "What is it? The babe?"

Her sister's face went white. "Yes. No. The babe is making me ill."

"Come then, I will help you to a room so you may rest. Oz—er, Mr. Lockwood?" She looked to him to make their apologies, but he was staring at something beyond them. She followed his gaze and could not credit the sight. Lord Tipton had just entered the room.

Devona returned downstairs once the worst of Irene's sickness had passed. Her sister was still weak from vomiting, so she had wanted to lie down until she felt better. A child not much bigger than a thought had done in the paragon. Devona promised herself that she would purchase the new family member a very special gift since it had accomplished the impossible. She was free of yet another chaperone.

She slowly eased her way through the crowd, smiling and nodding to each familiar face, her eyes scanning for Lord Tipton. What was he doing here? She had been told he had little use for his title, and less still for society. It was too much to hope the man broke one of his rules just to see her. The thought gave her a very feminine thrill. After all, he had kissed her. Her practical side also reminded her that he had not made any attempt to contact her after his confrontation with Brock. What if the last thing he wanted was to see her? Her heart skipped a few beats at the unpleasant thought. He might have already left the town house!

A hand shot out and stalled her before she could have broken into a run. "Whoa. You are going to break an ankle going at that pace." Devona's gaze shot up, shocked that she was so blind in purpose that she had almost dashed into Lord Nevin. Utterly mortifying! At twenty-eight, the handsome earl was reputed to cause the local ladies' hearts to race, and she included herself in that group.

Extraordinarily tall, the blond giant smiled down at her, his aquamarine-colored eyes twinkled with amusement. The rogue knew his effect on women. She inhaled, a weak attempt to settle her nerves. The dimple in his left cheek deepened.

"Lord Nevin, you startled me." She mentally kicked herself for sounding so dazed and breathless.

"Where were you off to?"

"I was, um, looking for someone."

Gold-tipped brown lashes lowered seductively. "Dare I hope such energy was meant for me?"

Devona forgot to breathe. Before she had met Lord Tipton, she would have declared Lord Nevin the most handsome man this Season. Second place did not lessen his devastating effects on her constitution. The man spent most of his life chasing women, not that any of them were running particularly fast. For some reason she could not fathom, he had decided to include her in his little pursuit games this Season. She highly doubted that he was considering her for his future countess. Her papa would have pounced on such gossip. No, she had an awful feeling that it was her reckless nature that had caught his roving eye.

"No—yes—I'm—" It was getting worse by the minute. She should just shut her mouth and move in the opposite direction. "I thought I saw someone I knew." *Good, one coherent sentence out. Now leave!*

"I spoke to your sister earlier. She gave me the impression you were lacking an escort for supper." Lord Nevin had yet to let go of her hand. "I would be honored to take you." He raised her gloved hand up to his lips. Twisting it palm up, he kissed, flicking the tip of his tongue across the open slit at her wrist.

Devona shivered. "Lord Nevin."

"Miss Bedegrayne regrets she must refuse you," Rayne drawled, behind them.

Taking advantage of Lord Nevin's surprise, she snatched her hand from his loose grasp. "Lord Tipton, do you know Lord Nevin?"

"Not intimately." Though his voice seemed controlled, the look in his eyes was predatory.

Lord Nevin sized up his rival. Without taking his gaze off Rayne, he asked, "Miss Bedegrayne, perhaps you would like to cool yourself in the conservatory?"

She looked to each of the men, feeling the instant hostility radiate from both. She had enough problems, trying to figure out how to help Doran, without having two men fighting over her. She glanced around to see if her friend Oz Lockwood was about. He might be the one to diffuse the situation. "I—"

Rayne clutched her elbow and guided her to his side. No one missed the proprietary gesture. "Miss Bedegrayne has kindly accepted my escort to supper. Is this not correct?" What his tone lacked in steel, he made up for it in his grasp.

Devona tried not to wince. "Yes, yes. My apologies, Lord Nevin. My sister was mistaken."

A silent message passed between the two men. Finally, Lord Nevin nodded. "Another time, then, Miss Bedegrayne. Tipton."

Rayne did not bother to wait for the man to depart. He steered Devona away, leading her to stairs that would take them to the refreshments.

Their partnering was drawing attention. She could feel everyone's speculative stares; hear their indistinct murmurs. "Thank you."

"For what?"

"Lord Nevin has become somewhat persistent this Season." When they reached the stairs, she was glad he still held her arm since her legs felt as wobbly as rubber.

"I would have thought your brother would recognize one of his kind and warned him off."

"Brock does not like these functions. He says they are for scheming mamas and fortune hunters."

Without a word he pushed her into an empty chair and wandered off to get her something to eat. As was the custom, he would stand by while she ate her supper. Later, he would partake in his own alone.

Rayne returned with a plate heaped with enough food for several large men. Handing her the plate, he leaned against the wall, keeping a glass of wine for himself.

"Perhaps we should call Lord Nevin back," she suggested, eyeing the heavily laden plate dubiously.

He did not bother to disguise his irritation. "Why would we want to do that?"

"Well, among the three of us we might do justice to this portion."

A reluctant grin tugged at the corner of his mouth. "Outside of enough, eh?"

"A trifle." She was pleased when he laughed outright. "Why did you say Brock should recognize one of his own kind?" Devona cut into a slice of ham. She wasn't hungry, but it was a respectable excuse for them to be seen together.

"Lord Nevin is not the man for you, Devona."

She warmed at the intimate use of her name, which was good since his glare was utterly chilling. "Why? He is handsome, titled, rich. Most women would be honored to have his attention."

Instead of anger flaring, he gave her a considering look. "This is important to you?"

"Not in the manner you think," she said, stung that he thought her such a superficial creature. "Besides, Lord Nevin just finds me amusing. Why else would he seek out Sir Thomas Bedegrayne's reckless daughter for a wife when there are so many other suitable candidates? If he was to choose a Bedegrayne, Wynne would be a better choice if you could convince her to have him."

Something lightened in Rayne's expression. In

another, she might have called it relief. "Your sister would not marry a handsome, flush earl?"

Devona wrinkled her nose. "Lord Nevin? No. Those smoldering looks may turn a lady's insides to jelly, however, she would refuse him for the same reasons that you believe he is not acceptable for me."

"Reasons?" he echoed.

"You said so yourself that he is very much like Brock. He probably spends most of his time drinking, fighting, gambling away his fortune, and womanizing. I would hate to be the one to ruin all his fun." She glanced around. "You forgot to get me something to drink."

"Here, take this." He offered her his wine, daring her to drink. It was a challenge she found difficult to resist. She took his glass and sipped, wondering if she was putting her lips in the same place he had. Her hand trembled, recalling how his lips had felt against hers.

A mischievous glimmer lightened his demeanor. "What's wrong, Devona?"

"N—nothing."

"Are your certain? The tips of your ears are a delightful shade of red."

In self-defense, Devona smirked. "I suppose it is too much to hope that if you can dress like a gentleman, that you can act like one as well!"

"Yes, it is."

Well, well, the man was teasing her. All those rumors about him being a ruthless, dangerous creature of the night must have been all nonsense. Rayne could be intimidating, and heroic, she mentally added, remembering how he had saved them at the gardens. Above all, he had been nothing but kind to her, even if he had refused to help her.

"I did not realize you moved in society."

He took his wine back, purposely turning the glass so that his mouth touched where hers had. "It is difficult to avoid people when living in a city."

"That is not what I mean."

"I know." Rayne stared past her, watching the elegantly dressed couples chatting around them. "And you are correct. I generally avoid such gatherings, unless it befits me."

Not understanding, she gazed up at him. "Like it does now, Lord Tipton?"

"Yes."

Devona had expected him to deny his heritage, as he had invariably done before. She had tried, and failed, in understanding why a man would deny his birthright. It provided him a position in society, respect, and opportunities. Rayne had walked away from all of it. Remarkable still, he had thrived. True, many here would not consider becoming a surgeon something to boast about, but he had made his choice, then had become the best in his profession. It made one think of all the possibilities, if he had chosen to embrace his advantages.

Rayne tenderly reached out, entwining his finger within the coil of one of the curls framing her face. He seemed mesmerized by her hair. Devona held her breath, not secure where his thoughts were taking him. If he tried to kiss her . . . No, he would not dare! Already, the people around them had noted his bold gesture. Someone in her family was bound to hear of it.

"W—what?" she asked, worried a little by the fierce satisfaction she saw in his expression. Her breathing improved when he reluctantly released her hair.

He pitched his voice so that only she could hear. "I have reconsidered your request for my assistance."

She fought back the urge to jump up and embrace him. "You did? Why did you not say something earlier? Is this the reason you came tonight?"

"Yes, and more," was his ambiguous reply.

Everything was going to be fine now. Relief was almost heady as the wine she had sipped. "I cannot begin to tell you how grateful I am. Doran will be thrilled to learn that you are willing to—"

"No."

His adamant refusal threw her off balance. Did he not just promise to help? Mentally regrouping, she considered her options, deciding to attack with guilt. "Without your help, Doran Claeg is going to die."

"I never said I would not help." Taking advantage of her stunned silence, he continued. "There have been a few changes in your plan."

"What changes?"

He leaned close enough for her to smell the wine on his hot breath. "I've thrown out your plan and have come up with one of my own."

Devona was too flustered by his announcement to react to the light kiss he placed on her temple before he pulled back. "It was a good plan!"

"No, it wasn't. I warned you before that the odds were not in Claeg's favor. What I have in mind isn't as dramatic, but your friend has a better chance of surviving."

The ball might have been in another country as far as Devona was concerned. All of her attention was focused on Rayne. "When do we start?"

"Why, Devona, we already have."

She thought for a moment. "Your emergence back into society."

"You are a clever woman. Sometimes too clever, eh?"

She ignored his taunt, considering the gesture magnanimous since he did all but tweak her nose. "So you attend a few balls, renew your membership at the clubs. How does that help Doran?"

"You are picking at threads, thus missing the grander scheme. You want me to help Claeg. Well, position is power, Miss Bedegrayne. My mother reminded me the other day that I rarely flex it."

"Your mother?" She gave up all pretense of eating and set her plate aside.

"Lord Tipton shoulders a certain authority that a mere surgeon cannot hope to achieve."

What he proposed staggered her. She had begged his help, and not only was he giving it, but he was making plans to change his life to achieve it. "It was not my intention to force you back into a life your abhor. I thought your skills in medicine could—"

"It is done."

Like a magician, he waved his hand, encouraging her to view the new world he had created just for her. Nerves started skipping along her spine while she instinctively searched for a means to escape.

"The real question is," he continued in a husky drawl, "are you willing to pay the price for my services?"

FIVE

Two hours later, Rayne was sitting comfortably in a hackney, looking forward to a warm fire and brandy. No more hired coaches for Lord Tipton, he mused. He supposed he should send word that the ones in storage bearing the family crest should be refurbished. When his mother learned of his latest actions, she would definitely conclude her son was under some sort of possession! He was. Her name was Devona Lyr Bedegrayne.

Naturally, he had picked her fair face from the crowd the moment he had entered the makeshift ballroom. She had adorned herself in light blue this evening. The gown was trimmed with silver net at the sleeves and silver-gilt thread at the waist and hem. The soft hue gave her skin a creamy glow that begged to be caressed.

She had had her long hair pulled up artfully and contained within a band of fabric to match her gown. A long gold pin, tipped with a large pearl secured the style. He could have spent the evening watching those fiery, silken curls dance and shift with every tilt of her heart-shaped face.

Rayne had not been pleased to observe her succumbing to the charms of Lord Nevin. Notorious, seductive bastard! Devona was too naïve to be interesting prey for such a surfeited villain. He won-

dered what kind of game Nevin was playing? It
would end tonight, even if he had to press his
point home by sword. At least she had dismissed
Nevin easily enough. Placated by the memory, he
relaxed into the bench.

Too clever for her own good, she had guessed
right away that his presence at the ball was due
to her. However, he had managed to surprise the
scheming Miss Bedegrayne by introducing a
scheme of his own.

"Are you willing to pay the price for my services?"

Appalled, she all but sputtered, "You want money?"

*"Some would consider gold an adequate dressing to
heal old wounds. Speaking as a surgeon, I can tell you
that there are other more effective means."*

"You speak in riddles, sir."

*"I speak of needs, Miss Bedegrayne. The means in
which to meet yours and mine."*

She shook her head. "You promised to help."

*"And so I shall. First, I need you to help me fulfill
mine."* He lifted her chin with his finger, his gaze held
hers. *"Are you courageous enough to assist me, Devona,
or has all this talk about saving Doran Claeg been just
that, talk."*

"I will do whatever you ask."

*"Bold, hasty words, my lady. As dearly as they warm
my heart, I confess, I am not such a blackguard as to
take your vow without revealing my intentions. I want
you."*

*Her mouth parted slightly. Shock warred with confu-
sion before a very feminine awareness gleamed in her
eyes.*

He had set himself up for failure by that truth-
ful blunder. If it would have helped, he would
have cut his throat and been done with it. A gently reared lady did not expect to hear such bold
declarations. Rayne had assessed her features and

thought she had too much color. Rallying what pride he had left, he had pressed onward.

"*I want you to help me regain my place in society.*"

She didn't even blink at his announcement. If she was disappointed, she hid it well. "*Oh,*" was all she said.

"*It won't be easy. Oh, no one will dispute the title is mine by right, but you will learn that I do not possess my family's support and that will complicate things.*"

"*I do not see how I can help you, Lord Tipton. My place in society is hardly coveted. At best I am amusing.*"

"*Then we shall make an interesting pair, you and I. Who better to take up with* Le Cadavre Raffiné *than the reckless Miss Bedegrayne?*"

"*You want them to think that you have taken me as your mistress?*" Her voice dropped to a horrified whisper. "*I would be ruined. My father.*" She shuddered. "*To be fair, he has been most tolerant. But this goes too far. I would be shunned. Cast into obscurity with no hope to marry.*"

For all her talk and joy of reckless adventure, she was still quite young, he suddenly realized. "*I thought you would do anything?*" he taunted, then felt remorse at her stricken expression. The unbridled jealousy he felt at her loyalty to Claeg had surged, overriding common sense. He needed her loyalty toward Claeg to be unflagging. It served his selfish purpose as it did that bastard Claeg.

"*What do you want of me?*"

Her solemn question cut into his flesh, as clean and precise as a scalpel. Victory had a bitter aftertaste. Cad that he was, it did not deter him. "*You. Your adoration. Your affection. Your friendship.*" Your heart, body, and soul. "*Not as mistress,*" he continued, ignoring the puzzled frown between her brows. "*Although, I am certain there will be talk. I want your support. Your betrothal.*"

"*You want to marry me?*"

"Just your word will do. Despite your penchant to challenge propriety, you and I suit each other well. At my side, you will lend a certain respectability that I have never achieved on my own. Later . . ." He shrugged. *"Well, we all know how fickle a young lady's love can be."*

Rayne had sensed she would have argued his point. He had all but thrown down a gauntlet at her slippered feet. Unfortunately, they had dallied too long at supper. Their association tonight, the rumors over the weeks, and his unexpected return to society were too much of a curiosity to ignore for long. Lady Geary had been the first to approach them. Her eyes full of conjecture and her painted mouth twisted in tolerant amusement, she had cornered, and then separated them. Each being pulled in opposite sides of the room, their prying, new friends had spent the remainder of the evening trying to glean news of the elusive Tipton and his intentions regarding Bedegrayne's youngest daughter.

Rayne knew he had left his audience wary and full of questions. He assumed Devona had done the same. It wasn't as if she were used to games of deceit. Rather, she just did not know what to think of him yet. He had done a fine job, keeping her inquisitive mind off balance.

Something rapped the side of the moving hackney, startling him from his thoughts. A tree branch, perhaps? He would have dismissed the sound if he hadn't heard the odd rap again, this time followed by a frightened yelp. Rayne stuck his head out the window only to see his coachman's body tumbling, flailing wildly on the ground as the coach blurred past him, a pole with a hook still speared through his clothing.

He heard a shout and saw a flash of light. Reacting solely on instinct, he ducked his head back inside before the pistol ball smashed into the window frame. The coach rocked perilously as the spooked horses picked up speed. Rayne rapidly assessed his circumstances. His coachman was gone, the horses out of control, and someone was doing his damnedest to make certain he remained right where he was. The coach pulled to the right, throwing Rayne across the compartment. He crawled his way to the front and knocked open the small opening that was used to direct the coachman. If this was a robbery, he would have thought the thieves would have taken over the reins by now. The seat outside was empty.

To remain inside was certain death. He had seen more than his share of broken bodies from such accidents. Coldness rushed through him. Whatever this was, this was no accident. Still, someone had gone to a great deal of trouble to make it look so.

He kicked open the door with his foot. Another ball struck the door before it snapped back into place. Considering the time it took to load a pistol, against one, even two pistols, he stood a chance. He heard shouts as the runaway coach roared its way down the street. The thunder and rattle of the coach's wheels pounded violently, matching the cadence of his heart's beat.

Rayne kicked the door again, this time springing out to grab an outer ring, and used his foot to hold the door open. Although flimsy, it provided some cover. The coach was going too fast for him to hear the discharge, but he felt one thud, then another against the door.

Deciding the odds weren't going to get better than they were at that moment, he straightened his crouched position and reached high for a

leather strap near the coachman's perch. Airborne dirt and gravel stung his face, and the wind
pulled at his clothes while he worked his way to
the front perch. Rayne moved like a blind man
slowly feeling his way to the higher purchase, not
knowing if the reins were secured to the coach
or if they danced beneath the deadly hooves of
the horses.

He would never know.

The coach bucked, its joints screaming at the
torture. Losing his hold, he fell backward into the
ink blackness of the unknown. His senses were
fully alert, focused for some sort of stimuli. The
impact gave it to him. The air punched out of his
lungs when he took the brunt of the fall on his
back. He slid across the abrasive surface, dirt, fabric, and skin fusing hot.

Then he was still. He couldn't breathe, couldn't
see, couldn't move, but his hearing was keen. He
listened to the thunder and the terrified sounds
of the horses as they rumbled past. A few heart-
beats later he heard the sounds of several riders
in pursuit. It mattered little now whether they
were friend or foe. Rayne forced some air into
his lungs and was grateful his body was beginning
to cooperate again. His back was starting to sting.
Soon it would give way to an awesome pain which
would remind him that he had survived. Scraped
and bloody, he dragged himself to his feet. The
sounds of his ordeal had long since faded, yet the
question remained. Who the hell was trying to
kill him?

At the Black Galleon, a small drinking tavern
off the Thames, no one paid much attention to
the four men huddled together. Drinks were in

their hands, although they seemed to be forgotten. The furious man, sometimes friend and benefactor, more lately the promising fist to their painful demise, was not pleased with their failure.

"He was trapped in the box." The angry man's voice was clipped and tight. "How did you let him get away?"

The man, who dared to defend them, was at least three stones heavier and had seen his share of danger. He also was smart enough to recognize that the man before him could be quite deadly. "You told us yourself the man was wily. He has a certain reputation and he lived up to it." He shrugged. "Next time he won't."

"Some say he has the gift of sorcery since he once mingled with the dead. Can call them up at will. Maybe they spirited him away," another man suggested.

The leader tilted his head, a gesture to suggest he'd consider the thought. Without warning, his foot lashed out from underneath the table and connected with the man's groin. The sound out of his mouth was barely a belch. He slid boneless out of his chair and out of sight.

"No wonder you can't kill one man. You have frightened children doing your bidding." He leaned forward, his menacing stare holding them in their seats. "Perhaps my faith in you is misguided."

The larger man bristled. "It's the manner you've chosen that's chancy. You never know if you are going to maim or kill with a coach. I think we should try a more direct approach to your problem."

"Fine. Do it. No mistakes this time."

The promise of death lingered like a bad odor between them. "What of the lass?"

The man frowned. The image of Miss Bedegrayne flickered in his mind. It laughed and
taunted him, then twisted into something hideous. She had linked herself with Tipton. He'd wager the man had done more than touch her with
his eyes. Damn him! There had been other plans
made on her behalf. Now, they would not do. All
these years she had held herself aloof and pure,
only to succumb to that monster's touch. The
thought could not be endured! Mayhap there was
some truth to him consorting in the dark magic.
It was an acceptable excuse to Miss Bedgrayne's
disappointing weakness to Tipton. His companions eyed him warily, knowing he was a thread
away from losing his control. His face hardened,
reinforcing his resolve in a mask of hatred.

"She has allowed herself to be tainted. She
must be punished."

"His lordship ain't receiving visitors, Miss Bedegrayne."

"See here, Speck, I am not a visitor. I am"—*His
betrothed?* No, she could not quite say the words
since she could hardly believe them. It was one
of the reasons why it was so important to see him
today. "I am his friend. If he knew I was here, he
would want to see me."

The gargoyle was in fine intimidating form this
afternoon. His pointed teeth gleamed with threatening intent. "I doubt it. Since he can probably
hear you squawking from his bed."

Devona straightened, preparing for the interesting verbal battle ahead of her when his words
sunk in past her pride. "Bed. What is the man
doing in bed this time of day? Is he ill?" She did
not hesitate or wait for Gar to smooth her way.

She just slipped under Speck's barring arm and went inside.

"See here, Miss Bedegrayne!"

Gar moved silently behind him. "Not a hand on her, Speck, or you will be dealing with me. There is little we can do, now. If your lord wants her out, he can manage the task himself."

Mortification and duty dueled in the older servant's eyes. "That woman. Your mistress—"

"Aye, she is." Admiration and respect glowed on his face, while they watched her grip her skirts and rush up the stairs.

"Rayne?" She rapped on the door then opened it, peering inside. It was empty. Where was he? This was her second visit inside his house. She always seemed to be reduced to a childish game of hide-and-seek to ferret him out. She approached another likely door. "Rayne?" She peeked inside.

Devona saw him on the bed, huddled under numerous blankets. She must have cried out. His eyes opened the moment she stepped into the room and ran to his bedside. "What is it?" She tugged off her gloves and touched his face. "You have a fever." Now that she was closer, she could see his face held a pinkish cast and his eyes were too bright. He was hot enough to make her frightened.

"J—just f—fever," he managed between chattering teeth. "Common reaction. Once infection s—set in. N—not too bad, I think."

"Infection? Are you injured?" He moaned, when she pulled back the blankets and saw the bandages on his arm and wrapped around his torso. Devona wanted to peek under the binding to see how badly he was wounded, but the linen looked clean and secure. Every movement seemed to bring him more pain, and she was just too softhearted to cause him more to satisfy her curiosity. She carefully tugged the blankets up to his shoulders. He shuddered, burrowing himself deeper. Dragging the nearest chair closer to his side, she sat down.

"Who did this to you?"

"I don't know."

He was too sick to remember, she thought. She felt the sting of tears and looked away then up to keep them from falling. The last thing he needed was a hysterical woman.

Reading her thoughts correctly, he slid a hand out from his warm cocoon. She eagerly clasped it; as if she could hold him to this earth by sheer will alone. "I'm not out of my head, Devona. I feel like someone has pounded nails into my bones, and my head aches. Symptoms, I can understand and expect. There is no need to worry." He nodded his head toward the cup on the table. "Since you've chased Speck away, you might as well help me with that."

"It's not my fault the man is so skittish." Devona brought the cup to his lips. He managed a few swallows before collapsing back onto the pillows. Her nose twitched as she sniffed the suspicious contents. "Not barley water."

"No. Cinchona bark for fever, saffron for its sedative effects . . . strong black tea to disguise the taste." He tried to smile. "What c—can I say? I like to experiment."

She noted the bruise and scrape on the right side of his face. "Did someone beat you?"

He managed a laugh, then groaned, his hand going to his head to soothe the pain. "What an opinion you have of me! I can assure you that until I met you, my life was quite sedentary." He frowned, mulling over the observation.

Following his thoughts easily, she said, "Do you think Brock attacked you?" It sickened her to believe her brother or anyone else in her family could have hurt him on her behalf.

"I don't know for sure. It was dark and I was trapped in the hackney. When the coachman was felled, I thought robbery. The lead balls punching into the door made me think it was a bit more personal." Not liking her coloring, he snapped, "Sit down, Devona. I cannot catch you if you faint on me."

She dutifully sat, not even checking to see if the chair was still behind her. Feeling chilled, she wrapped her arms around her body. "Brock is impulsive, loyal to his family. He was not pleased with you—us," she amended. "I will talk to him."

"No you will not."

She raised a brow at his tone. The beast was feeling well enough to bare his teeth. "It was my fault that Brock thirsted for a duel. When you wouldn't oblige, he sought out an unscrupulous manner to satisfy his revenge. He will pay, I swear it."

"Such a fierce, protective creature you are, Devona." His eyes took on an interesting light that had nothing to do with the kind of fever that burned within him now. "One might think you have feelings for me."

She fidgeted, then in typical Bedegrayne fashion reacted in the best defensive manner available. She ignored the comment. "If Brock is responsible—"

"Still taking on more guilt?" he softly queried. "I would think the burden those graceful, fine-boned shoulders carry now would buckle under the additional strain."

He thought her shoulders graceful? She almost melted at the compliment before she mentally shook herself. He was just trying to distract her. "If Brock shot at you—"

"And missed," he pointed out, although considering his present misery, a ball in a vital spot might have been the very thing he dearly wished. "Whoever is responsible, he and his companions were cloaked by the night. My injuries are the result of losing my grip and falling from the moving coach."

"Dear Lord, you must be scraped raw! You are lucky not to have been trampled by the horses." Her hand came up to her lips. "If you had not escaped, they would have—" She could not say the words aloud. If the mysterious men had caught him, he would have been murdered.

"They didn't. Although, they will wish they had, if I learn the names of those responsible."

Brock. Devona closed her eyes, thinking how there could not be a pleasing ending if either man had his way. This was all her fault. She accepted it, even if Rayne was too kind to admit it. Taking up the cup of physic, she made him take a few more sips.

"I was thinking of your plan." She purposely spoke lightly, pretending that he wasn't lying injured in his bed because he had dared to help her. "It was a sound plan, and might have worked. However, we have so little time, and now with you bedridden, I think we should make some adjustments."

His eyes narrowed to pewter slits. "I don't shake off that easily, Devona."

Rayne was angry now, but later he would appreciate the gesture. The knowledge gave her the courage to end their friendship. "You are useless to me. Forgive me for saying so." She set the cup down. Noticing a few drops of liquid on his lips, she pulled out the handkerchief tucked in her sleeve. He grabbed her wrist when she moved to blot the moisture.

"You came to me, first. Intruded on my privacy."

Why was he making this so difficult? She gave him her best patronizing smirk. "My mistake, Lord Tipton. I accept it, and know when to move on. Doran needs my help." Devona shrugged out the knots in her shoulders. "There are other surgeons." She had no intention of asking anyone to help her since she had learned firsthand the results.

He crushed her wrist. Ignoring her wince, he raged in his dry, raspy voice, "What are you planning to do, Devona? Hound and break into every surgeon's residence until you find the right man to help you?"

"If I have to."

The explosion she saw in his expression should have rocked the town house on its foundation. "You go too far. Even for you, Miss Reckless Be degrayne. Take up with another man? The devil you will! And I'm just the man to see to it."

Finally, frightened, Devona jerked her wrist out of his grip and took two steps back. Despite his illness, she could see why men considered him a formidable adversary. "I think not. Do not bother to call when you have recovered. I will not be home to you." There, she ended it. She should be feeling relief. She had never felt worse.

"Devona. Damn you. Come back here. This is far from finished. Devona!"

The desperateness and loss she heard when he shouted out her name almost made her turn around and run back into the safety of his arms. Almost. The tears she had held back slipped freely down her face. She raced out of the town house without looking back.

"Where did you go this afternoon?"

Devona glanced at Wynne and then returned her attention back to the small orchestra. They were playing a piece from Handel's *Water Music*, one of her particular favorites. There was such joy on the musician's faces, the music coming from something deeper than just their hands and breath bringing their instruments to life. She let the music sink into her, hoping it would soothe the soreness in her heart.

"Devona?"

"Sorry. I have not been attentive. Her Grace outdid herself this evening, I think. Did you want to play cards?"

Wynne watched her closely, the protective mother, searching for signs of illness. "This is not you, sister. What brought on the mulligrubs? Did you go see Doran again?" The question held no censure.

"No. I did, however, attend an interesting lecture on phrenology this afternoon. The lecturer, Mr. Christian Wohlman, is an esteemed disciple of Mr. Johann Spuzheim. I was most fortunate to locate a seat."

"So what happened? Did you have the lumps on your hard head analyzed and discover something frightening? That you are stubborn? An odd ridge that shows you will likely drive the ones you love to madness?" She touched her heart at Devona's suspicious sniffle. "Here now, I was but jesting. We have known for some time of your stubbornness and that the Bedegraynes are a mad lot, even without your help."

"The room was too crowded to gain an introduction to Mr. Wohlman. Oz was there," she added absently.

"All this drama, for a moment of sulking. Really, Devona, there will be other lectures."

"I was not sulking about the lecture." She spotted Lord Nevin in the distance. Devastatingly handsome enough to make any woman gape, he moved with catlike grace through the throng, toward the card room. He did not look her way. She was grateful since she was not in the mood to put up with his flirtation.

Wynne noticed his presence as well. Her lips tightened, and for a moment she appeared quite fierce, the ice queen, a few of the vanquished suitors for her hand had dubbed her. "Do you hope to gain that man's attention?"

The coldness in her tone snapped Devona's attention back to her sister's face. "I have it. The problem is what to do with it."

Wynne flushed, an uncertainty uncharacteristic to her nature had her carefully choosing her next words. "He is too old for you."

"He is eight-and-twenty."

"Too worldly, then. Heed me when I say that he is not for you."

For the first time, Devona noticed the high color in her sister's cheeks and the nervousness in each gesture. Was it possible? She had never guessed. "Who is he for, Wynne?"

"What? No one. A satyr is not a fit husband for any lady." Wynne dismissed the earl and the subject with a sharp nod. "Stick with the Mr. Lockwoods and Lord Tiptons of this world. They will be kinder to your heart."

"Lord Tipton? I thought you did not approve of him."

"Odd. Of the two men, he is the first you acknowledge."

"Wynne."

Relenting, she admitted, "Disregarding his reputation, I like him well enough. More so, since he kept my favorite sister safe."

"I saw him today. Before the lecture."

"Ah, the true reason for your melancholy. I need not point out to you that visiting him openly casts a certain speculation on your friendship." With the flick of her fan she discouraged an approaching suitor. Wynne softened the rebuttal with her siren smile.

"He has been injured, bedridden with fever. I think—I suspect Brock had a hand in this." It was a miserable confession, and the horrified expression on Wynne's delicate features conveyed acute denial.

"Brock? I cannot believe—"

"Well, I do. I tried to find him. I would have challenged him to deny it, but he was not to be found. Still the evidence is damning. He would not give up the idea for revenge, even after Papa had forbidden it. I think he and his cronies saw an advantage to appease their thirst and took it."

"Does Lord Tipton agree?"

Devona lowered her gaze to the closed fan in her lap. "I think so. He was so weak with fever. The notion that Brock had tried to kill him—" The helplessness almost overwhelmed her. "I told him to stay away from me. I would not welcome his attentions."

A flicker of amusement twinkled in her sister's

eyes. "You think to protect Le Cadavre Raffiné?
I'll wager his response was quite spectacular, and
very male."

She pressed her fingers to her head; the headache brewing was not to be ignored. "Stop calling
him that ridiculous name. He is not a corpse, and
from our brief encounters, I am not even certain
I would consider him refined." Before Wynne
could open her mouth, she snapped, "Regardless,
he is nothing to me!"

"If Brock is responsible, keeping away from
Lord Tipton will not prevent our brother from
exacting family justice, nor will it deter your feelings for the man."

Prepared to deny her sister's perceptiveness, a
movement caught her eye. "Oh, rot. He's coming
our way."

Wynne saw the source of Devona's dismay. Lord
Nevin. "Have you toured the conservatory? Her
Grace possesses a collection of exotics that must
not be missed." She stood, a blond warrior queen
readying herself for battle. "I will deal with the
satyr."

SIX

"Tipton." Brock sneered, the cards in his hand forgotten. "You look the very devil. If I had known you were in need of Hell's Gate, I would have reserved you a seat." The men around him snickered.

The seedy gaming hell off Drury Lane lured all types of young bloods and criminals, daring to wager their fortunes and their lives at the turn of the cards. Tired whores postured around the room, hoping to earn their night fees once lightened purses and drunken senses pushed the men from the tables and into their beds.

Rayne thought Brock appeared too well acquainted with the hazy atmosphere. All a man needed here was a good hand, a tankard never empty, and a warm, friendly doxy cooing in his lap. He could recall such times when he and his friend, Dr. Sir Wallace Brogden, had sailed around the world on the *Griffin's Claw*. Years ago, such idle decadence seemed satisfying. Now, he considered it a waste of a keen mind.

Despite the rumpled clothes and red-rimmed eyes, Brock was probably drowning in boredom. Rayne recognized all the signs of the waiting heir with nothing to do or prove in his life. Except,

Brock was not exactly looking bored at the moment.

"I thought you'd like to see firsthand that your efforts to kill me failed." Ten hours had passed since Devona had run from his town house. Bed and physic had improved his health. The fever was gone, replacing it with a weakness that sunk right into his bones. Rayne ignored it. Anger and a few other emotions he cared not to analyze kept him on his feet. He tightened his grip on his walking stick, trying not to show the group before him that he needed it.

Brock noted the slight sway in Rayne's stance. "You're drunk," he said, dismissing him.

His reply was to hook the front leg of Brock's chair and tip him on his snotty ass. Several of the men jumped to their feet, prepared to fight. Rayne held them in place with a glare. "This is between me and him. Let him be a man for once."

"If I didn't have reason to kill you before, by God, I do now!" He tried to roll over to gain his footing again.

Rayne held him in place with the sharp point of his stick. Sweat beaded on his forehead, an affirmation of the toll of his actions. "You tried. And failed."

"I don't know what you are talking about."

"A pity. Let me help you with your memory. When your own father would not support your desire to challenge me, you took it upon yourself to arrange a little accident. Pinning me in the coach would have worked if you had had a few more pistols. Lucky for me, besides being a coward, you lack brains as well."

Stunned, the younger man just stared at him, then loudly exhaled. "You think I am responsible?"

Brock's outrage was palpable. Rayne felt the first seeds of doubt. "You have voiced more than once your desire for my death."

"A duel, sir. For my honor and my sister's. I could maim you and be satisfied. Killing you would only inconvenience me."

He removed the stick he had pressed into Brock's throat. The man rolled over, pulling himself to his feet. "You might discover that trying to maim me is equally inconvenient," Rayne promised silkily. He indulged in a slight smile when Brock acknowledged the threat with a shaky nod of the head. "Where is Devona?"

Pride still strong, the younger man snorted. "If I knew, you would be the last I'd tell."

"Then think on this. She was beside me at the garden when that carriage tried to drive us underground."

"And it was you who was shot at later on. It sounds like someone is trying to kill you, Tipton. If he succeeds, he has my thanks." Brock spat on the floor between them.

"Your sister has her own enemies. She might share that danger, Bedegrayne. Whether you can stomach the notion or not, I shall be close. Very close," he said, giving in to the temptation to provoke the man.

Brock did not disappoint him. "You are the fucking devil's own, aren't you?"

"You know what they say, Bedegrayne. When you trifle at Hell's Gate, you are embracing all sorts of demons."

The conservatory was almost vacant when Devona arrived. Most of the guests had moved toward the front of the house, choosing dancing and cards to entertain them. She took her time, her kid slippers barely making a sound on the tiled floor as she admired the impressive conservatory.

It was a large structure. Glass and metal-framed walls with plaster columns holding up the ornate ceiling. Awed with the workmanship, she gazed up at the painted ceiling of a celestial battle of good and evil. The duchess obviously had an indulgent husband. Above the entrance there was a balcony, opening into the second story. Tangled vines draped the brick balcony like an old woman's comfortable shawl. She tilted her head back and stood on her toes to identify the statues. Fat cherubs. Very lovely. This was a marvelous sanctuary.

Laughter from above had her stepping out of view. She peered up, at a rustling sound; only the vines and a lifted leg of one of the marble cherubs was visible. Confident she would not be seen, Devona sat on the wooden bench next to her.

"No, no you mustn't," a woman from somewhere nearby moaned. "Even here, there are too many eyes and ears, my darling."

Devona covered her mouth with her hand to prevent them from hearing her laugh. She doubted the woman would be pleased to know how accurate her statement was. The man's murmur was indiscernible, yet she was enough of a romantic to guess he was trying to convince her to remain. Under the reflective glow of the four chandeliers suspended from the ceiling, this would be a wonderful place to be kissed by a beloved.

A couple appeared from the back of the conservatory, the lady struggling to put her curls back in place. Devona smiled at them as they passed.

They entered the library and she was alone again. Well, she amended, except for the heavy breathers on the balcony.

She had been kissed a few times, not even counting the devastating kiss Rayne had pressed onto her lips. She enjoyed the balls for the dancing, the crush of people, and the gaiety. It had never occurred to her to drag one of her dancing companions into the secluded flora and be kissed senseless. Devona eyed the room with a new appreciation. She would have to ask Wynne if she had ever enjoyed such a tryst.

There was a scraping noise overhead, confirming her amorous companions were still around. She felt trapped. If she continued her stroll, the couple in the balcony would know that she had been eavesdropping. To return to the ball would place her directly in the path of Lord Nevin, ruining all of Wynne's efforts. Indecisive, she bit her lower lip.

From the corner of her eye, she saw one of the pins holding her hair in place drop to the floor. Pretty glass beads were attached to the numerous pins in her hair, giving the effect of diamonds cast in a sea of cinnamon. Or at least that was the idea, she thought with a self-effacing grin. She leaned forward to retrieve the pin.

The collapsing bench propelled her forward. She shrieked, landing in an embarrassing sprawl. A shower of stinging bits of rock and dust covered her. It took her a moment to move, her mind trying to form a coherent thought.

Her head turned to the broken bench. It made no sense until she saw the broken head of a cherub grinning mischievously at her. Awkwardly, she stood. Her dress was ruined. Dirt marred the front, and there was a horrendous tear where her knees had struck the tile. Thinking of her knees made them start to burn. She took a few steps forward so she could see the balcony.

"Anyone there?"

The upper story was silent. She also noted the vacant corner where the cherub had once set. An accident. Just a terrible accident. Fine tremors shook her slender frame. How did a piece of heavy statuary suddenly fall from its perch with such deadly accuracy?

A noise to her left had her moving backward, deeper into the conservatory. Did she call this place a sanctuary? Feeling giddy with hysteria, she skirted several enormous pots packed with geraniums. Devona ducked behind the iron trellis, which created a living wall of ivy and flowering vines. She heard the shuffle of footsteps. No one called out or commented on the smashed wood and marble as one might expect.

A horrible thought struck her. What if someone had helped the cherub over the side? If it had been an accident, wouldn't they have called out a warning? Maybe it wasn't an accident, after all. Footsteps moving closer had her crouching and pressing deeper into the foliage. She held her breath. Why was it so cold in here all of a sudden? She couldn't stop shaking.

A man came into view. Or rather, his arm and part of his back. He stood, stock-still, listening. It would have been so easy to jump up and startle the man. She could have babbled on about playing a game with her companions, then hurried out of the conservatory toward the rooms holding light and laughter. She did nothing. Something about the way he held himself made her remain hidden in the shadows.

Minutes ticked by and neither moved. Devona

slowly let out the breath she had been holding, and just as carefully inhaled. Voices. Voices in the distance. Sudden laughter. Someone else was approaching. The man moved his arm, and then was gone from her line of vision. What the devil has just happened? She had the wildest urge to giggle.

There were more footsteps; this time pleasant conversation flowed with it. This time she did not care who saw her. The clawing need to run from this room and the house was overwhelming. Springing from her hiding place, she bumped against the wall of vines and straight into the arms of a man.

Devona screamed.

She struggled against the captive embrace, but strong arms had her effectively caged.

"Dear me! Devona, what is going on here?"

Wynne's shocked voice cut through Devona's hysteria. Her reserves spent, she sagged against the warm chest seizing the offering comfort. Wynne was here. She was safe. Devona tilted her head back, half expecting to see the dashing Lord Nevin.

Surprised, she all but gasped. The man holding her was just as appealing, maybe more so. The lines of tension in his face were cut deep by the shadows and he gleamed with sweat. He was also furious. Tipton. She never was so pleased to see him.

"Oh my, you all must think I am a real rattle-pate for carrying on so," Devona said, another variation of the apologies she had been issuing to anyone listening in the last thirty minutes. She held a cooling cup of tea her harried hostess had insisted she drink to settle her nerves. Rayne thought a good dosing of brandy would have been better.

"Those statues have resided in their places for years, and nary an incident," the duchess fretted. "Are you certain you are well? Maybe we should call for a doctor?"

"Lord Tipton has seen to me, and says I am fit. Is that not correct, my lord?" Devona could not quite meet his gaze.

Rayne knew she was trying to assure everyone, including herself, that she was fine. Every bit the lady, she sat primly, her spine Spanish steel, ignoring the fact that her gown was torn and dirty. Or that her hands trembled when she tried to smooth her disheveled hair. There were scratches on her face, hand, and knees. The latter was shown to him only under dire threat. She had taken the brunt of her fall on the right knee. The wound had still been seeping blood when he had smeared it with basilicum ointment and bound it.

"It was all a terrible accident. No one is to blame."

He doubted she believed a single word of it. He sure as hell didn't.

"Please, I feel badly that I have taken you from your guests, Your Grace. I have my sister to see me home."

"If you are certain?" The woman was torn by concern and the obligation to her other guests.

"Very. Thank you for inviting me." She smiled, encouraging the woman to leave. With a nod to all, the duchess departed for the library, closing the door behind her.

He would have laughed if he had not noticed Devona meant every word. The woman had just been stalked by some unknown assailant, but would not allow such a trifle like almost dying to put aside her manners. Typical. He took out a handkerchief and wiped his face. At least his fever had broken.

"Shall I ring for our coach?" Wynne asked, interrupting the silence.

"Might as well. I do not feel like dancing tonight." Devona touched her sister's arm when she turned away to hide her tears. "You are not to blame."

A sob broke over her breath. "I was a fool to send you out here. I thought if I dealt with Lord Nevin, he would leave you alone."

Rayne's interest perked up at the mention of the earl's name. "What's this about Nevin hounding Devona?" He'd call the man out tomorrow if he had anything to do with this.

She gave him a weary glance. "Old news, my lord. Wynne knew I was not in the mood to handle Lord Nevin's flirtation so she volunteered to distract him. No one could have predicted this would have been the outcome."

"Who else knew you were out here?"

"I—I do not know. I never spoke to anyone directly, but if someone had been watching me . . ."

Watching and waiting for a chance to hurt her. He did not want to add to her misery so he did not say the words aloud.

"I will go summon our coach." Wynne's gaze met Rayne's in silent understanding. "Keep her safe." After a quick, reassuring glance at her younger sister, she left.

"You should not be out of bed."

He almost grinned at the chastising tone. She was definitely feeling better if she was in the mood to skin him alive for his own careless behavior. "I thought I had a good reason."

Her brow arched inquisitively. "Pray tell. I am quite interested in this reason."

"You left me, Devona."

The succinct reason rendered her speechless, a rare state for a Bedegrayne. Seeing that she was improving made him feel better himself. "Did you really think I would allow you to walk out of my life so easily?"

She looked away. "I had hopes."

"Never, Devona," he vowed, ardently.

"Brock—"

"Is not an issue. I sought him out this evening." He did not bother to add where he had found him. After all, she was his sister.

"What did you do? What did he say? Please tell me you have not agreed to duel!" She was gripping her ivory fan so tightly he expected the delicate blades to snap.

Noticing that the ribbons on her slipper had loosened, he sat on his haunches in front of her and patiently began to retie them. "We haven't scheduled a duel on your behalf. Although, I might have given him a reason or two to call me out on his own."

"I do not see the humor in this, Lord Tipton! I forbid you to meet my brother."

Rayne smiled, resisting the urge to stroke her calf. He doubted she would appreciate his observations of her fine legs. "Still fiery, even when you're spooked, eh, Devona? Don't worry about it. I have no desire to face your brother. Even if he deserves it."

"Oh. Well, good." His compliance had taken the steam out of her scathing reprimand. "I assume he admitted to the attack then."

Wishing he could linger and admire her legs, he regretfully pulled her gown back into place. "No. Not specifically. He seemed surprised that there was a line of enemies just waiting to hasten my demise. He prays for their success."

"Brock did not mean it."

"Oh, I am most certain he did." He was not particularly disturbed by the fact. "His feelings will in no manner disrupt our plans."

Her shoulders sagged, along with her lagging spirit. "Rayne, I have not changed my mind."

"Nor have I, beloved. You are stuck with me."

The doors opened, and a burst of laughter and music floated on the air as Wynne entered. "Here, I borrowed this blanket from Her Grace. I thought you might want to cover your gown."

Rayne took the blanket, wrapping it around Devona's shoulders.

"That was thoughtful, thank you." Devona stood, wincing when she straightened her knees. "No more adventures for me. At least for a few days."

Rayne scooped her into his arms. Devona squeaked at his bold handling, but her arms went around his neck without hesitation. He looked pointedly at Wynne, expecting her to argue. Instead she reached for her sister's forgotten reticule and fan, then walked to the doors. He almost missed the hint of a smile she kept hidden as she sailed through the doors.

It did not go unnoticed that Le Cadavre Raffiné had Miss Devona Bedegrayne in his clutches again. With her mussed hair and torn gown, he was almost certain the *ton* would twist the scene and by morning word would be out that Lord Tipton had ravished Miss Bedegrayne in the Duchess of Lonsinger's conservatory.

He expected he would have the entire group of Bedegrayne males pounding on his door, demanding their chance to put a bullet in him. These demands for his death were starting to get tedious. Devona, too, would be quite upset by the turn of events. In typical fashion, she would set the blame on her shoulders. What she did not understand was that he never did anything without a purpose. Having her in his arms for the polite world to behold only quickened his plans. No, this could have not worked out any better, he mused.

They made their way through the crowd. Devona pressed her face into Rayne's neck, trying to pretend that the entire world was not watching her scandalous departure.

"I will be calling on your father on the morrow. Tell him to expect me." His deep voice rumbled in his throat, tickling her nose.

"I will do no such thing, my lord."

A woman from the crowd stepped forward. "Miss Bedegrayne, I shall call upon you when you are well," she called out to the departing couple.

"Meddlesome woman," Devona mumbled. "She wants to be first in line to gossip."

Eyes straight ahead, he cleaved his way cleanly through the guests. "Gossip is the least of your worries."

Oz Lockwood came forward, then kept pace with Rayne's stride since he was not in the mood to stop and chat. "Devona, I heard what happened. Are you hurt badly?"

"Nothing serious, Oz. I will be fit in a week, I swear."

Oz nodded absently, then glared at Rayne for doing his best to lose him in the wake of guests. His frown becoming more pronounced, he grudgingly inquired, "Tipton, anything I can do to assist?"

"Yes, get out of my way."

"Ooph!" Devona stared back at Oz, who had given up. She mouthed an apology. He shrugged and turned away. "That was beyond rude, Lord Tipton!"

"The man irritates me."

They were almost to the front hall. "I consider him a friend. All he wanted to do was help." She saw Lord Nevin when they passed one of the open side rooms being used for cards. If he was surprised to see her in Rayne's arms, his expression never revealed it. He lifted a hand in farewell.

"This is too embarrassing, by far."

"I will remedy it, when I call on your father tomorrow."

"Listen to me, you high-handed tyrant. I—" Her argument for the moment was forgotten when her attention fell on an older woman dressed in various hues of brown. Rayne had halted their progress so Wynne could collect their outer garments. Perplexed, she watched the woman. The woman looked somewhat familiar. A friend of her mother's perhaps?

"Let's not fuss about donning the cloaks. I would rather we just leave," she heard Wynne state.

"Allow me to follow you home."

"Thank you, Lord Tipton. An extra measure of security would be welcomed," her sister warmly said. They were moving again, almost out the door. The woman in brown turned, giving Devona an opportunity to see her face.

Good Lord, it was Lady Claeg!

* * *

"Truly, Devona. Lady Claeg, an assassin? Do you spend time pondering these insane thoughts or do they just pop into your head?"

Wynne pulled the drapes open. The morning sun filled the room. Dust whirled and danced on the incoming beams of light. Soon it would take the edge off the morning chill. "I thought after a night's repose, you would view the incident differently. I should have known better."

Devona kicked the blanket covering her down to the foot of her bed. This was not the first time they had had this discussion. She had mentioned it once in the carriage ride home last evening, again when a maid and Wynne had helped her undress and tucked her into bed, and now this morning. Her sister was no closer to believing her than she was last evening.

"The woman hates me, Wynne. She thinks I have somehow corrupted Doran. Perhaps she was the woman I heard in the balcony. When she saw me below, she could not resist." She tried to sit up, but Wynne pushed her back into the pillows.

Wynne chuckled. "So while she was rendezvousing with her latest lover, she decided to complete the evening with a murder attempt. You are a strange woman, sister."

A mutinous expression clouded her face. "She is strong enough to have pushed one of those statues over."

"And has a face like a horse, too. Who would ever steal her away and kiss her in dark corners? Give it up, sister. I cannot fathom Lady Claeg is guilty of either charge."

"Lord Tipton seemed to consider the idea."

"Well, Lord Tipton would seriously consider anything that you tell him. His position is too tenuous not to."

Devona fought her way back into a sitting position. "Meaning what?"

"Meaning Tipton is more clever than the other males that have come sniffing around you only to be rejected. Or do you think his sole purpose for speaking to Papa is to discuss politics?"

Her nose wrinkled as she waved the question away. "Oh, that. Do not concern yourself that I shall be leg-shackled before you. It is only a ruse to help Doran."

"Oh, really?"

Panic churned in her empty stomach. " 'Tis part of his plan. He needs me to—oh, Wynne, do you think he actually means it?"

Her sister gave her a pitying glance. "You may have been the one to shoulder your way into his life, but he is making plans to keep you there."

Entering the Bedegrayne household had felt a bit like entering the lair of a dragon. One half expected to get blasted by a wall of fire or stomped to death. The fact that neither occurred put Rayne on alert. Sir Thomas Bedegrayne, he was informed, would see him forthwith. Keeping his relief concealed beneath a façade of indifference, he followed the butler through a tight maze of halls.

The small chamber was pleasant enough, the intricately designed glass windows positioned to capture and reflect the sunlight. He had not been left alone. Wynne and a woman introduced to him as Aunt Moll had sat quietly working on their needlepoint.

His hand casually fingered the note in his coat pocket. Brogden's sudden return to England was curious since his friend had once sworn that nothing could lure him back. A half smile played across his lips as he looked forward to visiting one of the very few men he considered a friend again. Still, a man had priorities. He was certain the fact that Devona was his made the lady a very nervous woman.

The ensuing silence prompted him to ask, "Where is your sister, Miss Bedegrayne? I trust she has recovered from last evening?" Her absence concerned him, but it would not deter him from his purpose.

Wynne glanced up. "Consider yourself fortunate we forced her to keep to her bed for a day. All around, it should make your visit here much more amiable."

Rayne never was given the chance to probe the subtle warning. The butler had returned. Sir Thomas Bedegrayne was waiting to meet him.

He supposed he had imagined Devona's father to be an older version of Brock, shrunken and thin-boned by the ravages of age. The giant who held out a fleshy hand held no resemblance to the young man who desired his death.

Sir Thomas Bedegrayne was large, over six feet. Broad-shouldered and sporting a salt-and-peppered beard to match the unfashionable length of hair on top, he looked like the type of man more comfortable with a broad sword and a siege before him, than with playing the social games of polite society. Meeting the older man's gaze, Rayne saw at once where Devona had acquired her intriguing blue-green eyes. The older version skewered him as much as they assessed him. He could feel their sharp points all the way down his gullet.

"So you are the lad Brock says is up to every

rig and row with our Devona. Thinks he should call you out," Sir Thomas's voice boomed in the quiet room.

Rayne could not recall the last time anyone had referred to him as a lad, nor when he had felt like one. "I appreciate your understanding in the matter. I meant no insult to Devona or her family."

There was a speculative gleam in those flinty eyes. "Such flummery. I expect as much from the crop of fops that preen for my lovely gels. If the rumors are true about your circumstances, I am surprised that you found the time to attain the polish."

Acknowledgment either way was an insult. Rayne knew it, so did the shrewd old man. If Sir Thomas expected him to respectfully back down, then he would be disappointed. "If you know something of my life, then you know what I have today was born of sweat and sheer will."

"Stubborn, I give you that."

"Useful to the man who has been denied all gentle things because of a freakish twist of fate," he softly countered.

Sir Thomas ignored the blatant opening. He leaned back in his chair. "So you are old enough to understand the advantages of the softer comforts. Is this how you view my daughter Devona?"

"No offense, sir. I find little about your daughter that is soft or convenient."

"You arrogant pup!" The older man's blue-green eyes flashed outrage. "You telling me something is wrong with my gel?"

Rayne blinked. He suspected whatever position he chose, the older man would argue it to his advantage. "She is somewhat forward."

The oversized globe Sir Thomas had been

lightly stroking was sent into a reeling spin. "You calling my Devona fast, Tipton?" he asked, the edge to his tone was as keen as the look in his eyes.

"She pushed her way into my household at midnight to meet me. You cannot call her slow."

"It sounds like you need to hire sharper staff," Bedegrayne snapped.

Rayne placed his hands on the desk in front of him and leaned forward, his stance intimidating. "My staff isn't your concern. Devona is. The woman is quick off the mark and you, nor any other member in this household, has an inkling about how to handle her."

"Do you dare presume to tell me how to look after my gel?"

"I do." He paused, awaiting the explosion of temper. When none came, he continued. "Locking her in her room isn't going to correct something that is born of spirit. She needs someone who can appreciate her reckless tendencies, yet can channel them so the consequences are benign."

"By God, Tipton. Are you asking for her hand?"

Rayne found the older man's disbelief insulting. Shrugging, he said, "We deal very well with each other. She could do no worse."

"The question is: could she do better?" Satisfied with the insult, he moved on, not waiting for a response. "Why should I accept you? You are an outcast to your family, to society. You are a surgeon!" he said the last as if it were something quite vile. "I'll not have my Devona scouring the graveyards to satiate your need for dissecting corpses."

Rayne's left eyelid twitched. He rubbed his

thumb across the fragile skin to quiet the spasm. His lid twitched again. Trying to reason with a Bedegrayne was like reasoning with a corpse. Maybe he should reconsider his proposal. Marrying into this family could result in his commitment into an insane asylum.

"Sir, if you believe the role of a surgeon's wife is to play at being a resurrection man, then you know nothing of me or my chosen profession."

"You tell me marriage is what she needs, specifically marriage to you. Seems to me there is little in your life that is settled, Tipton. I hear that buck, Nevin, wants my girl. He has a title, one he plans to do right by."

Rayne resisted the urge to rub the tick. "If you need a title, I have one as well. Recently, I have taken steps to secure my position in society."

"Money?"

"On my own, I have built up a respectable fortune with several lucrative investments. When you consider there is the title, and the lands, even an old mercenary like you should be satisfied."

SEVEN

"So the old goat refused you, eh? I thought we had long concluded our lessons on finesse."

Rayne watched the ten-inch cream-and-brown-striped gecko creep up the length of his friend's arm. It perched on his shoulders, its broad flattened head turned in his direction, blatantly studying him.

"Considering your recent taste in companions, at least we can categorize mine as human."

Listening to his slightly older friend and mentor Dr. Sir Wallace Brogden's hearty chuckle, it might have been easy to dismiss the signs of illness. However, Rayne's abilities of keen observation were heightened by years of training. Where the casual observer might see lines of age in the thirty-two-year-old physician, Rayne knew they were carved by weeks, if not months, of intense pain. His occasional slurred words were not the result of an afternoon at his favorite club, but rather a liberal dosing of Thebaic tincture. He leaned closer, without being obvious. His friend's breath smelled faintly alcoholic and distinctly putrid.

The gecko adjusted its footing, then opened its mouth. A loud clicking sound disrupted the quiet.

"Apala is as sensitive as any two-legged female."
Brogden stroked his pet. "There, there, sweet."

"It appears I have been lost without your guidance these last five years. Perhaps you should remain in England for your recuperation. My
courting blunders shall be your entertainment,"
he said lightly, staring at his own reflection within
pupils so dilated there was only a thin circle of
brown.

"Ha! Indeed I well an' should, my friend.
Though I can't recall you having much trouble
with the ladies when we sailed together on the
Griffin's Claw." Brogden grimaced, trying to conceal his reaction by coughing into the back of his
hand. "Insatiable bastard," he affectionately muttered.

"Jealous?"

"As ever!"

Rayne grinned. The memory of a sultry night
in Bombay, a stolen cask of rum, and three very
creative and willing women silently replayed in
their minds. "English ladies are different."

"You sadly aren't meeting the right ones, Mr.
Tipton." Brogden wiped the moisture from his
red-rimmed eyes. "Maybe I should give up my
travels and show you how to really play with these
honey-water sweetened darlings."

Seizing the opening, Rayne gestured to the leg
Wallace had concealed with an artfully draped
shawl. "If you plan to chase the ladies then we
had better have a look at that leg."

Brogden blinked in dull surprise. "How did I
give myself away? Most don't notice. I usually arrange myself in this chair before I receive my call-
ers."

"I credit myself as having had a most excellent
teacher," Rayne said kindly. Without asking, he

removed the shawl and tossed it to the floor. Dragging a medium-sized mahogany case he had stowed under a nearby chair, he removed a pair of scissors. Competent hands gently cut away the dressing without disturbing the wound it protected.

Brogden sipped from the cup he held loosely in his hand. "So you are satisfied with this life you have made for yourself here?"

"I am content. Still I would—" He sucked in his breath as he peeled back the old dressing. "By God, Wallace, are you trying to kill yourself?" He stood, walking to the other side of the room to ring for a servant.

"As bad as that?" He peeled off the suction-toed lizard from his neck.

"Bloody bad enough to amputate, you stubborn arse!"

A tired-looking housemaid entered the room. "You rang, sir?"

"Your master is ill. Tell Cook to keep a kettle over the hearth. I need plenty of hot water and clean linens to bind his leg."

"Right away, sir!" She disappeared as quietly as she had entered.

"I won't lose the leg, Rayne."

He could see Wallace's resolve was as flexible as a fifty-gun frigate with a broken rudder. Deliberately, he rolled his shoulders, prepared to battle. "What good are two legs when you will be a corpse within a month?"

Brogden took a deep breath. He slowly blew it out. "Insolent, wet-eared scold. I know my business."

To irritate him Rayne silently raised a questioning brow and reached into his case for a small pair of forceps. He only got a response when he confiscated his friend's cup.

"Give me that!"

He ignored the command, concentrating instead on his task.

Choosing to gaze anywhere but at his injured leg, Brogden said, "It was a monkey bite, you know. 'Bout two months ago. Damn beast was someone's pet."

"Mmm."

Finally, unable to stand the silence, he roared, "Say something! I came all this way for you to see to it that I keep my limb."

"Maggots."

"What?"

Head bowed over the leg, he did not bother to look up. "You have maggots eating away at your leg, while the opium is eating at what is left of your brain." Rayne picked the offending creatures out, one by one, and dropped them into the cup. "Christ, what a mess! A ball to the heart would be quicker."

The housemaid appeared behind him, holding a large pot of steaming water and a fistful of clean linens. "Shall ye be needing some of the men to help ye, sir?"

Rayne raised his head and met the pleading gaze of his friend. This man had befriended him at the lowest point in his life when even his own family had forgotten his name. He had offered his protection, money when it was needed, and had taught him the skills so he could make his way in the world. Rayne tore his gaze off those begging, tear-filled eyes and forced himself to address the servant.

The agitated Apala clicked, "Geckogeckogecko."

* * *

"I thought I might find you here."

Devona was not particularly surprised to find Rayne at her carriage door. No, what was more surprising was the fact that she had avoided him this long!

"Good afternoon, my lord," she said, her fine manners automatically rallying forth as if they were meeting in a ballroom instead of Newgate Street. "Have many friends incarcerated here at the 'Gate?"

"Ladies who have criminals for suitors should not cast stones." He frowned at Pearl, who was doing her best to blend into the background. "What can I do to make you disappear?"

Devona stilled her maid's escape with a hand gesture. "Lord Tipton, I shall not tolerate you terrorizing my staff. Pearl stays."

His frown became more pronounced. "I desire a private discussion with you, Miss Bedegrayne, that will not be bandied about the servants' quarters this evening."

"Miss Brown is the very soul of discretion, are you not, Pearl?"

"Yes, miss." The maid visibly cringed under Rayne's perusal. "I think I could do with a bit of air, though." She scrambled to get out of the carriage.

"Lord Tipton, there is no need to bully anyone here!"

Gar suddenly loomed behind Rayne. His gaze held Devona's, but it was the heavily muscled footman whom he addressed. "You're late. I could have had my way with her twice over, before you interfered."

Devona's saucy little curls bobbed with the in-

dignant nod of her head. "Tipton, this is outside
of enough!" She looked at Gar, hoping she had
enough control over the young man to prevent
the inevitable fight. She was amazed to see a slight
embarrassing flush creeping from his neck up to
his face.

"Several attempts have been made on Miss Bedegrayne's life," Rayne continued in a quiet tone
that seemed more menacing than if he had been
yelling. "Have a care or deal with me."

The prominent lump in Gar's throat wobbled.
"Yes, milord." The footman held a hand out to
Pearl. "Come ride with me on top, Miss Brown.
We'll put the pink back in your cheeks." He
turned to Rayne. "Do you have a specific destina-
tion, milord?"

The simple question set fire to Devona's temper
as quickly as a stack of fireworks. Blast him. Gar
was her man! "There will be no destination," she
said through clenched teeth.

Pretending not to notice her agitated state,
Rayne climbed into the bench opposite her. "Miss
Bedegrayne is quite correct. I have no destination
in mind. Just keep driving until I signal you otherwise."

"Very good, milord." Gar closed and secured
the door.

Devona resisted the strong urge to stomp her
foot. What she really wanted to do was to plant
it firmly into his lordship's shin. Oh, the high-
handed gall of the man! "You presume much,
sir!"

"Just letting you know, beloved, that I take my
responsibilities as your betrothed seriously."

"Ha! Now I know you are addled. That incident
with the hackney was more damaging than you

anticipated. To refresh your faulty memory, I must remind you that my father refused your offer."

He shrugged, giving her an indulgent smile. "A minor bump in our plans. Your former suitors might have been intimidated by that old bull, however, I am not. He may bluster all he wants. In the end, you will be mine."

Devona tried to ignore the tingling thrill coursing through her body. Her shoulders could not prevent a small shudder. Since her traitorous body would not cooperate, she chose to concentrate on the practical side of their plan. Lord Tipton had not developed a great *tendre* for her. This ruse would benefit them both. His return to society could be used to help Doran, and herself as well. No one pursued a betrothed lady after all. And there were benefits for Rayne as well. She could show the *ton* that despite all the rumors about his past Lord Tipton was a decent man, honorable, and above all, quite ordinary. She suspected that if the polite world would treat him more like the gentleman he was, instead of some kind of supernatural creature, the embattlements he had built around his emotions would collapse. Only then would he allow himself to care for anyone.

"I do not think I like that look on your face."

She had been too occupied with her own thoughts to notice he had stopped talking. "Well, the face is mine. Either love it or you may leave," she blithely said, then stilled when he seemed to sincerely contemplate his options.

Their bodies rocked with the swaying motion of the carriage. When she thought she could not abide his silence another moment, he murmured, "I think I will stay, if you do not mind."

Those gorgeous long lashes of his lowered seductively, almost fanning on his cheek. He pulled at her in ways she could not fathom. It delighted her. It also terrified her. In a subtle movement, she leaned closer to him. Conflicting emotions whirled in her head. She wished that he would kiss her again, even if it were not the most sensible thing to do.

"Our betrothal will never work," she said to break his invisible hold.

"You think not?"

Again, there was a shift in the air around them, going from seductive to distant. Devona had not realized she had been holding her breath until it rushed from her lips. "My family does not sanction our union."

"It is of little concern."

He might as well have yawned. He did not place much faith in her papa's influence. "What of your family then?"

"I have no family," he said, the edge in that statement speaking volumes. "The few who claim a kinship to me would not dream of interfering."

"Oh." So he was not prepared to forgive his family, despite all the passing years. Devona stifled a sigh. One problem at a time, she told herself. "There is Doran to consider."

"I would rather not, if it is all the same to you."

"Lord Tipton, if you cannot be serious—"

"Rayne."

"Beg pardon?"

"As your betrothed, I think you should call me by my given name. Feel free to 'my lord' me in public. I am discovering there are certain rewards to becoming your lord. I will continue to savor each benefit."

Exasperated, she shook her head. "Have you considered that someone has been trying to maim or kill us?"

His eyes took on a shrewd cast. "All the more reason to keep you close."

"There is also the fact that a betrothal matures into another state. Marriage."

"I'm game if you are."

Devona had had enough of his glib retorts. She took her parasol and whacked him on the knuckles. His yelp gave her a certain satisfaction. It was all she could do not to laugh at his startled expression.

"Have you lost your head?" He snatched the parasol out of her hands before she could crack him again.

"No, but obviously you have. We cannot marry."

"Oh, on the contrary, I think our blessed union would simplify matters."

She did not like the expression she saw on his handsome face. It was part mischief with a healthy dose of determination. "Have I told you that I refuse to marry out of duty?'

"What reason do you give to Claeg's proposal? Guilt? Sounds like duty to me." He rolled her parasol between his palms. "Besides, no one makes a run for Gretna Green out of duty."

She sucked in a deep breath to fortify her. "We are not eloping!"

He nodded to himself, as if agreeing to an ongoing conversation in his head. "Let's see. The intended couple is present. We are presently traveling in a carriage. We have witnesses." He flipped her parasol handle up to knock on the trapdoor overhead.

"We are not going to Gretna Green!"

"I knew despite your tendency for recklessness, that you were a traditional girl at heart. You want a big wedding."

How had this conversation gotten so out of hand? "No. No!"

"A smaller wedding, it is. I suppose the families will be disappointed with the lack of fanfare."

The sigh he expelled, the telling anthem of a long-suffering male trying to please his woman, was enough to make her grit her teeth. "I think we should forget all about marrying one another. To become leg-shackled to a man who can drive me insane with just a few words does not sound like marital bliss."

"Only because your thinking is too linear, my sweet innocent." He offered her the parasol. When she automatically reached for it, he tugged, pulling her out of her seat and into his lap. "There are many levels of driving one insane, and I would like to have the freedom to explore each arousing level with you."

She struggled, feeling too vulnerable sitting in his lap. No man had ever been as bold. He did not use force to keep her in place. Instead, his mouth settled over hers, the shock of the electrifying contact stilled her attempts at escape. Sensing her surrender, Rayne pulled her so close she was certain he could feel the firm contours of her stays against his chest.

"Tilt your head to the side," he mumbled as he nibbled her lower lip, then moved on to the right side of her jaw.

Her experience with kisses was limited, and it never involved the mind-numbing embraces that Rayne seemed to prefer. Frowning, Devona wondered how many women he had to kiss to achieve such a mouth-devouring talent. The thought was disturbing enough to have her start to pull back.

"Stop thinking."

Using a light touch, he tilted her head himself.

She looked up, noting his eyes had a pewter glow to them. His gaze followed his finger as it moved up her jaw, halting at the yellow ribbons that secured her bonnet. She saw the intent in that smoldering gaze before he acted. A quick tug and the bow under her chin unraveled. Her hands flew up to prevent him from removing her bonnet, but she was grabbing air.

"Rayne!"

The bonnet landed on the opposing bench. "Such delicate ears," he marveled, using both hands to trace the intriguing contours. She shuddered at his touch. It was all the encouragement he needed. Threading his fingers into the intricate twist of her bound hair, he pulled her mouth to his, sinking them both into a deep kiss.

Such skill, she mused, thoroughly enjoying the feel of his warm lips on hers. Not certain of the proper etiquette when one was caught up in a torrid embrace, Devona clutched the light wool fabric of his coat. She dearly wished she were as bold as everyone credited. It would have been quite wonderful to have removed her gloves and touched his face, to test the firmness of his lips with her fingertips.

If Rayne had been aware of her thoughts, he would have heartily approved. It was enough that she was allowing him to cradle her on his lap. The fact she was kissing him back with guileless enthusiasm made him want to show her all the pleasures the sharing of their bodies could provide.

Slow down. Nothing worth keeping should be taken carelessly.

Even as the warning flashed in his fevered brain, he could not stop himself from slipping his right hand from her arm to her knee. The carriage dipped a wheel into a rut, and his roaming hand boldly plunged under the yards of skirt to caress her dainty ankle. Another tug of a ribbon and her slipper dropped to the floor. She laughed, unexpected and hysterical when he stroked his fingertips from her silk-sheathed toes to her heel.

"No one touches my feet," she declared in imperious tones, and then he ruined the effect by touching her feet and making her giggle again. "You brute. I would slay my brothers for less." She squirmed to kick her foot free from his merciless attack.

He thought she was the most beautiful woman he had ever beheld. Her hair was disheveled, her lips puffy from his ravenous attention, and her eyes dewy and wide from their shocking exploration. It made him want her more. "It will not do for you to think of me as an irritating brother. Perhaps I can think of something else to discourage that line of thinking."

Rayne kissed whatever argument was about to form on her lovely full lips. His hand moved from her ankle to her knee again, but this time the silk he stroked was her warm, enticing skin.

"This is not very proper," Devona said, gasping when he inched higher to her thigh.

"What is proper for society and what is proper for us, are entirely different matters." His fingers slipped within the slit of her linen undergarments, persistent, seeking, until he touched the satin curls between her legs. "You like the feel of my mouth on yours, do you not, my heart?" To prove his point, he brushed a kiss against her pouting lips, which he was beginning to crave as much as his next breath. "There are other ways to give each other pleasure. For instance—"

Rayne delved deeper in the small nest of curls and was rewarded with the sweet honey of her response.

Devona sucked in her breath; a small sound escaped her well-kissed lips. "I do not—This is not—Oh, Rayne!" Her hands reached up to his head, knocking his hat off with the gesture. Gloved fingers became tangled in the tied queue, and in her eagerness to explore she gave a handful of hair a hard tug.

"Ow."

"Sorry," she murmured automatically, not particularly aware of the action for which she was actually apologizing. She was too caught up in the sensations his mouth and hands were creating.

Rayne did not know how long he could endure the torment. The longer he held her, touched her, kissed her senseless, the more he desired her. His erect sex pressing against the confines of his tight breeches was a constant reminder of how much he wanted to remove his hand from beneath her skirts and bury himself deep into her welcoming warmth. Using his thumb, he caressed the blooming bud of her sex. The small circular motions made her squirm on his lap. He was not sure if she was attempting to draw closer or evade until she moaned. The low, begging sound of unfulfilled desire had him teetering over the edge of self-control more than anything before this.

"This is just a taste of what we could explore together." He kissed her closed eyelids before pulling her tighter to him so that his mouth was close to her ear. "I could replace my hands with my mouth." He noticed his breath was synchronized with hers, quick pants leading them to the razor edge of culmination. "After I have tasted the sweet dew of your passion with my tongue . . .

m—my teeth." Inspired, she sunk her teeth into his earlobe. He bit the inside of his cheek to prevent himself from instantly climaxing.

Whatever he was about to say, faded at the look of wonder on Devona's face. "I feel so strange. Stop. No wait! Oh, my God!" He kissed her deeply to muffle the scream that would have certainly been heard in a half-mile radius. She bucked against the storm of her climax. Locked in a tight embrace, he held her, the knowledge that he was the first man to ever show her such pleasures giving him a fierce satisfaction.

Devona buried her face into the fabric of his coat. She looked sleepy and exhilarated all in the same moment. "So that is what married couples do," she murmured. Rayne placed a comforting kiss on the side of her head. "I do not see what the big fuss is about. I found the entire event quite thrilling." She frowned, her brows drawing up in a manner he thought adorable. "Maybe that is the problem. If all ladies knew how wonderful this was, then we all would spend our times dallying out in the gardens and carriages instead of sipping warm lemonade at a ball."

The vibration of his silent laughter had her drawing back in question. She was so good for him. He had been feeling battered after his last meeting with Brogden. Cutting off a man's leg tended to make him not inclined to feel friendly, even if he had once considered you a friend. Devona's joy of life was like fresh water sinking into the barren dryness of his soul. "Before you start your own enlightenment movement for young ladies, I must confess there is more to the marriage bed than what you have just experienced."

"You jest!"

"A humble prelude," he said, trying to swallow

the smile that threatened at her disbelief. He did not want her to think he was mocking her. It was just the opposite. His heart and a major part of his pride swelled at her notion that there could be no more beyond their initial pleasuring.

"Oh." She paused. "Then there is no fear of me breeding?"

He did not even want to dwell on the emotions that surged at the thought of her becoming plump with their child. In his present, unsatisfied condition, he would have sold his soul to make the possibility an absolute fact. He took her small hand into his own, accepting the simple comfort her closeness offered. "You need to take me inside you to make a child. Has no one ever explained this to you?" He realized at her blush what a dolt he was. Of course not! Gently reared ladies did not sip tea and nibble on biscuits while they discussed their lustful rendezvous. What was more amazing was that she had allowed him to touch her at all!

"N—no. Not exactly." She appeared to be shamed by the admission.

"Don't. You slice me in two with that expression." Rayne held her face between his rough palms. "I have spent so much time in rough company that I have forgotten how to act like a gentleman. Devona, I treasure the combination of spirit and sweet innocence. It shapes what you are. Forgive me for my crudeness?" He would never beg forgiveness for touching her. If he had his way, he would be doing more than that soon.

She leaned forward to kiss him on the lips. The carriage dipped to one side and her lips landed on his chin. "You have been rude, stubborn, and high-handed." She kissed the insult away when he opened his mouth to protest. "You have also

been kindhearted, generous, and have saved my
life. A crude man? Never, my lord."

She laid her head on his shoulder. The quiet
action was telling. It meant that she trusted him.
At least Rayne hoped his assessment was more
than wishful thinking. In more ways than she
could guess, Devona needed him. He was willing
to save her childhood love, ignore Brock's challenges, and her calculating father's disapproval.
He would even endure the title of Viscount Tipton and all the burdens the rank implied, if it
meant that he could keep her willingly by his side.
Then again, he was just greedy enough to keep
her even if she was unwilling. A determined man
was a formidable one.

EIGHT

Rayne wearily sank into a large overstuffed chair. His valet, Stevens, appeared at his side and immediately began fussing about the scuff marks on his boots while he went about his task of removing them. Rayne thought the odd, slender man's voice held the quality of a buzzing insect. It was high, persistent, and in its finest form made the recipient want to smash it into an indistinguishable smear.

"Enough."

Stevens's sharp angular nose went high in the air, almost sniffing the command. "My lord, you have hired me to see that you are outfitted as a gentleman. Pardon me for saying so, sir, but you could not get yourself hired on as a cook's apprentice wearing garments as wrinkled and soiled as the ones you are wearing. Now if you will follow me upstairs, I will make certain there is a hot bath prepared and a freshly pressed dressing gown—"

"No."

The valet had taken a few steps before he understood. "Is something amiss, milord?"

Rayne rubbed his eyes. "Only your presence. Leave me, for now. Think of the extra dust I shall pick up in my hours of solitude. It will give you something else to fret about."

Stevens left without a word, something about which Rayne would have been surprised if the servant had acted otherwise. He paid his staff well to keep them quiet and honest, and to see to their duties with diligence. It was not his valet's fault that Rayne was in a dark mood. The man had only been doing his job. Normally, his fussy behavior amused him. Not tonight.

He had ended his day with a visit to Brogden's bedside. The visit had not gone well. What had he expected? The man had ignored all medical advice, keeping various skilled surgeons at a distance, in the hope that his friend would save his leg. Rayne had failed him. He reached for the glass of brandy Speck had poured earlier, warming it near the hearth. He filled his mouth with the liquor, enjoying the subtle burn on his tongue. Closing his eyes, he leaned his head back, resting it on a strategically placed pillow.

What scorched his pride was the fear that if he had been better skilled he might have been able to repair Brogden's leg. No, by the fates, he thought with a sudden fierceness, he had been correct to amputate. There had been too much gangrene. The man was fortunate not to have died from the poison. Even if he had been able to scrape away all the rotten flesh, there would have been nothing left to stitch together over the bone.

"My lord, a Mr. Bedegrayne to see you. Shall I send him on his way?" Speck asked, looking like he would relish the idea of vanquishing one of the Bedegraynes and succeeding.

Rayne glanced at the ornate clock on the mantel. It was past eight in the evening, a time when men were at their clubs or escorting their women to a ball. He would have preferred to send the young, angry man away. However, Brock played a small part in his plan to gain custody of Devona. If he was fortunate, he might survive the evening without gaining an appointment for a duel.

Bedegrayne filled the doorway, his pale green eyes flashing annoyance as he entered the room, with Speck following in his hostile wake to collect his coat and hat. A most thorough servant, the man was probably searching him for hidden weapons as well. Rayne was not particularly worried that Brock would shoot him in his study, but he had lived close to the rough fringes of life to be on alert.

"Bedegrayne," Rayne greeted him calmly enough to have the younger man visibly clenching his teeth. "So good of you to save me the trip of seeking you out." He nodded at the chair Speck was already positioning beside him. "Take the seat, and tell me what drove you from the gaming hells so early this evening?" With a subtle hand movement he dismissed Speck's protective tarrying. The butler silently departed.

"You can stuff your civility, Tipton. I am not as gullible as my sister."

"Which one? Lovely Wynne or the Bedegrayne changeling, Devona?" His steepled fingers linked then unlinked in a contemplative gesture. "The Bedegraynes breed such beautiful creatures. 'Tis a pity the sacrifice was a bit of common sense."

Brock, still refusing to sit, rested his hand on the top of Rayne's chair. "You surprise me, Tipton. I had assumed we would have to dance a bit before we got to the point."

Unblinking, Rayne met his opponent's gaze. "You have developed some eccentric tastes if you think I'd prefer dancing with you." He almost grinned at the barely contained growl Brock swallowed. He admired the restraint. It gave him some hope the young man had not been completely corrupted by the group of deviants he preferred.

"Since you respect the direct approach, how's this?" A concealed blade slid from his left coat sleeve, landing efficiently into his hand. The razor sharp edge hovered dangerously close to Rayne's throat.

One side of his mouth lifted into a parody of a smile. Speck was losing his touch in his old age to have missed the knife. For a man facing imminent death, he did not appear overly concerned. "It seems you have the advantage. The real question is, will you lose it?"

A lock of blond hair fell across Brock's face, giving him a rakish look. His angular features were drawn tight, and the hint of sweat on his forehead revealed that he was aware he was playing a game with stakes beyond his means. "You have mocked me and my family. You toy with my sister's affections. Do you think anyone would cry foul if I just slit your throat? I would probably be the toast of the Season."

"You are most likely correct." He mentally measured the length of the blade and the slim distance between his throat and the deadly point. "I think the only soul who would hate you for your deed would be Devona."

Brock sneered. "She is too innocent to understand the mind of men."

"You think?" he countered, taunting. "I guess it is the failing of older brothers to not comprehend that even sisters have unfulfilled desires."

"You touched her." The words were stark. Brock was feeling the full impact of his failure to protect his sister from the *ton's* fiend.

"I think men in general underestimate the alluring passion women keep bound up within them like a tightly tied corset. Take Devona—"

Brock's hand jerked, leaving a small bloody nick. "Obviously, you did, you callous bastard!"

The cut was negligible, but the young Bedegrayne was on the verge of having a stroke. Rayne decided to help him along. "A man would never ask for a more sweeter, responsive woman in his bed. The taste of her was as addictive as honey."

The last of Brock's self-control snapped. Red-faced with fury, he pulled the knife back to strike the fatal blow. The slight movement was all Rayne needed. His movements were as precise as a metronome. He grabbed Brock's wrist in a viselike grip, kicked his leg out, and knocked his opponent to his knees.

Sweat beaded on both their brows as they continued the silent struggle to gain control of the knife. Rayne surprised him by ramming the hilt of the blade upward into Brock's forehead. The burst of pain was enough to stun him. Rayne took the advantage and forced Brock's arm down. The blade slammed harmlessly into the padding of the chair.

"Devil take it, this is my favorite chair."

Livid, Brock, struggled against the firm grip on his wrist. "You lament over your damn chair, after what you did to my sister?"

Rayne gave Bedegrayne's wrist enough of a twist to have him wincing. He would have never resorted to such trickery if this family were a more agreeable clan. "What exactly do you think was done to your sister?"

"You bedded her!"

"A gentleman never tells, but then again, I've never been much of a gentleman." He gave him a wolfish grin. "If I had bedded your sister, she would still be there and you and I would not be wrestling on the floor trying to compare the size of our cocks." Just because he could, Rayne gave the younger man's wrist another bone-wrenching twist before he released it. "You should be ashamed to think so little of Devona. She is a generous, loving, beautiful lady. I am amazed you two are kin."

Brock eyed him warily, not certain how to proceed. "You are not her lover?"

"No." Rayne walked over to the table and poured two very generous brandies. He returned to Bedegrayne's side and handed him a snifter. "But you haven't posed the correct question. What you want to know is, did I touch her?"

"There's a difference?" Brock grudgingly accepted the glass with his uninjured hand.

"If you have to ask, then I would say your experience with the fair sex is nonexistent," he mocked, leaning against the chair. He privately wondered if he should remove the protruding knife from the chair before Brock got it in his head to gut him.

Remarkably, he did not rise to the baiting. Instead, he rolled to his feet with a cautious movement that had Rayne sympathizing. Almost. "I am giving up trying to figure you out, Tipton. You said that you had planned to seek me out. What were your intentions? Or is provoking me just a recently discovered amusement?"

Rayne offered him the opposing chair as if they had not been fighting for their lives just minutes ago. "Any enjoyment I receive is incidental. What I need from you is your tenacity. In my favor this time."

Brock sat, keeping his injured knee straight. "Why would I want to help you?"

"Because it is in your best interest to see that Devona is married off. Who better than I?"

"Oh I can list a score of men who would make a proper husband for our Dev, more so than the notorious Le Cadavre Raffiné," he said defiantly.

Rayne propped his elbows on his knees as he leaned forward. "Would these same men accept her if word got out that she was my woman?" He knew the answer; he just wanted to hear the words from Bedegrayne.

"You told me you had never bedded her!"

"This is the best part, Bedegrayne. Whether it is true or not, is not significant." He gave him a smug smile. "Regardless, she is mine. All I have to do is say so. There have been enough witnesses to put us together. The gossips will have her bedded to me before you can meet me on an abandoned dawn field." Brock viewed him as an adversary. He was also counting on him being a smart one.

"Damn," he mumbled, his posture slouched in defeat. "What do you want me to do?"

Approval beamed through Rayne's gaze. His new brother by marriage was not a complete ass, after all. "To do what you do best. Be a stubborn bastard."

Tea was served in the green and gold Worcester tea service. It had been in the family for several decades. It was also one of Devona's particular favorites. She needed something to keep up her spirits since her fellow conspirators appeared less than enthusiastic to be joining her in the small parlor.

Pearl had positioned herself at the window, peering out through the small opening in the curtains. Her nervous gestures and observations of doom were wearing on someone of Devona's temperament. Unfortunately, she needed the irritating woman. Wynne, in contrast, sat calmly beside Doran's sister, Amara. She offered a plate of biscuits to the quiet young woman and was politely rejected.

Inviting Amara had been impulsive, but necessary. Similar in height to Devona, her shoulders seemed unnaturally bowed from the continuous battering she took for being Lady Claeg's disappointing daughter. Her brown hair was gathered tightly into a bun in the back. The serviceable gray gown made her appear sickly. Devona wondered if the woman's hair had the tendency to curl like her brother's. Giving her a measuring stare, Devona's assessment was quick. A little clipping and curling to frame her fragile heart-shaped face, a hint of color to draw attention to her stormy dark blue eyes, some new fashionable gowns, and Miss Claeg would be enchanting.

Amara, uncomfortable with being the center of attention, sipped from her cup to hide her distress. Without looking directly at Devona, she asked, "I am still not certain why I am here today, Miss Bedegrayne."

Devona tried not to sigh. Obviously, Amara had every attention to keep their friendship at a distance. "Devona, please. And I shall call you Amara. It is such a beautiful name, do you not agree, Wynne?" She shot her sister a comply-or-else glare.

"Very," Wynne murmured, biting into a biscuit to keep from saying anything else.

"We have never been close, and I want that to change. Naturally, I understand if you cannot endure my company after all the terrible things

your mother has said about me." She thought
of the shock she had seen in the young woman's
eyes and hoped she had not misread the distress.

Amara clutched the teacup so tightly she was
likely to crack it. "I am not my mother. I know
you were only trying to help Doran." Her trou-
bled gaze was fixed on her cooling tea. "You did
not deserve the slap."

"Perhaps not so publicly," she said ruefully.
"However, I still insist on helping Doran with or
without your mother's blessing. Will you help us?"

Stunned, Amara forgot all about her cup and
openly gaped at Devona. "Me? What could I do
to help my brother? Mama said only a miracle
will save Doran from hanging. If Papa can barely
meet the taxes on the country house, a miracle
would surely beggar us." She blinked back the
sudden moisture on her lashes.

"I have a plan."

Pearl groaned. "Not more mischief, miss?"

"Quiet, Pearl." Wynne loyally commanded. "I
must confess, the hairs rise on the back of my
neck every time you mention one of your
schemes, Devona. Still your heart is in the right
place. What do you want to do?"

"First, we need to get rid of our watchdog."

Confusion glazed Amara's eyes. "A pet?"

"Our brother, Brock. He has been most annoying of late. If I did not know better, I would think
Tipton has had a hand in this." Devona dismissed
the notion with a shake of her head. The pair of
them conspiring together was too amusing.

Wynne dusted the crumbs from her fingers. "I
have a feeling Tipton rarely needs the assistance
of others to gain what he wants." She directed a
raised brow in her sister's direction.

Amara switched her gaze from sister to sister. "Tipton? As in Lord Tipton?"

"Yes." She faced Wynne. "If you are implying that Tipton is going to have his way with me, you are mistaken." She did not consider how her outburst sounded until Amara gasped.

"T—Tipton. The man they call the Refined Corpse?" the young woman squeaked. "They say he is dangerous."

"A tame man would never interest the *ton*," Devona assured her, distracted by her sister's observation. One thing she had learned was that Tipton had done nothing to improve polite society's low opinion of him, nor had he cared. "Brock has called him out numerous times. Papa has refused him. I seconded that refusal. Marriage to Tipton simply would be a disaster."

Pearl sniffed from her post at the window. "That's why we spent several hours driving 'round London while you cooed in the man's arms. Considering the sounds we heard, we should have made straight away to Gretna Green!"

Wynne laughed aloud. "That's the way to stand up to her, Pearl!"

Devona glared at her maid. "A fine time to develop some spirit, Pearl. You will need that bit of bone to help us." She could not help smirking at the woman's crestfallen expression. Cooing sounds, indeed!

"What exactly are you planning, Miss Bedegrayne?" If she was wary before, the news of Tipton being involved did little to calm her.

Pleased to change the subject, Devona turned a bright, convincing smile on Amara. "I could not help but notice how similar in size we are." She looked to Wynne for agreement. Her sister just shrugged.

"Well, yes, I suppose."

"Lovely features, just the kind of face I have always caught Brock admiring."

"Devona," Wynne said in a warning tone.

Amara blushed very prettily at the mention of the handsome Bedegrayne. "Your brother? He has never noticed me."

Devona frowned at that fact, then again, it mattered little for what she had planned. She clasped the other woman's hand as though they were best friends. "Have you ever considered using henna on your hair?"

"Hair dye?" Amara looked about, whether it was for confirmation or escape, no one was positive.

Devona ignored the fact Amara was trying to tug her hand free. "And curls." She lightly touched the ones teasing her cheek. "A hot iron would do wonders for your looks."

"I—I do not think—" Amara gave up her argument. Her slouch became more pronounced at her acceptance that she was no match for the Bedegrayne sisters. "No hair dye!" she mumbled.

Wynne was not as easily subdued. "What exactly do you have planned for us, sister?"

"Nothing too complicated. We will just have to free Doran from Newgate ourselves." She went on, oblivious to their shocked expressions. "The audacity of the plan proves no one will suspect it." Pleased with herself, she leaned back on the elegant sofa and nibbled on a biscuit.

Wynne was the first to recover. "I cannot wait to see Papa's face when you explain that his gels were locked up in the 'Gate because they possessed an overabundance of audacity."

"No one will get caught," Devona said, attempting to soothe their distress.

Her sister was not convinced. "If prison does not kill us, Sir Thomas certainly shall!"

"Young Brock, it was so good of you to attend our fanciful ball."

Observing that his sister Devona was occupied dancing, he felt it was safe enough to turn his attention to the middle-aged woman dressed like a cabin boy. "Lady Dodd, a most unusual ball. What have you called it?"

The woman's dark eyes gleamed behind her mask. "Oh, we are calling it Highwaymen, Pirates, and Various Rogues. Guess who I am?" She preened under his gaze.

Seeing most of the *ton* strutting around representing the cesspool of mankind made for a peculiar kind of evening. He tried to hide his amusement. "I haven't a clue, madam."

"Why I am Mary Read, lady pirate who apprenticed as a footboy to a French lady. However, I was born for high adventure and took to the sea."

Watching this demure woman playing the role of a pirate was too much for Brock. He rubbed his jaw to conceal his laughter. "Very effective."

Lady Dodd made rolling circles with her hand toward the ballroom before them. "You have your sister Devona to thank for this amusement. She was the one who suggested the theme, and I for one am eternally grateful."

Brock's gaze moved back to the ball, seeking out his sister again. He caught a flash of her as she maneuvered her way through a lively reel. Although he could not see her face, he knew her eyes would be twinkling and a genuine smile would gift each passing partner. He sighed. Yes, he could believe Devona had her hand in this bit of absurdity.

"Only my sister could look fashionable in masculine togs. Which derelict of society is she?" Judging from her clothes, the knave she played was at least one hundred years dead.

"Let me think," Lady Dodd said with a very unladylike tug on the slipping waist of her borrowed trousers. "Claude something. Du Vall." She beamed, pleased to have recalled the name.

"A flamboyant Frenchman?"

She laughed as if he had made a jest. "Your sister is original if nothing else. And who are you, young Brock?"

He tried not to wince at "young Brock." Some folks around kept forgetting he was five-and-twenty, a man fully grown. "Consider me one of the various," he growled.

"Marvelous, simply splendid!"

Brock was relieved to see Rayne appear suddenly at his side. "Tipton. 'Bout time you got here. Like I have little else to do but nursemaid my sister."

"Gentlemen, if you will excuse me?" Wide-eyed, and more than a little impressed to have Tipton show up, Lady Dodd curtsied then made her way to the ballroom to tell everyone of her special guest.

Dressed in black, Rayne appeared the perfect rogue without much effort. "Where is she?"

He cocked his head in the direction of the ballroom. "The fancy lace-bibbed lad in the silver-lined cape." Brock might not approve of Tipton for his sister, but one thing was obvious, the man considered her his own. He knew the moment Rayne had spotted her, just by the subtle narrowing of his eyes.

"White plumes on her mask?"

"Who else?"

"Someone, but not Devona," Rayne said with a cutting coolness that had Brock snapping his head in his sister's direction.

"Ridiculous!" He watched her lean forward to whisper something in Oz Lockwood's ear. The older man did not appear pleased when she accepted the arm of her waiting dance partner. Pivoting on one heel, he departed in the opposite direction of Devona. "I know my own sister, Tipton."

Tipton's pewter gaze flashed, the raw fury he held in control would have sent a less courageous man scurrying. "And your sister has never slipped the leash in your hand, right?" he asked. The sarcasm and the shame that he was correct had Brock wincing.

"See here, I have been watching her all evening." Feeling defensive, since he had mishandled her in the past, made him add, "Maybe a man your age should consider a pair of spectacles."

In low enunciated tones that made the hairs on the back of Brock's neck rise, Rayne said, "That woman is not your sister." He moved to prove his point.

"Wait." Brock grabbed him on the arm. "Devona has barely said three words to me this evening. She has not forgiven me for taking your side in this marriage business. Seeing us together will only make her dig in."

Rayne gave him a look of disbelief. "So she sulks."

Oz Lockwood blocked their course. "Bedegrayne. Tipton." He gave them a distracted nod. "I say, Bedegrayne, your sister is in a mood this evening. She dances with every man in the room as if her slippers have been bewitched. When I beg her for a moment of respite she whispers in French that she has sworn off all men who know her this eve." He stiffened, recalling her dismissal. "If I have offended Miss Bedegrayne, would you tell her to accept my apologies?" A nod to each of them, he headed for the front hall.

"Odd," Brock murmured, "I thought she was rather fond of Lockwood. In a friendship sort of manner," he felt compelled to add when he saw Tipton's expression.

"Sworn off all men who know her. Very convenient." Rayne sneered. He sliced a path through the crowd as cleanly as a ship's bow moved through water, his target the woman smiling behind the white plumed mask.

Sensing she was being watched, she turned in time to see their determined approach. Even with the mask hiding all but her mouth and chin, enough was exposed for Brock to see her displeasure. Had he not warned Tipton that Devona would be angry? Ha, let the man suffer the edge of her tongue. Mayhap he would reconsider marrying her.

Rayne grabbed her before she could make her escape. "Mysterious lady, I believe I have not had the pleasure."

Never lost for words, Brock was surprised when all Devona did was part her lips to speak then tightly close them. Now that he saw her close up in the candlelight, he thought the color of her hair was slightly off. Then there were the curls. His sister had a natural curl to her hair. It was obvious from the way some sections of hair had fallen that a hot iron had been used to create the effect. Not pleased with the renewed role of idiot brother, he snatched the mask from her face with enough speed that he had Rayne raising an approving brow.

Brock may have suspected a ruse, however the lady beneath the mask was a complete surprise. The stormy blue eyes that had gazed at him over the years with a shyness that he had always thought endearing were now sparking with the promise of violence. "Amara?" he said, his voice hoarse with shock.

Amara shook the sagging curls from her face. Her dainty chin held high, she glared at them as if they were in the wrong. Even Rayne appeared for the moment undecided on how to handle her. "I told her the hair dye would be a mistake," she snapped, daring them to contradict her. Brock, considering himself a man with some sense, figured he should check her for concealed weapons before replying.

NINE

"How long do you think Amara can keep Brock from unveiling her?" Wynne asked, pitching her voice so that only Devona could hear.

"Hours if she acts as I suggested." Sadly, Amara did not share Devona's enthusiasm for intrigue. She had balked at her disguise, vowing that the wearing of men's garments would call her mother's wrath down upon her. From Devona's perspective, Lady Claeg remained in a permanent state of ire. Talking her into using henna had taken all of her skills. Amara did possess a streak of stubbornness, which at any other time Devona would have applauded. Fortunately, she had more experience gaining what she desired. Brock had escorted a slightly bemused Amara, fully dressed in her male attire and complete with freshly dyed and curled locks, to the ball. Devona counted on her to play her role because her brother's freedom depended on it.

"Shall I take this basket, miss?" Pearl carried a large basket filled with bread.

"Yes, we shall all take one to press our purpose." Gar came up behind Pearl, carrying a small cask of beer on his shoulders.

"Does this plan of yours consider who shall rescue us in case we fail?" Pearl glanced at Gar, who only grunted. Neither one of them was thrilled to have been recruited.

"Do not sound so dour, Pearl. If we fail to release Mr. Claeg, at least we will have fed a few inmates."

"I wish I had your faith, miss."

Devona felt that optimistic thinking was the higher road to success. She refused to contemplate what would happen to them all if their mission failed. Papa was the least of her worries. How would Tipton feel about having a felon as his betrothed? She shuddered at a sudden chill. No, it was better to think about fooling them all.

"We have company, sister." Wynne grabbed her basket, prepared to support her sister in any manner.

A guard approached the gate they had gathered at, his harsh drawn features far from welcoming. "You there. This is no place to set up business."

Devona faced him. Wearing a warm smile, she walked to the gate. "Forgive us for being late. Two of the bakeries that promised to donate their goods abandoned our good cause. It took us most of the day to find a replacement." She did not waver under his suspicious stare. Instead she raised her hands to beckon her companions to join her. "The Benevolent Sisters of Charity would be disappointed if I could not carry out my duty. There are many within who do not benefit from family and friends. Our mission is to lessen their suffering." She tried to appear humble. When he just stared, she could feel the sweat bead on her forehead despite the relatively coolness of the evening. He did not believe her, or perhaps the hard man just did not care.

"Sister, do not forget the beer to wash away the

bitterness of their plight." Wynne approached the gate, radiating sincerity and looking like a true angel of mercy.

The guard scratched his head. "Beer, eh?"

"More than enough to go around, right, sisters?" Gar added, winking to include the guard in the camaraderie.

Wynne touched the gate, allowing her fingers to accidentally brush against the guard's fingers. He jolted at the contact. "We understand that the men who see to the care of the prisoners deserve a reward too."

"Ain't that the truth, sister." He eyed the barrel on Gar's shoulder. "How much do ye have there?"

Gar bared his teeth in a mock grin, knowing the gates of hell had just opened to them. "Enough to need a sturdy back or two."

Amara was all but thrown into the awaiting coach. Her useless attempt to brace herself against the door frame resulted in her sprawling facedown on to the floor. So utterly graceful, she thought. She groaned when someone yanked her up into a sitting position.

"Some might consider this kidnapping, Mr. Bedegraync." He grunted, and then shoved her across the bench to make room for him. Lord Tipton climbed in and sat on the opposite bench. "There were witnesses." She swallowed a bubble of hysteria when both men chuckled. So much for seizing control of the situation.

"How much time do you think we have?" Brock asked, giving Amara a chance to study his profile. Of the two Bedegrayne men, she had always thought him the most beautiful.

"We are working against a deficit, thanks to Miss Claeg's ruse." He fixed his piercing gaze on her. "So why do you not save us the burden of dragging you throughout London."

Prepared to do her part to save her brother, she drew herself up, appearing the perfect martyr. "Forgive me. I cannot help you."

"By tomorrow, all will know that you spent the night out on the town with two lusty gentlemen. Tell me, who would marry you after that?"

"Tipton," Brock warned.

"All you have to do, Amara—I may call you Amara—is tell me where my betrothed is and what she plans to do." He propped his elbow against the wall, lightly resting his jaw on his fist. And waited.

Amara could not fathom why this man enthralled Devona. He was too intense. Too predatory. Her gaze dropped to her hands fisted in her lap. "You can try to intimidate me all you want, my lords. Ruin me if you must, I cannot break my word."

Tipton's control slipped. Lashing out, he shouted, "What good is your word, Miss Claeg, when your silence places Devona in danger! Enjoy the moment, for if anything happens to her, my fury yields to no boundaries."

She paled at his threat. What was she to do? Devona had promised her plan would work. There was risk, to be sure, however even Devona would know the price she would have to pay for taunting the devil. She turned away from them and stared in silence out at the passing glimpses of shadowed civilization.

"Miss Claeg. Amara," Brock entreated when she flinched at the warm, large hand on her shoulder. "I understand a promise has been

made." He sent Tipton a look to keep him silent
on the matter, but Amara missed it. "I can admire
such integrity. It is something I have always liked
about you."

"You forgot to mention my gullibility, sir."
Amara's lips thinned. "If you think flattery will
sway me."

Tipton moved as if to pounce. "I have had
enough of this banter! Let's take her to my town
house. I possess items that will make even the
most stalwart gain their tongues."

Brock leaned his arm across her to block Tipton from touching her. "Threats of torture will
only scare her speechless, man. Bury your emotions for I need you to think of places we might
search."

Brock's features softened when he looked at
her. Amara reminded herself that he was ruthless,
too. He would do and say anything to gain what
he wanted.

"You have been growing up while my back was
turned, little one."

She bit her lower lip to keep from stuttering,
not realizing her innocent actions seemed pro-
vocative. Nor did she react to Brock's answering
flare of awareness in his pale green eyes.

"Bloody bad timing to play with a bit of skirt,
Bedegrayne," Tipton muttered.

"Find your own gel."

"That's what I'm trying to do, mate!"

Brock ignored him. "Your hair always reminded
me of polished mahogany." He leaned forward
and pressed his nose into her hair. "Mmm, and
smells of lemons. Nice."

Amara tried to temper the thrill of having him
so close that she could taste his breath. Unre-
quited love may inspire the poets, but for a young

woman it sentenced her to life as a spinster. "You are very good at this, my lord. Never have I heard such false words ring true. Doran always thought you Bedegraynes had the stuff for the stage."

Brock frowned at her lightly spoken words, feeling the sting of the backhanded slap. "I do not lie."

"Only when it suits you. Do not worry, sir, I understand it is the male way." She glanced at Lord Tipton, noting his incredulous look of disbelief at their exchange. She preferred it at the moment to Brock's false, flattering concern.

"Who hurt you, dove?"

Dove. It was a playful nickname of childhood. As a child it had made her feel special. It inflicted pain on the woman she had become. "I do not see how it is any of your concern."

Sensing this was a locked door she would not open to him tonight, Brock allowed the subject to drop. She saw a flash of his white teeth, and could not prevent him from twisting a curl around his fingers. "I vow, I cannot believe you permitted Devona to douse you in henna."

Amara thought back to the battle of wills she had fought with Devona and lost. She always lost when facing a Bedegrayne. "When she is on a mission, you know there is no stopping her."

The enlightenment she saw in both men's expressions had her silently cursing them both.

Brock gave Amara's shoulder a comforting stroke, but his triumph left her cold. "I only know of one mission which Devona seeks to accomplish. The saving of Doran Claeg. Is this how she lured the most sensible little dove I know? She swore your actions would help him?"

"What could she hope to gain at this hour?" Tipton wondered aloud.

Amara switched her gaze from one side to the next, attempting to keep the tears that burned her eyes from falling. Her mother had been right. The Bedegraynes were nothing but users. They employed their beauty and cunning to trip up the lesser mortals. She had been conned by a master. The bitterness she felt dried the oncoming tears. One day she would gain satisfaction from Brock Bedegrayne. Unfortunately, tonight she would sup on defeat.

"If you halt the coach and grant me leave, I will tell you where to find her."

Tipton rapped on the trapdoor to alert the coachman. Brock blocked her escape. "There is no manner in which you can convince me to allow a lady to walk the streets at night."

"As Lord Tipton pointed out, after word gets out, no one will ever consider me a lady. You have ruined me."

If Amara's tone lacked emotion, Brock made up for the passion in his. "By God, do you think I would allow a scandal to touch you for protecting my sister and her insane notion of duty?"

"That protection will likely get your sister in trouble if not worse."

"Still that tongue, Tipton, before I split it myself!" The coach had stopped. "Tell us what you know and we will collect Devona. Tomorrow, we will straighten out what the *ton* thought they saw at the ball."

Amara slipped under his arm and was out the door before he could grasp her skirt. "Such concern, Mr. Bedegrayne. You break my heart," she mocked. The tears in her eyes showed them both how ill-used she felt. "Devona is at Newgate. As you both thought, she has a plan to rescue Doran. Good evening." Her cloak twirled around her as she began her walk in the opposite direction the coach was heading.

She managed to get ten feet from the coach before the world tilted. She screamed, frantically reaching for something to steady herself and found purchase clutching Brock's muscled shoulders. "Put me down, you lying rogue."

Roughly he fought her, matching her struggles for flight against his determination to keep her. She never stood a chance. "I hate you." The tears fell as easily as her defenses.

Brock pivoted and strode to the awaiting coach. "I may be a liar and rogue, a man ruthless enough to rip off the wings of a helpless dove to protect my own." He pushed her into the coach. "Perhaps I even deserve your hate. Lord knows I don't feel great self-love for myself this night. You are hurt and angry. Let me repair the damage we've caused. It starts with not leaving you on the streets."

Tipton struck the trapdoor, signaling the coachman to continue. "We're going to have our hands full dealing with your sister. How do you plan to persuade your gentle dove to remain in our custody?" He laughed when Amara sunk her teeth into Brock's hand.

"Damn!" He flipped Amara around so that her wrists met behind her back. Holding her with one hand, he reached for a handkerchief. "I used to think you were such an even-tempered child."

She gritted her teeth. "I am no longer a child!" Both of them knew he had felt enough of her to verify that fact. "I shall scream until you release me."

"Tipton, give me your handkerchief," Brock said, finishing the knot binding her hands together. "I can only concentrate on one screaming, outraged female at a time."

"Doran Claeg," the gatesman called out to the dark ward. A ripple of sotto voce echoes answered the summons. "Wot so special 'bout this bloke?"

Since Wynne seemed to possess an amazing talent for handling the criminal element, Devona looked to her to push aside the man's suspicions.

"His name appeared on our list of special blessings. One of our benefactors knew him since childhood and asked us to make certain he personally received our gifts." The smile she gave him would have blinded the most cynical oppressor. The few coins she gave him did not hurt either.

"Doran Claeg!"

Wynne inclined her head close to Devona's ear. "He is in a ward. I thought you said he was in a cell. Pray, how do you propose we break him out with all of these witnesses?"

"He was supposed to be in a cell. At least that was what the map revealed."

"Map? What map?"

"I procured a map from an interesting street vendor—"

Wynne's elegant mouth dropped open before she could stop herself. "You bought a map from some street person? Are you crazy?" she asked with enough force to have the gatesman looking their way. She struggled to appear calm. "What did you think, that X marks the location of Doran Claeg? How could you be so naïve?"

Devona could not bear to see the disappointment on her sister's face. "I paid for a layout of the prison. I was assured it was a fair representation. It cost me sixteen shillings."

Wynne closed her eyes. To anyone else it probably looked like she was praying. Considering the circumstances, she probably was. "Okay. I would not mention this little detail to Pearl and Gar. I can assure you their nerves would barely abide the strain."

"I'm Claeg." Bleary-eyed, and looking drunk, the filthy creature swaggered up to the door. Devona was grateful Amara could not see her brother in his present state.

"Ye've visitors. A special blessing and other rot." The guard chuckled, ignoring the women's indignation.

"Blessings, Brother Claeg." Devona stepped forward, angling herself so the guard could not see her face. She placed a finger to her lips.

"What? Dev—Sister?" The look of surprise on Doran's face was such that she battled not to laugh.

"I was just telling Mr. Pringle here," Wynne delicately took the guard's arm and tried not to reveal her disgust. "That a quiet place to pray with Mr. Claeg is needed. This would give him the opportunity to help our man dispense the bread and beer."

"I don't know."

Wynne patted his arm. "What is the harm? You will have our man with you, and we are just three defenseless women."

"Ah, um . . ."

Devona gave Doran a wink before turning away. Never was she so grateful to have a sister who could muddle a man's mind with the touch of her hand.

* * *

"Since when did the Bedegrayne women take over a nunnery?" Doran demanded.

The anger was preferable to the listless drunk they had first encountered. "We never claimed to be nuns, we have just expanded on our charity work."

Doran sank onto the small bench, putting his head into his hands. "What have you done, Devona?"

"Nothing yet. With luck we will have you out of here soon."

Instead of being pleased, he appeared appalled. "You are planning to break me out of here? The three of you?"

Tired of defending herself, pride rose to meet his disbelief. "Not just the three of us. Gar is with us. And Amara is holding her own, keeping Brock distracted."

Doran's head snapped up. "Amara. Amara is here?"

"Not at the prison. She is pretending to be me at Lady Dodd's masquerade."

He pinched the strain building between his eyes. "Dev, love, when we spoke of my release, I thought you had plans that involved that odd surgeon. You mentioned nothing of risking yourself or my sister."

"Thanks for remembering me and Pearl, Doran. Wish I could say I am pleased to see you, too," Wynne said drolly, moving away from her post at the door. "I think it is safe to pray, Sister."

"Wynne, I thought you had more sense than indulging Devona and her schemes." He took the cup of beer she offered and drank deeply.

She knelt beside him. Dipping her handkerchief into his cup she dabbed at the small, oozing cut on his forehead. "How could I refuse when

someone else knows which heartstrings to pluck?"
She gave him a knowing look that had him flush-
ing under the dirt on his face.

"We do not have time to argue about this."
Devona reached for a long loaf of bread and
broke it in two. Baked within was a large file. "I
almost had heart failure when that guard broke
those first two loaves. I guess I am not the first to
smuggle tools into this place." She grinned.

Pearl stirred from her position. "Miss Wynne
had quite an effect on him. Daresay, your father
will have a question or two if that man comes calling."

"Quit teasing," Devona said, glancing back at
her. "It's time for you to strip." She ignored
Pearl's weary sigh.

Wynne grabbed Doran by the shoulders and
turned him toward the wall. "Now is not the time
to indulge your fantasies, Mr. Claeg."

He bit into the bread. "Why is she removing
her gown?"

"It is what's under it that we're after."

"Christ," he moaned. "You aren't planning to
dress me up in lady's underwear?"

Wynne's smile had little to do with humor. "As
amusing as that sounds, I fear we must forgo such
entertainment. Pearl wears trousers and a shirt
underneath her gown." She gave him an experimental sniff. "From the smell of you, I would
think a change of attire would be welcome."

Devona handed him the clean clothing. "You
have lost so much weight, Doran. If you cannot
conceal them under the rags you wear, we will
have to hide them elsewhere."

"Not that I'm not grateful, Devona. I am. Still,
what good is a change of clothes and a file in this
place?" he asked, sounding skeptical.

"Men have escaped this place, possessing even less than you have at your disposal." Wynne sneered. "I do not know why you want to save his worthless hide, Devona. The man is a quitter. He is already dead."

Doran jumped to his feet, blocking Wynne's dismissal. "What do you know of fear or despair, you sharp-tongued shrew? I'd wager you have to scrape the frost off your heart each morning just to get it to beat!"

Eyes flashing fury, her sister held her ground. "Go ahead and take that wager, Mr. Claeg, everyone knows what a coward you are. Even your own family has cut their losses!"

"Wynne."

Her angry focus switched to Devona. "You have always been too kindhearted to see how he has used you. Why do you think I am here? To save his worthless hide? Not in this lifetime. I am here to save you from yourself."

Doran was an old issue between the two of them. The fact that she had chosen now to bring up the subject had her jumping to her friend's defense. "You speak as if I do not know what I am doing."

Wynne grabbed her hand before she could stand beside Doran. "Well, let's take a good look at what we are doing. We have bluffed our way into the 'Gate. We are about to break out a man who has in my opinion taken advantage of your generous heart and most likely we will hang right alongside of him if we are lucky."

"Don't pounce on your sister when it is I who—" Doran tried to interject.

"Oh, quiet if you please, Doran. You have done quite enough in my opinion!"

Devona pulled her arm out of her sister's grasp

and took up Doran's in a show of support. "If you felt so strongly on the matter you should have not come."

"Still you defend him! I cannot decide who is crazier, you, him or me for being here." Wynne's tone all but dripped sarcasm.

"An interesting observation. Shall we put it to a vote?" Tipton asked, surprising the little group with his unexpected appearance. Pearl shrieked and ducked for imaginary cover.

Devona was the first to recover. Moving quickly to keep the distance between Doran and Rayne, she tried to think of some intelligent reason for her presence. The subtle tightening of Tipton's jaw told her he was not going to believe she was on a charitable mission. "My lord, you move in the oddest circles."

He opened his arms, and she went willingly into his embrace. "Another thing we share in common, my love."

"I do not think Amara is going to ever forgive you and Brock for treating her no better than trussed-up game," Devona said, not liking the silence between them. The evening had not gone as she had planned. Doran was still in Newgate, Amara was so furious she was speaking to no one, and her own thoughts of a reprieve quickly faded when Rayne announced to her siblings that he would see her home. Neither Wynne nor Brock objected so here she was at midnight, sipping brandy in his study. Even Speck was suspiciously absent.

"I do not particularly care if Miss Claeg ever deems to forgive me. Your brother handled her with gentler hands than I would have. He seems to have a soft spot for wide-eyed doves." He absently twirled the contents of his glass.

Devona blinked. "Doves?"

"Never mind. A private joke." He set his glass down on the table. "Forget your brother. Let's talk about your adventure."

It took every ounce of her will not to give in to the desire to rub the prickled hairs on the back of her neck. She would have preferred it if he yelled at her. This composed mask he wore made her uneasy. "I do not know what else there is to say. Having Brock lecturing me all the way back to the Dodds' ball has made me ill set on the subject."

An unholy gleam lit his face. Some might have called it humor, but she could not begin to fathom what he considered amusing this evening. "Indulge me."

She used the toe of her slipper to toy with the rug. "I can assume you are not pleased."

"Your instincts are correct. Would you like to tell me the why of it?"

"The devil take you, Tipton," she raged, overwhelming exasperation outweighing self-preservation. "You are not my father. I do not have to sit here and be chastised."

"On the contrary, my fiery temptress, you gave me that right when you accepted my betrothal."

"There would be no need for a betrothal if you had allowed me to carry out my plan." There was no point mentioning that their arguing had drawn the attention of the guard.

Rayne stilled. "Is that why you risked you life? To escape tying yourself to me?"

Devona met his gaze. His features were unreadable, yet she sensed his impatience for her reply. "You make it sound like I am the sacrificial virgin for the funeral pyre." She laughed, but she could not even coax a smile from him. "See here, Tipton, you were willing to betroth yourself to me to help me save Doran."

"And to protect you from harm," he softly added.

Flustered, she glanced away. "Well, yes . . ." She cleared her throat. "I thought I had hit upon a plan that would benefit everyone. Truly, you cannot want to marry me?"

Rayne did not answer her question. Instead, he cocked his head, giving her a considering stare. "You might have been able to pull it off, if you could have kept your sister and Claeg from tearing at each other."

The bubble of disappointment within her rose and burst. What had she expected? A declaration of love from him? Rayne might have a soft spot for her recklessness, but he was too scarred by his past to allow more than mild sentiment to guide him. She shrugged. "Wynne has never understood my relationship with Doran."

"Or she has understood it too well."

She motioned her hands in a mock surrender. "Not you too?"

Rayne dismissed the question by swallowing some of his brandy. "If Wynne has not been able to convince you, then I will not waste my time. Woefully, the man is at the heart of the matter. As the only trained surgeon in our little group, I intend to do what I do best." He swallowed the remaining brandy. "Do you know what that is?"

"Not exactly."

With a grace of a stretching lion, he pulled himself up and sat on his haunches beside her. "I am cutting him out of your life."

Before she could form a reasonable retort, he

stroked her ankle, distracting her. It was working.
A line of tingles traveled up her body, escaping
with the shudder of her shoulders. "I—um . . ."

He smiled, a bone-melting smile that made her
feel as fluid as a pot of face cream. "Shall I share
the details of my plan? Something you neglected
to do for me."

She refused to feel guilty for deceiving him.
When she tried to pull her leg out of his reach,
he tightened his hold. "You would have locked
me up in this study if you had known what I was
planning."

"Rightly so. Your exploit bordered on lunacy.
Succeeding would have only made you a danger
to society," he said, the edge to his voice could
have cut down to the bone.

The lash of temper had her recoiling. It was
the first time he had shown any visible sign of
anger toward her. "You make it sound as though
I do not have a sensible thought in my head."

"Oh, I consider you a highly intelligent female.
There lies the problem."

Insulted, she jerked her leg free and walked to
the chimneypiece. Devona glared at the jovial porcelain angel grinning at her. "Doran is no longer
your concern."

Tipton came up behind her. "Not for long at
any rate."

She turned and found he had her neatly caged
in his arms. "W—what will you do?"

"How much do you love Claeg, Devona? Is he
worth the price you will pay?" He caressed her
cheek lightly with the back of his hand. "You
stood in this room once on a night very much
like this and offered your soul as payment. Some
call me a devil. I have decided I will accept your
offer after all."

"Which offer?" His closeness was confusing her. His eyes reflected and glinted like a dull silver blade in the firelight. This time when she shivered it was not out of excitement but rather out of fear.

"A choice, my lovely Devona. I get to keep you, and Claeg . . ."

"And Doran?" she prompted.

"He gets to take my place as the walking dead."

TEN

"Hold him still," Rayne ordered, concentrating on pulling the last stitch through and knotting it. His patient had been the unlucky recipient of a jagged piece of crockery to his temple. The man would walk away with a nasty scar, but he would survive if the hemp did not catch him in a stranglehold.

"Strange business last evening," one of the trusted prisoners said, while he held the flinching patient.

Rayne reached for a piece of linen to dress the wound. "A small riot, I hear." It had been more than that according to another guard. At least fifty inmates had gotten their hands on files, the source of which no one was exactly certain. Although a small charity blamed for providing numerous barrels of beer to several wards was under suspicion. The ones who were not happy with getting pleasantly drunk and busting chamber pots were busy cutting their way through the rusting iron bars. One very productive ward managed to cut a large enough opening for several prisoners to escape. Two had been captured immediately; five others were still missing. Rayne shook his head. The way Devona's mind worked fascinated him. He could not be certain if she was trying to free Newgate's population single-handedly, or if it had been her ruse to cause confusion so Claeg could escape.

He had to stitch up a half-dozen other patients and help a fourteen-year-old girl give birth to her stillborn child before he was free to seek out Claeg. It might have been simpler to have allowed him to escape as Devona had planned. However, Claeg's early release would have messed up his own plans. Cold bastard that he was, he intended to use the man's dire predicament to gain Devona for his own.

Rayne could still see her expression when he had bartered the release of Claeg in return for her hand. He had never seen such a reluctant acceptance in her. Devona had appeared almost disappointed in him. He stalked down the dim corridor, nodding to the passing turnkey. What had she expected from the man everyone called Le Cadavre Raffiné? As far as he was concerned he was just living up to the name.

"I am Tipton. Is Doran Claeg waiting for me?" he asked the two gatesmen braced against the wall, passing a bottle between them. He had made certain Claeg would be isolated for their conversation.

"Inside. Is he ill?" one of the men asked, but he did not seem truly interested in the response.

Rayne stepped aside so the door could be unlocked and opened. "That's what I'm here to take care of." He was standing in the same room Devona had tried to execute her half-baked scheme. Walking over to the prone figure on the floor, he nudged him with his foot. "Wake up, Claeg."

He set the lantern down on the floor near the man's head. Claeg rolled over; his arm covered his eyes as if the light hurt. "Too much liquor to lessen your disappointment of last eve."

"Go to Hades, Tipton," Doran mumbled, groaning when he tried to sit up.

"If this isn't hell, it is at least the entrance hall. I heard that thanks to our mutual friend several prisoners escaped last evening. A pity you were not among the counted."

"No thanks to you!" Doran glared, then ruined the effect by rubbing the sleep from his eyes. "I could not believe you called the guards in on our gathering."

Rayne reached over and dragged the small bench closer to the light before sitting down. He rested his forearms on his knees and studied his rival. He may have been raised as part of the upper crust; nonetheless, the man had grown a little stale in his present surroundings. "Claeg, I would not pay a shilling for your pathetic hide unless I could find a use, like the patronage of my dissecting table."

"*Glorp!*" Doran reached for the sop bucket and vomited. Once his stomach settled he wiped his mouth with the back of his hand. "Sadistic butchering madman. I wager you kill more than you heal."

Rayne, able to appreciate the grim humor of the situation, laughed. "It is my abilities in the former rather than the latter which bring me to your side today."

Doran jerked himself upright, prepared to combat the dark specter of the *ton*. "My death would—"

"Not make the papers, nor stir the gossips' tongues. You are invisible," he said, not without some unwanted sympathy.

Denial flared in his young, defiant face. "Not to Devona. Last night proves that she would do anything for me, even risk her own life."

Rayne tapped down the rage he felt when he

considered the great risk she had taken to save her friend. Jealousy rose to take its place at the thought of her feelings for this unworthy fool. "All last evening proved was that Devona broke under the strain of your family's desire to blame her for your misdeeds."

Doran shook his head. "I never have blamed her."

A cynical curve turned his mouth upward. "Not aloud. You just reminded her every time she visited that everything you did, you did to obtain her. Then there is that bitch you call a mother. She has told everyone who bends an ear that Devona was the tart who seduced her poor hapless son down the road of sin. I even witnessed her striking Devona in public for defending herself." And maybe a bit more, Rayne thought, recalling the chunks of statuary at Devona's feet when he discovered her in the conservatory.

"No. I—" Doran pressed his fists to his temples. "My mother. She has never tolerated the Bedegraynes."

The helpless pleading in his eyes did not move Rayne. Devona had been hurt because of this man. Whether she wanted it or not, he would protect her.

"Devona never told me of these incidents," Doran lamely finished.

"Knowing your mother, you could have guessed what price she would pay for supporting you. It is now time to return the favor."

The younger man snorted. "Not much I can do from here."

"Perhaps not," Rayne agreed. "Devona once begged my services to revive your body once the hangman was satisfied."

Doran touched his throat, distinctly appearing sick again. "The stories about you, they are true?"

He did not care to share his own personal torments with this man. "True enough that I survived my own burial," he said so nonchalantly as to diminish its importance. "I have decided to help you after all, Claeg."

Blinded by visions of his fate, he stared sightless at a point beyond Rayne's shoulder. "Your arrival is a bit premature. The hangman has not summoned me."

"I find myself an impatient man. I am here to speed up the process."

Doran's expression of horror filled the silence as clearly as words would have if he had not been robbed of the ability to speak.

Rayne reached down and set the wooden case on his lap. Opening it, he withdrew a glass bottle. "A friend of mine's creation." He shook the bottle before Claeg's wide eyes, mixing the contents.

"What is it?"

"A means of escape. This tincture simulates death. All the benefits of the final repose without you actually becoming nourishment for the worms."

Doran stared at the bottle, mesmerized as if Rayne held a deadly coiled snake in his hand. "Why would your friend create such a substance?"

"Let's just say I have been fascinated by near death. He thought it would amuse me." He did not add that the man was a smuggler, and had use of the drug from time to time when what he peddled was flesh.

"H—how can I believe you? For all I know, this is some trick to get me to swallow poison." Hot, frightened eyes turned their attention to him.

"If I wanted to murder you, Claeg, I could have

slipped the poison into your beer last evening. At the very least it would have saved me the trouble of convincing you."

Doran gave him a shaky nod. He believed him capable of doing it. "Devona agrees to this plan?"

"Devona is no longer your concern."

Understanding replaced his wary expression. "My God, you do this for her. You want her for yourself."

"She is mine, Claeg. She has been since the first night she bluffed her way into my town house."

Doran eyed the bottle clutched in Rayne's hand. "You must think I am a threat to you. You are taking a personal risk to get rid of me, or perhaps none at all," he contemplated, thinking the bottle contained poison after all.

"Claeg, if Devona loved you, she would have handled the ribbons to Gretna Green herself. The only hold you have on her is guilt. Guilt because she could not love you enough."

The direct strike of truth had Doran rubbing the emotion from his eyes. "What of my family? Amara . . ." he trailed off.

Sensing he had reached the man, his expression softened. "If it comforts you, I will make certain your sister understands your choice. As for the rest . . ." His gesture spoke of what he thought of a man who would abandon his son and a mother's obsessive hold. "You must never return to England," he warned.

Doran took the bottle from Rayne. It offered him a freedom he had never dreamed to contemplate. "The choice of life or death. I never thought such power could be contained within my grasp."

* * *

The funeral for Doran Claeg was a small affair. To the grief of those who loved him, a seizure had taken his young life. Mr. Tipton had been summoned by the guards to assess his condition. However, the young man had been barely breathing, Tipton had told everyone who had asked. The gold he handed the keeper for first rights to Claeg's body had been profitable to all, even to the poor fellow who was receiving a decent burial, thanks to the Claeg family.

Welcome or not, the Bedegraynes had insisted on showing their support by standing at the grave beside the grieving family. Rayne had insisted on coming along with them. He stood by Devona, his warm, reassuring hand discreetly rubbing her lower back to remind her as she stood crying that Doran was alive and aboard a ship on his way to discover his destiny.

She appeared to be taking Claeg's "death" a little too hard, Rayne thought, irritated that he was feeling jealous of a supposed dead man. Or perhaps, she cried for another reason. Even now, she could be grieving about the deal she had struck with him. His hand froze its gentle ministrations and tensed. Wondering about her reasons would likely drive him insane.

Later, as everyone moved toward the carriages, Rayne watched Brock as he grabbed Amara's arm to force her to speak to him. She had pulled the veil from her face because of the heat. Even at this distance he could see the grief and torment on her delicate features. Whatever Brock had said to her angered her. Slapping his face, she walked away; the look in her eye had Rayne automatically patting the small, concealed blade he carried.

Brock approached them, the red imprint of her hand bold on his face.

"Are you okay?" Devona asked, reaching out to hug him.

"Yes. No." Brock shook his head. "She hates me."

"I thought we had managed to quiet the talk of that evening. I have told everyone that the two of you dragged her out of the ballroom because I was ill and needed her assistance." She dabbed at the remaining tears on her lashes with his handkerchief.

"There was still her mother to deal with. Her mother managed to cut off all her hair because of that damn dye you talked her into!"

Devona's hand touched her lips in shock. "I would have never thought—yes, I could. How could Lady Claeg be so cruel?"

"Doran is lucky to be free of her." Brooding, Brock watched Lady Claeg as she seized Amara in what had to have been a painful hold and all but pushed her into the carriage. "Amara is not going to have a good time of it, now that she is all Lady Claeg has left."

Wynne poured tea, comfortable with the role of hostess. "Papa told me Lady Claeg dared to threaten him. The Bedegraynes have been scratched off their invite list."

Brock pushed away his tea, opting to drink something stronger. "I doubt he stood for that woman speaking in such a manner to him."

"Actually, Papa restrained himself out of respect for Doran and his friendship with Lord Claeg," Wynne said, finally taking a seat next to Devona. "I am sorry, Devona, but I fear she blames you for Doran's death. And Brock is now responsible for ruining Amara, although I think

Lady Claeg would allow some of that blame to drip onto you. She truly despises you, sister."

Eyes bright with tears, she refused to permit to fall, she struggled to appear indifferent. "You cannot say I have not inspired it."

"Glenda Claeg is no longer your concern." Rayne's tone was steel, as he spoke from the doorway. "You and Doran are both out of her reach."

"Doran had to die to escape her clutches," Wynne observed, looking fresh and beautiful despite the black gown she had worn for the funeral. "What is Devona going to do?"

"Marry me."

Brock coughed, the drink he had been sipping went down the wrong way. Wynne arched an inquisitive brow, seeming almost amused. She calmly leaned over and pounded her brother on the back.

"I thought the betrothal stood only to help you move in society until you found a way to help Doran?" she asked.

"There is still the attempt on her life to consider," Rayne reminded them.

Brock, unsure of his role, cautiously added, "She has family to protect her."

"Now she has me. Tell them." He directed the order to Devona, mentally willing her to say the correct words to ease her family's fears.

"I love him. Scary reputation and all. I cannot think of another man who would tolerate my nature." She gave him a faint smile.

Devona's words punctured his control as if she had thrown spears instead of words at him. He gripped the painted wooden door frame to keep him from crossing the room and pulling her into his arms. Had she meant what she said? Or was her admission just her way to prevent her prying siblings from discovering their devil's bargain? Why did he want her so? All she managed to do was torment him. Her body, her mind, her heart . . . he would have them all, by God!

Wynne jumped up and hugged her sister, oblivious to the morbid tempest stewing behind Rayne's façade. "Devona, a love match. I am so pleased. But what of Papa? Irene? You know our news will never reach Nyle in time."

Brock rose. "Leave that to me." He walked over and offered his hand to Rayne. "I have an impression our father will be pleased with the match when everything has been presented to him. Welcome to the family, brother." His expression was clear. *Don't make me regret this.*

"Have you set a date? We will need time to prepare."

Rayne moved from his outsider position to Devona's side. "There is no need to fuss, Wynne. Devona and I are eloping, then on to my country estate. You may throw us a ball to celebrate our return if you like."

Since he had not revealed his plans to Devona, she was as surprised as her siblings. He had to admire the way she handled the announcement. With the exception of a faltering blink of her lashes, she looked every bit the bride on the verge of running off with her betrothed. He tucked a loose curl behind her ear because he had just given himself the right. Also, he needed to touch her, to reassure her silently that she was not making a mistake.

If her smile had been any brighter, Rayne figured they would all be sporting sunburns. "Our decision should not surprise you both," she said lightly. "A runaway love match. A fitting fate for someone of my nature, do you not think?"

* * *

Amara lay curled in her bed, yet sleep eluded her. She could not believe Doran was dead. All the risks she took, agreeing to help Wynne and Devona rescue Doran; it had all been for naught. She had been willing to face the wrath of her mother and father if her disobedience would have given them back Doran. Furious, she threw off her covers and went to the table. Efficient despite the darkness, she opened a small box and went about lighting a candle.

Grudgingly she admitted to herself that the Bedegraynes had not deceived her in their promise to cover what small scandal might result from Lord Tipton and Brock's unmasking and kidnapping her from the Dodds' ball. She should have known her mother would have placed guardians in her absence. She blew on the piece of tinder before touching it to the wick of the candle. Trust was a limited resource in her family.

She had been surprised that Brock would have dared to approach her at the funeral. He had held her arm, his handsome face weary and full of concern. It embarrassed her still that in an unguarded moment she had told him of her mother's wrath, of her ruined hair. She touched what was left of her long tresses. The length of it hung two inches from her ears. If the housekeeper had not entered the room when she had, Amara was certain she would have been sheared to the scalp. What her mother could not control, she destroyed.

A puff of wind made her turn toward the window. She took an involuntary step back at the shadowed figure of a man. "Brock?" she asked in a strangled whisper.

"If this is the manner in which Bedegrayne does his courting, I am surprised no outraged father has ever thrust a sword through his heart." Lord Tipton stepped closer into the small circle of light from her wavering candle.

She felt a rush of heat, more for thinking Brock Bedegrayne would ever come to her in the night, than facing Tipton in her nightclothes. "Forgive me, Lord Tipton, I never receive visitors in my bedroom, let alone undressed." Amara walked to the table, recalling there was a small knife in the drawer. She would defend herself if he approached her. "Just so you know. Mr. Bedegrayne has neither called upon me by day or night. I do not know why I thought . . ." She rested against the drawer. Behind her back she fingered the handle.

Her expression must have given her away. He gave her a gentle smile she thought him incapable of and sat in a nearby chair. "Take the weapon out if it gives you comfort, Miss Claeg. I have not turned into the local *milken* or have intentions of seduction. I bring you news."

Deciding her tiny weapon would do little to deter a determined Lord Tipton, she pulled the chair she had placed near her bed closer to his side. "I have heard you prefer to follow your own rules. However, making calls in the middle of the night seems a bit over the top even for you."

"Why does Bedegrayne call you a dove? With the tartness in your tone I think of something with a little bit more claw like a hawk."

Amara did not answer the question. She doubted his lordship came to discuss Brock's predilection for childish pet names. "You say you bring news?"

Tipton hesitated. "I hope I have not judged you

incorrectly, Amara. What I am about to tell you will put someone's life at risk."

"Really?" She could not think of why he felt the need to share such knowledge with her. Unless this did have something to do with Brock. She could not ask. To do so would reveal her feelings to a man whom she suspected knew exactly how to manipulate people, using their secrets. "The only person I ever cared about was buried today. I do not see how your news could affect me."

"You did not bury him."

Her mouth parted in horror. This man was a surgeon. He probably knew his fair share of resurrection men. "Has someone sold you Doran's corpse?"

"Come now," he snapped, his body rigid as if prepared to spring. "Don't faint on me, Amara. No one sold me his corpse," he said, smiling at some hidden joke. "I did take possession of his body."

"You speak in riddles, my lord."

"Doran did not die of a seizure. We only gave the guards a show so I could buy his corpse for my dissecting table."

The room reeled as she searched for her equilibrium. "Doran. He's alive." She could hardly bear to believe it, fearing it was a cruel lie.

"Yes, and presently on a ship sailing—" He paused. "I think it's wise that I keep that information to myself. I did promise Claeg that I would approach you when it was safe to do so and tell you not to grieve for him. He is satisfied with his choice."

Amara closed her eyes and the tears she was holding fell down her cheeks. "Will I ever see him again?"

Tipton frowned. "It will never be safe for him to return to England."

"I understand." Doran was alive, yet she was still alone. She, too, would have to be satisfied. "You risked much to tell me this. You have my thanks."

Not used to anyone's gratitude, he shrugged it off. "I keep my promises. I am leaving town and do not know when I will return. I did not think it fair for you to suffer in my absence."

Amara suddenly felt lighter. She had not known the weight of her grief until it was lifted. "I cannot believe you would leave Devona unattended for long." She had not been so caught up in her own troubles not to have noticed how the two of them had looked at each other.

Tipton gave her a rueful grin, reminding him that hidden in the shadows of his soul there was a man. One who felt, and maybe even loved. "After this night, I shall never leave Devona alone. I have applied for the post as her personal keeper."

Devona stood aside, waiting for the servants to carry in her trunks. Her hand squeezed her reticule. Within it, she held the certificate of her marriage. Her debt to Tipton had been paid. She was a married woman. A wistful longing twisted her heart. A hasty flight to Scotland had not been spun from girlish dreams. None of it seemed real without having her family by her side.

Dressed in a light blue gown, and her sister's new bonnet, which Wynne had insisted she keep, the ceremony had been quiet and swift. The parson's wife and the cook had been their witnesses.

Devona held her hand in the light so she could admire the ring Rayne had given her. The setting held two blood red rubies, just like two hearts, she thought, her romantic inclinations showing. Inside there had been an inscription. *Forever, I am thine.* If she had not made the deal with Tipton she would have considered the sentiment romantic. A wry grin revealed a dimple on her right cheek. Knowing her new husband, it was a reminder that she would never be free of him. The inscription proved something she had suspected on their journey north. It was proof that their sudden marriage had been under his direction for some time. She was not certain if she was pleased or frightened at the precision of the execution.

"Best wishes, mum." The departing men tugged on their caps and left the room.

She gazed about the room, wondering what she should do. They would only be staying the night. The room was sparsely decorated, the prominent piece of furniture being the bed. Many couples quickly married then moved upstairs to consummate their marriage before the pursuing family could separate the newly married couple. There was little they could do to annul the marriage if the bride could already be carrying her husband's child.

Devona doubted her family was rushing north to save her from Tipton. Papa may have been reluctant to offer his blessing to the match, but strangely, Brock had supported her decision. To her relief, her brother had ceased issuing those ridiculous challenges to Tipton. Wynne also had seemed genuinely happy for her. As for Irene and Nyle, they would follow their father's decree.

Her husband entered the room. Had she thought this room large? Standing in front of him, the two of them alone for the first time since they had spoken their vows, she felt the walls closing in on her.

"Do you have everything you need?" he asked. The simple task of removing his hat and setting it aside sent a wave of anticipation from head to toe.

"More than enough for one night." *Rayne.* She wanted to say his name aloud. She was his wife. There were no social barriers to distance them anymore. Only the pact they had made.

"I will save your precious Claeg if you are willing to pay the price."

"What do you want?"

"You, Miss Bedegrayne. Just you."

He gave her a questioning look as if expecting her to say more. When she remained silent, he glanced at the room. "Not exactly up to your standards, is it?"

Devona had not considered that he would be bothered by the accommodations. She was not a world traveler, but she possessed enough sense to accept that if she wanted to surround herself in luxuries, she should have remained at home.

"We have a bed and the sheets appear clean. As for food?"

His gaze strayed to the bed. "I spoke with the innkeeper. They will provide us supper and warm water to wash, if you choose."

Although she welcomed the idea of washing the grime of their journey from her face, she wondered how she was supposed to accomplish the personal task with a husband around. He did not expect to watch? Her eyes widened at the scandalous thought. She cursed herself for not consulting her sister Irene about what one does with a husband.

He must have sensed her distress. Uncertain of

its cause, he rubbed his thumb against her chin. "Devona?"

Lowering her lashes, to hide her response to his caress, she whispered, "Supper and w—water. Fine."

"Ah." He exhaled, drawing her rigid stance into his embrace. He pressed a kiss onto the bonnet she had yet to remove. "You are nervous, wife?"

"I have never been married before, my lord," she replied, her voice muffled since he had pressed her face into his chest.

"Devona, do you remember how you felt when I touched you in the carriage that day?"

She was glad he could not see her blush. "Yes." The warmth she felt was not on her face as she expected, but rather it was lower, deep within her.

"That was only the beginning of our exploration."

She drew back, eager to see his face. "Will we— do you expect—you will make me your wife tonight?"

"Of that, I have no doubt, my love." He laughed and gave her a tight squeeze before releasing her.

Seeing that he was prepared to stay within their room for the evening, she reached up to untie the bow under her chin. "We do not have to do this. My family will not contest our marriage." She did not underestimate her family's determination to remove her from Tipton's custody if they had been against them, whatever deal between them be damned.

Rayne glanced out the window before drawing the curtains. "I am not bedding you because I fear your family, Devona." He sent her a look that turned the warmth in her stomach into a bubbling cauldron. "My motives are completely selfish," he added.

Another ball was being given for the amusement of the *ton*. More music, more dancing, another hostess praying her efforts had made her the success of the Season. To walk through the crowded ballroom no one would ever guess the anger that was being hidden behind the smiles.

Word of Tipton's romantic flight to Scotland to marry the reckless Miss Devona Bedegrayne was the talk within the intimate circles. Some wondered if Miss Bedegrayne had been kidnapped, another ravished victim of the fiend. However, her family was supporting the match. Even hotheaded Brock Bedegrayne could not be counted on to put a ball into Tipton's beating heart.

The thought of Tipton touching her caused one to grieve and plot revenge, another to pray that she was mauled for daring to rut with the resurrected demon. Two angry, tormented individuals who unbeknownst to themselves were united in purpose. No one knew that behind the laughter each prayed for retribution and death.

ELEVEN

Their wedding supper had not turned into the private affair Rayne had imagined. When the innkeeper's wife learned of their recent marriage, she had insisted that they celebrate with the other guests. The cook had taken special care, he had been told by the innkeeper's wife, since there would be three newly married couples sharing a meal. They had supped on duck soup, trout pie, vegetable pudding, baked custards, and various fruits. For Rayne, he might as well have dined on bread and broth, for his appetite was of a carnal nature.

He leaned back in his chair, quietly sipping bramble wine and admiring his wife. Wife. He liked the ring of permanence of the word. He thought her most beautiful this night. She had changed her gown, the color reminding him of a tropical lagoon he had once seen. She had tamed her tresses into several fat curls which were pinned in place and framed with a matching band of fabric. Devona must have sensed his perusal for she halted in midsentence and glanced in his direction. She gave him a hesitant smile, then returned to her conversation.

He had wondered if she would change her mind about marrying him once Doran was secure and beyond his reach. Not that it would have mattered much. Whether it was by scandal or by duty, he had intended to have her. Too distracted by his own fears, he had forgotten that Devona was a righteous creature. If she gave her word, then she kept it. No matter the price. Doran Claeg was a fine example of how extreme his wife would go to keep her word.

Rayne scowled. Perverse as it might be, he wanted more than duty warming his bed. Although she was innocent, he sensed the passion in his young bride. Everything she did vibrated with it. He did not consider himself so removed from society not to have recognized desire and curiosity in her gaze.

Warily, she glanced in his direction. Rayne realized he was glaring at her, and tried to keep an expression of bored tolerance on his face. *Inept idiot,* he mentally chastised himself. One minute he was looking at her as though he could ravish her on the table in front of one and all, then the next he was scowling at her like she did not meet his approval.

Hell of a way to seduce your bride, ol' man! Brogden's strong, clear opinion intruded into his private thoughts. He could almost hear the man's laughter all the way from London at his clumsy handling of his wife.

"Here, let me help you," Devona offered the servant, taking an edge of the oilcloth and helping her smooth it across the floor. The maid had arrived with two buckets of tepid water for her sponge bath. She sent Tipton a nervous glance. The action was becoming habit lately. He sat in a chair; the tome he was holding had held his interest for the last thirty minutes.

Devona did not believe it for an instant.

Tipton had generously procured her a bath, but he was not leaving. She might be new to life as a married woman; still she could not imagine any woman bathing in front of a man.

"Right and tight, mum," the maid cheerfully said, oblivious to the tension radiating from Devona. "You'd be needing my help, mum?"

"Ah, yes!" Devona did not care if she did sound pathetically grateful for the woman's assistance. Perhaps between the two of them, they could figure out a way to conceal—

"No."

Eyes wide, she snapped her head in the direction of her husband's succinct reply. He stood. The forgotten book was still clutched in his left hand.

"I will see to my lady this night."

The maid accepted her dismissal with an understanding nod. "You got yerself a fine gent, mum." She lifted one of the buckets and poured some water into the washbasin. "Makes me think of me own wedding nights."

"Nights," Devona echoed, the grip she had on her skirts turning her knuckles white.

"All three of them." The maid winked at her. With a nod to Tipton she slipped through the door, leaving Devona to her own fate.

For someone who found herself rarely searching for conversation, she was at a loss as to what to say to her husband. She went to the towel horse and adjusted the towels she would use after her sponge bath. Devona nearly jumped out of her skin when she felt the touch of his fingers on her shoulders.

"This isn't an execution, Devona," he teased, turning her around so they were face-to-face.

"I know," she said, feeling ridiculous that she was about to succumb to a fit of vapors if she did not settle herself. "It is just that—" How was she to say it?

He playfully wrapped one of her curls around his finger, subsequently releasing it. "What, wife?" he coaxed.

"You have to leave!" she blurted out, and then quickly realized it was not the correct thing to say to one's husband on his wedding night. She had made a muddle of it, she thought, closing her eyes so she did not have to see the pain and anger reflected in his.

"Doubts, Devona?" Tipton silkily asked. "We had a deal."

That damnable deal! How humiliating it was to know she had secured a husband by an exchange of favors instead of hearts. Her eyes brimmed with tears. He was such a beautiful man. His hair had always fascinated her. She dearly wished she could stroke and revel in the coolness of it.

If he had courted her and proposed to her in a normal fashion, she would have been honored to accept. Standing before him, the reality was that beauty without heart was soulless. Could he ever think of her more than just as an amusement or something he claimed like the winnings from a gaming table?

"My lord, my word is as binding as your own."

He gave her a mocking smirk. "Obviously not."

He was going to make her say it aloud. A tear slid down her cheek. "I gave you a promise." Anger gave strength to her voice. "Mayhap you are the one who wishes to annul our vows."

He reached for her again, threading and locking his fingers through her hair at the back. Pulling her closer, he leaned closer so that their noses were inches apart. "A man would never challenge my word. You risk much, little wife. Have you forgotten that now I have the power to beat you for your cheek?"

Considering their present conversation, she could not believe all she wanted to do was close the gap between him and kiss him. It was too wanton. And amusing. The man speaks of beatings and all she could think about was feeling his warm lips nibbling at her throat.

"Did I say something to amuse you?" His eyes had heated to their pewter hue.

"Ah, no, my lord. It's just that I—" She wriggled out of his grasp, pulling away before she did something foolish like actually kissing him. "I want you to leave so I can take my bath. Even a thickheaded male should understand that a woman needs to do such things in private!" Her tone might have been frosty, but her cheeks were burning hot.

He laughed. The man truly dared to laugh at her misery. Her eyes narrowed as they searched for something light enough to handle, yet heavy enough to give him a good headache. He grabbed her arm when she stalked past him.

"Let go, peasant!" she hissed.

A judicious man would have backed away. Tipton was not such a man. Laughing still, he wrapped his arms around her until she was soundly ensnared. "I outrank you."

She sniffed. "Sadly, some breeding never shows. Release me."

"Never," he vowed. "I do not know why I doubted you. Never have I seen such a ferocious guardian of what is right. And that's what we are, wife. Right." Tipton pressed his face into her hair and breathed deeply. "You are such a bold creature, it makes me forget that you have never been with a man while I—"

If he mentioned the women in his past, Devona promised herself she was going to draw blood. "Yes?" This was not jealousy, she assured herself, this was a lesson in discretion.

Tipton must have recovered a dollop of common sense or it was the promise of pain in her eyes when he spun her around. "I have never had a wife." He kissed her on the lips and pulled away before she could enjoy it.

"I am serious, Tipton. I will not bathe in front of you. It is unseemly." She gasped when he plucked the fabric band from her hair.

"And you are always a pious model of proper behavior?" He tossed the band over his shoulder.

"I could give instruction to young ladies!" she replied, daring him to disagree.

Instead, he settled for seizing her hands. He began peeling off her gloves. "London can only handle one Devona Bedegrayne." One glove fell to the floor. He worked on the other.

"Wyman. Devona Wyman. I am Viscountess Tipton, you rogue. Will you stop playing with my fingers!" she demanded.

The other glove dropped. He had a dazed look on his face as though he had not considered that she had taken his name. "I do not think so. Turn around."

"Forget it, Tipton." His deep voice had changed into an intriguing drawl that made her legs feel boneless.

"Let me play lady's maid. You are my wife. I want to see you, all of you," he cajoled, turning her around himself.

Feeling the buttons coming undone, she tried to think of an argument against him being there. None came to mind. "I doubt that my sister Irene bathes in front of her husband."

"You are not Irene and I am not married to her." He kissed the back of her neck, causing a cascade of shivers to travel down her spine. "You and I do not fit the molds the *ton* herald as fashionable. We never have met our family's expectations. None of it matters here, Devona. With you in my arms, I welcome your recklessness. I demand it. There are no rules, no conduct that will be censured." The back of her gown opened. Rayne gently pushed the cap sleeves down so that the dress slipped and became a circle of fabric at her feet.

Free of her gown she felt vulnerable. No man had ever seen her in such a state. Rayne's hand splayed across her abdomen and guided her to step aside so he could kick the gown off the oilcloth. He could not seem to stop touching her; his hands were everywhere; her shoulder, her back, her arms. She felt like a brightly wrapped gift and he was enjoying the outer wrapping as he slowly unveiled the object within.

Tipton's fingers traced the whalebone of her long corset. "It must feel great to free yourself from fashion's trappings." He began to untie the strings.

"N—not really. I suppose women get used to them." After some time, the corset fell away, another protective layer vanquished. He turned her to face him so he could work on the buttons on her chemise.

"I think the first thing I noticed about you were your eyes. No, that's not right. It was your sassy tongue and audacity to sneak your way into my study."

His teasing made her laugh. He was trying to ease her fears of him, and his small kindness made her want to weep all of a sudden. "You were not pleased to see me. You had Speck throw me out."

Rayne did not seem bothered by her indignation. He unfastened the remaining buttons. "Only because I was afraid I would do something impulsive like locking the door and ravishing you."

"Please!" Devona playfully pushed at him not believing one word of it. She did not have the kind of beauty men would kill to possess.

She had not budged him, but her outburst brought out a mischievous glint to his eyes. "Well, since you asked so prettily." His fingers hooked the shoulders of the chemise and tugged.

"No," she pleaded. "This does not feel right, Tipton." Her hands covered his to prevent him from pulling the fabric down. He was still dressed and the notion of standing in front of him nude was disturbing.

"You are concentrating on the wrong feelings." Her hands tightened over his. "You have your clothes on."

"And rightly so, wife. This is your bath, love. I am merely your servant."

"Ha! Papa would have had a fit if I had summoned Gar to perform such duties." There was nothing in his stance or expression that suggested vassalage. Even if he denied himself the title, he was very much a lord. Her lord.

"I could easily kill any man who dared to look upon you thus." He worked the fabric from her fingers and pulled the fabric down, finally revealing shoulders, breasts, and abdomen. The fabric continued its revealing journey until it pooled on the floor. "Devona, you are so lovely. Not even in my dreams could I create such perfection." His hands hovered inches from her narrow hips. The control he exerted not to grab her roughly to him made them shake. "Your sponge bath, madam."

She turned to the washbasin, offering him time to study her backside. Tipton was looking at her strangely, and odder still was her reaction. Her chest felt so tight she could barely take a breath. Every movement she made seemed sluggish as though she did not have complete control of her body. She dipped a cloth into the tepid water.

"No. Allow me," he whispered hoarsely behind her. He took the cloth from her boneless hand.

She gasped at the first touch of the wet cloth against the back of her neck. "Just your servant," he murmured. "Close your eyes and enjoy the feel of the cool cloth against your skin."

"S—soap." The cooling wetness and the heat from his stroking hands was a startling, wonderful contrast. She instinctively leaned into him, reveling in his attention.

"Criticizing my skills already, madam," he teased, rewarding himself with a quick taste of her neck. "I endeavor to prove myself worthy." He dipped the cloth back into the water. He traced the length of her spine, then drew wet circles across her buttocks. "If I survive this," he groaned more to himself.

Devona did not look back at Tipton. She was content to listen to his movements behind her. The arrangement placed a certain detachment to their actions. He could become in her mind exactly what he said. He was her servant. The image was shattered when Tipton, growing bolder by her silence, moved the cloth from her back to her front. Water droplets sluiced over and between her breasts, tightening her nipples into firm buds. He moved in closer, his front lightly pressed against her nude back. The cloth followed the meandering trails of the droplets.

"Your shirt will be soaked." She noticed that his breathing had changed. The rapid, warm exhales tickled her right ear.

"Perhaps I should remove it?" he suggested, kneeling before her. The lightest touch of his hand had her turning to face him. "Would you assist me, madam?"

Her fingers all nerves, she grasped his cravat and pulled at the intricate knot.

"Easy, Devona. I value my neck as much as the next man."

He placed his hands over hers and showed her how to loosen the knot. Her husband expected her to be inexperienced with men, but her incompetence made her feel no less foolish. "It was not my intention to strangle you, my lord."

"Rayne."

The cravat came away, dangling loosely in her hand. "If you like."

His gaze roamed up the length of her body, up to meet her eyes. "Oh, I do. Very much so." He undid the three pearl buttons at his throat. "Help me, love."

Devona grabbed the sides of his linen shirt and together they pulled it over his head. He met her curious stare, awaiting her instructions. Now she understood why he was so fascinated by her body. Seeing him shirtless made her curious to see more of him as well. Forgetting about her own nudity, she stepped forward. A man's body was a marvelous creation, she thought. His shoulders were straight and firm, the muscles ropelike as they strained and pulled. He was almost as perfect as some of the statues she had seen in the museum. However, he was not made of cool, smooth marble. Rayne was heat and motion. "Is touching permitted?"

"Christ, yes, please."

Her fingers ruffled the hair on his chest; the hesitant gesture probably seemed flirtatious to him. How did one go about pleasing a man?

Rayne resumed washing her, the cloth bisected her stomach. He watched the water drip down into her downy nest of curls. "No rules, Devona," he murmured, bringing the wet cloth to the curls and pressing. It made her think of the time in the carriage when he had touched her there, sunk his fingers deep within her.

Devona threaded her fingers through the short hair on his chest. He sucked in his breath when her knuckle brushed against his flat nipple. She smiled when it reacted very much as her own had. "The night we met, your hair was unbound. May I?" She did not wait for his permission. A quick tug on the leather string and his hair fell to his shoulders. Her hand traced the shock of white standing out from the darker hue. "I heard this was the result of your accident."

If Rayne was disturbed about speaking of his premature burial, he hid it well. He pressed a kiss to her belly. "I noticed it the following morning." He shrugged. It was something he never dwelled upon or he had something else on his mind. She assumed it was both.

He placed a few more kisses against her belly, each lower than the last. His tongue swirled around her navel. "That tickles." She jerked back, but he held her, his strong hands firmly gripping her hips.

"Hold my shoulders, love. I plan to seek out all your ticklish areas." He buried his face into her nether curls and she almost screamed from the pleasure of it.

Rayne's hands rested on her hips, although he did not have to keep her in place. His little wanton had her hands so firmly fisted in his hair he doubted he could free himself even if he had desired it. He had wanted to gently introduce her to lovemaking, to slowly acclimate her to his hands and mouth on her body. She was not going to allow him to do this slowly. All he had to do was touch her and she burned like a flame in his arms.

Her cry of pleasure enhanced his own. He buried his tongue deep into the cleft between her legs, wringing another moan from her. Rayne cupped her buttocks in his hands, adding strength to her stance that he suspected was weakening as much as his own. Gliding up, his tongue flicked then swirled around the sweet nubbin of her desire. Her hands tightened against his shoulders, feeling the bite of her nails into his flesh. He welcomed her passion. Required it. When he buried himself deep within her, he wanted her caught up in the sensual journey.

He rubbed a finger, moistening it with her dewy response, then slipped it within her slight virginal passage. She flinched at the intrusion, then relaxed as if recalling the last time he had touched her. That time there had been no pain, only new pleasure. He hoped that this evening would be the same. He slipped two fingers within her, preparing her, testing her readiness for him. He felt like he had been waiting for her his entire life.

Devona shifted in his embrace opening herself
more to him. A growl of frustration vibrated in
his throat while he licked and playfully nipped
the gift she offered. Her body tensed, awaiting
the release his wife was just beginning to understand. His fingers plunged deeper, encouraging
the release he craved to give her.

"Ahh . . ." she cried out, her hands digging
into his shoulders then slackening when the cycle
of her climax came to completion.

Rayne pulled back, wiping the wetness on his
face with the back of his hand. Fierce possessiveness ran through him with the knowledge that he
was the only one who had ever given her such
ecstasy. He picked up a towel and wrapped her
trembling body.

She bent down, pressing her cheek to his. To
his delight, she laughed, the sound a closing fist
around his heart. "I do not think I can take a
single step," she confessed.

Rayne stood. Devona had yet to look him directly in the eye, a shyness having settled in her
demeanor. The different dimensions to her character fascinated him. He smiled, contemplating
the ways he could lure the wanton back. Scooping
her up, he carried her to the bed.

"I think your breeches are ruined."

He hid his smile with a kiss to her temple. "Still
worrying about my clothes?" He placed her reverently on the bed. "I guess I will have to humor
you and remove them." His hand reached for the
buttons at his waist. One by one he undid the
flap, his gaze never straying from hers.

"The candles?" Her voice had a wispy quality
as she watched him push his breeches down, revealing his very aroused state.

"Leave them lit. I want to see us together."

She nodded, her eyes now focused on his jutting manhood. He could see the uncertainty, the unspoken fears any gently bred lady would have. He would be a gentleman for her. He would handle her delicately, guiding himself slowly into her, no matter how much it would kill him to do so. She deserved this. He tried to think of something to assure her, that he was not some kind of beast that would leap upon her and rut until the madness had been purged. Even if that was how he was feeling at the moment. "If you will not trust your husband, you can trust the surgeon. This sort of union has been successful since the dawn of mankind."

She surprised him again by giggling. Before he could place blame on her amusement, she coyly admitted, "It was not the science I questioned, husband. Rather it was the size I marveled."

Rayne choked on his strangled laughter. He had never met a woman who could push him to the brink of pain and laughter at the same time. She aroused all elements of passion within him. "I insist you take full measure of it, wife." She was still laughing when he kicked aside his breeches and climbed into the bed beside her.

His closeness sobered her, but did not diminish the brilliance in her eyes. He tugged on the towel under her to bring her closer. Devona tilted her chin up in the defiant manner she had, as if challenging him to take her. He did. He lowered his face to hers and plundered her mouth. Her lips were full and pliant against his, returning the kiss. Covering her with his body, he coaxed her mouth open by gently squeezing her jaw. When she complied, he deepened the kiss. She stiffened at the intrusion of his tongue.

"Like this."

He licked her lips, then teased her tongue to mimic his movements. After an experimental flick or two of her tongue against his, she became enthusiastically caught up in the sensuality of the seemingly never-ending kiss. Together lips brushed, tongues licked, explored, and consumed. Her kiss-swollen mouth and the way her breasts rubbed against his chest was testing the limits of his control. His manhood, warm, velvet steel was already pressing against the wet nest of curls, seeking entry.

Devona pulled back from the kiss. "I cannot take a breath," she gasped. Her eyes dilated from passion had a glazelike quality to them.

He slipped a hand between them and parted the soft hidden folds, readying her for his entry. "Look at me, Devona. I want you to see what you do to me when I make you mine." Her eyes still had a dreamy haze to them, focused on his. What he saw there sapped the last of his control. She trusted him. Whether it was her body, her heart, or both he did not care. Rayne surged into her, with one definitive thrust. She automatically arched beneath him, a small sound escaping her lips. He stilled, his body viciously warring against the primitive instinctive need to pump until completion and the concern that he had hurt her.

"Are you hurting?" he asked, the question issued like a command. Needs were riding him too harshly for polite conversation.

"N—not exactly." She lifted her hips, trying to adjust to him being inside her. "Now I can understand why you never hear of this part discussed in the lady's retiring room."

Her movements made him slide deeper within her. He groaned. "Don't you dare make me laugh, madam. Some events deserve some veneration." He pulled out slowly, enjoying the way the muscles of her passage resisted his withdrawal. In a fluid motion with his hips, he filled her. This time her arching gasp was of appreciation.

"I would not dream of ruining your adoration," Devona said, giving him a sultry look that had his blood draining to the nether regions. "Pray continue, my lord."

Rayne had never imagined his wife was capable of such an expression. A man would sell his soul to have a beautiful woman stare at him in that manner. He only had to die and lose everything to have her. It seemed a small price now. "Put your hands on me, beloved," he murmured, increasing the tempo of his thrusts.

Devona's slender fingers clutched his upper arms as he moved, her body accepting his pressing weight. He could feel the sweat pool and run down his back as his exertions brought him closer to his release. Her eyes were closed now. She breathed through her mouth as he did, her breath as labored as his own. The replenishing wetness of her arousal assured him that she was more than enduring his ravenous penetration.

The tempo quickened, rising another level. Her hips lifted in a counter rhythm. Rayne gritted his teeth, a tingling at the base of his shaft warning him that he could no longer prevent the impending release. One hand cupped her buttocks, bringing her closer. Devona stiffened and cried out, but he was too caught up in his own release to notice. He ground his pelvis into her, the head of his shaft buried deep as he pumped his seed into her womb.

A blissful calm eased into his being. The tempestuous whirlwind of lust that had been tearing at him since he had first met her had abated. But not for long. He grinned to himself. Rayne eased out of her. He rolled on to his back, taking her with him. She curled up at his side, resting her head on the curve of his shoulder. Neither spoke. Words were not needed. His arm secured her to his side, a blatant act of possession. Listening to the lulling drone of insects outdoors, he fell asleep.

Devona retied the bow on her bonnet for the twelfth time in the last two hours. This was their second day in the coach. Although she had yet to issue a complaint, she felt she would go mad from the boredom. Tipton, preoccupied with his own thoughts, had silently stared out the coach's window. Each hour that brought them closer to his family estate, Foxenclover, the dourer his visage had become.

She knew nothing of his family. Tipton was rather closemouthed about the subject. If the rumors were true, his grandmother had died of heart failure the minute she laid eyes on him. Not long after, the Wymans tossed their second son off the family lands. His infamous resurrection had terrified the parish, and what could a family do but side with public opinion. Her mouth quirked into a mischievous grin. She would wager her monthly allowance that Tipton had enjoyed tormenting the entire lot.

"What are you plotting, love?"

She kicked at him playfully. "Why does everyone I know assume I spend my hours scheming mischief?"

"Because you are entirely too good at it."

"I cannot decide if I am being complimented

or insulted," she said, plucking at the ribbons of her bonnet again.

Rayne reached over and tugged the ribbons himself. "Stop fussing. I am not bringing you to Foxenclover so my mother can criticize your attire." He removed the bonnet from her head before she could stop him.

Assuming she could put herself back together later, she did not bother to argue. "Why are we going to your country estate?"

"I doubt anyone would find it unusual that I would like to show my new bride off to my family."

The explanation was reasonable. Too bad for him she did not believe one word of it. "I am not staff, Tipton. I am your wife. I think you owe me the truth. Everyone knows you despise your family for the way they treated you."

He gave her a considering look. "Listening to rumors again?"

"Only when no one will give me the truth," she said through clenched teeth.

Rayne rubbed his jaw, resuming his vigil at the window. "I should warn you that our presence will be resented. I will do my best to protect you from my mother's tongue."

"If this visit will bring out the worst in all parties, why are we bothering? Tell the driver to take us back to London."

"So soon after our marriage," he mocked. "They will say I could not tame the Bedegrayne flame." His gaze ignited as it always did when he spoke of bedding her.

"Oh." She glanced away, trying to quell her own body's response. She had learned in these early days of their marriage that there was little about her that did not stir her husband to passion. "Then choose another destination."

"Foxenclover is mine. I will not be run off."

He watched her in his intense fashion. It no longer made her uncomfortable. What she had once mistaken for intimidation was simply his way of focusing on his objective. He had wanted her from the beginning, just as he wanted her now. She had been too inexperienced to understand.

"I want you."

She checked the trapdoor above to make certain it was secure. "Here? I do not think so." She laughed, encouraging him to share in the jest.

He lifted her feet to his lap and efficiently removed her slippers. "Not much space," he spoke in a conversational manner, "but I think our creativity will compensate." His hand glided up her stockings to her thigh.

"Don't you dare!"

"Too sore?"

"No." She was, but she refused to discuss the subject.

His smile was reckless, as he worked her stockings downward. "Ah, a challenge. I promise you will not be disappointed."

True to his word, he saw to it that she was not.

TWELVE

By the time they were three miles from Foxenclover, Devona had managed to tidy up her appearance. The bonnet he had plucked from her head was firmly in place. If her cheeks were slightly flushed, she could always blame the confinement of the closed coach.

"No one will ever suspect you were ravished," Rayne assured her, growing more amused by her fussy behavior. "I told you, my mother is the one who must please you. Not the other way around."

Devona wrinkled her nose in exasperation. "She is your mother, Tipton." As if that explained everything.

"I mean it, Devona. If my mother or sister says anything upsetting, you are to tell me immediately."

She stilled. "You have a sister? You never mention her."

"You make it sound like I have been hiding a mistress from you." He did not understand why a man had to dissect his life for all to behold.

"Do you?"

"What?"

Devona licked her lower lip. The automatic habit had him wishing they had more time alone. He could still taste her on his lips. "A mistress, you dense man!" she said, her words barely audible over the roar of the blood in his ears.

"I would not worry about me stashing a greedy light-skirt or two."

"Two!"

He went on as if she had not screeched at him. "If all I was after was a quick tumble, I would not have gone to the trouble of luring you into marriage. No," he continued, privately glad she had not thought to plant her foot into his vitals, "I can see that keeping you satisfied will expend all my energies."

She looked far from pleased by his admission. "You should have mentioned your sister."

"Why? She is a child. It is not unusual for an older sibling to be disinterested. How close are you to—what's the name of your other brother? The one traveling." He did not bother to remind her that her family had tried and failed to protect her when Le Cadavre Raffiné had set his sights on her. It was better for him if she believed that she had had a choice in the matter.

Her expression grew more insolent. "Nyle. My brothers are grown men. When they are abroad they still remembered us by sending letters. Can you say the same?"

He could not, so he disregarded the question. "Do not concern yourself with my relationship with my sister. I don't." Sensing that Devona was sizing up his sister's plight as another Doran Claeg in need of liberation, he sought to distract her. "Look out the window. Foxenclover should be coming up on your left."

The search quieted her arguments as he had hoped it would. Her enthusiasm, sometimes childlike, but nonetheless honest, stirred a discontented humor within him. He could not remember having such naïve feelings, even when he was a child. Still, watching her practically hanging out the window, he wondered if the lack had been bred or drilled into him.

"Rayne, this must be your Foxenclover." She glanced back at him, her eyes bright with animation and excitement. "It looks old."

Giving into the urgency to hold her, he pulled her into his lap. His hand splayed across her abdomen, holding her in place while he gestured to the window. "See there." He pointed to a wall and part of the foundation. "That's all that remains of the original house. It burned to the ground around 1697. My grandmother said that it was in protest to William and Mary's clever window tax."

"What do you believe?"

"That my infamous ancestor was mad." He toyed with the swinging earring in her right lobe. "I hope I have not given you reason to fear having my children. Most likely the Wymans have bred out that tainted blood by now." His hand tightened on her abdomen. She could be carrying his heir at this very moment. The fierce elation made him feel light-headed.

"Oh, if your ancestor was responsible, I am certain he had a very good reason."

Already, her loyalty was switching to him. The unidentified emotion twisting his heart lessened. "Maybe he hated the house. The tax was just an excuse to get rid of it. I doubt the family will ever know." He shrugged, not particularly caring to probe his ancestor's dark secrets. "Whatever his incentive, he was caught up in the Palladian fever that overtook the time. I cannot recall the fellow's name, but he was a disciple of Burlington's."

The coach slowed, finally halting in the yard.

Only one man approached the new arrivals to see to the horses. Rayne opened the door himself and climbed down. Scanning the yard, he compared the Foxenclover in his mind to the neglected estate he saw before him. This had been what he wanted. The fifteen-year-old who had walked away from his family had wanted to see the lands fall to ruin. He waited for the rush of satisfaction to wash over him. He felt nothing. Nothing at all.

"Tipton. A hand, if you please." Devona's voice startled him from his frozen musings. He turned to help her down from the coach.

"I rarely visit here." The flash of shame came out of nowhere. Exposing Devona to this ugliness was like showing her the deformity of his soul. The downfall of Foxenclover was his revenge and his mother's prison. Rayne wondered what his optimistic wife would do if she understood the full extent of his hatred. Maybe the madness pumped through his veins after all.

"Hello," a cheerful feminine voice called out. The approaching woman, who, judging from her appearance, was most likely the housekeeper, waved. "Where are you folks from?"

Before Devona could reply, Rayne crisply replied, "I am Tipton. Kindly inform my mother of my arrival."

The housekeeper halted her stride so suddenly that she skidded a few inches. "Ah, sir, Lord Tipton. It is a pleasure to have you visit." She cast a worried glance at Devona. "I will tell her ladyship of your presence." She all but ran into the house.

"Really, Tipton," she chastised behind him. "What purpose does it serve to scare that poor woman half to death?"

"The fact that I can do it," he replied, aware

that his answer would starch up her spine. "Let's go see who else I can intimidate."

Entering the front hall, he noted it was clean and extremely bare. His mother, not pleased with her pauper state must have been selling off the statuary, paintings, and furniture that had once adorned the hall.

"It is quite—large."

The observation made him smile. It was so Devona. "It looks like it could use some furniture, maybe a few *objets d'art*. Thievery in the country has become astonishingly bold."

"I do not perceive this as a problem of boldness, but rather a lack of attentiveness. Particularly yours," his mother announced from the open doorway to their right. "I was about to have some refreshments. You both may join me." She retreated into the room, leaving them no choice but to follow her.

"Your mother?" Devona inquired softly.

"Too cheeky to be anyone else. Come, we might as well get this finished." Rayne crooked his arm and she accepted his silent offer by placing her hand on his arm. They walked side by side to the morning room, presenting a united front. For the first time, he would not be confronting his mother alone.

The room they entered was plainly his mother's domain. The cream colored paint appeared fresh and stenciled flower and vine panels accented the walls. The floor was bare wood, but it was scrubbed. His grandmother's favorite Indian rug had a place of honor in front of the hearth. He could not conceal the cynical smirk on his face as they passed an Adam's pedestal showing off a black basaltware urn. The Dowager Lady Tipton held on to the items that mattered to her, and cast aside the ones that did not. His gaze flickered to the finely displayed Wedgewood. Well, it was simple to figure out where she had allocated him.

"I did not know you had a mistress, Rayne. And I cannot fathom why you would bring her here." His mother sniffed as if breathing the same air as them would cause her harm.

He felt Devona's muscles tense, preparing for retaliation. He held her in place, not sure how she would react to his mother's casual insult. His mother had the instinct to judge her enemy and attack the weakest. At least he knew he came by his own gift for ruthlessness honestly.

"Madam, this house and land belong to me. I may do whatever I like. Sadly, you cannot say the same."

Eyes, a weary and older version of his own, narrowed. "I will not sit here and allow you to flaunt your whore in front of me. Not in front of Madeleina. Leave this house."

"Lady Tipton"—Devona stepped forward before Rayne could tell his mother what he thought of her mandate—"there has been a misunderstanding that I would like to rectify before one of you says something you will regret."

The older woman exhaled a harsh sound that could have been laughter. "I have never regretted anything I have ever said."

Devona moved away from Rayne and sat on the sofa beside his mother. "That is just pride speaking." She glanced at her husband. "Something I am certain you both have in common."

"Rayne, this is utterly priceless. A philosophical high-flyer. Wherever did you find this creature?" she asked, her false interest tainted by sarcasm.

"Enough!" Rayne shouted, his temper slipping its leash. "If you show nothing less than the proper respect due my *wife*, you and your daughter will find yourselves living in a cottage so small that you will have to entertain outdoors. Do I make myself clear?"

"So typical, Tipton." Devona's disapproval was a tangible wave that rose and crashed against his anger. "Only you could turn a simple wedding announcement into a threat!"

The cup and saucer in his mother's hands rattled. She carefully returned them to the cart. "Marriage. You married your mistress?"

"Miss Devona Bedegrayne was never any man's mistress. To insinuate otherwise will risk my displeasure. Poke at me if you must, but keep away from my wife."

His mother seemed to physically deflate before them. Her lips trembled as she tried to find her balance. "Why are you here? Certainly not for my blessing!"

Misunderstanding his mother's distress and bitterness, Devona tried once again to salvage their first meeting. "Eloping the way we did, there was no time to get the families together—"

The announcement seemed to shock her back into her old self. "You eloped to Gretna Green? Now it all makes sense. What did you do, Rayne? Spawn a bastard in her belly so her family had no choice but to sacrifice her to Le Cadavre Raffiné?"

Devona's hands clutched her reticule so tightly her fingers were white. She abruptly stood. "I do not care who you are. You have no right to speak of Rayne in that manner. Your son is an intelligent, wonderfully kind man. I married him quite willingly. I can only assume he received his character from his father since I have never met such

a mean-spirited creature with the mothering instinct of a snake!"

"Devona." Rayne tried to draw her away from
his mother.

His mother, never one to place herself at a dis-
advantage, rose from her seat. "Legal or not, my
opinion of your lady has not been swayed. You
and your whore may leave this house at once!"

Rayne's foot shot out, kicking the cart over,
shattering his mother's favorite tea set into frag-
ments. The sound brought the housekeeper scurrying into the room.

"I heard a horrible noise," the servant began,
looking about the room until her gaze settled on
the overturned cart. "Oh, madam, not the
Worcester?"

Rayne answered, since he finally had managed
to silence his mother's rabid tongue. "Regrettably
so, Miss . . . ?"

"Mrs., my lord. Mrs. Poole." Feeling unclear
about where her loyalties lay, she cast a quick peek
at her mistress. She found no reassurance. Her
mistress's attention was focused on the broken
porcelain.

"Well, Mrs. Poole, I assume from the appearance of this room that you are a good house
keeper."

"I know my job, sir!" she defended herself.

"It is always rewarding to see the efficient results of the wages I pay out to Foxenclover," he
remarked, leading Devona to the door. She still
looked furious. He figured she was biting a hole
through her tongue to keep mute. Soon he would
be able to comfort her and have her out of hearing range. "Our rooms are prepared, Mrs.
Poole?"

"Yes, indeed, sir. If you and your missus would follow me."

While Devona followed the eager Mrs. Poole, Rayne made the point of quietly closing the door on his mother.

Devona savagely tore off her gloves and threw them on the table. Lobcock! She had heard the rumors, had seen the way Tipton's face became shuttered at the mention of his family. What had she done? Attacked his mother! Frustrated and angry, she was already doing her best to destroy the knotted ribbons on her bonnet when Rayne strolled into the room.

While her eyes were burning with useless tears, she tugged on the knotted ribbon until it snapped. There, now even her pretty bonnet was ruined! Misery overtook the ire that had ridden on her back since she had first entered the morning room, causing her to all but collapse into a chair.

"I ruined my bonnet," she said, the tears she had been fighting back running down her cheeks.

He gently removed the bonnet from her head and placed it on the table. "I'll buy you a dozen to replace it." Kneeling on his haunches, he stroked the top of her hand.

She used her free hand to wipe away the tears. "Forgive me. I do not know why I am crying."

"Don't you?" His eyelids narrowed, an unsettling reminder of his mother. "I thought your reasons quite appropriate. You have just discovered your husband's mother is a horrid, unpleasant bitch," he said calmly, as if announcing the weather.

"Tipton!" She choked, thinking how strange it was to want to laugh at such a distressing time.

"You see? No more tears. Speaking the truth is always liberating." He moved away, seeming restless. "Do you want me to help you undress? No one would scold you for wanting a nap."

"Your mother will think I am in hiding."

"A clever tactician understands a well-planned retreat. Something tells me the new dowager needs to rethink her plan of attack."

She did not like the smug expression she saw. He was too pleased at the notion of upsetting his mother. "Why are we here, Tipton?" she asked, the edge back in her tone.

The question did not appear to surprise him. "I explained it to you earlier."

She gave him a queen-to-peasant glare that would have made Wynne applaud. "I heard what you wanted me to believe. I want the truth. After all, it is so liberating," she drawled.

"Devona, what reason can I offer when you have already decided on the words you want to hear?" He pulled her into his arms. "Forget the nap," he murmured, her body reacting to his husky demand. "We are alone and we have a bed. Guess what truth I want to explore?"

She did not have to guess. The outline of his erection was visible proof. The thought of undoing the buttons of his breeches herself had her pulse skittering. She pulled back emotionally before she could give in to the impulse. "I suppose even a horrible mother expects her son to do his duty for the title."

"Not really," was his succinctly blithe reply. He nuzzled her temple with his chin. "Wouldn't want the fiend to breed."

"What rubbish!"

He pretended not to hear her outburst. "Not that I haven't done my best to secure such success, eh, love?" His hot breath stirred a curl resting on her cheek. "How long before you will know if you are breeding?"

It was a personal question, something she was not prepared to discuss, even with him. Her nerves were too much at the surface for clear thought. It was also difficult to bury the deeper suspicion that his pleasure at impregnating her was due more to the news enraging his family than to the joy of making a life with her. When he behaved so attentive and charming, it was so easy to forget that their marriage was not based on love, let alone friendship. He had bought her. One life saved in exchange for hers. She had to remember that or the bruising she felt in her heart was going to be her constant companion.

"When did you bleed last?"

"Our wedding night!" She pulled out of his embrace and moved to the table. Picking up her bonnet, she studied the damage done to it.

Quietly, he approached her, his muscles tensed as if preparing to catch her if she tried to run. "That wasn't what I asked, and you know it."

She crushed the delicate bonnet when her hands contracted into tight fists. "What answer shall I give you, my lord? The truth or what you want to hear?" she said, using his own words to mock him.

"You have been nothing but honest—" he began.

"And you have been more than less, Tipton. Did you think I would be so besotted with you that I would not see?" Disgusted, she dropped the bonnet, but he seized her hands, preventing her from walking away.

"I warned you about this place, my mother." Tension made a muscle in his jaw throb.

"Yet you dragged me to Foxenclover. Why? I have asked myself. The answer is so obvious."

Rayne's pewter gaze darkened at her feeble struggle to free herself from his grip. "Please, share your revelation. You have found no value in my reasons."

"I have become a new weapon in your war against the Wymans, have I not?" She had managed to stun him, because her hands slid effortlessly from his grasp. "As a viscount, you could have married someone far better than me. Oh, I'm fair enough, so you could stomach the task of bedding me. And my family is respectable enough so when the game of tormenting your mother wanes, you can still hold your head up in society." Eyes dry, she met his furious gaze. "Maybe I should rest. I am going to need my strength to guard myself against all of you."

"You think too little of yourself if you believe that."

His hand speared through his hair. He removed the leather thong that secured his long hair in the back. With his long hair swinging free, she could not decide if she had married an avenging angel or a beguiling demon. Or maybe he had parts of each within him and that was what made him all the more confusing.

"Do you love me?" She died by inches, watching the agony contort his handsome face. "Let us just forget I asked."

His expression was filled with eloquent misery. "Devona, there hasn't been much love in my life. It is an elusive emotion, I am not even certain it is real," he spoke as if each word inflicted pain. "I have learned to count on the tangible. When

I cut a corpse open, I expect to see a heart, lungs, muscle, and bone. Love"—he lifted his hand in an idle helpless gesture—"it has no texture, no taste, nor odor."

"Shame on you, Tipton. Even I know men of science are dreamers." She felt so sorry for him. If he had not just ground her heart to ash with his boot heel, she might have moved to comfort him. Lucky for her, she was learning her bitter lesson early. She held still, not bothering to react to the surprise he did not attempt to conceal.

"I am no dreamer." The very notion seemed to offend him.

"Truly? What is a scientist, then, but a man who spends his time proving to the world that the unbelievable and unseen exists?" She returned to the chair and leaned over to remove her shoes. "Leave me, Tipton. Disillusionment is a bitter brew. Let's just permit this dose to burn in my stomach for a while."

She felt his hand on her shoulder, coaxing her to rise.

"Devona?"

It was difficult to resist the plea she heard in his questioning tone. Still, she had the Bedegrayne pride on her side. Without rising, she spoke, her gaze fixed on her shoe. "Although the act of impregnating me might hasten your mother's demise, I regret to deny you such pleasure this day. Seek your revenge elsewhere."

When she heard the sudden intake of his breath, she knew she had overstepped herself. The frozen silence in the room became unbearable. Making herself look in his direction, she watched his profile as he gazed at some activity from the window. His long hair free, he looked like some age-old conqueror. A man who had been fighting for his place in the world for so long that he did not know how to enjoy the simple pleasures. Deal or not, it had been a mistake to marry him.

"Tipton, what if we forgot about the bargain we struck. If it would please you, we could annul—"

"No!" The edge in his harsh reply was razor-sharp and she did not feel the steel bite until it was embedded to the bone.

Dry-eyed, she stared at the private battle he waged for self-control. His body literally shook as he used flesh and muscle to cage his feelings. "You once called me reckless."

"You haven't changed, madam," he snapped without thought.

"Can you not see how miserable I shall be, Tipton? I am not like you and your family. I find no joy in hurting others. As to the scandal—you care not of the *ton's* opinion and I shall never marry again, so shredding my reputation will likely push me toward notorious. It could be worse."

"Like staying married to me?"

Intuitively, she sensed answering either way would unleash the emotion he fought so hard to contain. "I believe you have regretted this business as much as I, but were too honorable to renege on the deal."

"Honorable," he said, tasting the word. "That sounds like a gentleman's term. I thought we agreed long ago that I lacked the attribute?"

Treading too close to the precipice of her own volatile emotions, she hugged herself. "I refuse to feel guilty," she warned, feeling as though he was stalking her, yet he had not moved from his position at the window.

"Why should you, I say? You came to me with

your plan of lunacy. You married me to ensure fruition. And now you wish to end our union because you have just realized the players in our little drama are a bit unsavory. I could have dressed this all up with pretty compliments and lies, but I find that I like you too much, Devona, to spare you."

"So this is all my fault? I should settle down and accept my fate since I chose the course." She shot up from the chair when he did not answer. "Poor Lord Tipton. Done in by a Bedegrayne. Ah, the scandal, the shame! Better yet, if I have such power over you, then I can end it. I will it!" So caught up was she in a fit of hysteria that she did not feel his hands gripping her arms.

"Tipton," he softly corrected.

Flustered by his opposing calm, her mouth fell open in surprise. "I beg your pardon."

"If I was done in, it was not by a Bedegrayne. You are Devona Lyr Wyman, Viscountess Tipton. My wife." The words rolled off his tongue as if he relished each syllable. "I refuse to debate who manipulated whom, suffice to say we are both wedded and bedded, Lady Tipton. I do not share, and I have an absolute rule about handing back anything I consider mine."

"You have not heard a word I have uttered."

"On the contrary, my hearing is sound. I do, however, have some concern about your own."

Misery churned and rose, closing her throat. "Coming here. Seeing you with her." She rolled her eyes upward, willing the threatening tears away. "I thought to save—it is not too late."

A queer light shone in his eyes, when his gaze locked with hers. "Oh, it is, my lady. Much too late."

To prove it to both of them, he lifted her high

until her lips pressed to his. God help her, she did not protest. Instead, her mouth parted eagerly against his. A tremor shook him as it rose from deep within his chest, before it found focus and release at their point of contact. Unbound energy surged and whirled around them, and she was so caught in the moment that she could not take a breath. He drank deep, his tongue laying claim to her mouth and the only thought that seemed clear was, *Take more!* Her vision dimmed, the need to give him more vied with her body's own life-sustaining demands. Whatever he was to her, adversary, friend, husband, or demon lover, she was unequivocally his.

THIRTEEN

The next morning, the empty breakfast room was less of a surprise and more than a relief. Devona did not expect any less from Tipton's family. If the *ton* thought her husband was odd, spending the evening under the wary eye of her new mother-in-law proved this penchant for drama and moodiness was derived from the blood. Crawling out of a smashed coffin at fifteen was simply atmosphere for this family.

Deciding to skip the morning meal, she moved to the back of the house and out the doors. She idly rubbed her temple, willing the slight headache away. Where was Tipton? After delivering that devastating kiss the other afternoon, he had left her alone. Apparently, he had been content that he had quelled all thought of her annulling their marriage. Appalling as it was, it was an accurate opinion. Her mood the rest of the evening had turned contemplative, but not once had her musings required his absence.

So distracted was she that the well-groomed flower beds had not made an impression on her. She had viewed numerous country gardens throughout her life. While she always found them pretty, she was never one to sit and contemplate their beauty. Halting several hundred yards from the house, she pivoted and studied her surroundings. The design was charming and well tended. It made no sense! The house had been stripped of many of its finer possessions, and it desperately needed repairs. Tipton's mother did not impress her as a woman who had the patience or inclination to nurture the fragile blooms. Then who? A loyal gardener?

She backed up, taking in the symmetrical beauty of evergreens sheared into pyramids and diamond-shaped flower plots. A looming shadow overhead made her look upward. It wasn't a tree, but a maze. And the entrance arch was a—"I do not credit this!"

The boxwood arch had been shaped into a dragon's head. His expression was taunting, daring the trespasser to walk into his open mouth. Now, paying attention, she could see the walls of the maze were his green serpentine body, winding and blocking the journey of the adventurer.

"Amazing."

"Glad you liked it. Want to come play?" The amused feminine voice floated down from above.

"From your ferocious, hungry grin, I imagined you to be male. However, since I have met the living dragon of Foxenclover, I can see the resemblance." Her hand came up, horrified by her slip.

A peal of laughter rustled the leaves. "Oh, I see you've met Jocelyn." There was more movement behind the wall before an enchantingly grimy young woman emerged from her hiding place. Tipton's sister? This woodland nymph was young, fifteen at the most. More child than woman, the girl beamed at her, her teeth almost white against her tan. Her light brown hair was coming undone from its hastily formed braid, and the telltale sun streaks and freckles revealed that she spent more time playing in the garden than practicing her school lessons.

"I thought you were Mother come to scold."

"No," Devona murmured, trying to fit this friendly child into the family puzzle. "My name is Devona Bedegrayne. Oof." She laughed, brushing her mistake aside with a nervous gesture. "Not anymore. I am Devona Wyman, now that I have married your brother. Rayne is your brother, is he not?"

The girl's complexion turned ashen as she scanned the garden. "Lord Tipton is here? He never visits." She took a step back into the maze.

"It is a pity his duties keep him in London," Devona lied, linking her arm with her new sister before she ran into the maze. "We are newly married, and I think he wanted to show his family off."

Brother and sister both shared the same light blue eye color and the resemblance was quite distinct when she snorted in disbelief. "I'll wager your acquaintance with Lord Tipton has been brief if you believe that! Did you elope? Mama and I have not heard news of the banns."

"No banns," she admitted, wondering how much of the tale to reveal. "We dashed off to Gretna Green. It will be an adventurous tale to tell our children." If they managed to remain married.

Devona located a bench to view the grounds and pulled the girl down beside her before she could think of a reason to escape. The child's demeanor had changed since she had learned of her brother's presence. Her movements were cat-like, and always searching as if she expected a greater beast to pounce on her. Devona frowned. She suspected her concerns were not far from the truth. Everyone knew Tipton held little tolerance for his remaining family. Staring down at this beautiful fey child, she could not fathom what this innocent could have done to deserve her brother's wrath.

"Who manages these gardens?" she asked. Of the thousands of questions swirling around in her head, the most trivial had surfaced.

Her chin snapped up to rival the challenging light in her eyes. "The gardens are mine."

The poor thing thought they had come to take away her imaginary world. Devona placed her hand to her heart to keep it in place. Whatever her husband's plans, she refused to sit by and watch him hurt his sister. "Of course the gardens belong to you. I doubt Tipton plans to remain here for long."

"No," the girl corrected. "The gardens are my creation. I dreamed them, and planted them. I tend them. They belong to me."

"Odd, I was saying something similar the other day."

Rayne's sarcastic drawl startled them. Devona automatically reached for the girl's arm to prevent her from running. She tightened her grip to keep her in place. "Good morning, Tipton. I was beginning to believe that I had been put out to the country and here we have not even been married a week."

Tipton's cheek ticked as if he was trying to conceal his grin. "I keep all my wives at my side for at least a month."

Devona did not bother to hide her smile. She was pleased that he had sought her out. "Well, the news relieves my anxious heart. Lucky for you I came across your sister. She is a hidden jewel, Tipton. No wonder you keep her from London.

Your male acquaintances would be begging you for an arranged marriage."

His sister stood, courageously accepting Tipton's critical scrutiny. "I meant no offense, sir. About the gardens belonging to me."

Devona quickly assessed the encounter as potentially volatile. Her inclination being to side with the weaker opponent, she stood and placed a protective arm around the girl. "Tipton, are these grounds not wondrous? They are your sister's design."

He was silent as if weighing the significance of her vocal stance. "I do not recall approving funds to restore the gardens," he finally said.

The girl gave a careless shrug, the stiff action betraying that she was feeling anything but nonchalant. "Talk of funds and distribution does not interest me. Only the gardens. If it has been a waste of time then it has been mine to waste."

"Then if I ordered that these beds be salted and burned, you will not care?" he asked, delivering the threat so calmly that even Devona was astonished by his cruel suggestion.

"Rayne!"

Hatred burned bright, but she remained composed. "You are master of Foxenclover, my lord."

Intrigued and perhaps slightly disappointed by the lack of the tantrum he had expected, Tipton cocked his head to the side, considering her as if she were a pawn on a chessboard. "You would not try to stop me, girl?"

"Madeleina."

The quiet correction had him stalling. "I beg your pardon?"

His sister met his cold gaze, matching it. "I have a name. It is Madeleina."

Noting the heightened color in her husband's

face, Devona piped, "You have such a beautiful name. Do they call you Maddy?"

"Only my friends."

The meaning was clear. They were not counted as her friends. How could she blame the girl? Tipton had all but promised to destroy something she cherished. It had to be some record. He managed to alienate his sister with the first words out of his mouth.

"Well, Madeleina," he spoke the words as if they were foreign to his tongue, "you have not answered my question. How would you stop me?"

She flinched at the question, but she stood her ground. "What would you have me say, sir? I am young, poor, and female. You hold the advantage." She turned to head for her maze.

"I have not dismissed you, girl!"

Madeleina glanced back. "Yes, you have, my lord. The moment you knew of my existence." With that parting shot, she ran, losing herself in her maze.

Rayne had managed to get Jocelyn to join them for supper. He would not tell Devona he had used threats to gain her cooperation. His lady wife did not appreciate his technique for handling his family. That was obvious from the way she had protected his sister. You would have thought the girl was her own, the way she had hovered protectively around her. No, gaining his demands without upsetting Devona would take cunning.

"What did you say to Madeleina? She refused to take supper at the table again," his mother asked, the first words she had bothered to utter since their private discussion.

"Perhaps she is ill?"

Rayne gave his wife a wry grin. He assumed she considered him the weaker opponent of this battle, or maybe she disliked his mother as much as he. Either way, he appreciated her attempts to distract the dowager from her quarry.

His mother sniffed, dismissing the question. "My daughter is never ill. Despite her penchant for living outdoors, I have managed to persuade her over the years to attend me at the table." Her faded brow lifted inquiringly at him.

"It appears your lessons have not taken, madam." He would be damned if he allowed her to manipulate the girl's absence as his fault. "Like all animals, I am certain when she is hungry she will leave her cover to feed."

Outrage mottled Jocelyn's face. He waited, half expecting lava to drip from her ears after the eruption.

"Madeleina is a lovely, sweet child. How dare you? She is no animal!"

"I do not think"—Devona began, but was cut off with a look.

"I do not care if you do or do not think, madam!" the dowager seethed.

"Silence!" Rayne slammed his fist on the table, the rattle of plates and silver echoing his annoyance. "My wife is off-limits, Jocelyn. You need to chew on something, I am certain Cook can serve you a satisfying bone. Or choose me, if you like." The smile he gave her was voracious.

"Since we are drawing battle lines, then I insist that your sister be left alone. You have managed thus far to ignore her existence. I wish you would continue to do so."

"Concern, Mother?" he mocked. "I never suspected there was this maternal side to you."

The dowager did not bother to respond to the

barb. Instead, she held his gaze and distinctly said, "Madeleina is not like you or I. If anything, she takes after your grandmother."

The comparison made him feel uncomfortable so he rejected it. He credited his grandmother for anything soft inside him. To consider his sister in the same manner meant that his treatment of her was as cruel as their mother's of him. Defensive, he struck out, "How do you expect any man to take her off your hands? You have allowed her to work outdoors like a common field laborer. Her skin is as dark as a woman from Calcutta and she had dirt under her fingernails. Has she had any schooling or has she spent her entire life scampering outdoors learning her lessons from the deer and hares?"

Devona burst out laughing, the tone a little on the high and nervous side. "Really, Tipton. You almost made me choke on my pheasant. I know you two derive great pleasure from needling each other, but I spoke to Madeleina. She seemed an intelligent, thoughtful child who has worked magic on the grounds. That maze of hers is spectacular. I can only imagine what she could do if she had some gardeners to help her maintain it. I doubt she could help the dirt under her nails or the tanning of her skin under the circumstances. She is truly an artist. Her canvas is outside, for heaven's sake!"

He almost smiled at the expression on his mother's face. She appeared torn between wanting to tear into him and the unfamiliar feeling of gratitude toward a woman she was determined to hate. After all, the bold chit had dared to marry her outcast son.

"Your sister has been tutored by me. If you find

her education unsatisfactory then you must accept the blame."

"Amazing," he marveled. "I cannot wait to see how you will pin her ignorance on me."

His mother took a contemplative sip of her wine. "If you recall, my last trip to London was to gain funds to send Madeleina to a school for ladies." She sent a glance toward Devona. "I am certain your wife understands that a polish is needed before she is presented at court."

Rayne had to admire her clever presentation. He had not even seen it coming. Days ago, he had warned Devona that his mother would size up her enemy before she attacked. His soft-hearted wife was now being used as a weapon against him. He could just hear his mother's quiet taunts. *How could you abandon your poor innocent sister? If she acts like a hoyden, who is to blame? Had I not begged you to assist in her care?*

The dowager had assessed Devona's weaknesses and figured that she was the perfect tool for manipulating her son.

Devona twisted her fork, toying with the meat on her plate. What he could only conclude was fear, tightened his gut at her next words.

"Tipton, perhaps we should pack up Madeleina and bring her to London. If her schooling is amiss, we could find her a tutor. My sisters and I would be willing to instruct her on the gentler arts."

"No!"

Whatever Jocelyn had expected from Devona, this was not it. In her artless manner, his beautiful wife had caused another good plan to go awry.

"My daughter remains at Foxenclover. It is her home. If you are willing to provide her the funds for schooling and a respectable wardrobe, I am certain we can weather her transformation from child to woman without anyone's assistance." The dowager focused on Devona during the latter part of her statement.

"No one would dispute that Madeleina is a re-markable child," Devona said, trying to soothe her. "I only suggested London because I thought the change would be stimulating to her creativity. Think of the museums, the concerts, and all the other amusements . . ."

Rayne closed off Devona's arguments from his mind. He knew from experience that there was little one could do to alter Jocelyn's decisions. That did not mean she could not be bullied and her authority stripped until she was just a whining nuisance in his ear. His first inclination was to tell his mother that his cooperation with this en-deavor was as likely as Devlin's resurrection from his fifteen-year-old moldering grave.

He stroked the edge of his dinner plate. A quick and ruthless execution of power was usually his preferred choice. His gaze caught the move-ment of his wife's fragile hand as she emphasized her point with a dancing movement of her fin-gers. The edge of his mouth lifted into a small smile. He must be smitten if watching her hands flutter, graceful as a butterfly's wings as they matched the chatter of her pouting mouth, made his heart ache. She noticed his attention and sent him a rallying smile before she plunged back into the discussion of bringing the insolent Madeleina to London.

He did not want his sister in his home, and more to the point, in his daily life. It had been so easy to forget her existence while she ripened and finally rotted her life away at Foxenclover. If

Devona had her way, the chit was going to be glaring at him from across the table every morning.

Damn. Perhaps he should allow his mother to win this battle and settle her with a proper allowance so he could retain a peaceful household. Besides, he had already set into motion his plan to bring another unwilling guest to his house. There was no doubt in his mind that Brogden would not eagerly embrace his invitation.

And yet . . . for him and Jocelyn to quietly agree on a subject was unacceptable. Sometimes throwing your money at a problem to make it go away was not the thing to do. It made life easier, true, but there was no satisfaction. Unfortunately, the only method of unbalancing his mother would entail him having to endure a penalty as well. However, he doubted Devona would see his side of it.

"I think my wife is correct. Your daughter will be traveling with us to London."

Devona clasped her hands together, pleased someone had agreed with her arguments. "Thank you, my lord. I knew you were a man who would bend to sound judgment."

He promised himself that she would never learn that he had come to this decision for less nobler reasons. Nor had he listened to a single word she had said.

"My brief glimpses of the child have led me to conclude that civilization has been sorely lacking in her upbringing. I look forward to instructing her myself."

"You make her sound as though she were some sort of animal viewing the menagerie from the wrong side of the cage," Devona muttered, not bothering to disguise her disapproval of the vein of his intention.

His mother's glare was no more encouraging. "You will not take my daughter from me, Tipton."

Rayne indulged himself by giving her a very arrogant grin. "I just did, madam."

"I shall simply kill myself. Then your husband will have to find another means of exacting his revenge on our mother." Maddy seized the gowns Devona had just offered to pack and sent them flying in all directions. "You cannot make me go with you!"

She spun wildly, a circle within the curved walls of her room. The three-story turret addition had been built over seventy-five years ago, a whimsy of one of the Lady Tiptons. She had chosen this room for herself when she was six. She had painted the walls a blue to mimic a cloudless summer day and over the years had added to it the encroaching garden that threatened to devour the blue.

Devona patiently bent down to retrieve the trampled gowns. "No one is kidnapping you, Madeleina. If you like, we could call this an adventure. When did you visit London last?"

Never. Though she loathed admitting that fact. As long as Tipton resided in London, then Mama would have never risked a confrontation. Indeed, Mama could bluster as fierce as the dragon she had created for the maze, but the truth was evident. Jocelyn was frightened of her son. How many times had her mother not called him a monster? From what Maddy had seen of her older brother, she was inclined to agree.

Pretending not to watch, she followed Devona's movements as she lightly touched the different painted flowers on her wall.

"This yellow was used for your dragon's eyes. What is it?"

As if she could not recognize it. *"Sedum acre."* Maddy sighed at the blank look she received. "Wall pepper."

"Ah," Devona said, moving to another flower. "And this?"

"Malva sylvestris or Common Mallow." Seeing through the ploy as an attempt to distract her, Maddy walked over and took the gowns from the viscountess's arms. "And that is, *Dianthus casius,* but I'm certain you know that. After all, I am such the village idiot that I need to go to town to learn all about civil-i-za-tion."

Devona chuckled at the way she had pronounced the last word and gave her a rueful glance. "You heard that, huh?"

In this household it paid to blend into the walls and listen to the conversations that excluded her. "Your husband has always made himself heard even in his years of absence."

"Maybe Tipton has finally come to do his duty by you." She pointed to a spiked leaf plant with small white flowers. "And this?"

"Don't you know anything about plants? *Ilex aquifolium* or holly." Maddy tossed the gowns on her bed and sat on them.

"Not as much as you apparently do. Who taught you?"

She shrugged. "Books mostly. Our neighbor on the western boundary, Mr. Hawkpit, has helped me over the years with cuttings." He and Mama had been carrying on a torrid affair for years, not that she was supposed to know. Sadly, she had not seen much of the man lately. She had overheard Cook tell Mrs. Poole that when Mrs. Hawkpit learned of the affair, she had threatened to split

Mr. Hawkpit's adulterous staff in two so there would be enough of him to go around. She snickered, understanding that when the women had spoken of Mr. Hawkpit's staff, they weren't referring to the hired help.

Maddy cast a sly look in Devona's direction. She decided to keep that bit of gossip to herself. Auburn Hawkpit had always been kind to her, a substitute father. The least she could do if he could not have Mama, was to protect him from Tipton. She shuddered, imagining what her brother would do to him just to add to their mother's misery.

"How long will you keep me from Mama?"

"Goodness, Madeleina, you make it sound like this is a punishment!"

Oh it was, but she was quick enough to know who was the pawn in her brother's little game. Devona was so different from Tipton. She was friendly, her emotions displayed so plainly on her face that Maddy suspected the young woman did not have a dishonest inclination. How in the world did she end up with the monster? "I have never been away from home. At least, not like this."

The viscountess drew her into her arms and gave her a reassuring hug. "You have nothing to fear from us, my sweet. All we expect you to do is to have fun."

"And become civilized," Maddy mumbled against the fabric of Devona's sleeve.

Her new sister drew back, laughing. "It will be a long time before you'll forgive Rayne those thoughtless words, am I correct?" She smoothed the wild wisps of hair from Maddy's face.

Her sober expression did not reveal the terror she felt at being left in the hands of her fiendish brother. He would kill her, just like he had killed his older brother. "I suspect my brother is very thoughtful in all things."

It was almost dawn when Jocelyn discovered her daughter's empty bed. Her first fear was that the girl had run away. Madeleina, despite Tipton's concerns, was a sensible creature. Running away would only delay the inevitable.

Taking up a lantern, she began her silent search of the gardens. There was no point alerting the staff. She would find her daughter on her own. The ground was slick and the heavy odor of wet vegetation made her nose itch. Jocelyn had never understood her daughter's fascination with the outdoors. She herself preferred the comforts that her favorite rooms provided: well-worn leather tomes, the clink of a china teacup, and the feel of a handmade rug from India. These were items she understood and appreciated. The one child who was hers was long dead, and the two who lived she did not understand.

Ah, the maze. Jocelyn clutched her dressing gown tighter with one hand as she worked her way through the maze. Madeleina thought her mama was not intelligent enough to figure out her clever child. Well, she would be surprised to learn this was not the first time she had wandered into her daughter's fantasy world.

"Madeleina!" she called out.

There was a rustle, then a wary, "Mama?"

"Who else would be playing in your maze at this time of the morning?"

It took another turn to the left and another two turns to the right before she entered the center of the maze. Maddy had had the sense to bring several blankets and a lantern for her outdoor slumber.

"Mama. You never rise this early."

"You were not in your bed."

Maddy pulled her knees up to her chest and rested her chin on the small table her arms formed. "I wanted to say good-bye to the maze before I left. Unless you have changed your mind about permitting me to go."

The hopefulness shining in her daughter's eyes made her feel ashamed that she did not have a stronger position from which to fight Tipton. "No, you will be departing as commanded." Commanded. The notion stuck in her throat so much that she thought she would perish from it.

"What if I ran away? Maybe Mr. Hawkpit could shelter me until they gave up and—"

"No." She softened her voice. "You have been denied so much because of who you are." And for that she would never forgive Tipton.

"You make it sound as if he has starved us. We may not be the richest family in the parish, or current on the latest fashions, but we have done well without him playing the bountiful protector."

Jocelyn closed her eyes. Madeleina did not remember her father or the life they had lived before Tipton had taken up his inheritance and began ruling their lives. They could have been the richest family in the countryside. Her daughter could have hired two-dozen gardeners and created an entire house out of trees and flowers if that had been her desire, if it had not been for Tipton and his interference in their lives.

"You are my daughter, Madeleina," Jocelyn vowed.

Confused, the girl gave her a sleepy-eyed blink. "Of course, Mama."

She pulled her up and gave her a shake. Startled, Madeleina clung to her, trying to find balance and understanding. "The serpent is taking you to his breast, my child. When you rest your head each night, study him. Learn his weaknesses. I thought it was another—" She stopped before she revealed too much. "Perhaps you will be his downfall."

Her eyes shining bright like morning dew, she held her daughter to her breast while dark wishes were murmured into Madeleina's hair. The dawn broke, streaking purple and red into the night sky. Such beauty. In Jocelyn's mind it was Tipton's life's blood spurting from his black heart.

FOURTEEN

The journey from Foxenclover had been un-eventful. Their unwilling guest had stared at Tipton as though he were a cross between a cannibal and an unholy creature every time he addressed her. Not that he had made much of an effort to converse with the girl. It made him a bit uneasy to have her around. Lord only knew what tales of horror Jocelyn had filled her silly head with. Despite the tales, Rayne had to grudgingly admit that his sister was not lacking in spirit. She might think he was the devil's disciple, but she was not averse to poking a stick in his eye.

"Oh, Maddy, see here." Devona pointed to the passing town house. "My family resides there. I cannot wait until Wynne and the rest meet you."

Somewhere along their journey, Devona had formed a fragile friendship with his sister. Knowing his wife, he realized that the girl had not had much choice. Once Devona set her mind on something, she could overwhelm even the most stubborn. He considered himself an authority on the subject.

"Where will we be residing?" his sister asked, her face pressed to the window. The masses going about their daily tasks had captured her attention from the moment they had entered the city.

"Not too much longer, pet." Devona gave her hand a friendly squeeze. "I am so glad you came with us. It will be so wonderful to have a younger sister."

The girl cast a wary glance in Tipton's direction. He stared back, his eyelids narrowing slightly, not even trying to allay her fears about him. Something akin to amusement stirred him as he watched her eyes widen and her forehead smack the glass when she turned back to the window. Perhaps having a little sister underfoot to torment would bring its own gratification.

Devona's foot shot out and struck him sharply in the instep. He reached down to rub the injured area. Damnable woman. One would think she could read minds. He nodded at her, attempting to look repentant. And the *ton* thought there was something supernatural about him! A woman's insight was more frightening than a close brush with death.

Speck had the door open and had his hand out before Rayne could offer to help Devona down from the carriage. "Good afternoon, sir. May I offer my congratulations on your recent nuptials, Lady Tipton."

Rayne stilled, waiting for the surge of emotion he had always tied to the name. Surprisingly, the dread and fury he expected remained dormant. He sought out Devona, but she was too busy pushing Madeleina toward Speck. It was a small thing, really. Yet it mattered to him. The title was hers now. There would be no going back for either of them.

"Speck, this is Tipton's sister, Miss Madeleina Wyman. Maddy, meet Speck."

Speck towered over her. "I never knew ye had

a sister, sir? And a small 'un at that," he said in a gruff rumble.

His sister serenely met the butler's rude stare. "You might want to practice that one in the mirror, Speck. I have gargoyles in my maze that are more terrifying." She walked past him, not awaiting his reply.

"Fancy that," Devona said, hiding the smile on her face with her hand as she hurried to catch up with the girl.

Rayne held back, waiting for Speck to finish giving instructions to the two underlings he had recently hired.

"What yer lady do? Shake the family tree to see who tumbled out?" Speck asked, taking a handkerchief out of his pocket to wipe the sweat from his face.

"I'm newly married, Speck. It is a husband's right to indulge his bride."

"Pardon me fer saying so, sir, but that young'un is full of spit and piss. A man like you should be planting his own brood instead of raising a girl who has been taught from the cradle to hate ye."

"That's why you are paid so well to watch my back." Rayne listened to the feminine chatter echoing from within his home. Such sounds were unfamiliar to him, but they weren't unpleasant. "The trip to Foxenclover was not what I had anticipated." Neither was Madeleina.

He started up the stairs. "Have you had any trouble in our absence?"

"Nary a spark. Expecting some?" Speck asked, his tone telling Rayne that he would relish it.

"I'm not certain. I have nipped the visible threads." He shook his head. "Just keep alert." He paused. "Has our other guest settled down?"

Speck's grin widened, showing his pointed

teeth. "The doc? It only took me and three others to stuff 'im in the carriage. One extra to pull 'im out. Hell of a fighter, even if you did whittle down his leg." The man spat and swiped at the spittle with his shoe. "He'll be wanting to see ye."

"It's a step up. His last wanting for me involved metal spikes, hot oil, and my body contorted in a creative, albeit, unlikely position."

He strode into the town house, leaving Speck chuckling in his wake.

Brogden responded to Rayne's soft knock. Pushing open the door, he entered the room, mildly astonished to see the bed empty and his friend sitting in a chair positioned at the window.

"I hear you caught yourself a wife, Tipton," the man said, his voice hoarse. "Ready to send her home?"

"Not quite." His lips quirked. "I have decided men like us could be improved on." Rayne slipped into the role of surgeon and studied his patient. Brogden was two and thirty and this moment he looked every one of those years, plus a few more. His beard stubble gleamed silver instead of matching the rich black on his head. His eyes were clear, he seemed alert, but he exuded a faint trace of his favorite opium tincture. Rayne grimaced, thinking his friend looked too thin. Brogden's frame had always carried an impressive bulk of muscle and the wasted form remaining was a disturbing contrast.

"And the lass is up to the task?"

"If she's not, at least I am."

Brogden laughed until there was moisture in his eyes. "I never had any doubt that you wouldn't know what to do with one of these English birds

once you found one who liked your homely face."
He straightened his good leg and pinched the
wetness from his lashes. "I noticed your viscountess was not the only lady climbing down from your
carriage. Did you manage to get yourself leg-
shackled twice?"

"Devona insisted we bring Madeleina from
Foxenclover."

"Madeleina." Brogden sat back and murmured
her name several times. "It makes me think of
hot sand on a beach and an even hotter woman
in my arms."

"Not that woman. She is only fourteen!" Rayne
said, his warning clear. His sister would think him
a real fiend if he threw her at someone as old
and scarred as Brogden.

Unperturbed, his friend's lips formed a secret
smile. "Depending on where you are in the world,
she's old enough to marry and have a baby hugging her hip. Unless"— He opened one eye. "Is
she your by-blow, Tipton?"

"Are you addled? I would have had to have
been her age to sire her!"

Brogden's clasped hands parted, palms up. "My
point exactly. A perfectly respectable age for making babies."

"Now that I'm back, I think we are going to
work on weaning you from your favorite medicine. It is rotting holes in your brain, my friend.
That *child* is my sister. Consider her off-limits."

"Sister?" He scoffed. "She is too pretty to be
related to the likes of you. Maybe she's your half
sister."

Tired and realizing he was being teased, Rayne
gestured to the remaining stump of the injured
leg. "I want to check the healing."

Affronted, Brogden sent him a look that reminded him of the man he had known eight years earlier. "I know my business."

Rayne settled on his haunches in front of him. "So much so that you had to cross several oceans to have me cut it off."

"Ouch!" His friend winced. "It's tender. Have a care." He looked away while Rayne pulled some scissors from his pocket and cut into the bandages. "How long is Madeleina visiting her dear brother?"

He frowned, not liking the way Brogden said her name. "Long enough," was all Rayne said.

"Damn, that hurts!" his friend growled through clenched teeth. Sweat began glistening on his brow. "Some host. You drag me out of my home because you did not approve of my care, and where does that leave me? Alone with no one to kiss me on the head and hold my hand." He laughed, but there was no humor motivating it. "Your lips are on the thin side for my taste. Why don't you call up your sister and she—*argh!*" His face flamed red while he choked on the pain. "Bloody sadist!" Brogden gripped the arms of his chair, all thought of taunting Tipton about the pretty lass with the swinging hair of rich, sweet molasses was forgotten.

Preparing herself for bed, Devona scooped water from the ceramic basin and scrubbed away the grime with her fingertips. Eyes closed, she reached for a nearby towel only to find it missing. She felt the soft brush of fabric on her opposing cheek.

"Very amusing." She turned her face into the offered towel and dried her face. "Tipton?"

"Are you expecting another?"

Finished, she tossed the towel at his chest. "Oh, there might be a man or two squirreled away if you prove to be annoying," she teased.

"I doubt it," he replied in all seriousness. "I think I have managed to ferret out and dispose of all your suitors."

"I vow, Tipton, you make it sound as if I had suitors hiding behind the drapery." Devona sat in front of the small dressing table. She scrutinized her face, trying to note the changes in her features since she had become a married woman. If there were any, she could not discern them.

"Do you always frown at your image?" Curiosity brought him closer so that he stood behind her.

"You will think me foolish."

"You? Committing a foolish act? Absurd."

Devona's mouth twisted into a smirk. "None of that or I shall be hunting up one of those hidden suitors."

Rayne held her reflective gaze in the mirror. "For the sake of marital harmony, I shall retract my previous comments."

She felt his strong, thick fingers nimbly sift through her hair and remove the pins that secured her braids. She loved the feel of his hands on her. He efficiently worked his fingers over her scalp; the accidental grazing of his nails was simply heaven.

"Why would I think you foolish?" his lulling tone questioned.

She blinked, having forgotten his earlier inquiry. A few caresses, and her mind became pudding. "Nothing, truly. I was looking for changes in my face."

He bent down and pressed a kiss on the top of her head. "You are too young to be counting wrinkles."

"I am not that vain," she said, even if it wasn't the truth. "I thought I would see something different. A change, if you like, now that I am a married woman." She shook her head to disengage his fingers from her hair. "I told you it was silly."

A gentle touch on her left shoulder made her shift her gaze to his on the mirror. His eyes of warm pewter possessed the means to touch her as effortlessly as if he had raised his hand. "Were you worried that others would see that I had bedded you, just by looking at your face?"

Getting irritated by the hint of laughter she detected in his tone, she picked up her brush and began stroking it through her hair at a reckless speed that should have created more tangles rather than smoothed them. "I did not expect to see a tattoo on my forehead for all to see, if that is your meaning, sir!" For spite, she rapped his knuckles with the wooden handle when he reached out to take it from her.

"Ow, you vengeful chit. Has anyone told you that you have the devil's own temper when you are vexed?"

Slowing the tempo of her strokes, she said demurely, "On the contrary. I have always been complimented on my wit and engaging manner."

"Perhaps only I can draw out your annoyance."

On her life she could not understand why the observation seemed to please him. "By all accounts, Tipton, I will have to credit you for that." Setting down her brush, she pivoted on her chair until she could look directly at him. "So, Tipton, with our growing family do you think we should contact a solicitor to help us locate a larger residence?"

The question visibly flustered him. "Growing?"

He gazed pointedly at her abdomen. "You—you said it was too soon."

Devona could not conceal her disappointment. "Still thinking a pregnancy would be a wonderful way to goad your mother? I hate to thwart you, but I was referring to Dr. Sir Wallace Brogden." Considering her husband's feelings on the subject of family, she hoped it would take years to conceive their first child. By then perhaps the notion of having a child together would be a joy in itself, instead of another tool to hurt his mother.

"Ah, yes," he faltered, trying to judge her present feelings. "I hope having him here will not upset you. Brogden has been a friend since I went abroad. He was a part of my life, when my own family could not bear the sight of me."

"There is no reason to explain, Tipton."

"He almost killed himself getting himself to London. I can only surmise the poison from his injury muddled his senses. He is a man of science and a good doctor. If he had been clearheaded, he would have seen that the leg needed tending."

Recognizing guilt when she saw it, she murmured, "His ill care forced you to cut off part of his leg."

Rayne kneaded the tension at his brow. "He thought by waiting that I could save the leg. I couldn't. There was too much infection. The maggots—" Noting her expression, he halted. "Forgive me, I forget that not everyone appreciates the details of my work."

"Does he blame you?"

"Some. Especially after the surgery. I only renewed his anger by having Speck bully him to the town house. But he needed my help, and I intended to see that he survived the amputation. Even if he was determined not to just irritate me."

"You never said a word about this. And here I was, doing my own bullying to get you to help me save Doran. Not to mention the attacks on our lives!" She stood. The weight of all the responsibility she had placed on his shoulders was beginning to strain hers. "No wonder you refused me at first. By all rights, you should have sent Speck to bully me into leaving you alone."

He opened his arms and she walked into his protective embrace. He had been protecting her all along. The thought that she had not been carrying her weight in their partnership made her feel miserable.

"No fretting, beloved. You'll bring on those wrinkles," he said, trying to tease her out of her melancholy. "Anything I did to help you with Claeg, I did for my own purpose. As my mother can attest, no one manipulates me."

"You took on Maddy," she pointed out, then could have kicked herself in the shin for reminding him.

"I did it to please you. And me, too, since I thought Jocelyn was going to have an apoplectic fit over the announcement." He stroked her hair, his hand continuing down her spine until he affectionately patted her bottom. "Sorry, love, if you think to reform my opinion of my family. However, since you did 'fess up about me bringing out your nastiness—"

"Your ability to vastly annoy me," she corrected, "and you are doing it now, my lord."

"Regardless, madam, I can stand here before you and not regret a single action I have taken on your behalf." He cupped her face and kissed her sweetly. "Having Brogden here won't bother you?"

"No. He is your friend. Since he is angry with

you, perhaps I can get him to disclose tales of
your past together," she wondered aloud. Enough
menacing glee was in her tone to have him chuckling.

"Not if I threaten him first."

He kissed her again. This kiss contained none of
the sweetness of the other kiss and left her hunger-
ing for more. Devona leaned into him. She
opened her mouth against his, allowing his tongue
to surge and seductively tease her own. Breathing
deeply through her nose, contentment rose deep
within her. The smell of Rayne, the taste and feel
of him, was becoming an ever-increasing need.
The more time spent with him, the more she
craved.

"One more thing," he whispered, the promise
that he would be inside her soon shone brilliantly
in his eyes. "When our child grows within your
womb, Devona, his creation will be the result of
my need to be a part of you. I'm a selfish bastard.
'Tis best you remember that."

"What is your impression of Maddy?" Devona
asked her sister Wynne three days after her return
to London. It had taken that much time to convince her husband that she would come to no
harm. Although no other attempts had been
made on their lives, Tipton was not convinced
their circumstances would remain so. Feeling like
a noble lady, she and Wynne strolled down Bond
Street with two trailing footmen as guards. She
thought her husband was the most protective man
she knew, even trumping her father, but she refused to remain a prisoner.

"Her manners are about as shabby as her
gown," her sister said after a reflective pause.

Dressed in a light green muslin walking dress with a yellow sarcenet spencer, Wynne exuded a confidence in her bearing that Devona had always found lacking in herself. If anyone could help her add the polish she had promised Jocelyn, it would be her sister. The gypsy hat of satin straw she was wearing concealed the thoughtful frown Devona suspected was in place.

"Are you hoping a few new gowns and the ability to execute the perfect curtsy will endear her to Tipton?"

"Not exactly. The wardrobe and the lessons are just the trimming. My intention is to make her real to him."

Wynne faced her, the disbelief clear on her perfectly sculpted features. "Now who is speaking nonsense?"

Spying the trailing members of their entourage, Maddy, Pearl, and Gar from across the street, Devona lowered her voice. "For years, Maddy has simply been a name, an undesired notion to reject. Avoiding Foxenclover reinforced that attitude. Unfortunately for Tipton, he has a wife who will not allow him to continue."

"You think throwing brother and sister together will make him change his mind?"

Devona stopped in front of a glove shop window. "I am not seeking a miracle. I just want him to understand that she has a long life ahead of her."

"And that means . . ." Wynne persisted.

"That's a long time to hate and fear someone." Devona's face brightened when Maddy joined them. "Did you find something interesting at Hookham's?" She usually took advantage of visiting the circulating library when she was in the area. Today, she had declined so she could have some time alone with her sister.

"A few." Maddy sent a look to Pearl. "Miss Brown was pleased to find a few copies of Mrs. Radcliffe's books. You would have thought she had found a handful of diamonds the way she carried on."

"I haven't read these tales," Pearl said defensively. "Besides, I saw the way you were clutching that old gardening book."

"That old gardening book was Horace Walpole's essay, 'Modern Taste in Gardening.' He discovered similarities between the post-medieval garden and those of the antique world. His observations were quite insightful, though I doubt you could appreciate them."

"That is enough, Madeleina," Devona interrupted before the pair of them could begin to argue in earnest. "Miss Brown may be in my employ, however she is your elder and you will display a more ladylike decorum when addressing her."

"Yes, ma'am." The glare Madeleina sent in Pearl's direction promised retribution.

Devona could barely contain a sigh. The Wymans were a combustible clan. Her appreciation for Tipton's self-control was growing each day.

"This is your shopping excursion, Devona," Wynne said, reminding everyone of their purpose. "Shall we do gloves or shoes next?"

"Neither. Maddy must be hungry after several hours of fittings. I propose we move on to Mayfair. Our new sister has never seen Berkeley Square and I think an ice from Gunter's would improve her mood."

"Truly?" Maddy exclaimed, looking more like

a child than a woman at the moment. "I would enjoy that very much, Devona."

"Do you think indulging her whims will benefit her disposition?" Wynne asked as they waited for their carriage.

She shrugged, not offended by the question. "Years of denial have left her hungry. I intend to feed her."

"Miss Bedegrayne, is that you?"

Devona turned, her hand lightly resting on the cool glass of lemonade as she searched for the person who had called out her name. Oz Lockwood walking briskly toward her, his walking stick sharply striking the wooden walkway with each step.

"Mr. Lockwood, it is a pleasure to see you again." She held out a hand and he immediately clasped it and bowed. "You of course are acquainted with my sister, Wynne."

"Mr. Lockwood," her sister acknowledged politely his quick bow in her direction.

"And may I present another sister, Miss Madeleina Wyman. Maddy this is a dear friend, Mr. Oz Lockwood."

Maddy looked up from her ice and frowned. "You look familiar."

Not pleased to be addressed in such a forthright manner by a mere schoolgirl, Oz irritatingly replied, "I doubt it, Miss Wyman. I rarely associate with children." Pleased he had put her in her place, he turned to Devona.

"Miss Bedegrayne, oh, forgive me, you are Lady Tipton now, are you not?"

She tried not to wince at the disapproving tone.

"You must forgive me, my dear, but your sudden marriage came as a shock to all of us."

"Really?" Wynne's smile should have frosted Oz's eyebrows. "Anyone close to the family could obviously see how smitten Tipton was with our Devona. I am certain you could understand how a couple in love is swept away by the romance of eloping."

Oz glowered at Wynne. "I was under the impression, Miss Bedegrayne, that Sir Thomas heartily denounced this match."

"Father was naturally disappointed that Tipton denied him the pleasure of marrying his youngest daughter off with the flourish suitable to our rank. Perfectly understandable, do you not think?" Wynne gazed directly into his eyes, her warning unambiguous. "Nevertheless, Tipton has the support of the Bedegraynes."

Devona tried to get her sister's attention, but she was too focused on putting Oz in his place. Wynne had never been very tolerant of Oz's peevishness. She had always said that the only reason Mr. Lockwood hung around them was due to his interest in Devona's hand. If this was true, the man had done a remarkable job hiding his intentions.

"Would you care to join us, Mr. Lockwood?"

Oz rolled his walking stick between his palms. "I had hopes of luring you away for a private discussion, Lady Tipton."

Wynne touched her hand before Devona could agree to the request. "Unfortunately, you have caught us at an awkward moment, Mr. Lockwood. You do understand."

Devona didn't, not one word. "What awkwardness?"

"My brother's displeasure," Maddy happily explained. She spooned another mouthful of ice into her mouth.

Ah, they had a point. She could not claim that her husband was a jealous man, but he did have some odd notions about her male friends. "We must continue our shopping, Mr. Lockwood. Another time, perhaps?"

Oz's lips had thinned to the point that his upper lip had disappeared completely. His hand tightened on the silver head of his walking stick as he leaned heavily on it. "Forgive me for intruding, ladies. I look forward to our next encounter." He nodded to Wynne, a small capitulation from the vanquished. "Lady Tipton." He moved on quickly, as if attempting to distance himself from their rejection.

"Oz Lockwood is harmless," Devona announced to anyone who needed reminding.

Pearl, who had remained silent throughout the exchange, shifted in her seat. "He's had his eye on you, it's obvious."

"Ridiculous. The man is my friend. I have known him for years."

Wynne signaled to Gar that they were ready to depart. "I would not try that pathetic defense on your husband."

Being the youngest, Bedegrayne was wearing on her cheerful disposition. "I am not naive, Wynne. Stop treating me like a child. You should be grateful for my intervention. I will wager Mr. Lockwood is, or will be once his anger diminishes." She took a bite of her ice then pushed it away.

"Grateful for chasing my friend away? Why should I be grateful?" Devona wondered aloud.

"That Lord Tipton doesn't murder Mr. Lockwood for approaching you for a private discussion." Maddy made her astute observation while she licked the pink smear of sweet confection from her lips.

"I am surprised you called this meeting at the club," Rayne said, taking the seat offered by Devona's father. "I had anticipated a more private setting."

"Like Wimbledon Common at dawn?"

A reluctant smile pulled at the corner of his mouth. "Something along those lines, although I expected Brock to issue the hotheaded challenge."

A blaze of indignation fired up in Sir Thomas's gaze. "What, Tipton, you think a little gray hair means I lack the teeth to punch a ball into your heart."

"No, sir. I suspect a man like you would simply forget about the invitation."

The older man leaned forward, his stance intimidating. "I'm no coward, Tipton, to plan an ambush. If I wanted you dead, you would be the first to know."

Rayne settled back in his chair. He liked the old Bedegrayne, even respected him. He could tell from which side of the bloodline the offspring had acquired their character.

"You expressed my thoughts better than I, Sir Thomas. My apologies if I offended you." He waited while a servant poured him coffee. "Your daughter is well. She hopes you will visit us soon."

"Come, Tipton, I did not invite you here for an idle chat."

Rayne matched the comment with an equally direct question of his own. "Why the imperial invitation, sir?"

Sir Thomas Bedegrayne slapped his palm

against the table and looked about the room. He glared at the few men brave enough to boldly stare in their direction. "A bunch of gossipy old women," he mumbled. "Did you know there is a bet in the books?"

Since Rayne did not frequent the club, he shook his head. "What was the wager?"

"That I would kill you the moment you returned to town with my gel." The older man's smile reminded Rayne of a wildcat playing with a snake.

"I plan to live a long life. Do you object?"

The smile warmed a degree. "Oh, I had my fantasies, Tipton. However, my boy Brock spoke up for the match. In fact, he insisted on it."

"I discovered Brock was a reasonable young man, once he stopped challenging me."

"It makes me wonder, though," Sir Thomas trailed off. His eyes widened at some undisclosed insight. "You have something on him. Something he didn't wanted bandied 'bout town."

"Brock's business is his own," he replied, sensing the ambiguous answer would infuriate his companion. Rayne did not have to wait long for the outburst.

"Lies and half-truths are the same in my book, Tipton," he grumbled. Bushy brows drawn together in an uneven line, he looked every inch the outraged father. "Drunk or sober, my boy has a functioning mind. What did you threaten him with to bring him in line?"

Rayne weighed his options. Bedegrayne appeared to be a sensible man. He doubted he would murder a man for doing right by his daughter. "I told him Devona was my mistress."

Sir Thomas laughed. "And he believed you? My

gels are ladies. Not one of them would risk their papa's wrath."

"I reminded Brock that it mattered not whether it was truth or fiction, the *ton* relishes such scandals. The downfall of the reckless Devona Bedegrayne would be a tasty morsel for the jaded."

The older man's eyelids narrowed as if he found something distasteful in front of him. "You would ruin a young gel because it amuses you? By God, you are as evil as they say."

"You forget. That lady is my wife. Her reputation is secure and I would call anyone out who says otherwise. We are on the same side, sir." Rayne got up. He was mildly surprised to see Sir Thomas do the same. "Since your daughter is safe in my hands, are we finished?"

"Not quite."

He did not expect the hammerlike fist his father-in-law planted in his stomach. He doubted he would have stopped him even if he had. A *whoosh* of air expelled from his lips. It was a respectable connection. Rayne doubled over, using his hand to brace himself against the table. His eyes began to water.

Sir Thomas leaned over so that his lips were an inch from Rayne's ear. "Don't think marriage is saving you from staring at me from across a dawn field. My gel has tender feelings for you so we will consider our disagreement at an end. Welcome to the family, son."

FIFTEEN

Maddy was still fuming as she marched upstairs. Who asked the mighty Lord Tipton to start acting like an older brother? She had been getting along just fine without him these last fourteen years. Her hand absently struck a door as she moved down the hall, fury almost blinding her. If she was so uncultured, perhaps he should just send her back to the country, where she could rusticate with the rest of his livestock. Her hand connected with another door.

"Enter at your own risk."

She froze. She had forgotten about the other guest in the house. She did not know much about him except that he was an invalid and a friend of her brother. Considering her present feelings toward her sibling, the last thing she wanted was to visit some boring old man and listen to his nauseating praises for the blackguard.

"Come on. If the thought of looking at it sickens you, can you imagine how being at your mercy angers me?"

The bitterness she heard in the mysterious booming voice should have sent her running to her room. Instead, she hesitated. What was *it* he expected would sicken her? She pushed the cracked door open and peered into the room.

"It's about time you got in here, you heartless

wench. Did you expect me to sleep on my arse? Come closer so I can get my hands around your spineless spongy neck." His severe features lightened in puzzlement, then to delight at his unexpected visitor. "Well, well, whom do we have here? Come in, come in."

Maddy chewed on her lower lip, wavering about what she should do. "I was warned not to disturb you, sir."

"You'll do on many levels, and I am in the fortunate position to have the time to contemplate each one of them. Please join me. My apologies for not rising to greet you formally."

"Lord Tipton will not like me being in here."

Brogden gave her a measuring look. "Neither of us gives a farthing what the lofty surgeon thinks. Come closer, pretty Madeleina. I do bite, but I'm adequately hobbled."

Her gaze followed his down to the stump he had concealed under a blanket. "How do you know my name?"

"By the usual manner. I asked." Cynical amusement curled his well-formed lips. "Do you want to see it? I'm thinking about charging admission. Dr. Sir Wallace Brodgen, physician and freak. Since I am feeling generous tonight you may gawk all you want." He reached to lift the blanket. Maddy boldly blocked his hand, then pushed it back down to his side.

"Forcing me to look at your wounded leg is not generosity. It is plain meanness. Is someone supposed to attend you? You thought I was someone else when I passed the door."

"Oh, the cruel Mrs. Winters. As cold as her name with a face that makes a monkey's arse appealing." His eyes widened when Maddy's hand covered her mouth to stifle her giggles. "How rude of me? Is a monkey's southern port acceptable?"

"I do not know. According to Lord Tipton, I am an uncivilized and ungrateful chit. I have been dragged to London to better my ways so I can be married off."

"A beauty like you needing improvement? Absurd. If you were older or I less jaded I would have to think of something to prove otherwise."

Sensing he was just being kind, Maddy just shrugged. "You are more tolerant than Lord Tipton." Deciding she was being rude, she added, "Thank you. Can I find your Mrs. Winters?"

"Actually welcome her to my room? Never!" His whiskey-colored eyes glowed in mock horror. She laughed at his expression.

"Fine. No Mrs. Winters unless she breaks down the door. So how can I help you?" Studying him, she guessed his age was close to her brother's. His face looked menacing, with the shadow of a beard highlighting his gaunt cheeks. Whatever had made him ill enough to take most of his leg had also ravaged his entire body.

Brogden glanced at the bed. "The bones in my arse—there I go again with my salty speech. I feel like the bones—"

"In your southern port," Maddy offered.

"Aye, those very ones." He grinned, the first genuine grin she had seen and she was stunned by how handsome it made him. "Those bones feel like they've been hammered into the chair. I was wishing for some relief in the bed." He shook his head as if coming to a private decision. "Maybe you should hunt down the disagreeable Mrs. Winters after all."

It was obvious that the idea had little appeal for the injured man. Pity swelled in her heart, but she swallowed it back down. She suspected Dr. Sir Wal-

lace Brogden possessed no tolerance for that particular emotion. "You could lean on me, if you
like."

"Thanks, lass. You are such a wee thing. I would
not want to hurt you."

Now she was feeling challenged. "Brace yourself on the chair. We'll need it for support to get
you standing."

"Your brother will cut off my other leg for
touching you, dearling."

"You aren't touching me. I am helping you. Besides, you were correct. I don't give a farthing
what Lord Tipton thinks."

His face shone with approval. "That's the spirit.
All right, Miss Wyman. I will have to put my arm
around your shoulders as an anchor. You promise
not to slap my face for being too forward?"

"Your face is safe, sir. I have not had a lesson
regarding impropriety yet."

Maddy slipped her arm around his, and he
locked his arm around her shoulders. Brogden
took a few fortifying breaths before he used the
chair to push himself onto his foot.

"Not exactly graceful."

"We are doing fine," she said through clenched
teeth, as though the action would add steel to her
gait. "What are you doing?" she asked when she
realized he was adding to their weight by dragging
the chair with each step.

"Counterweight."

The journey was an agonizingly slow one and
noisy. Both of them were breathing heavily. The
chair groaned and squeaked as it was dragged
then leaned upon for support. Maddy was surprised the entire household had not sought out
the curious sounds. "Almost there." She could

tell he was tiring. He was allowing her to accept more of his weight with every step.

"I'm hurting you and am sorry for it."

Several feet from the bed, one of the legs of the chair caught on a small woven rug. The snag threw their rhythm off and Brogden's weight pitched them forward. Maddy's startled cry was muffled against his chest as she landed on the bed with Brogden on top of her. He had struck his wounded leg on one of the wooden side beams of the bed and was swearing in such a manner that would have made a sailor blush.

"Sir, I cannot breathe!" Maddy pushed at his arms, a futile attempt to move him. An agitated clicking between them had her crying out, "Heavenly saints, what is this?"

Brogden groaned. He had the indecency to chuckle. "My lizard?"

"By God, you have gone too far, Brogden."

Lord Tipton's deadly pronouncement stilled her movements and managed to seep into even Brogden's pain-filled consciousness. Suddenly she was free from his weight. She sat up just in time to see a cream-and-brown-striped lizard run across the bed and disappear over the side. Her brother gripped Brogden with one hand while he slammed his other fist into his jaw. Brogden, unsupported, dropped like a stone onto the floor.

"You fool! Are you trying to kill him?" she shrieked. Scrambling off the bed, she crouched at his side. Brogden, dazed from the punch, meekly allowed her to cushion his head in her lap.

"You are my friend," Lord Tipton said, each word spoken in slow precision, reminding them all of the fury he was bridling. "I brought you into my home, caring for you as if you were my brother." He paced, glaring at both of them. "You repay me by acting like a damn satyr."

Maddy sucked in her breath. Realizing she was holding it, she blew it out. "This is the meaning of your outrage? You think he was tossing my skirts up? Or perhaps you think your friend is the victim? Maybe I was the one who seduced him into bed?"

Brogden tried to get her attention by lightly touching her cheek. "Sweet Madeleina, attacking your brother will not make him see reason."

His caress halted the ascent of her growing rage. She had the sudden urge to lean over and chastely kiss the swelling she saw forming on his jaw. "Are you well?"

Uncertain of the scene before him, her brother said defensively, "He was warned you were off-limits. It is indecent that you are here."

Disgusted, Maddy seized one of fallen pillows and eased it under Brogden to replace her lap. "To reason with a man one must find his mind reasonable. Forgive me for lacking the strength to aid you, Sir Wallace." She pushed passed Lord Tipton. "What my brother lacks in brains, he makes up for in brute strength." She slammed the door behind her.

"All she was trying to do was ease my suffering by helping me to the bed." He groaned when Tipton pulled him to his feet, and then lifted him in his arms to put him in the bed. "I haven't decided who was cast the villain in your sordid little drama, me or your lovely sister."

"Is Madeleina asleep?"

"No." Devona closed the door to the study. Rayne was sitting in a large chair near the fireplace, a glass of brandy clasped in his hands.

She walked over, took the glass out of his hands, and placed it on the mantel. "But she has stopped crying. I left her reading a book." She sat in his lap. He folded his arms around her and pulled her close. Rayne grimaced and rubbed his ribs.

"Did Brogden hit you?"

"No, I—it's nothing." He rested his cheek against her head. "I overreacted, Devona. I saw them on the bed and thought the worst."

"How badly injured is he?"

"Falling on his injured leg has reopened the wound. There was some oozing blood and fluid. If he remains in bed instead of moving about as if he were indestructible, he might survive."

"Maddy said that she was only trying to help him move to the bed since Mrs. Winters was elsewhere. She blames herself for what happened."

"And rightly she should," Rayne said, getting incensed all over again. "Why she chose to visit him in the first place is highly suspect."

Devona stroked his face, enjoying the texture of flesh and the beginnings of a beard. "You were lecturing her again, were you not?"

"I caught her digging into my medical case. She could have cut herself on a saw or blade."

She nodded in understanding. "You were afraid she would be hurt."

"Don't place any noble laurel wreaths on my head, Devona. I don't like anyone touching that case."

"Of course you were quite calm when you explained your concerns."

His smile was distinctly wolfish. "Hell, no, I took very large bites out of her hide. A little fear would do that young woman some good. Maybe she will think twice about walking into a stranger's private chambers."

* * *

Brogden propped himself up on his elbows at the first glimmer of candlelight from beneath the door. There was a soft knock, but it was merely a token of politeness. The door opened without waiting for his invitation. He could think of only one person who might seek him out this time of night.

"By all means, Tipton, please join me. Maybe you would like another chance at me while I'm down. Once I'm healed, you will need your own medical services."

"I am heartened by the news, sir." Madeleina stepped into the room, an aura of candlelight encircling her. "It is my understanding that my brother is considered an artist with the instruments of his profession. Whether alive or deceased, it makes no difference."

"You amazing, bold child. What are you trying to do? Your discovered presence will likely have me castrated." It was a noble act to chase her from the room. Tipton would not hesitate to protect his little sister, despite his protests of feeling the opposite. Still, it was a treat to see her pretty face. He pulled himself up into a sitting position to enjoy her visit.

She closed the door, then moved closer so no one could hear them from the hall. "I shan't stay long," she promised, sincerity practically radiating from her freshly scrubbed face.

"I rarely receive visitors this late of night." He didn't add, the ladies he had received or called on usually did not represent the dewy bud of innocence. "I figured Tipton locked you in the cellar."

"He values his rats too much." She held the candle closer and studied his face. "He told me he would beat me if he found me here."

Brogden was aghast. Protective or not, he was certain Tipton would uphold his threat. "Dear girl, why would you risk your brother's wrath?"

"I needed to see that he hadn't hurt you too much. It was my fault, and I could not bear the responsibility. The other reason was entirely selfish." She pulled back, eclipsing him in shadow.

"What other reason?" he demanded.

He thought he detected a hint of a smile before she turned to open the door. "Why, because he said I couldn't." She closed the door quietly behind her.

Laughing, Brogden pillowed his head on his crossed arms. The delightful image of the defiant Madeleina challenging her stubborn brother at every encounter was enough to entertain him for hours.

"This is just an excuse to make me miserable," Devona complained. She had been married a month. Her sister Irene was giving a ball in their honor to celebrate their nuptials. Instead of counting on Tipton as an ally to end this public showing, he had surprised her by heartily approving. The thought made her scowl.

"Stop grumping," Wynne chastised. "At least you have something to celebrate."

Feeling guilty, Devona glanced down to watch the *modiste* adjust the hem of her gown. Her marriage had placed a microscopic focus on Wynne's unmarried status. Having two unmarried sisters seemed acceptable. Being the remaining unmarried female Bedegrayne had made Wynne open to cruel speculation that there was something wrong with her. As usual, she handled the talk with dignified aplomb.

"You like, madame, yes?"

The gown was perfect, that wasn't the problem. "Yes, very much," she admitted. She gave Wynne a helpless look.

"The gown is wonderful, Nadine. Do you have enough measurements? I believe my sister is restless from all the standing."

The *modiste* briskly nodded. "Very good." She stood and helped Devona out of the gown. "I will send this to you. Tomorrow afternoon, yes?" she asked, her French accent distinct.

"On the morrow, then," Wynne agreed, seeing the woman out while Devona dressed.

"Allow me to assist," her sister offered when she returned. She efficiently secured the small glass buttons on the back of Devona's dress. "Where is Tipton? Hiding from all the female frippery?"

"He is seeing patients at the prison. Tipton is trusting all the details to Irene." Devona tossed a glance back in Wynne's direction. "The notion raises my hackles, if you want to know the truth. The man must be a sorcerer. Irene is smitten. It is appallingly disgusting to see her hang on his every word."

"There." Wynne stepped back, rechecking her efforts. "What is wrong with the family liking him? I trust you like him as well? You did, after all, marry the man."

"Of course I like him." She was beginning to think she loved him, too. "It just galls me to see Irene and Tipton agreeing about this ball. I do not see any reason for the fuss."

"Irene wants to show the *ton* that your marriage has the family's support. I can assume your husband is trying to amend the distance he has placed between himself and the polite world. It is an admirable gesture to protect you and your children from being ostracized as he once was."

Agitated, Devona paced the room. "It is more than that. I can feel it in my bones."

"You cannot still believe that Lady Claeg is behind that accident at the conservatory?"

"I saw her that night. The woman probably blames me for Doran's death." The lie was becoming easier to say with practice.

"She has Amara, and her position in society to consider. No, I think you are wrong," Wynne said dismissingly.

Tipton was up to something, Devona was certain of it. Nothing would convince her that the Bedegrayne family could meekly lead her husband around like he was a child's pony. He had agreed to the ball because he hoped to lure their mischief-maker out in the open. She feared they were the bait.

Behind locked doors a figure hunched over a writing desk, feverishly scribbling the news of the ball to honor the Tiptons. The letter would be of interest to the receiver. Its purpose was to inform, as per their bargain, but also to taunt.

The receiver thought the position of power was their own. Untrue. A correction would be made at the appropriate time. Only a weaker individual would hire someone to do their misdeeds. The true power was possessed by the messenger, the figure was certain of this.

It was a simple task to watch Lady Tipton from a distance. There were too many around guarding her to act. Lord Tipton's feeble attempts to protect her were a nuisance and at times entertaining. The figure accepted the challenge. A special

trap had been created for the elusive Lady Tipton.
And Lord Tipton, too. His interference would be
recognized and punished.

The figure sat back, satisfied with the letter. It
was an announcement and a warning. It was a
pity the receiver was too dim-witted to appreciate
the complexity of its true meaning.

The fiend would devour them all.

Carriages and pedestrians congested the streets
surrounding the Suttons' residence. According to
Irene, this declared her ball an instant success.

"I told you everyone would be too curious
about you and Tipton to refuse an invitation,"
Irene murmured, her blue eyes twinkling like the
deep blue sapphire and diamond necklace she
wore around her neck. "It is amazing how the
correct presentation can whitewash even the dark-
est reputation."

Devona wrinkled her nose in an unladylike manner. "Tipton did not create a scandal. He just did
not care what the polite world thought of him."

"Truly, Devona, you are a married woman. You
must remember that your position in society is
always tenuous. How you conduct yourself is con-
stantly scrutinized."

Devona bit her lower lip; otherwise she was going to tell her sister where society could stuff their
judgmental opinions. If she had listened to any
of them, she would have never dared to approach
Tipton. She doubted her sister would appreciate
the observation.

"Irene, perhaps you should put all of this wisdom down in a book." She smiled and waved at
her father. "I might even read it."

"Papa! Irene managed to lure you from your

clubs. It is a miracle to be sure." She kissed him on the cheek. "Brock promised to show up as well."

"Applied an ample dosing of guilt, eh?" Sir Thomas Bedegrayne gathered each daughter in his arms and gave them an affectionate squeeze.

Devona gave one of his side-whiskers a playful tug. "Only just enough."

"It is good to see you, Papa," Irene said, stepping away from his embrace. "You and Sutton are not permitted to hide in the card room for the evening. Devona, you are expected to circulate. Where is your husband?"

"He was delayed by a patient. He will be along soon."

"Excellent. Was his sister terribly upset not to be included tonight?"

Irene was already being distracted by a new arrival, but she answered the question anyway. "Maddy made a token protest. I think she plans to spend the night playing cards with Speck."

"Who?" Irene asked, confused by the two different ongoing conversations. "Oh, that's nice, dear." And she returned to the other participant.

"Come along, Papa. You should really see this champagne fountain. If everyone drinks this flowing river, the *ton* should be positively sloppy with affection for Tipton."

The hours swept by and despite the crush Devona was enjoying herself. She had lost track of her husband again, but she suspected her father had lured him and Brock into the card room. Irene had been correct. Presentation was important. Serve Tipton up with pineapples, champagne, and syllabub, and he would suddenly be hailed as a long-lost friend.

"Greetings, Lady Tipton. You are enchanting this evening."

Pleasure shone of her face, as she offered her hand. "Mr. Lockwood. It appears you caught me hiding at another ball."

Oz Lockwood bowed over her hand. "To win the lady's favor I bear a gift." He presented her with a cup of punch. "I had to scale a mountain of humanity to gain this. You may now show the proper gratitude."

Devona curtseyed. "My thanks, sir." She took the glass and sipped the warm punch. "Oz, it is so good to see a friendly face."

"Mine in particular or will any do?" he teased.

"Yours, of course," she replied automatically. Before she had met Tipton, Doran and Oz had been her closest male friends. Now Doran was gone and she was married. There was something calming about seeing that Oz had remained the same.

"The other day at Gunter's," he said, trying to be heard over the music and hundreds of other vying conversations, "I feared I had lost your friendship."

She shook her head. "My new household is taking some adjusting. We have taken on Maddy, who cannot decide whether or not she hates her brother. Plus we have an old friend of Tipton's who is recovering from the loss of his leg. Emotions are running high, and Wynne was only being protective."

"You are fortunate to have such a loyal family."

Yes, yes, she was. She had to confess that even stuffy Irene had managed to do the impossible. "I agree. However, I shan't tell a soul, 'else they would expect constant praise."

Oz laughed. "Never change, my dear."

Devona gestured to the chaos around her. "So,

Mr. Lockwood, is there a certain lady around who could entice you to become leg-shackled yourself?"

"I can think of a certain miss who might take me on," he contemplated.

"Who?"

"A man must keep some secrets. If she refuses, I would like to bear my rejection with some dignity."

A footman touched her on the arm. "Lady Tipton, your husband requires your presence."

"Where is he? Is something wrong?"

"I have no knowledge of that, my lady. You are to meet him outside, near the gardens."

"Thank you," she said, dismissing the servant. She took a sip of the punch then pressed it back into Oz's hands. "I have to go. Thank you for the punch. Promise to let me know when she accepts your offer."

Oz Lockwood waved her off. "I'll send you a note the moment the deed is done. Hurry on, I wouldn't want your husband angry at me for delaying his wife."

Haste was impossible. Devona slowly pushed her way through the crowd, acknowledging the people she was practically shoving out of her way. She welcomed the thought of stepping outside. The warmth from all the bodies packed in the room was making her light-headed.

She stumbled as someone pushed her from behind. Devona felt something scratch her on her exposed upper back. She touched the injury and her fingertips revealed traces of blood.

"I am so sorry, my dear," a woman slurred behind her. "My pin must have pricked you."

"You and her lord," a drunken companion quipped.

Devona ignored them both. It was taking all her

energies to focus on making it to her husband.
The heat was most intolerable, she thought, raising a gloved hand to her temple. She would be
soaked to the skin by the time she found the
doors to the outside.

She moved from person to person, gripping the
disconnected arm or hand as if it were a rope of
flesh leading her to Tipton. Hopefully, she could
reach the gardens before she disgraced herself in
front of all these people.

The walls rolled toward her and she cried out
in fear. Another push and she was through the
open door. Torches lit up the night. Their flames
were ridiculously long, their smoking tails attempting to lash at her. She staggered sideways to
avoid being burned alive.

"Rayne!" she screamed, running deeper into
the shadows. She kept running until she collided
with the brick garden wall. Closing her eyes to
keep out the horrifying images, she used her
hands to feel along the wall. There had to be a
gate, some way she could escape. The brick fell
away, and then there was cool iron in her grip.
She shook the gate. It was locked. Locked away
like Doran, she despaired, falling to her knees.
Devona was curled up like a child, sobbing into
her skirts, when Tipton found her.

"Some bastard drugged her," Rayne announced
to the somber Bedegraynes. Too caught up in her
nightmare to realize that the man she called for
was carrying her, Devona fought him and Brock
like a raving lunatic. They had tried to be discreet,
but there had been too many witnesses. It was evident that she had not seen the many guests standing about as she made her escape from her

invisible demons. His hands clenched into fists at the thought of her suffering.

"How's my gel, Tipton? Will this madness linger?" Sir Thomas asked, fearing the worst.

Rayne closed his eyes. "I assume the drug will dissipate in a few hours."

Wynne entered the room. "Her slumber is less disturbed. Maddy is at her bedside. She will call out if Devona awakens again." She sat next to her father and rested her head against his shoulder. "Do you know what caused these manifestations?"

"I don't know. There are numerous plants in the correct amount and combination that could create this effect."

Brock ground his fist into his palm. "Someone got to her. How did we slip up? I thought you hired extra men to watch the guests, Tipton?"

"What? One man to watch every fifty? There were too many bloody guests." He already blamed himself. Having Brock remind him was like putting an adze into his flesh.

"She should have been safe!" Brock raged.

"Tell that to your sister Irene. She should have been more selective with her invitations," Rayne snapped back.

Sir Thomas held up a hand. "Barking at each other isn't helping my gel upstairs. The deed is done. Tell me, Tipton, how do you think she was poisoned? Something she ate?"

"That would have been my first guess," Rayne confessed, seizing the topic as an alternative to pounding on his brother-in-law. "I was at her side when she took her supper. She ate nothing different from the other women. If it was in her food or drink, there would have to have been a mass dosing." He massaged the back of his neck. "No, I think our mischief-maker was a little more devious. There is a three-inch scratch on her shoulder."

Wynne confirmed it with a nod. "I saw it earlier. You think something sharp was dipped in the poison?"

Sir Thomas's brows lifted. "Like a button, or the edge of a fan?

"Or perhaps a ring?" Brock suggested.

"It could be any of those items or something we have not thought of," Rayne said wearily, the strain of the evening showing on his face. "Too many people could get close to her. I blame myself."

Wynne made a protesting sound. "We must shoulder the blame as well. It was our family who insisted on this ball."

"If I had suspected Devona was the intended target all along, I would have refused Irene's offer."

Brock glared at Rayne, the fury rekindling in his gaze. "Then why did you accept, man? Hell, you encouraged my twit of a sister!"

"Because," he starkly admitted, "I thought I was the intended target."

Consciousness came slowly to Devona. She felt as if a great weight had been pressing her down into the black depths of the deepest ocean. Suddenly free, she was rising through a graying scale of elusive shadows to the bright dawning of awareness. She opened her eyes. The first thing she noticed was that she was in her night rail. She stared at the lace on her sleeve as if she had never seen it before.

"Praise be, you're awake, mum," a maid exclaimed, carrying a tray in her hands "I was supposed to try to wake you and make you eat some broth."

She cleared her throat, noting it was dry. "I am not hungry. Some tea would be nice."

"Right away, mum." The maid placed the tray on a nearby table. "Everyone will be so pleased your senses have returned."

Devona quietly watched her pour the tea. Her thoughts were still a fuzzy jumble. "Have I been sick?" She accepted the cup and took a few tentative sips.

The servant gave her a pitying look. "Poor lamb. I'll get the master. He'll put your mind at ease."

Minutes later, Tipton rushed into the room. She had never seen him in such a state. His clothes were wrinkled and it appeared that his last shave had been days ago. "What a sight! Either you have misplaced your valet or he has taken up gin."

"Neither, my lady." Seeing that her cup was empty, he refilled it. Sitting beside her, he stared at her like a starved man deprived of a meal. "How are you feeling?"

She pressed her lips together into a pout. "Confused. What is going on here, Tipton? Am I ill?"

"What is the last thing you can recall?"

"Well, let's see." She thought for a moment, "The ball, of course." Her eyes widened at a sudden insight. "Don't tell me I fainted in that crush? How embarrassing. I suppose you overreacted and rushed me home. Am I correct?"

"Partly." He pressed his fingers to her throat, trying to assure himself with her pulse. "Do you recall becoming ill?"

She frowned. "Perhaps. I think I told Oz that I was hot."

"Oz Lockwood?"

"Yes. You know he is a friend." She narrowed her eyes. "Why are you looking at me like that?"

"Someone drugged you that night. Brock and

I carried you out of the house, screaming like a madwoman."

An intangible thread of memory increased her unease. "I don't recall any of this." She tried to think of something, anything. Fear counted its way down her spine. "You said, 'that night.' How long have I been insane?"

He kissed her lightly on the lips. "Not insane. Unconscious. You passed out three hours after our return home. It's been two days, Devona."

She silently mouthed the words. Two days were gone and she had lost her memory of that night. "How?"

"There is a mark on your back. We think someone came up from behind and scratched you with something that had been dipped with the drug. Whatever it was, it had to have been potent."

Devona stared off, trying to put together the wisps of memory as if they were a complicated puzzle. There was laughter all around her. A woman. And something. It was sharp. The pieces turned, then fitted together perfectly. "A pin," she said aloud. "A woman bumped into me. She apologized because her pin had scratched me."

This news seemed to revitalize Tipton as readily as a night's rest. His body hummed with excitement. "Who was it? Would you recognize her if you saw her again?"

"I—" She shook her head. "Her image escapes me, Rayne. It is akin to looking through a piece of piping. Everything is at a distance, and I can only focus on pieces of the memory. Forgive me for not being much help."

He took the cup from her and placed it on the table. "There is no need to apologize for my irresponsible behavior, beloved." Self-loathing hardened his features. "Your family has been quite forgiving, considering I almost got you murdered. Brock has restrained himself from issuing forth a single challenge."

Devona shifted her position so she could rest against his chest. The rhythmic hammering of his heart was comforting. "You did not know—"

"The hell I didn't," he growled. "Nothing has happened for weeks. I thought, perhaps, we were too well guarded. Keeping you safe was important. However, I could not allow our mischievous friend to go unpunished for his deeds." He tightened his arm around her. "I swear, I thought I was the intended victim. When I found you outside, screaming my name, I . . ." his words faded as the emotions from that night threatened to consume him.

Devona tilted her head so she could see his face. She had never seen him look so tortured. His bloodshot eyes were sunken and shadowed from fear and lack of sleep. His beard stubble tickled her hand when she reached up to stroke his cheek. "Still taking on the world single-handedly? I thought we were partners. Was that not part of our bargain?"

"To Hades with our bargain!" he fiercely declared. "You are my wife. I'm supposed to protect you." The hand resting on his leg clenched into a fist. "Some protector. Maybe you should return to your family."

She pulled back, not believing his words. "Return me? Like an unacceptable purchase? I'll be the laughingstock of the *ton!*"

"Devona, that wasn't what I meant."

The more she thought about the suggestion, the madder she became. "You would like that, would you not? You have regretted our union from the start, and a little incident like getting poisoned gives you the perfect excuse to bow out."

"Little incident? You could have died."

"Fine. Embellish the facts, forgetting the point that I did not perish."

"I'm supposed to be grateful?" he bellowed.

Stricken, she put her hand to her heart. "Oh, I suppose having me die would have tidied up this mess quite nicely."

Rayne sprung off the bed. "Madam, you are driving me mad."

Devona sat up on her heels. "Just try to send me back to my father. I vow all of London will hear of it. Think of the scandal."

He had been stalking away when she issued her threat. Her words made him pivot and march back to her. Dragging her into his arms, he gave her a shake to gain her attention. "You silly idiot. Do you think this is some sort of lark? I want to keep you safe."

She lifted her chin and squarely met his gaze. "Sending me back to my father is not the answer. Besides, I do not want to put him or the others in danger."

Some undefined emotion flashed in his eyes. "I see you have no problem placing me in the path of risk." Rayne loosened his grip on her arms.

She pulled away and wrapped them around his neck. "We're partners. The bargain has been struck."

He grimaced, not pleased with the reminder. "There will be no more wandering about on your own," he warned. "I promise to take better care of you."

I'll protect you as well, my love, Devona silently vowed.

She sealed the pledge by kissing him on the lips.

SIXTEEN

"What are you doing here?"

Her brother had not bothered to look up from his work. His back was to the door and Maddy would have sworn she had been quiet.

"I asked you a question, girl. Are you deaf or just impertinent?"

She moved closer to see what he was shielding with his body. "Probably the latter. What are you doing?" She peered over his shoulder and gasped. "Is that—that's not—human?"

Tipton's lips curved in grim amusement. "Mr. Kelly would be hurt to be referred to in such a manner. A man who sacrifices himself for science should be respected."

An old sheet had been thrown over the lower half of the dead man's body. Maddy placed the handkerchief she had been holding to her nose. Seeing a half-naked corpse was not distressing in itself, as much as viewing the large gaping hole that used to be his chest. "The smell is just dreadful. How can you tolerate it?"

"It is amazing what you can put up with when you have no choice."

It did not take the wisdom of age to know his statement could be applied to many circumstances, herself included. "Why do you do it? Cut up the dead, I mean."

Tipton glanced at her, but her attention was focused on the corpse. "What would you say if I told you I do it because it amuses me? According to the rumors, I linger at deathbeds trying to capture their ~~souls then sup~~ on their hearts."

Seeing him hovered over a corpse, she could see why people would believe such tales. There was something eerie about a man who preferred the dead to the living. "I cannot believe Devona would bind herself to a fiend."

He chuckled. "Shallow praise, indeed. And indirect. What do you believe, Madeleina?" his voice echoed in the quiet, tomblike room.

She resisted the urge to hug her ribs, a useless attempt to banish her feelings of trepidation. "I think you enjoy your reputation too much."

His brow lifted at her observation. "My wife has accused me of the same." Efficient hands probed the chest cavity.

Maddy forced her gaze to return to his face. "Mama said you changed after the incident."

"The incident. You make it sound like I committed an unforgivable public faux pas. My family buried me alive. It was blind luck there were two greedy men waiting around my grave to dig me up. Otherwise, this conversation would not be taking place."

Maddy flinched at the bitterness in his tone. Once there were two brothers who bore the Wyman name. One was long dead, the other dead in heart, and she really knew nothing of either. "There was a sickness. It took many in the parish. Everyone thought they were going to die. Their mistake was understandable."

Tipton halted his exploration. Dropping the

small metal probe into a basin, he turned to her, his bloodied hands clamped into fists. "You know nothing. Your view has been tainted since your birth by Jocelyn."

"I speak not of our mother, but of our grandmother."

"Mum? She died when you were barely out of napkins."

His voice and posture had subtly changed at the mention of their grandmother. There was at least one family member worthy of his affection. "I am surprised you were aware since you did not remain at Foxenclover or in England for that matter."

He muttered something under his breath that she could not understand. "If you believe I had a choice, you are mistaken." He picked up his instrument and began to work again. "I will tolerate you in my house because my wife wishes it. Do not mistake the indulgence as an opportunity to befriend me. I have no desire to know you, sister."

Had that been her intention? If so, it had been an unconscious one. Still, his words struck at her like blows. She did not know she had allowed her heart to become as exposed as Mr. Kelly's. "You despise me. Why? What have I ever done to you?" she demanded.

"You exist."

Maddy sucked in her breath and took a step back. She had never been so openly hated before. "You blame me for something I had no control over? It would make more sense to blame our parents."

"I have shocked you," he observed, unmoved by her distress. "Truth is a rare commodity at Foxenclover. If it comforts you later when you cry into your pillow, I will admit that it is not you personally whom I despise."

"Small comfort to go along with my shallow praise." She blinked, almost surprised to feel the tears sliding down her cheeks. Idiot. She never cried. "You speak of truth, hate, symbolism, and choices, but you are forgetting one thing." She took a few breaths to keep from crying openly in front of him.

"What?"

"Cowardice. You ran away from your home and birthright. It is much easier to blame an unborn sibling, or a grief-stricken mother and grandmother than to face up to the fact you were too weak to do your duty by them!"

Tipton glared at her. In her wild imagination, she could almost feel his tightening fingers at her throat. He certainly seemed as though he were sizing her up for his dissecting table. "Your conception was nothing more than a replacement. A replacement for the beloved son who had died, and the one they thought possessed by the devil. It must have been such a disappointment to them that you were born female."

Words to battle words. Her family was good at striking a killing blow. Maddy lifted her chin, showing that he had not broken her with his cruel statement. "I have always known my place, my lord. I remained and survived despite it." She picked up her skirt and walked to the door, bearing a graceful dignity that would have made their demanding mother proud. "Hide behind your hate, Lord Tipton. I am not desirous of gaining your brotherly tenderness even if you served it up on a gold plate."

Coward!

The word seemed so ruthless and cold in his

dreaming brain that it jarred him to consciousness. The brief chat he had had with his sister
must have disturbed him more than he thought.
The audacity of that girl! She knew nothing of
his life, how it had been after Devlin had died,
with the surviving members of his own family warily staring at him like he was some sort of fiend,
as Madeleina had called him.

There was a vein of truth to her words that
bothered him. His mother seemed protective of
his sister. He had always assumed that she had
benefitted from their mother's affection. Was Jocelyn still grieving for Devlin? So much so that it
shadowed the joy of giving birth to a daughter?

Mum would have loved having a little girl to
hold and spoil. He imagined she filled the new
baby's life with love and attention, allowing her
own daughter to bury their father, who soon followed the favored son and the absence of the unwanted second. Had Jocelyn's disappointment
been great enough that she heartlessly reminded
her third child of her failure for not being born
male? Mum must have died when the girl was four
or five. She had been around long enough to be
a kind memory, but not long enough to protect
her from their mother's tongue. Was that the reason his sister chose to live outdoors, her gardens
and surrounding woods her haven? It was the one
place their mother abhorred, the one place
Madeleina could find her peace.

Good Lord, he thought, rubbing the grit from
his eyes. His sister battled him even in his mind.
If he kept at it, by dawn he would be at her door,
begging her forgiveness. He was fair-minded
enough to accept that his dislike of her was un-
reasonable. He did not know her. He did not care
to know her. If he opened his heart to her, he

felt that it would mean he was forgiving his mother as well. He was not prepared to go that far. Not now. Maybe never. Madeleina was raised without her brother. She did not need him to become a grown woman.

Rayne rolled out of bed. He needed to do something or his sister's words were going to haunt him the rest of the night. Not bothering to cover his nakedness, he padded over to the door connecting his room to Devona's. She had been asleep when he retired, and he had not wanted to disturb her with his restlessness.

He entered the room, not needing a candle to light his way. Quietly he stopped beside her bed. She was asleep on her back, her arms resting above her head like a trusting child. Even in the darkness, her pale skin gleamed like pearls in the moonlight.

His sister forgotten, Rayne gently peeled the blankets back. Her nightdress was seductively draped over her right hip, exposing her legs. Just the sight of her aroused him, he mused, feeling his rod fill and rise as Devona's luscious form beckoned. Of all the decisions he had made in his life, the taking of Devona as wife had been his brightest.

Not wanting to disturb her just yet, Rayne eased onto the bed beside her. Stretching his long frame out the full length of the bed, he rested his head on his arm while he considered the simplest means to remove her clothing. His first thought was to cut the nightdress off her. However, the last thing he wanted was for her to wake up and see him hovering over her wielding a knife. Knowing Devona, the imagined delightful romp in bed would end with him requiring stitches.

Instead of giving in to the urge to just rip the

garment off her, he decided to apply some of that
great patience for which he was supposedly
known. Hooking his finger under the hem, Rayne
inched the fabric up, halting when she kicked
fretfully at the discarded blanket he had pushed
to the end of the bed. She sighed, slipping back
into a deeper state of sleep.

Rayne released the nightdress. The majority of
the fabric was piled up on her chest, leaving her
exposed from the waist down. He wanted to see
all of her, but he would have to wait.

Smiling, he placed his hand on her stomach.
He had never awakened her thus, and looked forward to her reaction. With the barest touch of his
fingertips, he explored the under curve of her
breast. Delighted by her shivering reaction, he
snaked his hand deeper under the fabric so he
could circle one nipple, then the other. As he expected, her body was already aware of him. The
turgid nubs prickled at his caress. He swallowed
thickly, wishing he could put his mouth to her
and suckle. During their brief marriage, he had
learned that he could almost bring his wife to the
brink of pleasure just by suckling her breast.

Devona moaned and tried to shift away from
him. He stilled her by throwing one of his legs
over hers to anchor her in place. Leaning over
her, his tongue replaced his fingers. Her breasts
were beyond his taste for now, so he traveled
southward down the center of her abdomen. He
playfully swirled her navel, then dipped his
tongue into the center. She laughed aloud, and
he lifted his head to see if he had awakened her.

Her eyes were still closed, but he could see the
lingering smile on her lips. Becoming serious, he
nuzzled the soft nest of hair between her legs,
inhaling deeply the musky fragrance that filled

him with such potent lust it bordered on pain.
Rayne brushed the rigid length of himself against
her leg, sensing there would be no end to his
torment until he could bury himself deep within
her. Stifling the urge to groan, he scooted lower
until he could lick the tender skin of her inner
thighs. Devona said something under her breath
and kicked out with her left leg.

Rayne used the movement to his advantage by
shifting his position so that he was lying between
her parted legs. Now on his stomach, he leaned
over and kissed her right knee. The fine hairs on
her legs prickled under his gentle worship as he
moved up her leg. This time when he came to the
soft folds of her sex, he parted them and put his
mouth on her. His intention was to prepare her
for him, however she was already wet. He tasted
her, his tongue flicking the tender tissue within.
Devona cried out as she lifted her pelvis. Rayne
cupped her buttocks bringing her closer to him.

"A dream," she murmured.

He lifted his head. "No, beloved, paradise." In
one strong movement, he pulled her under him
and plunged into her. She cried out again, the
surprise of their joining as intense as the wait had
been for him.

The time for leisurely love play was at an end.
His patience broke from its invisible tether and
the frenzied need for her flooded his system. Her
eyes were locked with his and her fingers gripped
his muscled forearm. Not being able to give her
time to adjust, he set the rhythm of his thrusts at
a pace that minutes later was making her breathless. She arched beneath him, as if to draw him
in deeper. He groaned, biting the inner tissue of
his cheek, hoping the pain would hold off his impending release.

If he could spend his life within her, it would never be enough. Rayne felt her tense beneath him, and sensed her own pleasure would soon be upon her. His body tightened and fine tremors shook his frame as he tried to fight his body's natural response. Gazes still locked, he pressed a hard kiss to her open mouth. His tongue penetrated her as his rod did, each giving and taking pleasure. The metallic taste of blood from the small wound in his mouth mixed with sweetness he had come to associate with her.

She pulled away from the hard, relentless kiss and took a fortifying breath. His mouth latched on to her exposed neck and she bucked wildly beneath him. Lost in the ecstasy of her release, she writhed as if to escape him. Vigorously, he pounded his thrusts deep within her, no longer able to hold back as Devona's soft, womanly form beckoned to him on a primitive level. Frantic, he hugged her to his chest, sinking his teeth into her shoulder. Rayne's release was as violent as his need for her. Hot, forceful, and seemingly endless, he pumped his seed into her.

The disturbing dreams that had brought him to her bed were forgotten. Keeping himself inside her, he rolled onto his back so she would not be burdened with his weight. He groped for the sheet and flipped it over them, though the last thing he felt was cold.

Devona snuggled her nose against his hairy chest. "Paradise," she murmured.

His hand stroked her head. "A magnificent dream. Go back to sleep." With one hand caressing her back and the other propping up his head, Rayne remained awake. If Devona had lifted her head, she would have seen the intense resolve etched on his features.

The lover had been pacified for the moment, but the protector had surfaced in his stead. Someone was trying to hurt her. Whoever was behind this must have thought they were quite safe hiding in the shadows while plying their deadly mischief. Rayne could be equally ruthless. Mingling among the common inhabitants of London had its benefits. He would use the contacts he had to find the person responsible. And he would. Their foe either grossly underestimated the lengths to which he would go to protect his wife, or they knew exactly how far he would.

"I cannot decide if Tipton sent you here because he is too furious to see to me himself, or if you are a peace offering."

Devona smiled as she tied off the stitches she had sewn into the bandages to keep them secure. Taking up her scissors, she snipped the thread. "You must forgive Tipton. He is just learning how to be a brother. I fear he overreacted when he saw you—" She paused, thinking the phrase, "on top of Madeleina," sounded slightly indelicate.

Obviously amused by her discomfort, Brogden laughed. "Embracing his sister?"

Relieved by the substitute, she returned his grin. "He realizes now that it was an unfortunate misunderstanding of the situation."

"Don't you believe it, sweet lady. Tipton knows me better than most. I should be grateful all he tried to do was take off my head."

Devona liked Dr. Sir Wallace Brogden. He was not much older than her husband; however, when she looked into his eyes she would have sworn he had crammed an average man's lifespan into thirty-odd years of living. There was something ancient about him, a mystery that intrigued and teased like the greenish gold flecks that twinkled at her from the brown depths of his eyes.

"You've known Rayne a long time."

It wasn't a question, but he answered it as if it were. "Since he was fifteen. He's journeyed far from the lad they dragged onto the deck of the *Griffin's Claw.*"

She stopped gathering up the soiled bandages. "I thought leaving London was his choice?" She dropped the linen into a discarded bowl of soapy water.

Brogden's eyes widened in disbelief. "He didn't tell you about the sorry state he had managed to get himself into?"

"I know he was mistakenly buried alive. That his family was afraid of him after his resurrection."

He snorted. "I can't confirm if it was a mistake or not, but that mother of his preferred him in the grave to having him sharing their supper." He motioned for a pillow that had dropped onto the floor. She picked it up and stuffed it behind him. He sighed his contentment.

"The story has circulated throughout society for years. There was some rubbish about demonic possession, but upon meeting the dowager myself, I would wager she's had more dealings with the underworld than my husband."

Admiration shone on his face. "Now I see why Tipton nabbed you. For a bitty little thing, you are quite feisty."

Delighted and embarrassed, she brushed the compliment away with a wave of her hand. "I figured even a fifteen-year-old Rayne could tolerate only so much hysteria before he became disgusted and left."

"You're right about the disgusted part, although he had more motivation to leave than his feelings. He could leave or allow them to commit him." Apala, deciding Devona was harmless, crept from her hiding place under the pillow. She rested on his arm, flicking her tongue over each eyeball.

"An asylum?" she said, aghast.

"The grandmother was against it, but she was only one voice. Young Tipton ran off as soon as he was recovered from the sickness."

Rayne would not appreciate the pity she felt for him. How heartless could a mother be to have run off her only surviving son so soon after burying his brother? Her grief must have induced a temporary madness. It seemed the only plausible explanation. "So he boarded a ship to seek his fortune."

Brodgen stretched his arms. "Nothing so romantic. He hooked up with a gang of boys bent on thievery. He was so green he was caught on his first attempt. With the choice of the gallows or transportation looming, it seemed fate was steering him back into the grave he had cheated."

Devona nibbled her lower lip, realizing how little she really knew about her husband. The man had not been exactly forthright about his past. Of the two options, it was simple to predict which had occurred. "Where was he transported? Jamaica? Barbados?"

Brodgen rubbed the stubble on his jaw. "Actually, neither."

"How the devil . . . ?"

Enjoying her confusion, he smiled. "Devil or guardian angel? Take your pick. We know which one the *ton* chose. He was a lucky bastard all the same. What most folks don't know is that a friend of his father's interceded on young Tipton's behalf. The man was part owner of the *Griffin's Claw* and saw to it that he was on board before she sailed."

"Rayne has never spoken of him." Or about any of this. Why should he? He married her as part of their devil's bargain, not because there was love between them. Her spirits plummeted. At least he wasn't burdened by the emotion.

Misinterpreting her frown, Brogden explained, "The man died years ago when we were in India. He set up Tipton nicely by willing his shares of the ship to him." Becoming concerned, he felt he needed to add, "There now, I would be worried if he spent all his time telling you tales of his past. A pretty jewel like you is meant for stolen kisses and sweet compliments. His struggles to manhood aren't for a lady's ears."

Devona grimaced, feeling as though he had just patted her on the head. There had been too many times in her life that someone had shielded her from indelicate subjects. Her corset was not the only thing holding her upright. She had a spine as well! "Dr. Brogden, if you are not comfortable discussing my husband, please say so. I can see that Rayne has lived an extraordinary life, and he bears the scars for it. You will do well to remember that pretty little jewels are, merely, hard rocks."

"Did I sound that condescending?"

"Enough for me to seek out a hard rock," she admitted, softening her threat with a smile. "I do not understand why I like you, Dr. Brogden."

The charming smile he bestowed upon her would have made any female's pulse skitter. He absently rubbed his heart. "Just Brogden. Or Wallace if you like."

"Brogden then." She stood to leave. "I have to see to Maddy. We have struck a bargain. She will endure one hour of household lessons if I will spend the equal amount of time improving the small gardens out back."

His expression turned indulgent at the mention of her sister-in-law. "You will never tame her nature. Wild creatures never adapt well to cages." He scooped up his ugly bump-riddled pet and kissed it on the head.

Surprised he had given Maddy more than a cursory thought, she nodded. "I want her to have a choice, too."

Pearl was coming up from the kitchen when Devona ran into her on the stairs, her arms overflowing with soiled bandages, scissors, and a bowl of soapy water.

The servant rushed forward. "I've got it." She grabbed the bowl just before it slipped from Devona's grasp. "You shouldn't be tending the doctor yourself. It isn't respectable."

"I have no plans to announce the news in the *Times,* so let it be our secret."

"And here I thought marriage would uncurl that wild hair of yours," Pearl mourned. They continued down to the kitchen.

"Do not fret, Pearl. I have his lordship's permission to look after Brogden. It was his instructions I was following."

"And why would he be trusting you to doctor his patient," she scoffed.

Devona wrinkled her nose while they walked under the drying herbs. "Since the patient is a physician, where is the harm? Have you seen Maddy?"

Cook angled her head in the direction of the door behind her. "She is out back playing with a kitten."

Cook was a large woman in her fifties. She had raised eight children on her own, and was confident of her abilities to tell the Tiptons what she would and would not do. Instead of igniting Rayne's temper as Devona expected, her husband liked the brisk, straightforward woman. The fact that she could cook was favorable to all.

"Those aren't for me. I don't do laundry," she reminded them. "I was hired for cooking and that's all I'll do." She continued to peel the onion in her hand.

"Nelly has done a fine job laundering," Devona began.

Cook tossed the onion in a pot and picked up another. "Silly twit."

Hoping the comment was for the absent Nelly, she cleared her throat. "That may be, but these are for you." She placed the linens on the worktable and pushed them toward her.

The servant eyed the bundle. "You planning to eat these?"

Pearl opened her mouth to silence the uppity cook, but Devona stilled her by touching her arm. This was her household, and she felt it was her job to maintain domestic tranquility.

"As long as Dr. Brogden is in residence we will need your assistance. And really, they do fall under your duties," she promised.

Warily, Cook poked them with her knife. "What do you want me to do?"

Feeling she was going to win this domestic battle, Devona's eyes sparkled mischievously. "Cook them, naturally."

Pearl was still mumbling her discord fifteen

minutes later. "You should have allowed Speck to backhand her for such sass. I would have paid him a shilling to watch him do it."

"Truly, I never noticed this streak of violence in you, Pearl." Devona decided she would show Maddy how to plan the menu for the week. She glanced back at her sister-in-law. She was dirty from sitting on the ground, playing with the stray kitten. Red welts from its claws marred both her hands and arms.

"Before we start, why do you not go change your gown and wash the filth out of those scratches. You'll end up under your brother's medical care if they get infected."

Maddy appeared properly horrified. "Ah, the real threat. He would probably bleed me just to get rid of me."

"Madeleina!"

Maddy brushed a kiss to her cheek. "I shall not be long." She rushed up the stairs to her room.

"I do not think you are the proper guardian for that impertinent child," Pearl observed, her skepticism clear.

Devona hugged her. "Of course I'm perfect. I know all the tricks."

"Beg' pardon, Lady Tipton," the approaching footman interrupted.

"Yes?"

"This note arrived for you."

Curious, she took the letter. There was nothing identifiable about the wax seal. "Who delivered it?"

"Just a boy. No one important." He bowed and left her staring at the letter.

"What is it?" Pearl peered over her shoulder.

"I am not certain. Go on to the drawing room. I will meet you there." Devona stood frozen in the hall, the letter clasped firmly in her hand. She was being foolish and paranoid. So someone had sent her a note. It was most likely from a friend. The private assurances did not calm the whirl in her stomach.

Taking a deep breath, she broke the wax wafer and opened the paper. Nerves made her fingers tremble. She read the letter once, then again because she could not believe the contents.

"It's a lie," she whispered. It was better to believe it than to consider that every decision she had made had been based on ghastly deception.

SEVENTEEN

Several hours later, Rayne stood in the same spot where Devona had stood, wondering where his wife had run off to. Oily panic slid down his spine, but he ignored it. It was not as if she had disappeared to meet her lover. Something had prompted her to leave the house unescorted and he was determined to tear the house apart to find out.

He heard Speck come up from behind. "Anything?" he asked, purposely keeping his voice even.

"I spoke to the two footmen we hired to look after Lady Tipton. Eddy said a boy delivered a note for her."

Finally, he fiercely thought. "She spoke to this boy?"

Speck's ugly face scowled into a frightful mask. "She never saw him. One of the footmen handed her the note."

"The bastard got to her somehow," Rayne growled. "And one of my men handed it to her on a silver salver."

"You can't be sure on that, milord. Maybe the note was harmless. One of her friends inviting her to visit?"

She would not disobey him. He thought he had

made it clear to her that their common enemy had gone beyond trifle mischief. "Check around. I want the boy if possible. If not, I want that note."

"Aye, sir."

Satisfied, Speck would carry out his orders, Rayne headed for the drawing room. Maybe she was out visiting friends. It would be like her to drop everything and rush to assist someone.

He punched through the doors, enjoying the sound of them rebounding off the walls. Pearl, Wynne, and Maddy jumped at the intrusion. All the women appeared as if they had been crying, as if Devona were truly lost to them. Their acceptance of his silent fears only fed his fury.

"We have no time for a social visit, Wynne."

His sister-in-law's cool glare was the perfect counterpart to his heated one and just as effective. "You know very well why I am here, Tipton. Pearl sent for me the moment she was certain Devona was missing." Wynne stood, her mask of composure faltering. She fought to keep her lips from trembling. "You said no one would be able to hurt her again. You swore she would be safe here."

Her words might as well have been jagged pieces of glass. They cut into him and he bled. He mentally cursed her because she was correct. She must have realized how cruel her comments seemed, or perhaps he was not up to the usual effort of concealing his emotions. Either way, the stiffness in her beautiful face lessened. The tears she had been holding back leaked down her cheeks. God, the last thing he needed was to witness Wynne giving in to despair!

"Yell at me, Wynne. Call me an arse, 'cause I deserve it. For God's sake and my own, don't cry."

Awkwardly, he pulled her into his arms and allowed her to cry into his favorite dark blue coat.

Brock burst into the room, unannounced. "Damn it, Tipton, is it true? Has Devona been kidnapped?" A look of horror came over him as he noticed Wynne crying. "Something has happened. What have you heard?"

"Nothing," Rayne replied. "Your sister thought she would make me feel better by ruining my favorite coat."

Wynne choked on a sob and she stepped out of his embrace. "You know I want to do my part." She managed a watery smile. She walked into her brother's waiting arms. "Has someone sent for Papa?"

Brock kissed the top of her head and gave her a comforting hug. "I have Gar searching the clubs. We'll find him."

"And Devona, too," she prompted.

Brock and Rayne's gazes locked. A nonverbal oath passed between them. "She'll be found."

"She wanted to show me how to prepare a weekly menu," Maddy's soft voice broke through the tension in the room. "I had been playing outside and was dirty. She told me to go change. If I hadn't maybe—"

"Oh, you poor dear," Pearl cooed, taking up his sister's hand and giving it a comforting squeeze. "Dirty or clean, the note was going to arrive. Your presence would not have changed the outcome."

Rayne understood her guilt. He stared down at his sister, realizing a few words from him would absolve her of the responsibility. He glanced at Brock and Wynne. Whatever their differences, the Bedegraynes brushed them aside in time of need. Family supported family. It was a lesson Devona had taught him. A lesson he had never learned from his own.

"Pearl is correct, Maddy. If the note is responsible for Devona's absence, then you could not have stopped her." He felt ashamed by the unabashed surprise and gratitude he saw in his sister's eyes. He tried to clear his throat, but the rising lump prevented it. "The woman's will is a reckoning force to battle when she is on one of her rescuing crusades."

"Is that what you think?" Wynne asked. "You think she ran off to help someone?"

Rayne rubbed then pressed the pressure at his brow. "I don't know. At the moment, it is easier to believe she is off on some reckless adventure than to contemplate that some bastard has her."

"Who could have her?" Maddy asked, not understanding what was going on around her.

"Someone who likes to play in the shadows. If he has managed to catch her, then the game should change. I expect a note shall arrive for me as well."

Brock stirred. "A ransom?"

Rayne shrugged. "Or to gloat. Either way, he's a dead man."

"I consider it an honor that you have sought out my assistance, Devona," Oz Lockwood confessed beside her as they traveled by coach. They had left London hours earlier, and were heading south to an undisclosed village. "I am rather interested to see your husband's response to your latest adventure. As Lady Tipton your behavior must bear up under the scrutiny of the *ton*."

Devona's teeth set at the mention of the resulting gossip and potential scandal of her actions. If the contents of the letter were true, then her jaunt into the country escorted by Oz would only be the spark to the comparable powder keg of deception.

Regardless, she did not feel comfortable enough to voice her fears to Oz. "Lord Tipton has been quite indulgent. Besides, the only people who know of this are you and I." She gave him an inquiring look. "I assume I can trust you to maintain your own counsel?"

"Naturally, my dear. Neither Tipton nor anyone else is aware of your intentions?" He sounded incredulous.

"No," she forlornly murmured, turning toward the window to watch the passing landscape. There had not been much planning involved. Too stunned by the news she had received, Devona had simply walked out the front door. She had walked the streets with no thought of direction or funds to pay her way. It was fortunate she had stumbled into Oz before her inattentiveness had put her under the wheels of a racing carriage.

"Can you talk about it?"

Devona did not pretend to misunderstand. "Not now. Soon." It was a lie. She had promised herself that she would not say the words aloud until she could do so without tears. A lifetime from this moment was too soon. Every time she thought of Tipton's treachery, her heart broke.

"Sitting around like a bunch of old women will not find my gel!" Sir Thomas blustered to the somber group.

"Papa, Brock, and Tipton have been searching the streets for hours," Wynne said, defending the men. "The night brings its own dangers."

Her father pounded his hand on the table. "And my gel is out there."

He only stated the obvious, but Wynne understood. The helplessness of the situation was wearing on everyone's nerves. Tipton sat in the corner, looking haunted. Both the men had searched all the possible places Devona might have gone, then they moved on to the improbable. Neither garnered even a clue to her whereabouts. It was as if she had vanished. "You should eat," she told Tipton. His plate had remained untouched for half an hour.

The grief she witnessed in his expression tore at her heart.

"I cannot. Thomas is correct. I should go back out there. Devona is probably frightened that I have not found her. She could be hurt." Misery was a lump in his throat, which he could not swallow. "I will only go insane if I remain."

Grim-faced, Brock shoveled his food into his mouth like an automaton. "Eat. You'll be of no use if you don't have the strength to help search for her." He glanced at his father. "There must be twenty men out there searching for a trace of her. If there is a clue to her whereabouts, we'll find it."

Wynne nodded encouragingly when Tipton took a bite of his stew and washed it down with some ale. "I took a tray to your guest. Dr. Sir Wallace Brogden has a forthright manner of speaking to a lady. I was torn between laughing and slapping his face."

"It won't work, Wynne."

She tried to look innocent. "What am I doing?"

Tipton, not looking as pale as he had minutes before, stared at her from over the rim of his tankard. "Distracting me," he succinctly replied. "Ev-

erything and everyone can burn brightly in hell
for all I care."

If anyone knew of hell, she figured Tipton
would be the one.

Devona and Oz secured rooms at the inn. It
was a sensible action. They needed a place to
sleep and a meal, Oz had reminded her. The
thought of food sickened her. This was just another delay which left her nerves pricking her
arms like a needle making loose stitches in a piece
of cotton.

"You picked at your meal, dear," Oz admon-
ished. "You aren't becoming ill. Shall we seek out
a doctor?"

Devona flinched at the suggestion. "I am just
tired, that is all. I think I shall retire."

Oz immediately arose, good manners and concern showing. "Have we reached our destination?
I'm all for intrigue, but don't you think it is time
to tell me why we have raced across the countryside? You have to admit that I have been a patient
and faithful conspirator."

She owed Oz an explanation, but she couldn't.
Not yet. Besides, she was regretting her hasty decision to bring him along; however there had
been little choice in the matter. He had rented
the equipage, paid for the rooms, and their meal.
Yes, she owed it to him to finish the rest of her
quest this evening alone.

"Tomorrow. After I have rested."

Oz abruptly nodded, not pleased by her answer
but not pressing her. "Of course. I will knock on
your door early and we will have this out.
Agreed?"

She kissed him on the cheek. It was an apology and a farewell. "I will see you in the morning."

No one at the stables questioned her request for one of their horses to be saddled. While waiting for the task to be accomplished, Devona rummaged through the items in the hidden compartment under the seat of their hired coach. The wooden box she removed contained a pistol. Noting that the box also contained the implements to prime it, she closed the box and tucked it under her arm. She had no idea what to expect upon her arrival. Bringing the weapon seemed prudent.

The directions and markers committed to memory, she rode off into the night with the full moon to light her path. Amazingly, the night journey did not frighten her. Numbness had overcome her and it was a blessing. Was this how her husband lived? Did he go through life, seeing the world through unemotional clarity, which permitted his ruthlessness? Poor Tipton. Empathy and forgiveness were out of reach when one felt nothing at all.

The silhouette of the house rose up before her. She did not know the history of the abandoned great house. The owners could have perished without an heir to birth another generation of descendants. Or perhaps they had been penniless and could not repair the section of the house consumed in the long-forgotten fire. Its reasons for vacancy mattered little to Devona. Still, clutching her boxed weapon, she halted the horse and slid off the saddle. She tied the reins to a nearby branch. The horse seemed content to remain to nibble at the leaves.

It was time. Devona set the box on the ground and kneeled before it. Flipping the latch, she opened the lid. She lifted the pistol, frowning at the weight. This was made for a gentleman's hand, most likely Oz's, although he had never mentioned the weapon. He probably had not wanted to frighten her. The metal gleamed in the moonlight as she examined it. Oz had underestimated her once again. She understood the necessity of protection. Violence provoked violence. It did not negate it. The question was could she aim the pistol and pull the trigger?

The surrounding insects' lulling buzz concealed the awkward sounds she made while she prepared the weapon. Her unpracticed efforts took longer than they should have, but when she stood, the pistol was primed to fire.

Instead of walking through the front door, she made her way around to the back. The pistol level, she used the walls of the house to keep her from stumbling. She discarded the notion of entering by way of the burnt wing. The floors could be crumbling or nonexistent. It was too risky to guess under the moonlight. She continued, following the back wall until she came to a pair of doors. They were locked. Devona wiped a pane of glass with her hand and peered. The reflective moon on the glass prevented her from seeing beyond the blackness.

There was no light or signs of life within the dead house. Perhaps this had been a cruel prank or a clever ruse to lure her away from Tipton? Doubt bathed over her like moonlight, leaving her cold in its wake. She trembled despite the relative warmth of the evening. *Brace yourself, Devona. You have come this far. If it is a ruse, then touring an abandoned house is nothing.*

She went back to the gutted wing and began searching the grounds. Devona was not certain what she would find, but if it was thin and long it would suit her needs. It took her ten minutes to find the rusted piece of metal. Holding the L-shaped piece up against the moonlight, she judged it thin enough for her purpose. Moving back to the locked doors, she shoved the metal into the small crack between the two doors. It would have been easier to break the glass. Nevertheless, until she could prove her midnight jaunt was a hoax, she intended to be careful.

The rusty metal resisted, then slid into the crack. Devona changed her grip, and then pulled the metal upward. As she had hoped, her makeshift tool caught and popped the inner latch. Her lips pulled into a humorless smile. What would Papa think of his daughter turning into a housebreaker? What of her husband?

Oh, Rayne. I know you desired me. I felt worshiped every time you pulled me into your arms. You had learned to take what you wanted at such a young age. Was there any limit to the lengths you would go to to maneuver me into your bed?

She abruptly closed her mind to the answer, keeping the anguish at bay. The moonlight only lit her entry a few feet into the room. She silently moved through the room. Thankfully, it was tidy so if she avoided the darker shadows of covered furniture, she was less likely to trip. Along the wall to the left was a long table. Devona slid her hand across the dusty surface until she felt the recognizable shape of a candlestick. Placing the pistol on the table, she pulled out the wide shallow drawer, looking for a tinderbox.

Minutes later she had the candle lit and the pistol back in her other hand. There was an open door to her left. The candle allowed her to move more confidently as she searched room after room.

Forty minutes later, her breath was uneven and her gown clung to her from perspiration. She made her way down to the first landing. Relief was making her feel giddy. Empty. No one was in the house. Devona sat on the last step, depositing the candleholder and the pistol on the upper step. Wisps of hair had loosened from her coiled braid. She was dirty, tired, and her nerves had been rattled. Yet she was alone. She covered her face with her hands, resisting the urge to cry out her relief. To give her hands something to do, she smoothed back the loose strands of hair and tucked them behind her ears.

The sudden sound below froze her actions. Devona held her breath and listened. Silence. A rat. Or maybe an old tomcat prowling for his meal. *Thump-thump*. Hands trembling, she picked up the candle and fumbled to get the proper grip on the pistol. She had thought she had checked the entire house. She must have missed a storage room or root cellar or at the very least an accessible crawl space. Common sense told her to leave, but she refused to give in to her fears. Besides, it was just a cat, she was certain of it.

Retracing her steps to the back of the house, she rechecked the rooms. If there was an entry to a cellar, she would find it. She started in the kitchen. Nothing. She moved on to the pantry, then on to the dining room servery, which was a connecting hall more than anything else. The next door was the dining room. No, it would not be there.

Perplexed, Devona pivoted to recheck the pantry. One foot stepped into a bucket and it was

enough to unbalance her. She pitched forward,
reaching out to break her fall. The white cloth
cover she grabbed puffed then floated down to
cover her after her cheek struck the floor.
Stunned, she sat up. The candle, still lit, was burning an impressive brown hole into the cloth. Spit
and flour! She picked up the candle and immediately slapped at the glowing edges with her
hands. The last thing she needed was to set the
house on fire.

A flash of light caught her peripheral vision and
she shrieked at the sudden movement. The frozen
figure stared back at her. She barely recognized
her disheveled image. A mirror. The cloth she had
pulled down on herself had covered a mirror. Her
mind had accepted it, but her pounding heart
would not ease. Pulling herself up, she set the candle on a wooden press so she could cover the mirror. Devona winced when she put her full weight
on her ankle. It hurt, but it would not prevent her
from getting out of this house. Picking up the covering, Devona limped to the mirror. She pulled
the heavy frame toward her to secure the cloth in
place. Her hand felt air instead of the wall she had
expected. The mirror concealed a doorway.

It was impossible for her to lift a mirror that
size. Maybe she could drag it. With the help of
the covering and sheer willpower, she rotated the
mirror one hundred and eighty degrees until it
rested against the wall. Swiping at the cobwebs
sticking to her face, Devona reached for the candle. The light revealed another hall with two
doors on each side. She tried the first door, expecting it to be locked. Surprisingly, it twisted easily in her hand. She pushed the door. It creaked
as it swung wide.

Holding the candle high, she stepped into the

room. Her nose twitched at the terrible stale odor. It was some sort of storage room, she decided, walking around a large covered cupboard.

"Help."

The weak plea raised the hairs on the back of her neck. Frantically, she realized she had left the pistol on the floor in the servery. Fool! The candle lit an aura around her, making her an easy target for her new companion. He, however, was cloaked in the dark shadows of the room.

"Who's there?" she sharply inquired.

"Here," the disembodied voice beckoned.

Stepping further into the room, the light threw menacing shadows on the walls. There was rubbish everywhere, and the fetid smell was getting stronger. Putting her hand to her nose, she moved closer to the man. He was sitting on a bed, his head bowed. His greasy light brown hair gleamed in the light. She noticed his wrists were manacled, and a heavy chain connected his arms and one cuffed leg to the bed. The man was chained like an animal and from the looks of him had been left to starve.

"Who did this to you?" she demanded.

Filthy and weak, the prisoner lifted his head and flinched at her weak candlelight.

Regardless, Devona would recognize the man in any condition. She staggered backward. "Oh no. It cannot be true. Doran."

"Mama," Maddy exclaimed, rising from her seat. "What are you doing here?"

The dowager turned her cheek, anticipating a proper greeting from her daughter. Maddy kissed her then took her hand, leading her to the table.

"Did you think I would abandon you, child?"

Jocelyn asked, inspecting the morning room's occupants seated at the table. Tightness thinned her lips, showing disapproval at what she beheld.

Rayne did not rise from his seat. He resumed chewing as if he could actually swallow down a meal and enjoy it. Whatever had lured Jocelyn from her precious Foxenclover had nothing to do with him. He glanced at Maddy, who made a fuss about finding a place for their mother. Maybe he should send the girl home and be done with them. The sun had broken over the horizon and was now burning high in the sky. There had been no word from Devona. Everyone swore she had walked out of the town house on her own. He was left wondering if the choice not to return was hers or another's. "Maternal visits are unusual, Jocelyn. What brings you to town?"

The Bedegraynes looked at one another in mute communication, trying to understand the animosity in his tone. If his wife had not enlightened them regarding the estranged relationship between mother and son, then Rayne would not. He was not the sort to reach for a handkerchief and cry out the unfairness of his life to his in-laws.

Jocelyn took the vacant seat offered by the footman. Tension spread and coiled around them as mother and son confronted one another. Maddy carried a plate filled with items she had chosen from the sideboard. From the quick, wary glances she was darting in his direction, Rayne could see his manner had dimmed his sister's pleasure at their mother's unexpected visit. He gripped the knife he had in his hand so vigorously he could feel the detailing cut into his palm.

"I agreed to sending Madeleina to London. I did not say that I would not visit her from time to time." The dowager pierced Wynne with a curious stare. "Is this one your mistress, Tipton?" she inquired politely, causing a stir of exclamations at the table. "She has a look about her that is appealing to a man's weakness. How ever did you convince your wife to set a place for her at your table?"

Rayne doubted his mother believed the nonsense she was spouting, although she had rallied the Bedegraynes to defend Wynne's honor.

Sir Thomas glared at Jocelyn as if she had sprouted three heads. "Are you mad, woman? My daughter would tolerate no mistress hidden or not, even if Tipton was foolish enough to dishonor her in such a manner."

"Thank you, I think," Tipton murmured.

Brock's scowl mirrored his father's. "Madam, you owe my sister an apology."

"I suggest you make your apologies, Mother. Brock likes to issue challenges when he is angry."

Jocelyn's eyes narrowed. "What sort of people are you forcing my daughter to associate with?"

Rayne parted his lips to tell her, but Maddy spoke before he could speak.

"Mama, you are insulting Devona's family." She made the quick introductions to Sir Thomas, Brock, and Wynne. Despite the men's anger, politeness overruled and the dowager received stiff acknowledgements from them.

Jocelyn nodded in Wynne's direction. "It appears I misunderstood the situation, Miss Bedegrayne."

If Wynne had expected a sincere apology, she hid her disappointment well. A night of restless sleep did not prevent her from seeing the amusing side of the situation. "I have never been accused of being a man's mistress before," she mused, her delicate brow lifting at the notion. "I am too tired to decide if I should be truly offended or not." She shrugged off her father's astonished expression.

Maddy clearly looked relieved that the Bedegraynes were prepared to ignore their mother's insulting comments. "Here, Mama, I prepared the plate myself."

Something softened in the older woman's features. "Thank you, Madeleina." Maddy laid the plate in front of her, then moved back and settled in her own chair.

"Were you worried, Mother, that I had sold off your daughter to slavers?" Rayne taunted. Her very presence seemed to provoke him.

Jocelyn remained calm, refusing to take the bait. "Not precisely." She dabbed an invisible speck of food with her napkin. "I am surprised your wife is not in attendance." A perceptive woman, she noted Rayne was not the only one who tensed up. "Good heavens, pray do not tell me that you have already managed to run off that fiery creature. I am astounded. Truly, if there was a woman who deserved Le Cadavre Raffiné, I would have wagered Devona Bedegrayne was that woman."

Rayne was used to her appalling lack of decency. The Bedegraynes, however, were not. They stared at the dowager in varying degrees of shock. To his amazement, it was Maddy who rose to his defense.

"Mama, I expected better of you. Devona and my brother have been very generous by inviting me to their home." The fact that she had been bullied and used as a pawn to spite their mother was carefully overlooked. " 'Being judged as a gracious lady cannot be taught in lessons, it is bred into her and divined by her actions'," she quoted from some reference known only to her and to their mother. Jocelyn's cheeks heightened in color.

Wynne sipped her coffee. "A lovely saying, my dear."

Brock muttered something unrepeatable under his breath.

Rayne stared at his mother. "Why do you assume she has run off?"

Jocelyn's attention switched from Maddy to him. "I do not know. Has she?"

He began buttering the slice of bread on his plate. "My wife could just as easily be upstairs resting. Or maybe she just walked out of the room at the mention of your arrival."

The direction of the conversation was not in her control and it was obvious that his mother did not like it. Her gaze shifted and assessed the Bedegraynes' interest. "If your wife was present, a place for her would have been prepared at the table."

"So she is asleep."

"Why would she remain in bed with her family visiting?"

"She could be ill."

"Oh." She absorbed that for a few minutes. For the first time in his life she actually appeared to be ashamed of her behavior. "Will she improve? You have not called her family to her deathbed?"

He had lowered himself to playing one of her endless games. Disgusted, Rayne shredded his bread and tossed the remains on his plate. "No, madam, you were correct. My wife is not here."

Becoming more confused, especially when Maddy reached over and held her hand, Jocelyn asked the question that was consuming all of them. "Where is she?"

The Bedegraynes still feared she was in the hands of some villain. Rayne was beginning to have his doubts. If she had been kidnapped, would there not have been a ransom note by now? Maybe they had gotten it wrong. The note Devona had received must have contained information about him. Something so vile that it made her flee his protection.

"Tipton, where is your wife?" his mother persisted.

He shook his head and stood up. Whether the information in the note had revealed the truth or lies, his wife had not trusted him. She ran away instead of confronting him and demanding his side of it.

The thought that she might even fear him staggered him. Had he not shown her from the beginning that she could trust him with her worries and problems? Exhaustion rolled beneath the surface of his enforced calm like the waves of a tropical storm. The battering was relentless, and at times he thought he might die from it.

This was grief. He felt as if someone had buried him alive again. His heart was racing; the air felt too hot and thin, and no one could hear his screams. If he could not find Devona, he feared he would feel like this for the rest of his life.

"Tipton, are you still with us?" Sir Thomas asked, his voice more subdued than usual as if he, too, sensed that Rayne had reached the brink of his emotional fortitude.

"We have to find her, Thomas," Rayne replied. Before the moist earth and airless darkness claimed him again.

EIGHTEEN

Devona sat up, an unnamed urgency startling her awake. Blinking, she looked around the room, horrified she had slipped into a restless slumber. Her candle had burned down to a puddle of wax hours ago, if the filtered light from the hall was any indication. It was morning and she was no closer to freeing Doran.

Some rescue, she thought depressingly. The man was still chained to the bed. She had searched for the key, but his jailer must have kept it. Doran could not help her. He burned and shivered with fever. She had not heard him speak rationally since he had called out to her.

Her first thought had been to ride back to the inn and awaken Oz, but she had quickly discarded the idea. She had been too shaken by her discovery. The idea of riding out into the night frightened her. Every tree and shrub that cast a shadow on the landscape could possibly hide a villain. It had been humiliating to admit her cowardice. She had to consider Doran as well. In his condition he could barely lift his head let alone fight off his captor. So Devona had remained. She had uncovered in her search for the key a broken table leg. Hugging it to her chest, she had positioned herself near the entry. If anyone walked through the door, she had intended to club him. It had sounded like an admirable plan until the candle had burned out and Doran's rhythmic raspy breathing had lulled her to sleep.

Doran moaned then mumbled something. She weaved around the pieces of splintered furniture and boxes. Kneeling at his side, she touched his head with her palm.

"Cold," he muttered, plainly disagreeable.

"You have a fever, Doran. Do you know where you are?"

His eyes were still closed and the words that passed his chapped, swollen lips reminded her of his delirious state.

"Do not fret, Doran. I will think of a way to get you out of here. You know me. I have a talent for dreaming up plans." Her friend did not answer, nor had she expected him to.

"Finding that key or something to turn the lock will be easier now that it is morning, do you not think?" Her stomach rumbled. Devona patted it, thinking of the supper she had barely sampled. "I suppose it would be too much to hope that there is a lovely breakfast laid out on the sideboard." She sighed, rechecking the area beyond his reach for the key. "We might have to do without food, Doran, but you could use something to drink. Cook would have insisted on making you some beef marrow broth."

A low moan vibrated his chest.

Interpreting it as a response, she made a sympathetic sound. "How thoughtless of me. I am certain even tasteless broth would be welcome. Let's start with water, and we will work up from there as you improve." Devona threaded her way back to the door. "I have to leave you for a while. I will search the grounds for something to free you. If I fail, then I will be forced to ride back to the inn for assistance."

The pump in the kitchen was not cooperating, so she drew the water directly from the well. The bucket she found nearby was most likely used for that same purpose. While lugging the water back to Doran, Devona scanned the grounds, looking for anything that could be used to break open the locks. She held a hand to her eyes and gazed at the horizon through her fingers. Time was running out for them. Whoever had placed Doran here might come back to check on him.

She resumed her walk to the house. Even now she carefully chose neutral words so she did not have to admit the truth aloud. If this part of the letter turned out to be correct, then she had to accept that the other damning statement was also true. Rayne was responsible for Doran's starving exile. Her heart lurched as she hurried through the house. She could not contemplate the personal betrayal. For now, she had to figure out how to get Doran out of this house.

It took Devona time to figure out that if she dipped a cloth and wiped Doran's lips and tongue, even in his unconscious state he would swallow some water. She patiently kept dribbling water onto his tongue until he choked. Using the cool cloth to wipe his face, she said, "I am so sorry, Doran." *If I hadn't sought him out, you would still be in Newgate and I . . . I would not be in love with him.*

The admission had her jumping up from her kneeling position. "I have to go find help, Doran." For all she knew, Tipton could have guessed her destination and was riding to her this moment. "Oz is at the inn. We will return with the tools to free you." Feeling that her chest was too tight, she stopped, forcing her lungs to fill with air. "Soon. I will be back for you soon."

Her poor neglected horse was still waiting for her by the tree. She climbed up onto the saddle. "It appears I must apologize to you as well, horse. Water, oats, and a good brushing for you, I swear, as soon as we reach the inn."

Two miles down the road she encountered Oz Lockwood on horseback.

"Devona, you have taken more years off my life than I can afford," Oz chastised. "Running off in the middle of the night. I did not know what to think, especially when your husband—"

Her complexion faded to chalk. "Rayne? Rayne was at the inn?"

"Yes, of course. Did you think he would not find you, you reckless girl? Your brother Brock accompanied him. We have been searching the countryside for a sign of your whereabouts." He waved his hand at the dust their horses had stirred. "He went north, Brock west, and I, south. You may be fortunate that I was the one to find you. Tipton was mumbling something about your lovely backside and his hand."

"Dear God!" She gasped, wishing she could indulge in a fit of vapors. "When, when did you see him, Oz?"

Oz's forehead wrinkled in confusion. "Tipton? An hour if I had to guess. Devona, dear, you look terrified. I fear it is a male tendency to voice our concerns in terms of violence. However, once Tipton sees that you are unharmed and properly repentant, he will forget all about his threats."

An hour. Was Rayne really pretending to search the countryside north, or was he heading this way? "Hurry, Oz, there isn't much time!" Devona spurred her horse back in the direction of the

abandoned house. Oz shouted his objection behind her, but she did not slow her horse for an
explanation. Seeing Doran chained to the soiled
bed would be enough.

Fifteen minutes later, they reined up in front
of the house. Oz was off his horse first. "Devona,
if you think hiding from Tipton will not put him
in a fine rage, then you must be suffering a mental upset. Is this where you went last night?"

She allowed him to help her from her horse.
"I have something to show you." Ignoring the lingering pain in her ankle, she all but ran around
to the back of the house.

"Devona! I did not plan on a leg race this
morning."

She could hear him following her, so she continued moving through the house. Her heart
pounded out its beat with each rapid step. They
were going to get Doran out of this house before
Rayne discovered them. Oz's surprised intake of
breath took some of the tension from her shoulders.

"My word, is that Claeg? Th-the man died in
prison. I attended his funeral." The room was
windowless, so Oz pushed the door open wide,
allowing as much filtered light as possible to fill
the room. "What has he told you?"

Wretchedness rose in her. "Nothing. He is half
starved and delusional from fever. I do not believe
he even knew I was here to help him."

"I do not understand any of this." His eyes
bulged when Doran groaned. "How many dead
men do we have walking among us?"

Devona could see Oz was frightened to see
Doran alive. He appeared as if the wrong word
or sound would send him scurrying to his horse.
She needed his help, and that meant telling him

the truth. Never taking her gaze off his face, she explained how Doran was able to escape Newgate.

Oz nodded slowly, taking time to sort through her confession. "Tipton's plan was clever. I cannot fathom what went awry. No offense, Devona, I know Claeg is a treasured friend, but the man is a harmless simpleton. Who would do this to him?"

Her tears burned her cheeks like molten glass. She found voicing the rest of her confession more difficult than she imagined.

"What is it?"

Her lips parted, but the anguish that escaped was soundless. She swallowed and tried again. "It was Rayne. He's the one." Speaking it was a thousand times worse than thinking it. She doubled over, keening her grief.

In a nervous gesture, Oz removed his hat, blotted the sweat from his forehead and temples, and settled the hat back in place. "Uh, Devona." He gave her an awkward pat on the shoulder. "This is a grievous charge. Perhaps you are mistaken? Claeg had engaged an unsavory lot. One of them could have—"

Bilious rage reared, causing her to lash out her frustration. "Do you think I want to believe such a thing? I stood before God and took him as my husband and my lover." Her gaze shifted to Doran. There were bruising and oozing sores where the metal cruelly cut his flesh. "Rayne told me Doran was on a ship. He should be hundreds of miles from England, and yet here he is. What conclusion do you reach?" Excess energy had her standing, then searching the contents of the room again.

"What you are suggesting is outrageous, Devona, even for Tipton. What would the man have to gain by doing this?"

She overturned a box and began sorting through the contents. "At the time, he was trying to convince me to marry him. It is only a guess, but maybe Doran had tried to warn me about something." She pushed over a larger wooden crate.

"What the devil are you doing?"

"The key. There must be a key hidden somewhere, though I have yet to find it. If not that, then maybe something to break the lock." Devona met his gaze. "There isn't much time for us. If Rayne is guilty, then he could be riding onto the front lawn as we speak."

The warning goaded Oz to lift the white dust cover protecting the chair next to him. "I say, my dear, do all your schemes make ducks and drakes with your life? If you value our friendship, next time skip me as a player."

It was Oz who found the key. While pushing a small table out of the way, he had disturbed the wainscoting. Further examination revealed that part of the design concealed a hidden compartment. Inside there were several bags of gold and the elusive key.

He handed her the key. "Why don't you unfetter Claeg while I check the grounds. It is a pity I did not come by coach, for I fear our unconscious companion will be difficult to carry."

Taking the discarded table leg for protection, Oz left the room.

Devona knelt beside Doran. "We have the key. Soon we will have you out of here and into a warm bed with a motherly type to fret over you." She pushed the key into the cuff lock on his leg and twisted. The metal popped open, revealing the damaged flesh beneath. She must have cried out because Doran's eyelids lifted. Bewildered, he focused on her.

"Doran. Do you know who I am?" she begged. Noticing that his tongue moved in his mouth, seeking moisture to relieve the dryness, she cupped her hands into the bucket of water. Ignoring that most of it was dripping through her fingers like a sieve, she brought her hands to his lips. He murmured for more, so she repeated the process twice.

"Who am I?"

Doran licked the drops of water from his lips. "Dev," he whispered, his voice husky from abuse. "How?"

"A very long tale." She motioned to the manacles. "Can you lean forward a bit so they catch the light? I am having trouble with the lock." Devona bowed her head and concentrated on her task.

"T-Tipton?" It took so much strength to get the word out that he collapsed back into the shadows.

How Doran must hate him, and her, too, but she did not permit the sad thought to stop her from twisting the key. One wrist was free. She focused on the other. "I figured it all out. I know what Rayne did to you and am more than sorry for it. We will get you out of here," she assured him, smiling at the distinctive *snick* of the other lock being disengaged. "I do not plan to drag you out on my own. We have a friend to help."

"Get y-your—"

She heard a noise at the door. She turned to see Oz, the table leg resting on his shoulder. "Oz, our patient is awake and making sense."

"Is he now?" Oz said, smiling.

Devona turned back to Doran. "Riding astride might seem beyond your capabilities. However—"

"Tipton!" Doran vehemently forced the word past his swollen lips.

Devona frowned, worrying he was still delusional. She reached out to touch his cheek for fever. Her hand never connected.

The table leg Oz was carrying was made from walnut. It was a fine, sturdy piece. He arced the table limb high, and then swung it at her head. He did not flinch at the sickening thud of connecting wood, flesh, and bone. Her limp body sprawled forward over a mewling Doran Claeg.

Devona awoke with a metallic taste in her mouth. She was lying on her stomach; her face resting on the most disgusting mattress she had ever encountered. That would account for the dreadful taste in her mouth, she grimly mused.

Lifting her head magnified the hammering pain at the back of her head to intolerable proportions. Resting her cheek on the mattress she took deep breaths to fight off the rising nausea. It did not work. She vomited up a clear light green liquid. Only when her violent spasms dwindled to dry heaves did she lay her head back on the ruined mattress.

"I thought he had killed you."

She slowly tilted her head up. So consumed by the pain and sickness, she did not recognize the man on the bed with her. Embarrassed that she had an audience for her sickness, she was appalled to see that she had thrown up not on the bedding but on the man's legs.

"Forgive me. I could not move when the sickness came."

The man appeared equally ill. He took his time to speak. "Your hands. Bound. Behind you."

Listening to his halting words triggered her sluggish memory. "Doran?"

"Yes." His breathing had a slight rattle to it. "So sorry, Dev."

Tears stung her eyes. If the effort wouldn't have aggravated her head, she would have cried. "Things are a little foggy for me, Doran. What happened after the roof dropped on my head?" Humor surfaced in the oddest places, but in this instance she did not smile. It *did* feel as though the house had come down on top of her.

"He hit you."

She assimilated the statement. She sorted through the "he's" in her life who would have dared. Not Papa, she thought; he had not spanked her since she was a small child. Brock and Nyle were too busy living their own lives to bother her. Rayne? Ridiculous, he—

"Rayne struck me down," she whispered, the idea taking root to fill in the holes in her memory. "He caught up with us. He tried to stop me from freeing you." The horror of the memory made her feel sick all over again. "Oz?"

"Oz. Hit you." Doran's expression hardened, giving her the impression of white marble. "You. Expendable now."

"How indelicately put, Claeg," Oz Lockwood pronounced from the doorway. "Every lady enjoys the belief that we men would perish without their company. Even our independent, reckless Devona." He made a small, disappointed noise when he noticed the mess she had made. "Not such the lady, it seems. I thought at first that I had killed you outright."

She gritted her teeth and resisted the urge to

scream when he gripped her shoulders and
pulled her into a sitting position. The ceiling
slammed into the wooden floor as she mentally
tried to find her balance. Her breath came out
as quick pants while she fought back another bout
of nausea.

"Well done, my lady. I have always admired
your fortitude."

The dizziness she felt added to the unreality of
the situation. "Oz, where is my husband?"

"I suppose his whereabouts depend on what
you did when you received my note." He sat on
a crate. "I was gambling on you not confronting
him. I had hoped the shock of learning about the
black-hearted deeds of your husband would send
you running off to save your childhood friend.
Did you leave him a note damning him for his
treachery or did you simply use my note to explain your sudden disappearance?"

Rayne was innocent. It also meant he was not
coming to save her. He was probably half crazed
wondering what had happened to her. Devona
closed her eyes, feeling the dual sharp prongs of
shame and guilt. Empty-headed fool! He had
warned her that someone was trying to tear them
apart. She had refused to listen. Instead she had
walked into a carefully laid trap. "I cannot recall."

Oz stretched forward and calmly shoved her
head so that it rebounded off the wall. Shooting
stars streaked across her vision. Devona felt the
bile rise in her throat.

"The truth, my dear."

"I cannot. The blow to my head has confused
me." She winced when he reached for her again.
"I will be fortunate to know my own name if you
keep bashing my brains into pudding!"

The familiar smile he fixed on his face chilled

her to the bone. She recognized evil when it was grinning at her, promising the pain had just begun.

She had to keep him talking. It would give her time to figure her way out of this mess. "I do not understand any of this. I thought we were friends. Was it because I married Rayne?"

Oz laughed. "Such conceit," he mocked. "Your brains must be muddled. I was the one who pushed you toward Tipton."

The swelling at the back of her head throbbed like the cadence of a drummer. Maybe she did have some of the facts wrong. However, she still had enough wits to not give him any information that could hurt Rayne. "Because of Doran?" she guessed.

"You are trying my patience, Devona."

She glanced at Doran. He was conscious but in no better condition to help her. "Rayne said that Doran had left England. How did you learn that his death had been faked?"

Oz shook a finger at her. "I was surprised Tipton bothered rescuing your precious Doran. I would have left his worthless hide to rot behind the 'Gate. But then I saw the genius of Tipton's actions. He gets rid of a possible competitor for your affections and becomes the reluctant hero of your heart. Brilliant."

"There was more to it," she argued.

"I almost permitted Claeg his exile," Oz admitted, "but he was a thread that had to be snipped."

Doran sneered. "Gullible."

Oz cocked his head in the other man's direction. "I intercepted him on his way to the ship. He believed me when I revealed that I was a participant in his great demise. I told him that you wanted to see him once more before he lost himself in the world. I played up the part of how you planned to sacrifice yourself to the marriage bed just to spare your beloved friend's life." He raised his hands and bowed his head. "If I did not have more lucrative plans, I would have considered the stage."

Devona shivered. "This elaborate ruse must have taken months to plan."

"Years. It was one of the reasons I ingratiated myself into your close circle of friends. At first glance I realized your looks and temperament would work to my advantage."

Because her hands were bound, Devona manipulated her shoulder upward to rub the tickling sensation behind her right ear. She glanced down to see bloody smudges on the shoulder of her gown. "Were you responsible for the runaway chaise at Vauxhall?"

"The driver was more concerned about his next cup of gin than securing his animals. An unfortunately timed discharge of powder created a realistic accident."

"The poisoning? The woman who jabbed me with her pin?"

Oz clasped his hands together and touched his lips. "A stroke of luck. I handed you tainted punch."

"Bastard," Doran growled. He was ignored.

"My intention was to drug you. Tipton in his arrogance thought you were beyond my reach. He needed to be taught a lesson and your abduction would have fit nicely into my plans. There was a man waiting to carry your unconscious form from the garden." He sighed. "Regrettably, I misjudged the dosage since you refused to drink the entire cup. You were hallucinating and conscious far too long. Tipton and the others reached you before my man."

She chewed on her lower lip. "Rayne feared I was the villain's target," she mused. "He was wrong. I am just another pawn."

Oz beamed approvingly. "Excellent. I would have been distressed if I had damaged that quick little mind of yours. Toying with Claeg has been amusing, but our boy could never match your wit. I never understood why you supported our gloomy poet."

"To do that you would have to understand the meanings of friendship, loyalty, and honor." Devona stiffened, prepared for his retaliation. He threw her off balance by laughing.

"My dear, appealing to my civilized nature by issuing a backhanded insult will not work. I chose my goals early in life and the instruments just as carefully." He stroked her cheek. "You have blood coming from your ear. Is the pain in your head intolerable?"

"Why?" she asked, turning her head so that she did not have to feel his fingers on her face. "You enjoy knowing that you've hurt me?"

"On the contrary, I abhor violence, particularly when it involves a woman. I just want to make certain you can keep up with me."

Devona focused on appearing to be what Oz expected her to be—a frightened, injured woman. "The rope is cutting into my wrist and my fingers are numb. Untying me would make little difference. I doubt I could walk three feet without falling. Running would be impossible. Please, Oz. A little mercy would not shift the power in my favor."

He stood and hope surged through her. Expecting him to produce a knife when he reached behind to remove something from the waist of his breeches, her eyes widened at the sight of her pistol. She had forgotten she had lost it when she tripped in the dark.

"This was never meant for a lady's delicate hand." He checked to see if it was primed. He made an approving noise. "I assume Brock taught you how to handle a weapon. I wonder if you could have fired it."

"Want to put me to the test?" she dared, giving him a glare that assured him she would like to aim the sight directly at his heart.

"I regretfully decline your offer, my lady, just as I must deny your request for untying your bindings." His apologetic demeanor was more appropriate for a ballroom than a dirty storage room where he played his life and death games. "This is my show. My rules. Rule number one."

Oz aimed the pistol at Doran. "Snip." He pulled the trigger. The discharge was deafening in the small room, blocking out Devona's scream.

Snip all threads.

The ball struck Doran's throat. There seemed to be an explosion of gore and spraying blood as the lead ball separated the fragile column of bones in his neck. Her face and gown were washed in a sea of red. Through tears and blood she watched Doran convulse, the gurgle of liquid bubbling from the gaping wound in his throat quieted to an eerie hiss. His eyes had locked on hers in those final horrifying moments, becoming fixed. She did not recognize the wild, high-pitched sound that filled the silence as her own tortured screams.

She had never seen anyone die. Even when her mother took that fatal blow to the temple while chasing a three-year-old Devona, her family had sheltered her the best they could. She certainly had never imagined witnessing the murder of one of her best friends.

"Madman! Fiend!" she shrieked.

Oz's eyes seemed to glow, piercing the lingering smoke that floated around them. "That instrument served its purpose. I have given him dignity in death that he never could attain in life. He was dead even before I pulled the trigger."

Devona struggled against her bindings. He was going to kill her. *Snip.* As soon as her value expired, he would aim the pistol at her heart and the organ would explode into chunks of useless matter only a cook could appreciate. The bones in her wrists and shoulders twisted and popped under the strain, but the rope held.

"Do you want to know rule two?" He stepped closer.

Inwardly she cringed at his approach, however, her expression was tranquil when she asked, "Why bother adding rules when rule one is so tidy?" Oz reached for her skirts. She yelped and pressed her back to the wall. "No," she yelled, kicking at him to prevent him from grabbing her legs. She did not think she could bear it if he violated her.

"Hold still."

Mindlessly, she fought him. She managed to land a stunning blow to his stomach. Instead of holding him off, it impelled him to capture her. He seized her ankles and dragged her across the mattress. With both feet caught, she kicked his arms and his chest. He grunted and staggered back a step. It was enough to make him release her right leg. She arched her back and drove it upward. Her heel connected with the underside of his chin. Oz's head snapped back, and his arms flew up to steady his gait. It did not help.

He collapsed like a fan. Devona rolled to her side, then pulled up to a sitting position. Oz was on his back. His eyes were closed.

Fighting off the increasing dizziness and nausea, she stood. Her swaying stride would not win any races, but she managed to get to the door. With her hands bound, escaping by horse was impossible. She would never be able to outrun him. The truth did not dishearten her. There was another option. She might be able to elude him by hiding in the woods. If she was patient, she could return to the house and find something to cut through the rope. He would have taken the horses by then, but it did not matter. She would crawl on all fours back to Rayne if that was her only choice.

Rough hands mercilessly speared her hair, locked, then jerked her backward. The pain dimmed her vision to the size of a nail's head. His hand still gripping the back of her head, he rolled her into him so that her body pressed against his.

"Lady of fire," he murmured. "I should have spared you and kept you for my own."

Revulsion rose in her throat, but she swallowed it. Her very survival was at stake. "It is not t— too late, Oz." She cried out in pain when he tightened his grip.

"I know you love that resurrected outcast, Devona. Save your breathy lies."

In their brief struggle, she had managed to hurt him. A trickle of blood oozed at the corner of his mouth. She had also disturbed his well-crafted façade of a gentleman. His clothes were rumpled. There was a tear at the seam of his shirt and his cravat was in an unidentifiable tangle. Blood and dirt marred his usual immaculate appearance. Devona felt a fierce rush of satisfaction at the ruddy swelling under his chin where her foot had struck him. It wasn't enough. Nothing but death could balance the misdeeds he had committed against her friends and family.

"I have yet to tell you about my rule two." He pulled her close so that another breath closer their lips would touch.

Tears leaked passed her temples and into her hair. "I hate you."

He continued as if he had not heard her violent declaration. "Rule two: when choosing the proper bait, do not stint on the presentation. There must be beauty, succulence to tease the palate, and value beyond price. Are you priceless to Tipton?"

Rayne had never failed her. She understood that now. They shared a similar type of loyalty and reckless spirit that would force him to find her, even if the cost was his life. Oz would not have him, she silently vowed. She had to find a way to stop him before he staked her out as bait.

Devona's refusal to answer had angered Oz. He punished her by pressing a bruising kiss to her lips. The pressure he exerted on the swelling at the back of her head to keep her from turning away was too much for her. The peripheral blackness closed to a point of light then winked out completely. She embraced the dreamless darkness.

NINETEEN

Proof that his wife had not run from him willingly arrived at the door in the afternoon. Four large, tired, unrelenting men interrogated the boy who had been paid to deliver the note. Disgusted that the sobbing boy could not bring him closer to solving Devona's disappearance, Rayne had returned him to the streets. It had not been loyalty that had kept the child quiet. He simply did not know who had requested his services.

When he thought on it, Rayne felt as though Devona had been lost to him for weeks. In truth, it was barely a day. If he had not known someone had been stalking her all along, it would have been simple to believe that she was away on a country visit.

Brock, Sir Thomas, Wynne, and now Brodgen sat brooding in Rayne's study. Jocelyn, frightened by the situation, begged him to allow Maddy to return immediately with her to Foxenclover. He did not protest. They were a distraction. It was also safer. There was no point providing the kidnapper with another viable target.

"Read it aloud again," Brogden requested. They had spent the last hour contemplating the contents of the note. The brief riddle was meant to frustrate and mock, yet offer a clue to Devona's whereabouts.

Wynne cleared her throat and read

Hail the reborn prince of maggots!
Choking on hallowed earth and stale air
His baptism, a gravedigger's golden piss.
Vile outsider!
Cast out to distant shores,
No coin, knowledge or time absolves,
Thy shroud-bound resurrected heart.

"Cheerful," Wynne observed. " 'Tis unfortunate the scrawling script could not conceal the disgusting contents." She glanced at Rayne. "Tipton, did we accidentally receive a political commentary about our Regent or did the anonymous poet have you in mind?"

"No mistake," Rayne replied. "How many people do you know who have been buried alive?"

Brock shook his head. "It makes no sense. There is nothing in those lines about Devona."

"Perhaps the riddle was just the teaser," Brogden suggested. "Our villain enjoys pulling the legs off a spider before he smashes it under his shoe."

The corner of Rayne's mouth lifted slightly. "I do not approve of the analogy to the spider, but I can appreciate the opinion."

"Nay, you all have it wrong!" Sir Thomas bellowed. He paced the room, looking as though he wanted to tear the room apart. "There is nothing missing. The clue is in what is stated, though I cannot fathom why the chap didn't speak the words in plain English."

Wynne's brow lifted as a thought came to her. "This person hates you. You have been his goal from the beginning."

Rayne ground the palm of his hand into his left temple. "I haven't exactly been the favorite son in polite society. Name one enemy, and I could match it against twenty. Give me that paper."

Wynne handed him the note, and they all watched as he reread it again. Devona's life depended on him interpreting the foul riddle. He mouthed the first few lines of the text. "I agree with you, Wynne. The words chosen convey a mocking hatred."

Brock interjected, "Someone not pleased that you survived."

"So you bump my family up onto the list of suspects," Rayne said, not particularly upset. "We are no closer to singling out a villain or a location."

"Location," Brogden repeated. "If you ignore the emotion and insults, what location does the riddle offer?"

"My grave." Rayne straightened his slouch. Renewed energy coursed through him. "The riddle points me back to the parish churchyard close to Foxenclover."

Devona rested on her side across the coach's bench. Her bound wrists and ankles, and the cramped position prevented her from kicking at him. It also discouraged escape. She caught glimpses of trees and sky, however there was nothing in her line of vision that gave her a hint about their destination.

The bumpy ride did little for her stomach. Having spewed up what water she had consumed that morning, she had nothing to offer the retching spasms that wrenched her insides. At least the sickness forced Oz to remove the gag. The last thing he wanted was for her to drown in her own vomit.

Oz replied to the unspoken question in her eyes. "Soon, my dear. Your part is almost finished."

Panic flared inside her and Devona did not try to conceal her fears. "Have you sent Rayne a letter telling him our destination?" He had left her bound and gagged when he took the horses back to the inn. Two hours later he had returned by coach. She quickly had learned that the coachman's loyalties sided with his employer. The servant had even carried her twisting bound form into the coach.

Her determination to glean information from him amused Oz. He was enjoying her efforts to foil him. "You keep forgetting, Devona," he said, his eyes twinkling. "I have had months to plan this moment. Don't worry, your husband has seen my note and if he possesses a modest amount of intelligence, he should be racing to your side."

"Why is Rayne so important to you?"

His lids narrowed in anger. He clenched his hands into fists and briefly she worried he would strike her. "I would be more concerned about your role in my plan, rather than the fate of your husband."

"We were friends, Oz," she pleaded softly, willing him to relent and spare Tipton. "We could strike a bargain. I swear Tipton would not seek retribution. Doran is already dead and buried by his family so no one would have to know you killed him." *Forgive me, Doran.* "You could leave England."

The coachman called out. The jostling coach slowed to a gentle bounce, then stopped. All Devona could see was the gathering large gray storm clouds. The blue sky had been blotted from her view. Also, gone was her chance to talk Oz out of the fate he had slotted for her.

"Allow me to help you." Oz gripped her upper arm and pulled her into a sitting position.

Devona peered out the open door and frowned at the graveyard. "Where are we?"

"It all began here. I thought it appropriate that it ended here as well." He climbed down from the coach and automatically offered her his hand.

She was trapped. Resisting his summons would only result in punishment. Devona scooted closer to the door and did not pull away when he grasped her arm to help her down.

"Is the rectory empty?" Oz asked his approaching coachman.

"Dead as the 'yard."

"Fine. Head over to the shed, you will find the tools we need."

Devona watched the coachman walk to the small storage shed. "Dead as the 'yard. Did you have the vicar and his family murdered?"

He took hold of her arm and pulled her deeper into the graveyard. "I told you. I am not a violent man. The vicar and his family are away on a holiday. I was fortunate to have a friend to see to the details."

She stopped. "An accomplice? A corrupted soul who does not understand that he will be as dead as Doran. Even John Coachman here." She raised her voice so the returning man could hear. She eyed the pick and shovel he carried on his shoulder. "Do you expect him to dig his grave before you push him in it?"

The coachman's blank expression became speculative. Oz caught a fistful of her hair and yanked hard. He was rewarded with the appropriate response. The immense pain drove her to her knees. Her cheeks puffed with air while she struggled to overcome her latest punishment. She would fall on her face if Oz released his hold.

"Trying to cause mischief?" He tugged hard.

"No, Oz." She squeezed her eyes shut, not thinking her abused head could endure another attack. "P—please."

Keeping his fingers locked in her loosely bound hair, he hoisted her to her feet. She choked on a stifled sob. "Evan knows as you do that the only people who should look over their shoulders are the ones who have outlived their usefulness."

To her relief, he released her hair, allowing his hand to rest on her upper back. "Come along. I tire of these delays." They continued walking, threading their way around dozens of monuments. The manner in which he scanned each stone told her that he sought a specific grave.

"Paying respect to the dead, Oz?"

"More along the lines of luring." He halted, signaling to the coachman that he was to use the shovel at this site. "We may be slightly early to pay our respects, however, you may want to get yours over with since I cannot promise you will be around at the proper time."

Devona looked on while Oz scratched the moss from the stone. Rayne Tolland Wyman. The letters jumped out at her despite time's best efforts to conceal them. Rayne's grave. "I wonder why his family never knocked over the stone?"

"Maybe they had hoped he would return to it."

All of them turned at the sound of an approaching horse. A single horse pulling a gig came into view. A woman held the reins, but she was unidentifiable from a distance.

Devona glanced at Oz. He seemed undisturbed by the newcomer. A moment later it occurred to her. Oz had a female accomplice. "No one believed me when I told them Lady Claeg had been responsible for pushing that statuary over the ledge in the conservatory. She had made no secret of her hatred."

He noticed her disappointment that the lady in the gig was not an innocent arriving to tend her husband's grave. "You should be happy the woman is expected. Another body would weigh heavily on your tender conscience."

She gasped, wondering how she could still be shocked by Oz's actions. The vision of Doran choking on his own blood haunted her every time she closed her eyes. "Considering Lady Claeg's great love for her son, I doubt she will feel inclined to assist you when she learns of Doran's tortured execution."

"Oh, I agree." He laughed at her astonishment. "Lady Claeg is a horrid creature. Her peculiar possessiveness of her son and her outlandish behavior to all she considered a rival for her son's affections has been at best, diverting. If she were here, she would likely wrestle both you and me into the grave Evan is digging."

Her spirits were already wallowing in the grave. "That isn't Lady Claeg."

"No." He raised his hand to the mysterious lady. She set aside the reins and climbed down from the gig, each step bringing her closer to the bleak gathering. "Madam, come join Lady Tipton and settle her concerns. She feared I had set Lady Claeg upon her."

The woman tilted her face upward, her somber features quite distinct. Devona did not realize she was swaying into a faint until Oz's firm hand halted her descent and steadied her.

"Who is this Claeg woman?" Lady Jocelyn

asked, her eyes widening at the disheveled condition of her daughter-in-law.

"A mother who recently buried a son. I am certain you can understand."

Jocelyn's gaze held Devona's. She seemed to be cataloging every detail, from her torn dirty gown, and lack of shoes, to the dried blood on her face then up to the snarl of hair, the sad remains of her pretty hairdressing. "What is she doing here?"

"Did you think your son would walk into an ambush, solely by request? I needed an attractive lure."

"You never mentioned anyone else getting hurt."

Oz's eyes hardened; the sound of the shovel striking and hollowing out the grave filled the silence. "You have not needed to be privy to all the details, nor have you shown any desire to be enlightened."

Jocelyn seemed to want to protest, but she remained mute.

Devona had no such problem. "What kind of mother would conspire to have her son murdered? What did he ever do to deserve this?" she demanded. Oh, if only her hands were free! Her blood pounded with rage. She felt strong enough to rip them all apart using her hands and teeth. Her intent must have shown on her face, because Jocelyn gave her a wary glance before stepping out of her range.

"An avenging angel to complement your demon, Lady Jocelyn," Oz noted. "It is a pity you will never hold the passionate offspring the pair might have created."

Devona cried, "No!"

The statement also shook Jocelyn. "You have

no need to keep Devona here. Your trap is baited, Mr. Rawley. My son is coming for her."

"Rawley?" she echoed. "Lady Jocelyn, do you not even know the name of your henchman? This is Osmund Lockwood."

"My dear, I claim both names. Lockwood is my middle name. When I set myself up in London, I was worried Tipton would recognize a family name."

"Family." She gasped, the meaning of the events becoming lethally apparent. "Next in line. Damn you both."

Oz patted her cheek. "Always an intelligent girl."

Devona charged her mother-in-law. "How you must hate him! I know all about your attempts to lock him away in an asylum. You must have been disappointed when he ruined your efforts by running away."

"You cannot understand what I went through back then. I had just lost my firstborn, and soon after my second. The grief consumed me!" Jocelyn's liquid gaze pleaded for her to understand.

"God in his mercy returned one of your sons."

"The wrong one!" she wailed. "Devlin and I shared a bond that I never had with Rayne. He was an odd boy. Even as an infant, he would stare at me through his eerie silver gaze as if I had somehow failed him."

"And you think doing this will help him? You are as mad as he is," Devona declared, switching her gaze to Oz.

"I am not insane, Devona," he protested. "A madman loses control and direction. Trust me, I am very sane."

Jocelyn stepped closer to Devona. "Rayne will not die." She dug into her reticule and removed a small blue bottle. "I have a gentleman friend who enjoys his gardens as much as my daughter. His favorite exotics have some very interesting effects. I distilled this myself. A few drops and you will have the most restful sleep."

She eyed the bottle as if Jocelyn clutched a poisonous snake to her breast. "My God, you do not believe that foul brew will be used to correct any sleep disturbances?"

"If he had remained in India," Jocelyn continued, "none of this would have occurred. Rayne could have been declared lost at sea and the title would have gone to Mr. Rawley. A fair allowance would have been agreed upon and we could have lived out our lives happily. Madeleina would have been raised in a manner deserving of her rank."

Instead, Rayne had returned and amused himself by cutting his mother off from the funds she had obviously coveted more than her second son. His actions might have been considered petty, but Devona understood now the reasons for his cruelty. She trembled, grieving for the lost chance of giving him the love and family he had so long been denied. Lady Jocelyn had underestimated her distant relative. The ruthless man would bury more than one body this evening.

"The killing will not stop with Rayne, Lady Jocelyn."

"Killing." She blinked. "Heavens no, my dear. There shall be no murder." She held up the bottle. "A few drops induces sleep, a bit more a deathlike state for a period. When the person revives, there is a forgetfulness. The severity depends on how much of the drug was consumed. Mr. Rawley will simply encourage my son to drink from the bottle, I assume in exchange for your freedom. He will then place Rayne on a sailing ship headed for an exotic destination. My son will begin a new life,

Mr. Rawley will have his title, and I will have the funds to give Madeleina a dowry that will attract a respectable husband."

Devona thought the entire scheme despicable. The notion that it could succeed terrified her. These evil people were plotting to steal her husband's life and memories and there was not a single thing she could do about it. Rayne would forget her. He would be lost to her forever. A low keening sound came up from deep in her chest.

"I do not think Lady Tipton agrees with your plan, Jocelyn," Oz murmured. "Now that I have had a chance to consider it, neither do I." His fist shot out and smashed into the older woman's temple. She collapsed onto the pile of freshly dug earth. She remained unconscious.

Although she bore little love for Rayne's mother, the vicious attack automatically had her asking, "Why? She has delivered up her son. I would think you would be showering her with gold."

"Evan, permit me the use of the shovel." Oz took up the offered shovel and tested the feel of its weight. "It was Jocelyn who first sought me out all those years ago. She was irritated by her son's closefisted ways and the greedy woman thought dangling the title in front of my eyes would ensure my cooperation. It did, for a time." He leaned down and picked up the small blue bottle. It disappeared into the inner pocket of his frock coat. "Listening to her babble on about her plans reminded me that what was to be halved could be mine as a whole, including her precious, innocent Madeleina." He brought the flat side of the shovel down across her head. Once. Jocelyn's body quivered, then became deathly still.

Dropping the shovel, he swaggered over to Devona. She was so appalled, it took her a few second before her body acted on what her mind screamed.

Run!

She managed to sprint past four headstones before he caught her. His arm snatched her waist and her forward momentum pulled them down. Oz rolled her over and straddled her, sitting firmly on her pelvis. "A new plan, Devona. This one ends with your beloved husband dead and in his grave."

"No," she seethed. His added weight pressing down on her bound arms made them feel as though they would pop from her shoulders.

"Despite what old Jocelyn thought, Tipton was never going to live out his life on some exotic island. I have decided to amend my plans for you." He braced his palms against the dirt on each side of her head. "You were to join your husband, Devona. However, the notion of killing you does not sit well with me. I am rather fond of you. And as I mentioned, I avoid violence when necessary." He withdrew the bottle from the hidden pocket in his coat. "Your family will learn that you experienced a terrible accident. Involving a coach, I think. It will strip you of your memories, my dear. Sad and tragic, it's true. Fortunately, I will be on hand to help you through your difficult ordeal."

"Monster!" she hissed, trying to buck him off by arching her hips. "No one will believe you."

He removed the tiny cork. "Look at you. Your gown is filthy. You have a nasty head injury where you struck your head when the coach rolled down the embankment. Yes, your family will believe me. Now open wide. A few sips and you will sleep like an enchanted princess. Perhaps I will even make you my viscountess."

"No—" She opened her mouth to tell him what an evil beast he was and then realized her mistake. Oz took advantage of her weakness and forced the bottle between her lips. The vile bitter liquid filled her mouth. Twisting her head she spat some of the liquid out. The inside of her mouth burned, telling her that it would be impossible to get rid of all the poison. Oz was just as determined as she was, and he had the advantage. He jammed the bottle between her lips again, this time using the other hand to constrict her neck. She could not expel enough air to spew the liquid out. Terrified of losing her mind, she used her tongue to push the drug out. A glance told her the bottle was empty. Oz noticed it, too, and threw it away. More liquid dribbled from the corner of her mouth.

"Swallow, damn you!"

She fought valiantly, a woman driven to save herself and the man she loved. It wasn't enough. Oz, still gripping her neck, lifted her and slammed her head into the soft dirt. The impact was not hard enough to hurt her, yet it served its purpose. Devona's throat automatically convulsed and some of the liquid went down. Rayne! She had failed. Oz lifted her head again and the gray storm clouds dropped from the sky to blind her. More liquid burned the back of her throat as it went down. She no longer felt Oz's strong fingers strangling her. Strangely, she felt nothing. No pain in her head, no desperate need for air, even the heartache of her loss seemed to ease. The storm clouds settled over her like a warm blanket. She no longer was frightened. Relaxed, she succumbed to the inviting void.

TWENTY

They were walking into a trap. Rayne knew it, just as the villain who took Devona knew that he would do anything to get her back. Brock and Sir Thomas accompanied him, as did Wynne. The Bedegrayne men had been resistant to the idea of her placing herself near the danger. He did not have time to argue. He stuffed the ill-tempered group into the coach and allowed them to fight it out on their journey.

In the end, he was pleased by the decision. Wynne Bedegrayne was a sensible woman. Her soft feminine tone firmly cut through the male outrage. "We do not know what Devona has endured. Some matters are best confided to another woman," she had explained. No one had debated the issue.

The hours passed in silence. When the sun dipped below the horizon, Wynne went about the task of lighting the coach's inner lanterns.

"Tipton, I have given this some thought," Wynne began, sounding hesitant to offer her opinion. "Rushing into the graveyard may be exactly what this madman wants. Besides, you cannot be certain she is even there."

Sir Thomas stirred, awakening at the sound of Wynne's voice. "What's this? You think you know more about these matters than us men? Next you will be demanding we hand over a pistol so you can be the first to spit in the bastard's eye?"

"And you are an expert, Papa? I will wager there are cobwebs in the barrel of that fine pistol you have tucked in your waist." She ignored her father's discreet scrutiny of his weapon and focused on Rayne. "This graveyard is close to Foxenclover, correct?"

"Our lands border the rectory. Why do you ask?"

"Maddy," she starkly reminded him. "And your mother. If this man's intent is to destroy you, do you think he would resist taking your kin? I realize your feelings for your mother are not the least sentimental, however your sister—"

"Enough," Rayne interrupted, the image of his sister's proud, defiant face surfaced in his mind, haunting his conscience. "Your point has been made. Your concern is reasonable, and the logic of it irrefutable. We are fortunate that you are on our side."

Brock's grim features shifted in and out of shadow with the swaying movement of the coach. "Damn, but I have to agree. I would take all three, figuring your feelings for one if not all would lure you into an ambush."

If there would be an ambush, Rayne planned on being the instigator. When they were a half mile from Foxenclover, he signaled for the coachman to halt. "An approaching coach this time of night will alert him of our arrival. We will continue to the house on foot." He glanced up through the trapdoor at Speck's ugly face. "Speck, you remain behind with the coachman. If there is no trouble, then we will return and continue to the graveyard."

"Aye, milord."

He climbed down from the coach. He tilted his face up, a warm, misting rain beaded on his face.

"At least the rain will help mask our approach," Brock muttered.

Rayne blocked Wynne's descent. "Perhaps you should wait with Speck until we know what we will discover?"

Wynne brushed aside the suggestion. "If Devona is there, then she will need me. If not, then I will remain behind to keep vigil along with Maddy and your mother."

He nodded. Devona would want Wynne to attend her. The pair of them shared a bond his own upbringing left him ill-prepared to comprehend. Sir Thomas emerged after his daughter, patting his concealed weapon. Wet powder would be careless and in these high stakes, quite deadly.

"Speck, I won't waste my time telling you not to ride in if you hear shots."

The servant spat. "Good. My hearing ain't sharp when you start blathering idiocy."

"Keep low. I would regret shooting you." Rayne warned. He opened his medical case and removed a scalpel. Taking out his handkerchief, he wrapped the cloth around the razor-sharp blade and stuffed it in his boot. He wasn't particular about which implement or whose hand saw to the task, what mattered to him was that the man who took Devona be punished.

Not wanting to risk a lantern, they made the trek to the house blind. Their movements were cautious and at times noisy. No one present was claiming to be an expert at stealth.

The house was unexpectedly dark, they noted, while they crossed the front yard. Assuming one door would do as well as another, Rayne boldly

walked up to the front door. The door opened
easily, an even blacker darkness beckoned within.

The exertion and the cooling rain made
Wynne's teeth chatter. "Could they have gone visiting?"

"Possible. It appears Jocelyn has hired a negligent staff." He entered the front hall. "Wait there
until I can find a candle or lamp." A few minutes
later, the hall glowed from the light of an oil
lamp.

"Should we call out?" Brock whispered.

A thud from overhead had Rayne putting his
finger to his lips. *Thud!* Removing his pistol from
the protective folds of his cloak, he moved toward
the stairs.

"Wait!" Sir Thomas urgently invoked. "What if
it is a trap?"

"What if it is Devona?" Rayne countered. He
had no patience to debate this with the elder Bedegrayne. "Stay here and protect Wynne. Brock,
assist me." Not waiting for their agreement, he
swiftly climbed the stairs.

The men heard the noise again. It came from
the room at the end of the hall. Mentally, he re-
viewed the layout of Foxenclover and immediately
concluded his sister's tower room was the room
they approached.

"Please, Mama." Maddy's sobbing plea was
faint behind the door. "Whatever I did, I apologize."

Rayne imagined it was her tiny fist that pounded
futilely at the door, each stroke weaker than the
last. The lamp revealed a chair had been jammed
against the door. The key still in the keyhole
gleamed in the light.

Brock opened his mouth to alert Maddy of

their presence. Rayne silenced him by slapping his hand over the younger man's mouth.

"It could still be a trap. Let's check the other rooms before we free her." His sister's broken sobs tore at him in a manner he never thought possible. Perhaps it was because he could easily place Devona as the frightened woman behind the door. Brutally, he shut the interfering thoughts from his mind.

The quick search of the other rooms revealed nothing suspicious. Maddy, too tired to pound on the door and beg, had been reduced to soft, incoherent crying. He removed the chair. The action brought Maddy to the door.

"Mama?"

"It's Rayne." The key turned, the door opened, and suddenly his arms were full of a very hysterical, albeit grateful sister. Her face pressed against his chest, his name a muffled litany.

The men's gazes met. "She's not here, Tipton."

Brock's grief could not compare with Rayne's desolation. He pulled Maddy from him and gave her a shake. "Where is she?"

Confusion and the urgency in her brother's voice quieted her. "Who? Mama?"

"No. Devona. Has she been here?"

Through swollen red eyes she searched both men's faces, judging their sincerity. "Why would you expect to find Devona at Foxenclover?"

Brock took her by the arm and broke the siblings' contact. "Wynne was wrong. We need to get to the graveyard."

Maddy sniffed, wiping the tears from her eyes. "Has everyone gone mad? First Mama, now you two."

"Tipton, you might want to come down here," Sir Thomas called out.

His sister in tow, Rayne and Brock went downstairs. Maddy ran into Wynne's waiting embrace.
The mothering comfort brought forth more tears.
"Papa is in the drawing room," Wynne murmured, petting his sister's hair.

"What has happened?"

He heard Maddy ask the question to Wynne as
he and Brock went to view Sir Thomas's discovery.
Two maids and Mrs. Pool were lying on the floor."

"Dead?"

Sir Thomas picked up the housekeeper and
placed her on the sofa. "No, although they are
giving an impressive representation of it. I cannot
rouse them. There are three others in the kitchen."

Brock picked up a discarded teacup and sniffed
the contents. "Drugged, I'd guess."

Rayne had seen enough. "Did you find my
mother?"

Sir Thomas's reply did not hearten him. He returned to the hall where the women had stayed.

Maddy ran to him. Trembling, she grabbed his
hands. "Wynne told me everything. You will find
her. I feel it."

"The staff has been drugged, Maddy. What
does Jocelyn have to do with all of this?"

She did not flinch, nor did she collapse into
tears as he expected. Instead, she held her head
up courageously and expelled a shaky breath.
"Mama. She said we were celebrating. There was
tea, biscuits, and even currant cake."

He did not give a bloody farthing what was
served at their little party. "Then what?"

Her brow furrowed. "Nothing, really. I spoiled
Mama's party by getting sleepy. I thought she
locked me in my room to punish me for my unladylike behavior."

"Not likely," Brock mumbled, coming up behind them.

Wynne's lips parted in amazement. "You cannot believe my sister's disappearance and your mother's strange tea are related."

"Let's just say Jocelyn has some explaining to do." Rayne addressed Maddy. "Do you know where our father's pistols are kept? Good, I want you to show Wynne." He locked gazes with his sister-in-law. "Do you know how to load a pistol?"

"Insulting, I tell you," Sir Thomas charged, joining the group. "Male or female, Bedgraynes know how to defend themselves."

"I'll stay and look to your sister and the staff," Wynne promised.

"Speaking of the staff, you and the gel might want to check on them. One of the ladies moaned and rolled to her side."

"I will check on them immediately, Papa." Her hand clasped in Maddy's, Wynne paused in front of Rayne. "Find her and bring her home."

"Only death will keep me from her."

A small smile teased her full lips. "We want to keep you too."

"Be well, brother," Maddy murmured shyly, allowing Wynne to lead her away.

"I do not know what evil lurks in the blackness this eve, but it cloaks my wife. I propose we light our path with lanterns. I intend to kill what I aim at."

They returned to the coach and shortened the journey to the graveyard. Once again they halted the coach. Dim light beamed from the rectory windows. There was enough light to discard the bold notion of approaching the grounds with lit lanterns. There was no reason to offer Devona's kidnappers an easy target. The vulnerability of light went both ways. Rayne would be able to see anyone who stood in front of the windows.

Reaching the building, they crouched against the side wall. His heart was pounding in his ears, and he assumed the excitement he saw in his new kinsmen's eyes mirrored his own.

"I think we should separate, each taking an entrance. One of us is bound to catch the kidnapper unawares."

Brock wiped the mist from his face with his sleeve. "We have to get out of this rain or the pistols will be worthless."

Sir Thomas was still attempting to catch his breath. "What if one of us is captured?"

He did not see fear in his father-in-law's eyes. There was a steely determination in them that promised he would sacrifice his life if it would bring down the kidnapper.

"No heroics. If you are taken, then wait for us. The distraction will be to our advantage."

Sir Thomas nodded, looking slightly disappointed. "I will go right."

"Brock, you take the left. I want to check that small building. Try not to shoot one another if you circle around."

The men separated and faded into the darkness. Rayne paused to light the lantern. There was no warm glow of inviting light coming from the building. Choosing a side window, he held the lantern up to the glass. A huge saw hung down from one of the wood beams. The building was probably used to store tools. It might even be a workplace for a carpenter to build coffins.

An indefinable chill passed through him. He had managed to avoid this graveyard for fifteen years. It had rained that night, too, he remembered, but then it had been a violent storm with thunder and lightning stabbing the starless obsidian sky. His rebirth had cost him his family. Devona and the rest of the Bedegraynes had replaced the one he lost. He refused to allow another stormy night in this graveyard to spin the wheel of fate to determine if he would win this time, or lose.

He did not hear the man. One minute he was alone, the next the man was a blurred image in midflight. His head collided with Rayne's chest and they both fell to the ground. Fighting instincts heightened, he shoved the man off him and rolled to the left. Any hopes that the tackle had knocked out his attacker were diminished when the man dived for Rayne's knees, bringing him down on his back.

He tugged at the strings securing the black cloak. It no longer served to hide him in the night; perhaps he could use it to deflect the blade the other man wielded. Rolling the thick fabric over his arm, he leapt backward avoiding the arcing blade. The second attempt he used his padded arm to block. The attacker seized the knife with both hands, utilizing all his strength and weight to bring the blade downward.

Both men were breathing heavily, a silent struggle of strength and sheer will. The man's gaze dropped, and Rayne knew what had caught his attention. The pistol tucked into his waist. The surprise attack had prevented him from drawing it. The belief that this man could lead him to Devona kept him from using it.

His attacker experienced no such dilemma. Freeing one hand, he reached for the weapon. Rayne took advantage of the man's torn priorities. Instead of reaching for the pistol, he focused on the knife. Allowing the blade to cut into his padded arm, his other fist shot upward, connecting with the man's wrist. The attacker cursed at the distinctive crack of breaking bones. His countering swipe to steal the pistol knocked it into the mud. The man dove for the weapon. Rayne fell on top of him, praying the rain had ruined the powder.

Instead of reaching for the pistol, the man clawed at his throat. His frantic twisting bucked Rayne off. He straddled him, prepared to deliver a vicious blow, but his arm stayed cocked when he saw the reason for the man's struggles. The burden of Rayne's weight and the man's broken wrist had altered the angle of the knife and had driven the blade into his neck. It had entered three inches below the man's left ear and was buried deep within the intricate tangle of veins, arteries, muscle, and bone. He was still breathing, so he had managed to avoid cutting his windpipe.

Rayne dragged him up by his shirt, his relentless gaze probing for the man's attention. "Where is my wife?" He slapped him when his eyes threatened to roll white. "I'll remove the blade and leave you to drown in a puddle of your own blood. Tell me where she is, and I will use all my skill to save you."

The man's lips twitched. Rayne leaned closer to hear the dying man's last words.

"T—too late." The man fainted from the loss of blood.

Furious, Rayne stood, wondering if the man referred to himself or Devona. He stooped over to pick up the pistol. There was a slim chance it was functional.

"I fear the rain has ruined your fine weapon," a man spoke behind him. "Even so, it pays to be prudent. Throw the pistol to the ground, Tipton."

The newcomer stood just beyond the light of his discarded lantern.

"Your lady needs you, Tipton," he urged. "The weapon."

Reluctantly, he opened his hand and allowed the pistol to drop. He did not need it. He was angry, desperate, and just mean enough to dispatch this man with his bare hands. "Where is she?"

Laughter came from the darkness, drawing closer as the man stepped into the light. "Close. Real close," Oz Lockwood promised, the barrel of a pistol peeking out from his greatcoat. He correctly read Rayne's thoughts. "I have not dropped this one. Is Devona's life worth risking to prove the condition of this weapon?" There was a hard edge to his mocking smile. "I thought not."

Disgusted, he wiped the mist from his face. "She never realized you were dangerous. Hell, she probably invited herself along on her own kidnapping."

"You have come to understand our reckless Devona very well. So beautiful and a spirit to match. If there was a lady to breach your defenses, I wagered she would be the one to do it."

"Do not attempt to convince me that my wife conspired against me, Lockwood. I will not believe it. What puzzles me is the why of it. I do not know you. I have led a quiet life in London," he mused, keeping his gaze on the pistol aimed directly at his heart. "If you encouraged Devona to seek me out, then it cannot be for her affections. So why?" Brock and Sir Thomas would come across them soon. All he had to do was keep him talking.

"You are a creature of fate, are you not? An illness, death, a miraculous resurrection, and the discarded second son became Viscount Tipton."

He could not help smiling at the ridiculously brief account of his life. "There was pain, grief, loss, and redemption too," he dryly added. "You seem remarkably obsessed and informed about the details of my life."

Oz shifted, redistributing his weight. "We have never been formally introduced. You might recognize me by my full name: Osmund Lockwood Rawley."

Despite the poor lighting and rain, it was obvious that the man expected some reaction to his revelation. Rayne purposely kept his expression blank. Oz had taken so much from him; he refused to give him one more damn thing. "Under our present circumstances, do not expect me to be pleased to meet you."

Oz faltered, the lack of recognition seemed to stun him. "My name. Rawley. Do you not know it?"

"Should I?" he asked, barely concealing a yawn. The moment Oz Lockwood Rawley became careless he was a dead man.

"The title was mine, you resilient upstart!" he shouted. "There had been talk of you dying in India—"

"A few close calls," he modestly admitted.

"Then you returned to London, prepared to live out your life scoffing at the title I would have killed to possess."

Rayne watched the barrel pointed at him waver. His muscles coiled, readying for a sudden attack. Oz, noting his intense concentration, readjusted his aim. "You already have—killed, that is."

Determination hardened the man's jaw. "A few.

Doran Claeg for one." Oz nodded his head, satisfied that he had managed to surprise his nemesis. "Ah, I see you did not expect my little confession. Poor Devona. She was beside herself when she learned her childhood friend was not off exploring the world as her husband had sworn. She found him half starved and chained like a wild animal in the bowels of an old ruin."

Rayne flinched, the truth of why Devona left him battering at his self-control. She thought he had lied to her about Claeg. For a time, he had emerged as the real monster polite society whispered about, and she had *believed* it. "Naturally, as a concerned friend, you helped her escape the fiend she married?" The urge to strangle the man consumed his thoughts.

"She came to me," he boasted. "I planned it brilliantly. I sent an anonymous note revealing your misdeeds. Devona insisted on traveling to the mentioned locale and I could not in good conscience allow her to journey alone." He sighed. "She was heartbroken when she found out that the information about Claeg was true."

Rayne's eyelid's narrowed to mere slits. He was so focused on Oz that he matched him, breath for breath. "So, cousin, you covet my title? Come and take it."

"Why do I have to take it when your delightful mother offered it to me?"

The news that his mother played a part in this scheme did not surprise him. "When?"

Oz shrugged. "The first time I heard from her was when she was arranging to commit you to the asylum fifteen years ago. She had inquired, and realized I was next in line after you. That lady loves her pretty house, and the money that goes with it."

"She contacted you when I returned, I assume."

Passionate about his triumph, the pistol's aim shifted and bounced at every gesture. "I have always been there, Tipton. Why do you think Foxenclover has been stripped of its treasures? You may be cheeseparing, but you provided enough funds for the care of your mother and sister. Unfortunately, you did not account for my requirements."

He blinked at the audacity of the man. "You blackmailed her."

Oz's teeth clenched as if recalling what he had endured dealing with the dowager. "Being denied my birthright was costly for Jocelyn. When you returned, she was so terrified of you that she finally agreed that a fifteen-year-old mistake needed to be corrected."

Brock came stalking out of the surrounding blackness. His clothes were rain-soaked and smeared with mud. Blood dripped from a wound at his temple. "Fart-catching cully," he muttered, swinging the shovel in his hands.

Bloody hell. Bedegrayne was going to get one of them gut-shot. Rayne moved at the same time Oz twisted around to confront Brock. The flat side of the shovel struck Oz in the face as his finger reflexively pulled the trigger. The explosion was deafening. Rayne hit him from behind and the action also took Brock to the ground.

"A little late in coming, Tipton. Now get him off me."

"Where did the ball hit you, Bedegrayne?" He was already turning the facedown Lockwood over.

"Not me." Brock sucked in his breath at what was left of Oz's face. "Lockwood must have bungled the loading."

"Bring the lantern closer," Rayne ordered. He did not need the extra light to show him that Oz was badly injured. Whatever the reason, the pistol had literally exploded in his face. Pieces of wood and hot metal had punctured his left eye and sheered off a ghastly amount of flesh, exposing gleaming white glimpses of cheekbone.

Bedegrayne swore and cupped a hand to his mouth. "Even stitched back together he'll look like some sort of hellfire creature." He stared on as Rayne unknotted his cravat and began wrapping the long cloth around the injured man's head.

"I will need yours as well." He slipped the end of the cloth under another layer to keep it in place. "Talk to me, Oz." The man was conscious, and his pain beyond a man's endurance. When he parted his lips, blood gushed and soaked into the cravat. "You will most likely die if we do not try to sew up these wounds. First, tell me where Devona is hidden and we will get you to the rectory. I have my medical case in the coach."

"Want—want to die."

"Fine," Rayne snapped, "I would not stand between a man and his God. Where is my wife?"

He shuddered. "At peace."

Brock slapped his cravat into Rayne's hands. He glared down at the injured man. "Lockwood. It would give me the greatest pleasure to draw out your pain, till madness makes you peel the other half of your face off. The bastard cracked me in the head with a bloody shovel," he explained to Rayne. "He probably knocked my father out too. I vow he will get no peace until he pays for what he's done to our family."

"No riddles, Oz. I have no patience to explore your perverted views. I want you to tell me where Devona is or I will abandon you to Brock's negligent abilities." Rayne checked his patient's pulse. "Sometimes when the trauma is severe, the brain cannot cope and it begins to depress normal functions."

Brock spat at Lockwood's feet. "If you mean he's dying, good riddance."

"This weather is not helping his condition. Unlike you, I hope he lives long enough to tell me where he's taken Devona." Rayne rose to his feet. "Carry him to the rectory. There isn't much you can do except to question him again if he awakens." He picked up the lantern and the shovel. "You might want to look for your father. If Oz greeted him with this shovel, call out for me. His head may not be as hard as yours."

"Where are you going?" Brock asked.

"To search the graveyard. Devona might be tied up and gagged somewhere close."

Rayne felt he had no choice but to leave Oz in his brother-in-law's care. Head injuries were fickle. Some wounds bled heavily and still the patient survived, where other smaller wounds killed the patient outright. If Oz survived, he would be recovering in Newgate. If the infections there did not kill him, the hemp would.

"Devona!" he yelled. Holding the lantern out in front of him, he scanned each gravestone. Most were small, but their shadows were large enough to conceal a slender woman. He also kept a firm grip on the shovel. If Oz had any more accomplices roaming the area, he wanted a reliable waterproof weapon. "Devona!"

After he finished searching the graveyard, he would move on to the copse of trees beyond. She was close and unharmed. He could feel it. The light washed over another stone. This one made him pause. Nightmares of drowning in a river of rain, the smell of inebriated resurrection men, and the smell of corpse-packed earth still awoke him at odd times over the years, his mouth opened in soundless terror and cold sweat drenching the sheets. He forced himself to say the words aloud.

RAYNE TOLLAND WYMAN
OUR LAMB AT PEACE

At peace. Those were the last words Oz had spoken before he lost consciousness. Another riddle or was he speaking the truth? His eyes widened in horror as he nudged the soft earth with the toe of his boot. *Too soft.* He lowered the lantern and surveyed the area. It was difficult to ascertain in the darkness and rain, but the ground looked freshly dug. He dropped to his knees and pushed his hands into the earth. The first inch or so was mud, however the dirt beneath was dry and soft. *A newly dug grave. At peace. My God, Devona!*

He screamed her name. The madman had buried her alive. He could very well imagine the horrors tormenting her. If he wasn't too late. He couldn't be!

"Tipton," Brock called out from the other side of the graveyard. "Lockwood is conscious and asking for you."

"I will see him in hell," he shouted back, not slowing his frantic digging. "Find another shovel. That demonic bastard buried her alive."

He heard Brock's roar of denial, then his heavy footfalls as he went to search for a shovel. Rayne vehemently hoped Oz was still alive when he was finished. He would see to it that Lockwood took her place.

Think, Tipton, he thought. Just like that night fifteen years ago. Resurrection men can get a body out without disturbing much of the gravesite. *Concentrate on the head.* He could splinter the lid and pull her out. *She will be fine;* he tried to assure himself. He survived, so will Devona. The shovel struck wood. Lying on his stomach, he scooped the crumbling dirt out with his hands.

"Rayne."

He could hear the tears in Brock's voice. He tamped down the surge of raw emotion. "Clear away the excess dirt. I don't want it to fall on her face when I break open the lid."

"Maybe you're wrong. This could be your old coffin?"

Rayne was in no condition to calm Brock's fears. "The wood is new," he said, his teeth clenched as he drove the edge of the shovel into the lid. "If this had been mine, this lid would have been breached." He slammed the shovel into the wood again. A crack formed in the center. Again. Again. Again. Three crevices the width of his thumb opened. He bisected the damage by smashing the shovel horizontally.

Tossing the shovel aside he got down on his knees and shoved his fingers into the cracks and pulled. A jagged piece of wood broke off. He threw them to the side and attacked the next section.

"I see her!" Brock added his strength to the labor, creating a large enough hole to pull her out. "I can't tell if she's breathing."

Neither could Rayne. "Stand aside." He took the shovel and rammed it into a stubborn section of wood. Three hits and Brock was able to pry it off. Enough. She was so still. *At peace.* The phrase taunted him.

"Your sister wouldn't dare die on me. She hates to disappoint me." He braced his legs on either side of the hole and gently dragged her out of the grave. Brock brought the lantern closer as Rayne laid her out on the ground.

"Is she alive?"

He put his ear to her chest and listened. His eyes closed in relief. "Yes. Devona." He tapped her on the cheek. She did not awaken.

"What's wrong with her?" Brock asked, picking up the lantern when Rayne scooped her into his arms.

"The air might have been too stale," Rayne said, more frightened by her unresponsiveness than he was admitting. "I have some smelling salts in my case. Let's return to the rectory and get her warm."

Brock matched Rayne's hurried stride. "My father is standing guard over Lockwood. It turns out his head is as hard as mine."

He did not reply to the banter. All his concentration was focused on willing Devona to stop terrifying him and awaken. They met a stern-faced Sir Thomas in the sanctuary.

"Lockwood, blast his soul, is dead." Sir Thomas appeared to visibly age in front of them when he saw his unconscious daughter. "Will my gel live?"

"Yes," he vowed. The two of them had a bargain.

"I'll get your case," Brock offered, disappearing through the door.

Rayne placed her on the floor. He touched her everywhere, searching for a reason why she was not awake. He felt the large bump at the base of her skull. Lifting her up and folding her over his arm, he pushed her matted hair back, trying to view the damage. "Let's hope Devona inherited your hard head, Sir Thomas. She took a blow to the head as well."

"She's a Bedegrayne. My gel has a harder head than most."

Rayne agreed. "There is a great deal of blood on her," he observed, placing her carefully on her back again. "I cannot find a source. It must belong to someone else." Claeg.

"The salts!" Brock burst through the door. Speck followed behind him, carrying several blankets.

Rayne opened the bottle containing a combination of ammonia and various oils. He waved it under her nose. No reaction. "Wake up, love. This is no place to spend the night." He held the bottle under her nose.

Devona's nose wrinkled. Her breath hitched, and then she started coughing. Rayne pulled her to a sitting position, bracing her back with his arm.

"Horrid," her voice rasped, trying to catch her breath.

Rayne kissed her forehead. He thought it was the most beautiful thing she had ever said.

A day later, Rayne caught Devona sneaking out of bed. "I know you said a week, Tipton. However, I cannot bear it. My back hurts and I have slept enough for a lifetime." She did not remember Oz sealing her in a coffin, nor the ride back to Foxenclover after they had revived her. The thought made her shudder. Lady Jocelyn's mysterious herb concoction had sedated her. Whether through faulty chemistry, or application, the bitter liquid had not erased Devona's memory as the crazy woman had promised it would. The blow she took to her head had done more damage. While her husband and brother had frantically unearthed her grave, she had blissfully slept through the horror.

"Have you been remembering?" he politely queried.

He was dressed in buff-colored breeches and a cream-colored shirt. His beautiful silky hair she so loved was neatly tied back. To look upon them now, one would never guess what they had endured the last few days.

"A few more details," she admitted, shrugging. "Brock tried to answer some of my questions earlier, but I stopped him. Some answers are best forgotten." Like Oz taking her place in the grave.

"I am sorry about your mother."

Devona had concluded that years of unrelenting grief over the death of her son, Devlin, and then her husband, had placed Lady Jocelyn's mind in a fragile state. Her own greed and lust to defeat the son she feared and loathed had shattered what remained of those tangible threads of sanity. Perhaps she had truly believed she could have discreetly disposed of Tipton without killing him. Or maybe that was what she had wanted to believe. No one would ever know with complete certainty.

"She deserved her fate."

To others his comment might have sounded callous. She knew that buried beneath his indifference, guilt and pain simmered. Devona wanted to offer him comfort. She doubted he would thank her for it. Regardless of his protestations, learning that his mother had encouraged Oz's obsession for the title must have cut him deeply.

Speck had discovered her battered body in a small workroom. Lady Jocelyn had been punished for her crimes. It would be a long time before her children would be able to forgive her treachery and perhaps allow themselves to grieve.

Rayne propped his arm against the window and gazed down at the view of the gardens. Devona knew he saw Maddy weeding her precious flowerbeds.

"You have been avoiding me." There, she had said it.

"I wanted you to rest." His wry glance skimmed her from head to toe, admiring the seductive way the thin fabric revealed as much as it concealed. "Brock and your father have refused my advice as well. I should have known better than to order about a Bedegrayne."

"Wyman," she lightly corrected. "We made a bargain. I intend to uphold my end of it."

He visibly sagged at her announcement. "I thought I had lost you. First when you disappeared from the house, and later as I stood over the earth covering you." He rubbed his eyes and inhaled. "I bullied you into our bargain." He hesitated, a guarded expression replaced the pain she had glimpsed. "My family has visited enough misery on yours. What if I said that I did not want to remain married just for the sake of a bargain?"

He was pushing her away. Looking into those mysterious pewter-colored eyes, they might as well have been separated by an ocean. Rayne had spent half his life distancing himself from love. He would sacrifice his chance of having a wife, a home, and his own family if she did not stop him. This was one rescue of which no one would accuse her of being reckless. Getting on her feet, she moved closer to him. Her gait was still unsteady from the effects of the drug.

"What if I agreed? After all I have experienced, I think I deserve a marriage not bound by past bargains," she murmured, the flash of emotion he could not hide from her gave her the courage to continue. "What if I demanded a new bargain? This one made for love?"

He caught her and pulled her close. "You love me? Not for Doran's sake? Not even for mine?"

"You know us Bedegraynes." She smiled up at him. "Never a more stubborn clan."

"Wyman, Lady Tipton," he corrected, brushing a kiss against her lips. "My beautiful beloved. I thought you were a maddening piece of baggage the night you barged into my study and demanded that I help you." He swept her off her feet and carried her back to bed. He placed her gently on the mattress then stretched out beside her.

"I thought you were wickedly handsome." She sighed, reaching for the bit of leather that bound his hair and tugged. It gave way easily and his hair curled slightly against his shoulders. She threaded her fingers through it and he leaned into her touch.

His eyes, this time glowing the lightest blue, touched her as tantalizingly as his roaming fingers. "I love you." The words rushed out as he kissed the lace at her throat. "I promised your father that I would give you a dozen children to keep you too busy to revert back to your reckless ways."

Devona laughed. Yes, they would have children. Beautiful babies possessing her cinnamon-fire hair and his keen icy blue eyes. Together with their extended family, they would rebuild Foxenclover, this time filling it with love.

"Well, hopefully I will not have to give up all my reckless tendencies." To prove her point, she teased the outline of his mouth with the tip of her tongue. He growled, claiming her mouth in a devastating kiss.

Rayne pulled back to nibble her lower lip. "Not all of them," he amended. Smiling, he rolled her on top of him, encouraging her to demonstrate her uninhibited nature. Devona happily complied.

Le Cadavre Raffiné had rediscovered his heart.

ABOUT THE AUTHOR

Barbara Pierce resides near Atlanta, Georgia, with her husband and three children. Readers may write to her at: P.O. Box 2192, Woodstock, GA, 30188-9998. Or visit her website at: http://www.barbarapierce.com for updates on her next book.